Soviet Sources

Soviet Sources

Robert Cullen

THE ATLANTIC MONTHLY PRESS
NEW YORK

Published simultaneously in Canada
Printed in the United States of America

Library of Congress Cataloging-in-Publication Data

Cullen, Robert.
    Soviet sources/Robert Cullen.—1st ed.
    ISBN 0-87113-358-X
    I. Title.
PS3553.U297S6   1990   813'.54—dc20   89-29428

The Atlantic Monthly Press
19 Union Square West
New York, NY 10003

For Ann

1

HE awoke with the smell of cigar smoke and stale beer in his nostrils. The rhythmic, grating sound of shovels scraping against the pavement outside told him snow had fallen during the night. He opened his eyes. The grey light coming in the window told him he had overslept. He got up. The thud of his brain hitting the inside of his skull told him he was approaching the time of life when he would have to start taking better care of himself.

Naked, Burke stepped to the window, trying not to upset the fragile equilibrium in his head and stomach, and opened the curtains wide. Through the double panes of glass, he could see that a frosty, grey haze hung over his quarter of Moscow, fed by the smokestacks of the Sacco and Vanzetti Pencil Factory a quarter mile to his south. In the distance, the spire of Moscow State University seemed to shimmer, as if heat waves were distorting the view. Burke rubbed his eyes. The spire straightened up and grew still.

He desperately hoped there would be hot water this morning. He walked into the bathroom and turned on the shower. The water ran cool, then tepid, and finally hot. Burke gratefully stepped under it and stayed there until his joints felt looser and his head throbbed less.

He had a lunch date, he remembered, so he shaved and looked for a suit and tie. The corduroy looked a little rumpled, but warm. He put it on. Feeling a little better, he tried to straighten up the apartment. He threw the beer bottles down the trash chute. He emptied the cigar butts from the ashtray and threw them after the bottles. The smells made him faintly nauseous. He had promised himself to cut way back on beer, but someone had found a couple of cases of Urquell Pilsner on sale at the back door of the Praga restaurant and brought them to the game. In Moscow, in the wintertime, Burke took his luxuries where he found them. He folded the poker table and stowed it behind a bookshelf. Five hours of competition, till two in the morning, had left a small wad of winnings on the dresser. He counted it. Thirty-seven dollars and twenty-five cents.

On the nightstand, reproaching him, sat a copy of *Crime and Punishment*, in Russian. His New Year's resolution had been to get to bed early and read ten pages of Dostoevsky every night, to sharpen his Russian. More than a month had passed, and his bookmark still looked like an appendage of the front cover.

He went to the kitchen and found some instant coffee, turned the flame on under the kettle, then changed his mind and turned it off. The thought of sitting in his kitchen alone and waiting for the water to boil made him restless. He'd get his coffee from Olga at the office. He put on his blue parka and took the clanking, shaking elevator to the lobby, then braced himself and went outside. In the courtyard, he took deep breaths. When the weather was right, on a clear, sunny day, the winter air could be a tonic that banished headaches. This air was a little too grey, but it still helped.

The courtyard at No. 7 Kutuzovsky Prospekt was a vast parking lot. Husky women and bent old men were shoveling snow and washing the tenants' cars. Steam rose from their buckets. Only foreigners lived in Burke's building. They could afford the service.

Burke started his red Volvo easily; judging from that, it was at least a few degrees above zero. Threading his way between the banks of dirty snow and the jagged ranks of parked cars, he drove out past the *militioneri* hut at the compound entrance. *Militioneri* watched the foreigners leave their apartments in the morning. They watched over their offices all day to see who went in and out. They watched as the foreigners returned home at night, checking them in like sheep in a pen. Peter the Great had first decreed that foreigners must live by themselves in special ghettos and Vikenty Ponomaryov, for all his *glasnost* and *perestroika*, had not decreed otherwise.

There was another *militioner* standing watch in a little brown hut at the entrance to 18 Kutuzovsky, a grimy twelve-story building of dun brick that formed another island in the Moscow foreigners' archipelago. Burke did not acknowledge his greeting nod as he drove into the courtyard, parked, and entered the *Washington Tribune* bureau. It had once been a one-bedroom apartment; the largest room was Burke's office. In all of Moscow, it was one of his favorite rooms. It had a brown teak desk from Sweden and a matching bookshelf that filled an entire wall with reference books. An imitation Persian rug from the foreigners' store at the

Mezhdunarodnaya Hotel covered the floor, and there was a massive old leather sofa for the all-nighters when big stories broke. Portraits of past Soviet Politburos were taped to the walls, along with framed copies of *Tribune* front pages.

By tradition, each departing correspondent hung a copy of his best front-page story on the office wall. Most of them recounted momentous events in Soviet history: Khrushchev's ouster, the deaths of Brezhnev, Andropov, and Chernenko, and the election of Vikenty Ponomaryov as general secretary. A few correspondents had left behind copies of pieces they had dug up on their own initiative, such as a feature about a day spent in a Siberian salt mine. Burke regarded the collection of front pages as a challenge. He wanted the one he left behind to reflect both a momentous event and his own enterprise. So far, he'd covered a lot of big events—elections, Supreme Soviet sessions, a summit meeting. He'd dug up a lot of features. But he still didn't have the story he was looking for, and at the rate things were going, he couldn't predict that he would. January had been a boring month.

Burke's new secretary-translator, Olga Semyonova, had the coffee brewing. Olga had black hair, black eyes, and the kind of high cheekbones that attested to the presence, somewhere in her family tree, of a member of the Mongol horde that conquered Russia in the thirteenth century. He once had heard one of the other translators in the building call her "Tatar," and he had seen her bristle. Her documents said she was Russian, and she had the body of a Russian peasant girl—buxom, but still teetering on the fair side of corpulence. She had told him she was divorced, with a six-year-old daughter. She had graduated from the Institute of International Languages, majoring in English, but had never been in an English-speaking country.

She reported on him, of course. All the Soviets who worked for foreigners were required to. But he did not have the feeling she relished doing it, so he didn't hold it against her. Besides, she was pleasant and quiet. She kept the files well organized. And she seemed actually to like making coffee for him. Better a spy who contributed something than a lazy and inefficient one, like some of the other correspondents had.

"Good morning, Colin," Olga said in Russian, as Burke sat down. "How are you?" There was no intimacy in her use of his first name. She used the formal, plural form of "you" in addressing him, which was *vy*. Very few Russians Burke knew addressed him with the singular, intimate form, *ty*. As she leaned over his desk to place the morning edition of *Pravda* before him, Olga allowed her breasts to brush softly for a moment against Burke's shoulder. This, like the coffee, had become part of their morning ritual. Burke wondered whether her supervisor had instructed her to seduce him for some reason, or whether she was doing it on her own, in hopes that he would bring back jeans and stockings from his vacations in the West. Burke's next shopping trip to Helsinki was scheduled for March. He would find out soon enough.

"*Vsyo normalno*," he replied to Olga, looking at the paper, not at her. Then he caught himself, turned around, and smiled at her. "Thank you," he said. Olga smiled back and went for the coffee.

Burke turned to the newspaper. *Glasnost* had given birth to almost daily press conferences by Soviet officials. They provided correspondents with, if not the truth, at least some live quotes. But Burke still preferred to sift for news the old-fashioned way, beginning with a close reading of *Pravda*. The lead story this morning reported on an exemplary workers' collective in an oil field in western Siberia that had leased its patch of land from the state under the new *perestroika* rules and exceeded its production quotas. So why, Burke wondered, were there still long lines at all the gasoline stations?

He turned to the top left-hand corner of the page, to the editorial. Under the heading "It Is Necessary to Reform Management," it rehashed an old speech by Ponomaryov, which called on factory managers and local party leaders to stop relying on central directives and begin taking more initiative, all within a socialist framework, of course. Burke noted that Ponomaryov was quoted by name in the second paragraph, and stopped reading.

The news lay at the bottom of the front page, under the classically flashy *Pravda* headline "Message from V. P. Ponomaryov to a Delegation of American Scientists." The text read:

Moscow. Tass. Feb. 18. V. P. Ponomaryov, general secretary of the Central Committee of the Communist Party of the Soviet Union and president of the Presidium of the Supreme Soviet of the USSR, addressed the following message to the delegation of the Union of Concerned Scientists of the USA, currently visiting Moscow.

"Esteemed gentlemen:

"I heartily welcome you to Moscow and thank you for your letter of concern about the prospect of the militarization of the cosmos. Unfortunately, I cannot receive you personally because I am suffering from influenza. However, permit me to say that the entire Soviet people shares your concern for the maintenance of peace on earth and the preservation of the cosmos as a zone of peaceful research for the benefit of all mankind. The foreign policy of the Soviet Union has consistently

and unswervingly supported these goals. Unfortunately, the same cannot be said for the policy of the USA, which still vainly seeks to use the
cosmos as a platform . . ."

Olga returned and put a mug of black coffee on the desk.
"Anything interesting in the paper this morning?" she asked.
"You bet your ass," Burke said in English.
"Bet your ass?" she asked him.
"Yeah. Bet your ass."
"What does this mean, 'bet your ass'?"
"It's just a common slang expression that means, approximately, 'To
be sure!' " he told her. He knew he was going to tease her, and he felt
vaguely guilty about it, but the story about Ponomaryov had exhilarated
him too much to care.
"What does it really mean?" she asked, dubious.
"Well, it comes from Middle English. People used to ride asses, of
course, and sometimes they would race and the winner would keep both
asses. You've read the great ass-racing scene from Chaucer, haven't you?"
"Oh, yes," she said, nodding too emphatically. "I think I remember
studying that now."
"I'm sure you did," he nodded.
"And it's polite to use it?"
"Oh, yes," he assured her.
Pleased, she smiled and walked out of his office, murmuring her new
phrase under her breath.
Burke swiveled in his chair to the windowsill where he kept, in a
rough pile, the most recent two months' worth of *Pravda*. He thumbed
through the recent issues until he came to February 10. Its front page
showed Ponomaryov pinning the Order of Lenin on the beribboned chest
of a cosmonaut. *Pravda*'s pages had not reported an appearance by the
general secretary since that date.
Burke returned to the paper and found another story for the *Tribune*'s
front page at the bottom of page 3. There, in a black-bordered obituary,
the paper eulogized a World War II hero, Marshal Timofei Rodimenko.
Burke skipped over the usual encomiums about the marshal's valor in
defense of the Motherland and went to the list of those signing the
obituary, which came at the end. As usual, for someone of a marshal's
rank, the general secretary's name led the list: V. P. Ponomaryov. Then
came the rest of the Politburo members in alphabetical order: Andrushin,
the KGB chief; Denyeprov, the Ukrainian party leader; Fyodorov, the
foreign minister; Kluchevsky, the defense minister, and on down to

Ulyanovsky, the party secretary charged with overseeing ideological purity. Something seemed missing, and Burke read the list again, comparing each name to the names on the Politburo membership roster taped to the wall. He whistled softly to himself. Pavel Morozov, Ponomaryov's closest ally on the Politburo, the man in charge of appointments to all key government positions, had not signed the obituary.

He picked up the phone and dialed the number for the Foreign Ministry spokesman, Vasily Grishin. It was busy. He tried again to make sure he had dialed correctly. Still busy. He tried Grishin's alternate number. Also busy. *Perestroika* would succeed, he thought, when Moscow had a civilized telephone system.

Burke dialed the home number of Fyodor Orlov, his best contact in the Congress of People's Deputies. The Congress was not in session, but Orlov usually had good information. No answer.

He tried Valentin Skorov, one of Grishin's subalterns, whose particular job it was to act as nanny for the Americans in the press corps. Skorov occasionally had been helpful in the past. The phone rang for a long time. Just as he was about to hang up, Burke heard a murmured "*Da.*"

"Mr. Skorov?"

"That's right." Russians, by long tradition, only reluctantly identified themselves when they picked up a telephone.

"This is Colin Burke from the *Washington Tribune.*"

"Yes, Mr. Burke. My favorite newspaper." Skorov had worked in Washington.

"I wonder if you could tell me how long the general secretary has been ill?"

Skorov laughed. "Sorry, Mr. Burke. I know only what you do. Apparently, he has the flu. If you want further details, I suggest you contact his office."

As far as Burke knew, Ponomaryov's personal staff never gave out information, but there was no point in complaining about it to Skorov.

"All right," he said. "And can you tell me why Mr. Morozov did not sign the obituary for Marshal Rodimenko?"

"Didn't he?" Skorov said, again with an arch little chuckle. "I'm afraid I hadn't noticed. I suggest you ask his office as well."

"Interesting," Burke said, hoping that Skorov would ask him why it was interesting. But Skorov said nothing.

"All right then?" Skorov asked, cheerily.

"Yes. Thanks," Burke said.

"Any time, Mr. Burke," said Skorov, and hung up.

Burke dialed the only telephone number he had for the Politburo, which, as far as he knew, connected him to a receptionist somewhere.

A woman answered. "Yes," she said.

"Is this the Politburo?" Burke asked.

"Yes," she said.

He identified himself and asked to speak with someone who might have more information about Mr. Ponomaryov's flu.

"Call the press office at the Foreign Ministry," she said, and hung up.

Burke stood up. If he was going to get anything more than what everyone would read in the papers, he would have to get out of the office and dig for it. The usual sources were giving nothing away easily. But that was fine. It meant that whatever he could learn would be exclusive. His editors wouldn't see it first on television. And, with Andrei Kuznetsov as a lunch partner, he might very well learn something.

He had a couple of errands to squeeze in before lunch. He reached into his desk drawer and took out a vial of white pills and a package wrapped in brown paper. From the middle shelf of the bookcase, he extracted the most recent issues of *Newsweek* and *Playboy*. He stuffed all of that into a briefcase and put his parka on to go out.

It was going to be a busy day. The Russians were committing news.

2

ANDREI Kuznetsov occupied perhaps the only office in Moscow with a *Playboy* centerfold openly displayed on the wall—Miss October, 1983. She had blue eyes, enormous breasts, and a white bearskin rug. Few Muscovites would dare flaunt such a picture, but Kuznetsov cultivated an image of decadence. He knew that most Russians, no matter how devoted to order and discipline, secretly admired and envied a successful libertine.

Kuznetsov, at fifty-three, qualified for the role. He was short, mustachioed, and approaching 270 pounds. A table in the barroom of Dom Zhurnalistov, the Moscow branch of the journalists' union, was known as "Andrei's Table." Whenever Kuznetsov entered the room, the barmaid, unbidden, placed before him a flask with five hundred grams of vodka and a plate of hot bouillon with Siberian meat dumplings called *pyelmyeni*. The lucky ones among those present would be invited to sit at Andrei's Table throughout an afternoon and early evening, listening, perhaps, to the proprietor's tales of his travels through the brothels of Hamburg, Amsterdam, and New York. Occasionally, he would rise at eight o'clock, walk ponderously, but straight, to the street, where a black Volga would be waiting to take him to the government television studio at Ostankino. An hour later, he would appear on the evening newscast, *Vremya*, earnestly and flawlessly reading a commentary that generally managed to give a veneer of logic to the orthodoxy of the moment.

The party, not without reason, valued this talent. Late in the Brezhnev era, it had made him a candidate member of the Central Committee—in title, at least, one of the few hundred oligarchs who ran the country. In the Ponomaryov era, his official status had slipped. Holding on to high party posts began to depend, in some measure, on a man's ability to win election to the Congress of People's Deputies. Kuznetsov had stood for election, and found that a lot of his countrymen would simply not vote for a man perceived as a party propagandist. That had not really surprised him. In fact, he rather sympathized with their point of view. Falling back into the status of mere journalist had not disturbed him. He still appeared on television, though much less often. He still received, and accepted, invitations to occasional conferences abroad. He still found it a rather comfortable life.

This morning Kuznetsov was engaged in the sole aspect of his work that truly appealed to him, writing his weekly column for *Izvestiya*. Occasionally, when a younger journalist, sitting at Andrei's Table, had the temerity to suggest that Kuznetsov's television commentaries were a bit, well, orthodox, Andrei would never disagree. "Read my column," he would say. His younger colleague would nod. And then at a party some night, with the television news turned on to provide background noise, the colleague would tell a young lady, "Andrei Petrovich was telling me the other day that he does that just to establish his political reliability. Then they let him write what he wants in *Izvestiya*."

What Kuznetsov wanted to write this week was a balanced piece about the Americans' Strategic Defense Initiative. He agreed with the party line that SDI was, at its core, an attempt by the Americans to achieve the ability to launch a first strike against the Soviet homeland. But he also believed that if the Soviets would finally, irrevocably abandon the view that the ABM Treaty banned SDI, they could get a strategic-arms treaty. Then, one of two things would happen. The American Congress would starve SDI to death for lack of funds. Or the Americans would bankrupt themselves in a futile attempt to put a roof over an entire continent. There was no way to lose.

But how to say so? The piece would have to be delicately done—strong in its condemnation of the Americans, oblique in its criticism of Soviet policy. It was the kind of delicate writing that Andrei Kuznetsov did better than any journalist in Moscow. Normally, it would have been the occasion for a pleasant morning's work.

But this morning, Kuznetsov could not concentrate. He had known that Vikenty Ponomaryov was ill; his friends on the Central Committee staff had begun whispering about it as soon as the general secretary stopped showing up at the office. But he had not known that the Politburo had decided to speak publicly about it, and this disturbed him. Even more troubling was the removal of Pavel Morozov. Morozov was not a friend of Andrei Kuznetsov; he was a stern Communist moralist from Siberia whose goal in life had seemed to be ridding the party apparatus of drunks and thieves, and Kuznetsov fell all too often into the former category. A man like Morozov easily made enemies. But purging the deadwood from the apparatus was Vikenty Ponomaryov's goal, too. Why had he not protected Morozov? Kuznetsov could draw only one conclusion. Vikenty Ponomaryov's strength, whether political or physical, or both, was rapidly ebbing.

The telephone interrupted Kuznetsov in midreverie. He picked it up. "I'm listening," he said.

"Comrade Kuznetsov?" a male voice said.

"Yes."

"I have a call for you from Comrade Andrushin. Please be kind enough to wait a moment."

Kuznetsov sat upright. Why would the chairman of the KGB be calling him? Kuznetsov had met Igor Andrushin years ago, when they were both working in the international department of the Central Committee secretariat. Once, they had split a bottle of vodka; Andrushin had never invited Kuznetsov to drink with him again. It would not have been seemly for Kuznetsov, with his lesser stature in the party, to invite Andrushin for a drink. For an instant, Kuznetsov wondered if he was in trouble. After a brief examination of conscience, he dismissed the idea. His position in the party was solid. His offenses were not, in the end, political. The days when a Soviet journalist would tremble at the notion of talking to the chief of the KGB were, thankfully, gone, he told himself. And besides, if he were in trouble, Andrushin would no doubt let a subordinate handle the initial contact.

"Andrei Petrovich," Andrushin greeted him in his strangely nasal voice. "How are you?"

"Fine, Igor Vasilievich. And you?" Kuznetsov replied.

"I am quite well. But there are some matters I wish to discuss with you. Would it be convenient for you to come to my office?"

"Of course, Igor Vasilievich. When?"

"If you could come right now, I would be most grateful," the KGB chief replied. "You will find a car waiting for you at the entrance to your building."

"I'll come at—," Kuznetsov began. Then he heard a click. Andrushin had hung up.

The journalist sat quietly for a moment. He lit a cigarette without thinking about what he was doing. He got up and put on his muffler, his coat, and his sable *shapka*. Leaving his office, with the cigarette burning in the ashtray, he locked the door and walked down a long corridor lined with offices much like his own. He found he had to go to the bathroom. So he went to the men's room, which smelled of old cigarettes and urine, and took off the coat and the *shapka*. But he sat on the toilet for a while and nothing came of it.

He took the elevator to the ground floor and walked out onto the concrete plaza that lay between *Izvestiya* and the crowds walking by on Gorky Street. A black sedan, its rear windows shielded by beige drapes, stood idling on the plaza. He opened the rear door and got in. As soon as he had closed the door, the driver, his head buried beneath a rabbit-fur *shapka*, put the car into gear and they glided quietly away. They turned left, down Gorky Street, toward the Kremlin. At the foot of Gorky Street, within sight of the onion-shaped domes of Saint Basil's Cathedral on Red Square, they headed uphill past the buff facade of the Lubyanka, which tourists still regarded as the headquarters of the KGB. Fifty meters farther around the square stood a new building of polished grey granite. In the rear, a steel door rose silently, revealing a tunnel to an inner courtyard. Without slowing down, the KGB driver entered the court-yard. Then he stopped, got out, and opened Kuznetsov's door. The journalist got out.

Kuznetsov followed the silent driver to a doorway twice his height, recessed deep within the north wall of the courtyard. The driver pushed, and the door opened noiselessly. Kuznetsov entered a small reception hall. The driver walked past a uniformed guard in the blue epaulets of the KGB. They entered a Finnish-made elevator and ascended quickly to the second floor. Kuznetsov emerged to find a long, high-ceilinged hallway; a woven red runner covered its parquet floor. Directly across from the elevator was a large double door, unmarked, covered in brown leather. The driver strode across the hallway, thrust open the double door, and motioned Kuznetsov inside. The journalist heard the doors close behind him.

He was in another small reception room. This one had a single desk, a picture of Lenin on one wall and a picture of Marx opposite Lenin. Kuznetsov noticed that no portrait of Vikenty Ponomaryov adorned Igor Andrushin's anteroom.

A male secretary sat behind the desk. "Good morning, Andrei Petrovich," he said. "Please go in."

Kuznetsov's bowels told him to wait.

"Is there a toilet?" he asked.

The male secretary's face showed nothing. "Third door on the left," he said, pointing down the hall. Kuznetsov walked down the hall, feeling foolish, to the men's room. It smelled clean, as if no one ever used it. He sat on the toilet again, but again nothing came of it, and he buckled his pants and returned to the anteroom.

The male secretary opened another set of leather-lined double doors. Kuznetsov was in a large, sunlit room, with wallpaper of white satin and curtains of shirred silk. Pictures of Marx, Lenin, and Dzerzhinsky were on the walls. Before him stood a long conference table of polished birchwood. At the opposite end, like the transept of a church, stood a gleaming desk of the same height and the same blond wood, unadorned save for three red telephones. And, standing behind the desk was Igor Andrushin.

None of this made the least impression on Andrei Kuznetsov. His attention was arrested by the presence of a thick-shouldered man sitting in the corner formed by the conference table and Andrushin's desk. On each epaulet of his brown uniform tunic gleamed a single, golden five-pointed star. He was Marshal Nikolai Petrusevich, chief of staff of the Soviet army.

"Good morning, Andrei Petrovich," Igor Andrushin was saying. The KGB chief's thin lips opened in a smile. He was a tall, stoop-shouldered man, haggard, with a fringe of white hair over a bald dome. In his baggy blue suit he looked like a kindly, but unworldly, professor of physics. In fact, he had been working for the party since 1942, when he joined the Communist underground in his native Byelorussia. Kuznetsov had heard that as a boy of sixteen, Andrushin had killed seven Nazi soldiers. Whether this was true, or simply a persona the KGB chief had created for himself, Kuznetsov did not know.

"Please sit down," Andrushin said, motioning him to the seat across the table from the military man. "You know Marshal Petrusevich, of course."

In fact, Kuznetsov had met the general on occasion, at Central Committee and Supreme Soviet meetings. Petrusevich was the first man without experience in the Great Patriotic War to attain the rank of chief of staff. As if to compensate for this, he was one of the only military heroes to emerge from the mess in Afghanistan. His tank brigade, in one memorable day, had killed seven hundred *dushmani*. Petrusevich nodded his leonine head of grey hair in Kuznetsov's direction, but did not speak. The journalist sat down.

"The marshal and I were just discussing a military problem that threatens to become a problem of state security," Andrushin said. "Would you like tea or coffee?"

"Tea, please," Kuznetsov said. He would have preferred vodka.

Andrushin picked up one of his red phones and ordered tea.

"The problem," the KGB leader went on, "is unfortunately with the young people who are entering the armed services these days. Not enough discipline. They resist authority. They try to wiggle out of assignments to places like the Far East. The Lithuanians insist that they serve only in Lithuania. Some try to evade serving at all."

Petrusevich spoke for the first time. "I don't mind telling you, Andrei Petrovich, that if the West were to probe for weaknesses in our positions in East Germany today, there would be no assurance that they would not find some."

They looked at him expectantly, as if waiting for him to contribute something to the conversation. Kuznetsov wondered why Andrushin and Petrusevich were putting on this little show for him. Did they want to hear him advocate discipline? That would be too easy. He said the safest thing he could think of.

"I thought that sort of thing came mainly from some of our southern republics?"

It was a polite reference to the Muslim areas of the southern Soviet Union. Because the population in those areas continued to grow, while women in Slavic areas adamantly refused to have more than one baby, the pool of recruits was filling up with swarthy young men who spoke little or no Russian.

"No," Petrusevich responded. "Those kids may not speak Russian too well. Let's be honest. Most of them can't speak it at all. But they do what they are told. The problem is with Russian kids. Ever since we got out of Afghanistan, when they don't like something their officers tell them to do, they complain. Sometimes they write letters to the party or to the newspapers, demanding that reform and democratization be extended to the armed forces."

"We've never printed one," Kuznetsov said. Was that what this meeting was about?

"We know that," Andrushin interrupted. "The point is that this country has discipline problems, not just in the military. I'm afraid the party, in its effort to stimulate the creative energy of the people, may have underestimated the extent to which even our modern Soviet people are willing to take advantage of a loose hand."

The doors to the office opened again, and the male secretary walked in, carrying tea and cookies on a tray. As he watched the tea being poured, Kuznetsov wondered if the words he had just heard were the same, more or less, as the words that had preceded the Politburo vote to retire Pavel Morozov.

Petrusevich rose. "I must be going," he said. "Andrei Petrovich. Igor Vasilievich." With a slight bow, he turned and left the room behind Andrushin's secretary.

Igor Andrushin turned to Kuznetsov. "Once again, thank you for coming. Would you like a cigarette?" He reached into his pocket and pulled out a pack. Andrushin, who could have smoked Dunhills or Marlboros, chose to smoke plain Russian *papirosi*, homegrown tobacco wrapped in crude cardboard tubes. Kuznetsov, who preferred Kents, was glad for a chance to do something with his hands. They were, he noticed with irritation, a bit damp. He accepted the *papirosa*, took a match from the box on the table, and lit it.

Andrushin, he noted, seemed to be watching the operation intently. Then he spoke. "I asked you here in hopes that you would do me a small favor."

"If I can," Kuznetsov said. He looked for an ashtray. There was none.

"Good. As you know, there will be a great deal of speculation in the Western press about the illness of Comrade Ponomaryov. We want to guide this speculation along truthful lines."

"Of course," Kuznetsov said. The ash on the end of his *papirosa* was growing longer.

"You will, I understand, be having lunch this afternoon with an American journalist. Is that correct?"

Kuznetsov did not bother to ask how Andrushin knew this. "Yes, Igor Vasilievich. At the Praga. One o'clock. With Colin Burke of the *Washington Tribune*."

Kuznetsov's ash was about to fall off. He considered using the teacup or the saucer for an ashtray and decided against it.

Andrushin nodded. His eyes were opaque.

"This is not your first such lunch?"

Kuznetsov realized that Andrushin knew the answer to the question.

"No, Igor Vasilievich. He asks me to lunch every month or two. I usually accept."

"You get invitations from lots of foreign journalists. Why accept Burke's?"

In truth, Kuznetsov found it useful to have a number of acquaintances in Washington, which he often visited and found quite expensive, given the niggardly hard currency allowance he was given. Dining on an American newspaper's expense account there made it possible to buy things with his meal money. So he allowed himself to be cultivated. But that was not an explanation fit for Igor Andrushin.

It occurred to Kuznetsov that Andrushin was going to tell him that Burke was an American intelligence agent. He reviewed all of the conversations he had had with the man. He could not recall saying anything he shouldn't have said. But then, there were sometimes mornings when he couldn't recall anything. He reached for a cookie with his free hand. He decided to play it as dumb and innocent as possible.

"I've found him to be one of the . . ." He paused, searching for the right word. " . . . well, brighter Americans. Arrogant, like most of them. Speaks pretty good Russian, which a lot of them can't." This was true enough.

He swallowed his cookie whole, then wished he hadn't. He wondered how he must look to the abstemious Andrushin, stuffing sweets into his mouth with one hand and sucking up smoke from the other. His ash, he noticed, was so long it was beginning to droop.

The KGB chairman nodded, neither approving nor disapproving.

Kuznetsov lowered his cigarette below the table and dropped the ash into the palm of his other hand. Then he thrust the ashes into the side pocket of his coat. He continued to talk.

"Other than that, I don't know too much about him. He's tall. Thin. Not bad looking. I don't know of any family." He stopped, feeling he was beginning to babble.

If Andrushin noticed Kuznetsov's difficulties with his cigarette, he gave no sign.

"We have some information that may interest you," he said. He took two red file folders from the blotter on his desk and passed them across the table to Kuznetsov. "Take a look at these."

One folder was thin, its color slightly faded. On the outside, Kuznetsov read: "Burke, Colin 1967–72." He opened it. He saw a yellowed clipping from the *San Francisco Chronicle*, dated September 26, 1967. It was about a student riot at the University of California in Berkeley. There was a picture of an angry young man with long hair and a headband, fist raised, speaking to a crowd of students. Behind him, off to one side, stood a much younger Colin Burke, possessor then of a drooping mustache.

Kuznetsov was impressed. He would not have thought that the KGB, though it had an office in San Francisco, would have such extensive files on American students.

The next clipping was an editorial column from the *Daily Californian*, which, someone had noted in the margin, was the "student newspaper" at Berkeley. The masthead identified Colin Burke as the paper's editor, and the editorial endorsed an elaborate plan for one hundred thousand American students to refuse to cooperate with the draft, throwing the courts into chaos.

"A student radical?" Kuznetsov asked.

"Of a shallow, egotistical American sort," Andrushin said.

There were a couple of similar clippings from the *Daily Californian*, then a few bylined articles from something called the *Berkeley Barb*. Kuznetsov skimmed one of them. It apparently was a detailed list of the undercover narcotics agents employed by the local police.

Kuznetsov stifled a smile. Such gall!

"What is the *Berkeley Barb?*" he asked.

"It was what American students called an 'alternative newspaper,' " Andrushin explained. "Supposedly, an alternative to the bourgeois monopoly press. Ideologically, quite childish."

Kuznetsov nodded.

"We compiled the first file as part of a project initiated when it seemed to some members of the Politburo that the American Left might really become a revolutionary movement. Of course, not being grounded appropriately in a disciplined, Leninist view of the world and the role of a revolutionary vanguard, it could not. Fully half the people we monitored destroyed themselves with drugs. When that became apparent, we dropped the project."

Andrushin's rhetoric surprised Kuznetsov. It had been years since he had heard a sophisticated person use phrases like "revolutionary vanguard." What was going on here?

"And Burke?" the journalist asked, trying to keep the conversation on safe ground.

"He apparently fell onto the second path taken by the so-called radicals. He joined the bourgeoisie."

Andrushin leaned back a little in his chair and spoke with the air of a professor leading a seminar of bright, but still callow, graduate students.

"Most of these 1960s radicals were rebelling against their parents. Burke's father, according to our records, was a modestly successful real estate developer. So Burke grew his hair long and studied Russian in college and opposed the Americans' Vietnam aggression—to spite him. Or some such reason."

Kuznetsov opened the second folder, which was thicker and newer and marked, "Burke, Colin 1989–." The first entry was an application for accreditation in the USSR. Scanning it, Kuznetsov could see that Colin Burke had left the *Berkeley Barb* in 1973 and gone to work for the *Oakland Tribune*. Six years later, he had joined the *Washington Tribune* and moved to

Washington. Under dependents, he saw, there was a sixteen-year-old boy who still lived in California.

"Notice the home address," Andrushin prompted him. It was 809 G Street SE, Washington.

"It's a townhouse in the Capitol Hill district, which is a neighborhood that used to be for workers and has become an enclave for the wealthy. Burke has become a property owner. We may assume that he worries about blacks moving into his neighborhood and lowering real estate values because of panic sales by white bigots. He has, as the Americans say, sold out." Andrushin smiled for the first time. "I think this makes him an excellent subject for this little operation."

Kuznetsov hesitantly smiled back, nodding. The rest of the folder consisted mainly of copies of every story and every message that Burke had sent from Moscow to Washington. At the end of the file were some written evaluations by KGB case officers. Kuznetsov began to scan them.

"No need to read it all," Andrushin said, reclaiming his attention. Kuznetsov dutifully closed the file. He was relieved. Burke was apparently not a spy.

"The main thing you need to know is that Burke has not had a story on the front page of his newspaper for more than a month. For an American journalist, this is a long time. Their egos—and their salaries—depend on getting their names on the front page. He will be anxious—eager, really—to believe what you are going to tell him."

Kuznetsov nodded. What was he going to tell Burke?

Andrushin shifted in his chair and came to the point. "As I said, the little item in *Pravda* today is going to cause a lot of speculation about the general secretary's health. Naturally, we want to channel that interest in the right way."

Kuznetsov nodded.

"The American can be counted on to ask you about it. We want you to tell him that the general secretary has had a stroke, that he is recovering, and that he is handling business from the Politburo clinic at Kuntsevo."

Kuznetsov wondered momentarily whether what Andrushin was telling him was true. It was certainly plausible. But a second thought soon overtook his curiosity. He wanted no part of a KGB operation. When he opened his mouth, he tried to wriggle away from it. "Why do you think he'll believe me, Igor Vasilievich?"

Andrushin was a step ahead of him. "Because you'll say nothing about the general secretary while you are in the restaurant. Refuse to answer. Then, on the street after lunch, you will offer the information. The American will assume that you were afraid to be candid in the restaurant because you feared that the table was bugged. He will conclude that what you tell him on the street is the truth."

For the moment, Kuznetsov could think of no alternative to stifling his uneasiness, nodding, and agreeing. Much had changed in the Soviet Union under Vikenty Ponomaryov, but a Politburo member was still a Politburo member, and the chief of the KGB was still the chief of the KGB.

Andrushin, like a lot of older party leaders who had never been to the West, tended to overestimate the influence of factors like salaries and property values when predicting American behavior. That was his Marxist blind spot. But in this case it didn't matter, Kuznetsov thought with grudging admiration, because Andrushin's little operation would attack the real American vulnerability: individual ego and ambition.

Well, it would not be the worst thing he had ever done. And he could foresee no negative consequences for doing it. Refusing, on the other hand, would make an enemy he could well do without.

"All right," he said, nodding again. "I'd be glad to help, of course."

Andrushin rose. The meeting was over. "Thank you for coming, Andrei Petrovich. I have long been an admirer of your work and of your contributions to the party. I hope that we may find a way to make your contributions even more significant in the future."

Kuznetsov thought briefly of asking Andrushin what he had in mind. The only jobs in the Soviet Union that could be considered a promotion for him would mean restoration to membership in the Central Committee and a post supervising the media. Those were not, or should not have been, in Igor Andrushin's power to grant. He considered asking what had happened to Pavel Morozov, and what the true state was of Vikenty Ponomaryov's health. Then he decided against both questions. He would be told when the party, or Igor Andrushin, decided that he needed to know.

Kuznetsov walked out, took the elevator downstairs, and found the same car and driver waiting for him in the courtyard. The driver sped smoothly back through Dzerzhinsky Square, down Prospekt Marx, and up Gorky Street. Kuznetsov barely noticed the passing scene. Was Andrushin trying to exaggerate Ponomaryov's illness? Or cover it up? What did Andrushin mean by "even more significant contributions" to the party? And when, since the end of the Great Patriotic War in 1945, had the KGB and the army ever agreed on questions of state security?

He found that, once again, he felt he needed a toilet.

3

"YOU look terrible," Tatiana Kornilova said. "You need something to eat."

"Thanks," Burke said. "You look as beautiful as ever. Too bad you can't cook."

Tatiana sniffed like a duchess. "You should have seen me forty years ago." At sixty-odd, she had a *babushka*'s stubby, barrel-shaped body, her hair was iron grey, and her face bore all the lines that a Jewish girl born during the *Stalinshchina* could expect to have, if she were one of the ones who reached old age. She wore a shapeless flowered housedress, thick grey socks, and bedroom slippers. Her knobby shins were almost chalk white.

"Here are your pills," Burke said, handing her the vial. She nodded and slipped them into a commodious pocket in her housedress. "And here are some things Anton sent. He wants me to tell you—I believe his exact words were—to 'give up that schmuck and come to New York.' "

She thanked him and took the package, containing books from Anton and some sausage and tomatoes that Burke had bought in the farmers' market. She placed it, unopened, in an inconspicuous corner of a bookshelf. They sat on opposite ends of the sofa in the book-lined room that comprised Tatiana Kornilova's home. The room was so small that Burke could almost reach across it to touch the desk opposite the sofa. She had piled the desk high with papers and books; little scraps of paper protruded from the books' pages like the fringe on a rug, marking her notes. She was writing a history of the Jews under Stalin. The radiator at the end of the room was pumping out dry heat, and although the small *fortochka* above the window was open, Burke felt stuffy. A few weak shafts of grey light came in through the window.

Tatiana Kornilova was one of the Muscovites who had invented the dissident movement. After Khrushchev's fall, most of the Soviet Union sullenly, stoically had accepted Brezhnev's reversion to a halfhearted form of

Stalinism. A few people had not, and Tatiana, a widow with a teenaged son, found herself instinctively drawn to that group. She was a cofounder of the Helsinki Watch and one of the first refuseniks. When some dissident was arrested, she was the one who called the American correspondents to tell them. When someone went on trial, she was the one who showed up outside the courtroom to bear silent witness. Finally, after Vikenty Ponomaryov came to power, she and Anton got permission to emigrate.

But Tatiana had shocked everyone who knew her by refusing to go. She had, she explained, fallen in love with a Russian man who refused either to marry her or to leave. Anton had left, but not before prevailing on Burke's predecessor to serve as a courier for the nifedipine pills his mother needed for her angina—and an occasional book by an author the Russians had not gotten around to rehabilitating—which he mailed to the *Tribune* bureau via the American embassy. Burke had inherited the charity duty, then grown to like it.

"Tell Anton to mind his own business," she said.

"Okay," Burke said.

"So why do you look like such a mess?"

"So why are you the only Jewish grandmother in Moscow who can't cook?"

"I asked first," she said.

"Clean living," Burke said.

"I bet. You need to find a wife and settle down. Or you'll be dead before you're forty."

"I tried that once. And I'm already past forty."

"You look older."

"Thanks a lot. I feel better already."

Her eyes narrowed. "I mean it. It's not good for a man to be alone. You don't look happy."

Burke rolled his eyes. "So introduce me to some nice Russian girl, Tatiana."

She laughed. "If you were a nice Russian boy, I would. But more worry you don't need."

She stopped smiling. "Aren't there any women in your life?"

"Just you, dear," he said, straight-faced.

She did not laugh.

"Well, to be honest," Burke said, "sometimes I meet a woman—another reporter, maybe, or a tourist—who's passing through looking for a . . ."

He stopped, trying to think of the Russian for "one-night stand." He couldn't.

" . . . single night," he continued. He raised his eyebrows and tried to summon a boyish smile. "I let them take advantage of me."

Tatiana looked at him solemnly. "Is that all you want?"

She was the only person left in his life who talked to him that way, and for a moment, he found it hard to respond.

"Well," he finally offered. "It's all I can manage." Even to himself, Burke sounded brittle about it.

She looked at him, a little like a conscience, and said nothing.

He changed the subject. "Read the paper yet?"

She nodded soberly. "It's very troubling."

Tatiana, Burke knew, had been a history teacher before she became a dissident. He had found her to be one of the smartest observers of Soviet politics in Moscow.

"Why?" he asked.

Tatiana assumed a didactic mien. "The newspapers have only twice before reported illness in the party leader," she said. "In 1922 and 1923, Lenin, you know, had a series of strokes."

Burke nodded.

"*Pravda* and *Izvestiya* never used the word 'stroke.' They did mention things like 'exhaustion' and 'circulatory problems.' Everyone who saw Lenin could tell he was dying. The newspapers never said so. They reported steady improvement. Meanwhile, Stalin was accumulating power."

"And the other was Andropov?"

She nodded, like a teacher with a reasonably good pupil.

"In 1983, Andropov dropped out of sight for several months. Finally, just like today, there was a report that he had a cold. A couple of months later he died. It turned out that his kidneys hadn't worked for a year and he was undergoing dialysis all that time."

"Do you really think Ponomaryov could be that sick?" Burke asked. "He seems so healthy."

Vikenty Ponomaryov was sixty, a sturdy, florid son of a peasant. As far as Western observers could tell, he drank little and never smoked. He was famous for working long hours.

"It's hard to say," Tatiana said. "The press has been a little more honest for a while. But on something like this, they'll write what they're told to write, *glasnost* or no *glasnost*. If the deputies were in session, someone could ask, and maybe they'd have to answer him. But they're not due back till April." She paused, weighing her information and its sources.

"How long has he been out of sight? A week?" she asked.

"Eight days," Burke responded. "It's a long time between public appearances by his standards, except for vacation times. Do you think he could be taking a vacation?"

"He took his long vacation last summer," Tatiana said. "I doubt that he'd take another. He's too busy trying to persuade the rest of us to work harder." She smiled. They both knew how much success Ponomaryov had had in that endeavor. Every time she went shopping, the lines reminded her of it.

She shook her head. "He could actually have the flu. But I suspect not. If he really had the flu and would be back at work soon, they'd say nothing. I think it means he's really sick."

Burke nodded. He was inclined to agree with her.

"What about Morozov?" he asked.

She frowned. "That's what really worries me. Let's assume that he's been thrown out of the Politburo. That's what it meant in '82 when Kirilenko's signature didn't appear under an obituary. Let's also assume that he is Ponomaryov's man, since he joined the Politburo after Ponomaryov was general secretary. Who voted against him? Why couldn't Ponomaryov protect him?"

"Because he's really sick?"

She nodded grimly. "That's the way I read it."

"You're worried," he said, after a few seconds of silence.

"Of course," Tatiana said. "I'm not one of those idiots who think all of them are the same." Burke assumed she referred to the Soviet leadership. "Ponomaryov is not the savior you make him out to be in the American press. But we've had lots worse. We could again."

"Like who?"

She shrugged. "There's no way to know. Stalin parroted Lenin's line till Lenin was out of the way. Khrushchev parroted Stalin's line till Stalin was out of the way. Some of the ones who are parroting Ponomaryov's line now also parroted Brezhnev's. Who knows what they really think?"

"Not me," Burke said, rising. "But I'm afraid I have to get going and try to find out."

Tatiana got his parka from the hook near the door. Leaning over, he brushed his lips against her lined cheek. She was less than five feet tall.

"Thank you for the medicine and the package," she said. "Don't wait for the next package from Anton to come by again."

"Call me when you learn how to cook," he grinned, and she smiled back as she shut the door.

4

GREAT heaps of grey cloud hunkered in the sky; the winter sun was a feeble glow from somewhere behind them when Burke left Tatiana's building. Reaching in his pocket, he checked to make sure he had a few *dvuchki*, the two-kopeck coins that operated the public phones. In the old days, before *glasnost*, when just talking to an American could be dangerous for the average Russian, a correspondent called all his contacts from pay phones. Now, Burke and his colleagues made most calls from their office phones, bugged or not. Most of their sources were either government officials or people like Tatiana, whom the authorities knew all about anyway. But there were still some people Burke called only from pay phones. It was a sense that he had about which contacts required discretion and which did not.

Burke drove east, toward the center of town, for about a kilometer, then parked in front of a vegetable market with a couple of well-used public phones. A long line of stocky women in greasy overcoats and felt boots stood waiting to buy the turnips and cabbages that were their winter vegetables. Burke got out and went to the phone. He took from an inner coat pocket an address book; since Moscow had no telephone directory, Burke had compiled his own. He guarded the little book more carefully than his passport. Again, it was a sense of discretion.

Under *P*, Burke found the number for Vasily Pankratov. Pankratov was on his list of people to contact today, and although he had nothing to do with the Ponomaryov story, there was no reason to put off calling him. Putting a *dvuchka* in the coin slot, he carefully dialed. A woman answered. Burke dropped his *dvuchka* down the slot.

"Vasya, please," Burke said.

"You've got the wrong number," the woman replied, and hung up.

Burke was sure he had dialed correctly. He tried the number again. This time there was no answer. He hung up and dialed the number a third time. His fingers were getting numb. He cursed the cold and Soviet public services. Moscow's pay phones, he had found, delivered the correct number about one time in three. This morning they were running true to form.

Burke occasionally thought about how much more pleasant his job would be if, just in the winter, he made all his calls from his office phone. But he didn't. Burke observed few rules. He tried, as best he could, to avoid becoming a conveyor of falsehood to his readers. He picked up his own checks. And he did what he could to protect his sources, even if it meant using Moscow pay phones and freezing his fingers. It was a tattered excuse for a code of ethics, but it was all he had.

On the third try at the phone, a man answered. Burke dropped the second of his *dvuchki* down the coin slot. "Vasya," he said.

"Yes," the voice replied.

"Vasya, this is Colin. Is this a good time to drop by?"

"Colin, hello! Right now?"

"Yes."

There was a pause. Burke wondered what Vasya was thinking.

"All right. In ten minutes."

"Good," Burke said, and hung up.

He returned to his car and sat for a moment, letting the reliable Swedish heater warm him up. Then he drove a kilometer in the wrong direction, until a blue sign signaled permission for a *razvorot*, or U-turn. He sped back toward the center of the city to Bolshaya Bronnaya Street, where Vasya lived in a big, three-room apartment near the Dom Kino, the club for workers in the film industry.

Burke had met Vasya Pankratov at a press conference called by the State Cinema Committee to publicize yet another joint Soviet-American production of *Ten Days That Shook the World*. Vasya was an actor of sorts; he got a continuing series of second leads in productions at Mosfilm, the state movie company in the Lenin Hills overlooking the city. Vasya also fancied himself a singer in the manner of the late and wildly popular Russian bard Vladimir Vysotsky. Vysotsky had died during the 1980 Olympics; ten years later, crowds of mourners still covered his grave with flowers every day. Like Vysotsky, Vasya dressed in black and accompanied himself on the guitar. Unlike Vysotsky, Vasya had never quite caught on. His lyrics lacked the barbed humor of Vysotsky's; his voice lacked Vysotsky's vodka-roughened sincerity. And in the era of *glasnost*, people didn't have to listen to a singer to hear some political satire. But Vasya persisted, certain that the bards' time would come again. On the side, he did a black-market business buying, restoring, and selling antique samovars, mostly to foreigners. He was, in Moscow terms, a Renaissance man.

An old woman, the *dezhurnaya*, sat on guard inside the entrance to Vasya's building. She looked at Burke's obviously Western nylon parka with wary suspicion. "Where are you going?" she demanded.

"To Pankratov's," Burke answered briefly, hoping that if he said as little as possible she might think his accent was Estonian or Polish—and not report an American visiting Vasily Pankratov.

He opened the black mesh door of the elevator cage and stepped in, shutting the door with a clank. The elevator ground slowly to the sixth floor, where Burke got off. Crossing the dim landing, he pressed the buzzer for apartment 14. There was a scuffling sound, made, Burke knew, by slippers on a wood floor. Vasya opened the door.

Vasya was wearing a faded red velvet smoking jacket over a pair of jeans. Though there were lines at the corners of his blue eyes, his chest was boyish and hairless. Burke hung up his parka on one of the wall hooks inside the door. Obedient to Russian tradition, he slipped off his shoes and found a pair of slippers from the assortment strewn on the floor of the entrance hall. Then he followed Vasya into the living room.

Vasya Pankratov's apartment was among the best Burke had seen in Moscow. Only the party elite, he imagined, lived better. The living room had two large windows facing south, toward Gorky Street. There were a few pieces of graceful, prerevolutionary furniture, and an impressive collection of icons on the walls. Vasya's pride, a Japanese compact disk player, sat in splendor in a dark mahogany bookshelf. Burke briefly wondered how many samovars he had had to sell to buy it.

Sitting down, Burke opened his briefcase and took out the two magazines. He dropped them onto Vasya's coffee table.

"Marvelous!" Vasya said. He opened the *Playboy* quickly and inspected the centerfold. Then he tucked them both into a desk drawer. "Thank you, Colin."

"Not at all," Burke said. "So, how have you been?"

"The same," Vasya said. "Things are getting worse at the studio. Mikhailkovsky's new film is still on the shelf. It's okay to be critical of Brezhnev or Stalin, but not of Ponomaryov. And they won't, for some reason, let my last film be entered at Cannes. It's not fair, Colin. If my films were seen, I would be invited to work in the West. If I worked in the West, I would be rich and famous by now."

Burke had seen Vasya's last film. He did not imagine it would have done well at Cannes, but he said only: "That's too bad, Vasya."

"And how about you, Colin? What are you working on?"

"Right now, trying to figure out what happened to Pavel Morozov. And what's wrong with Ponomaryov."

"Has something happened to them, I hope?" Vasya said.

"If you read the papers, Vasya, you'd have seen that Morozov is no longer among the Politburo members signing obituaries. Presumably, he's out. And Ponomaryov has admitted to being ill."

"Well, whatever it is, I hope it's terminal," Vasya said with a vaguely feminine toss of his head.

"Vasya," Burke said gravely. "I'm shocked. These men are the direct lineal descendants of Lenin. The precious wisdom of Marx comes down through them to you. They have brought *glasnost* and democracy to you."

"Fuck them. They pay billions of rubles to Cuba each year and give us sugar shortages," Vasya said, but cheerfully, presumably because he had a *na levo* source of sugar for himself. "But enough of politics. When are you going to write something about films?"

Burke had been waiting for this question, which Vasya generally asked. "As a matter of fact I'm working on something. It's about these articles I've been reading on the crackdown on people showing Western films on videocassette players. It sounds like an interesting business. And I'd like to meet someone in it. Do you know anybody?"

"Someone who shows Western films on video?"

"Yeah."

Vasya was silent for a moment. Then he spoke. "Well, I do know someone. Name is Shurik. But I can't let you call him. If you like, I'll talk to him. If he's willing, I'll tell him to call you."

"All right," Burke said. He gave Vasya one of his business cards. Vasya stuffed it into a pocket in his robe, then returned to his own agenda.

"Colin, I've come across something you absolutely must see."

"A samovar?"

"Sterling silver. Belonged to a prince before the Revolution, and I've restored it to mint condition."

Vasya had been trying for months to get Burke to buy a samovar. Burke was not interested. But he didn't want to offend a useful contact.

"Vasya, you know I can't give you dollars." Conveying foreign currency to a Soviet citizen was a crime.

"I don't want dollars, Colin. I want a video camera. Even if you don't want the samovar, you can sell it to any antique dealer in London for five times what the camera costs you."

"And how am I going to get it out of the country?" There were customs laws against exporting antiques.

"Get someone in your embassy to send it through the diplomatic pouch."

"I don't think so, Vasya," Burke said.

"Colin, just see it. Let me run over to my workshop to get it. It will only take ten minutes." Vasya's workshop was a small apartment off the Leningrad Highway. He had inherited it from an ex-wife, who, by his account, had died tragically in an auto wreck.

Burke looked at his watch. There was still an hour before his lunch with Kuznetsov. "All right," he said.

"Marvelous!" Vasya said. "I'll have Marina make you some tea." He turned toward the bedroom. "Marina!" he called.

"I'm getting dressed," a woman replied from the bedroom.

"Who's Marina?" Burke asked. There were often women at Vasya's apartment, but Burke had never seen the same one twice.

"She's an actress at the Mayakovsky. Quite talented. Too headstrong to keep around, but just right for an interesting evening," Vasya said, grinning complacently. He put on a sweater, socks, and boots.

"Marina, dearest!" he called to the closed bedroom door. "I'm leaving my friend Colin. Would you make him some tea?" Without waiting for a reply, Vasya left.

Burke walked into the kitchen. A kettle sat on the chipped white stove, and there were matches and a tin of English tea on a shelf above it. Burke filled the kettle half full of water, turned on the gas, lit a burner, and put the kettle on it. Then he sat down at Vasya's kitchen table.

In the hallway, the door to the bedroom opened and a woman emerged. She was tall; her slender legs were bare beneath a woolen skirt. Hair the color of honey spilled from a loose chignon and fell in tendrils down her long neck. She had blue eyes.

The woman did not introduce herself. Frowning wordlessly, she walked to the stove and saw the kettle. Then she turned to him.

"Who put the water on?" she asked.

"I did," Burke said.

Her face softened. "Thank you."

"Not at all."

"You're a foreigner," she noticed.

"Working on my accent, though," Burke said.

"It wasn't the accent," she said. "It was putting the water on. Not something a Russian man would do."

She pulled some cups from an overhead cupboard and Burke watched the muscles in her calves contract as she stretched to reach them. Then she turned to Burke.

"What did he tell you about me?" she asked.

"Hello," said Burke. "It's a pleasure to meet you, too."

She managed to scowl and blush simultaneously. "I'm sorry. It's nice to meet you." She turned back to the kettle.

"He told me that you're a good actress," Burke said. "That your name is Marina."

The woman sat down at the table across from Burke. She said nothing.

"My name is Colin Burke."

"A pleasure," she said. She did not look pleased. "I suppose he told you I was looking for a *propiska*?"

A *propiska* was a Moscow residence permit. "No," Burke said. "Are you?"

"Yes," she said. "And he was happy to find out about it."

"How do you mean?" Burke could guess. But he had as much morbid interest as the next person in someone else's sad and sordid secrets.

"None of your business," she snapped.

"I'm a reporter. It's part of my job to find out how people live. I have a license to be nosy," Burke said, trying his best boyish smile.

"Do you want to write about me?"

"No," Burke said. "I'm just nosy."

"Well, I'm not normal."

"I'm sure you're not," Burke said. "But humor me. I'd be too shy to ask if I weren't a reporter." This was true, too. Burke knew it was also disarming.

Marina walked over to the stove. The water was boiling. She brought two cups to the table. As she poured, Burke noticed that she had long, elegant fingers.

"All right," she said. Once she had made up her mind to answer his question, she held nothing back. "I need a *propiska* because my husband decided he wanted me to live with him."

"I don't understand," said Burke. "Your husband wanted you to live with him?"

"You're a foreigner. Why should you understand?"

"So tell me."

"I'm from Nyerungri," she said. "Do you know where that is?"

"Isn't it the new town in Siberia where they have the big coal mine?"

"In Nyerungri we say that they ought to test bombs there because if they make a mistake and the place disappears, no one will miss it."

"So what does that have to do with your husband?"

"Since I was a little girl, I knew I had to get out of Nyerungri. I applied to the Institute of Theatrical Arts in Moscow. I was accepted. Vasya was right when he told you I am a good actress."

"So what happened?"

"At the end of your fourth year at the institute, the graduating class puts on an audition show. All of the directors of the Moscow theaters come to see it. They take the people they want for their companies. I got sick that spring and had to miss the audition show. Without an audition, I got no job offers. With no job offers, I had no *propiska* to live in Moscow after I finished the institute. With no *propiska*, I had to go back to Nyerungri."

"That's terrible," Burke said. "So you married a Muscovite to get a *propiska*?"

She sipped some tea. "It was not that simple. It costs money to arrange a marriage. Two thousand rubles." Two thousand rubles was about a year's wage. "I went back and moved in with my mother. I took a job driving a truck near the pit."

"Why didn't you work in a theater there?"

She sniffed. "They are boors there. I wanted to work in Moscow. After two years, I had saved the two thousand rubles. I came to Moscow. One of my girlfriends from the institute had found a man. He is forty-seven years old, he drinks, and he has been twice married and divorced; his wives threw him out because he's a pig. The arrangement was that we would sign the marriage papers. I would get my *propiska* as his wife, and he would get his money. But we would not see each other after that."

"But it didn't work?"

"For a while it did. I moved in with my girlfriend. I found a theater group; we put on plays in the basement of an apartment building. One night, the Mayakovsky director came to see us. He thought I was 'splendid.' He invited me to work informally with his company. Then he gave me a role in *The Dacha*. You've heard of it?"

"Yes," Burke lied. "I've been meaning to go see it. It's hard to get tickets."

"They will always give tickets to an American correspondent," Marina said. "They want publicity. They want a foreign tour."

"How did you know I was an American and not English, say, or German?"

She smiled for the first time. "Your coat. Your shoes. Eddie Bauer or L. L. Bean?"

"Eddie Bauer," he acknowledged. "So what's your problem?"

"A few weeks ago, my 'husband' came to see me. He wanted me to live with him. He said he is getting old and he wants a son. I refused. So now he has begun divorce proceedings against me. When the divorce is complete in two weeks, I will lose my *propiska*. He says he will inform the police that I am living in Moscow without one. I will have to go back to Nyerungri."

"But you're working at the Mayakovsky now. Can't they help?"

"Not right away. They say they have to wait until there is an opening in the official ranks of the company. Someone will have to die or retire or get another job."

"So you're looking for a bachelor to give you a *propiska* in the meantime. Is Vasya the one?"

She scowled. "He let me think he might be. But he's a bastard. This morning he brought up money. And I'm damned if I'll pay to go through this again. Besides, I haven't got any money—not enough for him, anyway."

In the back of his mind, Burke remembered the dictum that a man should never get involved with a woman who has more problems than he does. Moreover, throughout his time in Moscow he had made it a practice not to socialize with Russian women. When he met them, he told them he was still married to a woman who could not abide living in Moscow and had remained in Washington. It eliminated the women looking for a husband with dollars.

But he liked this woman. He liked her determination. He liked her blunt, cynical honesty. He liked her long bare legs.

"I wish I could help you," Burke said.

"Are you married?"

Burke found that he wanted badly to return her honesty with honesty. It had been a long time since he'd last felt that way.

"I was," he said. "When I was younger. I'm not now." Then he laughed. "But with all your problems, the last thing you need is to marry an American."

Before Marina could reply, Vasya returned. In his arms he carried a cardboard box, and in the box, covered in newspaper, was the samovar. Vasya put the box on the table.

"Where's my tea?" he asked Marina.

"The water's boiling," she replied. "I'm sure you can take it from there." She went back to the bedroom and closed the door.

He grinned at Burke. "See what I mean? Headstrong." Then he lifted the samovar from its box and placed it on the table.

"Not bad, eh?" he said.

Burke, who knew nothing of samovars, nodded. "It looks very nice."

"And it's genuine!" He turned the samovar upside down and pointed to an engraved crest. "See. The Buryakovsky seal. One of the best of the Petersburg silversmiths."

Marina reemerged from the bedroom, with stockings and shoes on. She took her coat from the hook on the wall and began to put it on.

"I'm sure it's a great samovar, but I really am not sure I'm interested in one right now, Vasya. I'll think it over," Burke said. He stood up. "I've got to be going, too. Thanks very much." Trying not to seem hasty, he got up and followed Marina into the hall and put on his coat. Vasya trailed after him.

"Call me then," he said.

"I will," Burke promised, as he slipped on his parka and shoes. "Don't forget to talk to Shurik."

Vasya kissed Marina on the cheek. "*Proshchai*," he said. The Russian word was usually translated as "good-bye." It literally meant "forgive me." Burke thought the literal meaning was appropriate.

"See you," Marina said to Vasya, and then she and Burke were out the door.

They rode silently down to the lobby and walked outside. "Can I drop you somewhere?" he offered.

"No, thank you," Marina said. "I'll take the metro."

She turned to go. "Wait," Burke said. "When's the next performance of *The Dacha*?"

"Tonight," she replied.

"I'll try to get a ticket," Burke said. "But sometimes I can't quite understand all the dialogue. My Russian isn't that good. I need someone to help me afterward. Can you do that?"

Marina smiled. "Your Russian is all right, Mr. Burke. But I would be happy to help you. Strictly so you can write an article about us, of course."

"Oh, strictly," Burke said. He smiled back.

"All right," she said. "I'll see you twenty minutes after the performance in front of the theater."

She turned and walked toward Gorky Street, where the metro was. Burke waited until the plume of frost from her breath had dissipated, then walked in the opposite direction toward his car.

5

BURKE was still thinking about honey-colored hair when he pulled off
Kalinin Prospekt near the Praga restaurant and noticed all the yellow and
blue police cars. Half a dozen of them clogged the north end of the Arbat,
Moscow's pedestrian mall. Burke squeezed his car into a space next to a
bus. Looking into its windows, he noticed that it was full of *militioneri*,
sitting and waiting.

He got out of his car and walked up to the nearest *militioner* on the
street.

"What's going on?" he asked.

The *militioner*, bundled up in a greatcoat and a grey *shapka* with a
brass badge, looked at Burke silently for a moment, his breath steaming
from his nostrils. Burke was about to turn away when he spoke.

"Hooligans," he scowled. "We're protecting hooligans."

"What do you mean?"

The *militioner*, lapsing back into silence, half raised a heavy grey arm
and gestured in the general direction of the Arbat.

Following the gesture, Burke walked down the snow-covered mall.
All of the people, he noticed, were walking purposefully in the same
direction. It felt like the streets around a stadium just before a game.
Rounding a slight bend, he saw where they were going.

A crowd of perhaps a thousand people stood in the packed snow in
front of the Vakhtangov Theater. He saw scattered placards among them.
People, singly and in twos or threes, were streaming across the snow to
join the mass, like iron filings skittering toward a magnet. Most were
young men, Burke noticed, in dirty parkas, with thick hands and blocky
Russian shoes. Here and there he could see a vodka bottle making its way
through a circle of instant comrades. *Militioneri* stolidly ringed the area,
doing nothing to interfere with the growing crowd.

Burke pushed through the fringes toward the vortex of the crowd,
standing on his toes, straining to see what was going on. He passed a man

with a placard, and he turned to read it. RUSSIA FOR THE RUSSIANS! it said, in big red letters.

Then, in front of the pale green facade of the theater he could see a man with a long grey beard and a bullhorn, standing on a soapbox. Judging by his flushed face and the cords standing out on his neck, the man was almost yelling. But whatever amplification the bullhorn gave him did not compensate for the crackling static that accompanied it.

"With reverence for the land . . . ," Burke heard him say. He could only understand fragments. ". . . could grow enough to feed all Russia. . . . Instead, the Jew, Milstein, plans to send Russian water . . . fields in central Asia . . . flood our sacred heritage." Burke pulled out his notebook and began scrawling quotes.

"You could hear better from up here, Colin," a voice to his right said in English. Burke turned and saw Victoria Carlson, the cultural affairs attaché from the American embassy, standing on a bench a few yards away. She beckoned to him with a hand sheathed in black leather. "There's room," she invited. And she shifted to the right, creating a small space between herself and the *babushka* standing next to her.

Burke decided it would be churlish to refuse. He shouldered past a few people. She extended a hand and helped him up. She was wearing a coat of a fur that looked like sable. A matching hat covered her gleaming blond hair, which fell into a wave precisely halfway down her neck. Her makeup, as always, was carefully understated. He caught the faintest trace of a perfume.

"Thanks," he said. "What's going on?"

"It's a Pamyat rally," she said.

"I thought Pamyat was dead," Burke said.

"It has been, for the past three or four years. Not anymore."

He looked around. The crowd seemed to have doubled in the few minutes since his arrival.

Pamyat's anti-Semitic, Russian fascism had been one of the least attractive revelations about Soviet society in the early years of *glasnost*. "Still a bunch of harmless culture lovers?" Burke asked.

"Yes," she said, looking at the man with the bullhorn, not at Burke. "Still."

"Who is that guy?"

"Ivan Ivanov."

The name was so common it had become the Russian version of John Q. Public. It was like Everyman.

"I thought he was in exile."

"He was. Three years ago, they expelled him from the Artists' Union and took away his *propiska* and sent him back to where he came from, which is a village somewhere in Yakutia," she said, still staring ahead. "Obviously, he's back."

On the other edge of the crowd, Ivanov entered his peroration. "I speak in the name of all Russians here, comrades," he said in measured tones. "We demand that the party stop the rape of Russian land!" People applauded, their hands muffled by their gloves. His voice grew stronger. "We demand the preservation of Russian culture!" More applause. Then he shouted, "Russia for the Russians!" The crowd picked up the chant. People kept a muffled time, clapping their gloved hands and stamping their feet in the snow, their eyes bright. Ivanov abruptly stepped down from his soapbox and disappeared in the mass of bodies in front of the theater.

The crowd on the Arbat waited for a few minutes, expecting something more. When nothing happened, they began to drift away.

"Interesting," Victoria said.

"Extremely," Burke agreed. "What do you make of it?"

"Well," she said, "all I know is that this is a peculiar time for Pamyat to start holding rallies again."

Burke nodded. "How'd you hear about it?"

"You aren't the only one with sources," she said.

"And I guess you protect yours, too," Burke replied, stepping down from the bench.

He turned to give her a hand, but she was already down on the slippery pavement. His swinging arm knocked her slightly off-balance, and he caught her by the elbow and steadied her. For a moment, she was directly in front of him, their arms linked, and she was smiling with bright white teeth. He could have sworn that she stayed there long enough to see that he had felt something, then took a step backward.

"Unexpected chivalry," she laughed. "Thank you."

"From a knight erring, I'm afraid," Burke said.

"Errant, Colin. I think you're quite errant."

"I'll take that as a compliment. Thanks," he said. He was used to politicians buying some goodwill with flattery, but he wondered why she was doing it. She hadn't seemed the type.

"Really," she said. "You've been writing some nice stuff."

"Thanks again," he said. "Which way are you headed?"

"Back to the embassy," she replied. "Going that way?"

"No, I've got to meet someone at the Praga. And I'm late."

"Too bad," she said lightly. "Well, it was nice to see you." She smiled again.

"Thanks. Nice to see you, too."

They parted, and he walked back up the Arbat, confused, as always, by Victoria Carlson. Standing with her in front of the bench, he had been sure he was picking up a flicker of interest in her eyes. And that was not the first time. She lived in his building in the foreigners' ghetto. She was pleasant, and she was glad to help him when he wrote about a play or an art exhibition. They occasionally found themselves partners at diplomatic dinner parties. He had suggested dinner together once and received a friendly, but definite, no. He had not asked again. Maybe, he thought, she was committed to someone back in the States. Maybe someday he would ask her about that.

Proletarians never saw the best restaurants in Moscow, unless they happened to work in them. The Soviet elite dined in private clubs, like the prerevolutionary mansion that housed the Writers' Union. Or, they ate in special dining rooms, rather whimsically called cafeterias, attached to their ministries, just as if they were factory lunch halls. As a result, Moscow had no good restaurants except for a few cooperatives that catered to foreigners and *fartsovshchiki*. The people with power and the people with money almost never had occasion to eat in a state-owned restaurant. What did they care?

Faced with this choice, Burke had suggested the cooperative 36 Kropotkinskaya for his first lunch with Andrei Kuznetsov. It was not that the food there was good; it wasn't. But the headwaiter at the co-op, most of the time, answered the telephone, took reservations, and honored them. In this, he was far ahead of his state-owned competition.

Kuznetsov had insisted on the Praga. He said he liked the Praga's *pyelmyeni*, a Siberian dumpling. Cooperatives, he did not have to point out, could not serve alcohol. And as their lunches became a regular event every month or two, Burke had simply accepted his choice.

The bells in the Spassky Tower at the Kremlin were chiming one when Burke entered the Winter Garden Room on the fourth floor of the Praga. A waiter in a wrinkled tuxedo showed him to a table at the edge of the deserted dance floor. Ten minutes later, Andrei Kuznetsov hove into view. Moving slowly and delicately, like a blimp in search of its mooring, the journalist made his way to Burke's table. Burke rose to greet him.

"Andrei Petrovich," he said. "It's nice to see you again."

"Thank you," Kuznetsov said, lowering himself into his chair. He did not return the compliment.

The waiter returned as they looked over the menu.

"I would like five hundred grams, bouillon with *pyelmyeni*, and chicken Kiev," Kuznetsov said. The waiter approved.

Burke, ordering from the menu, asked for sturgeon and mineral water.

"No sturgeon," the waiter said.

Burke knew that at the Praga, the appearance of a dish on the menu could mean that the restaurant once had it, had it today, or might have it in the future. It was by no means a binding offer. "What kind of fish do you have?" he asked.

"There isn't any," the waiter replied.

"All right," Burke said, smiling. "I'll have the chicken Kiev, too. Mineral water."

He enjoyed the fact that Kuznetsov, who had traveled in the West, knew how inferior the service was.

He might have asked Kuznetsov about his family, but they had never talked about families. Kuznetsov, in the Soviet tradition, chose not to reveal personal details to a foreigner. Their lunches were business transactions. Burke asked Kuznetsov about Soviet politics. He took what Kuznetsov told him and weighed it together with all the other information he collected. Kuznetsov occasionally asked Burke what the Americans thought about sea-launched cruise missiles or the Middle East. Burke tried to oblige. Neither would ever publicly identify the other as a source. They informed one another's thinking.

"So," Burke began the conversation, "what will *Izvestiya* say about the demonstration I just saw out on the Arbat?"

Kuznetsov stopped buttering a piece of bread and looked at him suspiciously from under heavy eyelids. "What demonstration?"

"Pamyat," Burke said. "You didn't know about it?"

"No."

Briefly, Burke told him about the crowd on the street and Ivanov's speech. "Who's Milstein?" he concluded.

Kuznetsov sighed heavily. "Milstein is a scientist who is in charge of the Central Committee section that deals with water resources."

"He's Jewish?"

"That's what's stamped in his passport. But he is a good member of the party and I am sure he is an atheist. I know him."

One of the oldest controversies in Soviet politics involved plans to take water in northern Russian rivers and pump it south into the parched agricultural lands of central Asia—where the people were darker and not Russian. It had been approved under Konstantin Chernenko, rejected

under Vikenty Ponomaryov, and was now being talked about again as a
sop to the restless Muslims.

"So Pamyat blames the water diversion program on Jews?"

"Not just Pamyat. A lot of people think there is some scheme to
destroy old Russian churches by building dams and flooding them. They
think water diversion is just an excuse. The Politburo is under heavy
pressure to replace Milstein."

This was good stuff. "What's your opinion?"

Kuznetsov looked straight at Burke. "It makes me angry. When I was
at the university, I lived through Stalin's plot against the Jewish doctors.
It was . . ." He stopped, searching for the right words. ". . . unworthy
of us. I think we are beyond that sort of thing."

"So why has Pamyat come back?"

Kuznetsov shrugged. "I don't know." He did not look as if he wanted
to pursue the topic.

In America, Burke would never have stooped to interviewing another journalist. But this was Moscow, where the journalists, despite
glasnost, all drew state paychecks. Kuznetsov was a peculiarly Soviet
phenomenon—half journalist, half government spokesman. And what he
said generally struck Burke as a lot closer to the truth than what he heard
from the spokesmen who conducted briefings at the Foreign Ministry.

"So what will *Izvestiya* say?"

"I hope we will not say anything. I don't want to encourage them."

"Can you make them go away by pretending they don't exist?"

The waiter arrived with a teapot and two cups. Kuznetsov carefully
poured himself half a cup. Burke noticed that the liquid inside was, as
usual, clear. Under Vikenty Ponomaryov's campaign for sobriety, restaurants were not supposed to sell vodka before 2:00 p.m. But there were
exceptions to every rule.

"Probably not," Kuznetsov said with a slight smile. "But that is why
journalists get to drink at lunchtime." He looked at Burke and raised the
cup. "*Na zdorovye*," he said, and downed the drink in a single gulp.

Denied a graceful opening to what he really wanted to discuss, Burke
plunged ahead. "Well, you know, it's just that your newspaper in the past
few years has become so forthright . . ."

Kuznetsov said nothing and poured another shot.

". . . that when it starts ducking subjects and becoming oblique
again, it's hard to—to readjust."

"Meaning?" Kuznetsov did not look happy with the direction Burke
was taking.

"Well, for instance, the obituary on Rodimenko was pretty oblique."

"He was an old man. He died. And so?"

"Well, I noticed that all the Politburo members except Morozov signed it."

"Perhaps he did not know Marshal Rodimenko," said Kuznetsov, his face blank.

"Or perhaps his position has changed."

"Now you're engaging in speculation, Colin. This is something journalists in socialist countries do not stoop to." Kuznetsov turned his lips up just enough to acknowledge that what he was saying was nonsense.

The bouillon with *pyelmyeni* appeared. Kuznetsov buried his face in the bowl.

Burke was disappointed, though not surprised. Soviet officials rarely, if ever, agreed to talk about the inner workings of the Politburo. He decided to persist.

"And then there was Ponomaryov's saying he had the flu."

"You found that interesting?" Kuznetsov paused, halfway through his *pyelmyeni*. "That someone in Moscow has the flu in the wintertime?"

"Yes. I don't recall ever seeing a similar statement by him. The last time I can recall such an admission was Andropov's saying he had a cold in 1983. A few months later, he died."

Kuznetsov ventured a smile. "I didn't know you were such a student of our history."

Burke noticed the flattery, and chose to ignore it. "Is Ponomaryov seriously ill?"

"If you were a good student, you'd know that, unlike you, we practice a collective leadership. Whether one individual falls ill or not is not a matter for the press to speculate about."

The Russian poured himself another shot of vodka.

"Have some," he invited.

Burke shrugged. Clearly, this interview was going nowhere. "Okay," he said.

Kuznetsov poured a couple of ounces of vodka for Burke. Burke took a sip. It seared his lips and tongue.

"I'm sorry, Andrei Petrovich, but to an American, when the leader of one of the superpowers is sick, it's news."

"You are not in America, my friend. You are in the Soviet Union. And here we have an old Russian proverb: 'Don't butt into someone else's monastery with your own prayer book.' In this monastery, journalists do not speculate about the health of their leaders. And they do not sip and leave vodka in their glass, even if in this case it must be in a teacup."

The chicken Kiev arrived. Heavily breaded and overcooked, it lay on Burke's plate like a piece of sandstone. Burke picked up his teacup. "To your health," he said to Kuznetsov. "And to that of the general secretary."

Kuznetsov smiled. Burke turned his cup up and the vodka slid quickly down his throat, spreading warmth. He looked down at his plate; after the vodka, the chicken seemed a little more appetizing. There was something to be said, Burke decided, for the old Russian traditions.

Kuznetsov looked with distaste at the equally unappetizing chicken on his own plate.

"You know," he said to Burke, "after the inevitable triumph of communism, my only hope is that we spare three or four capitalists so that there will be at least a few good restaurants."

Burke laughed. Kuznetsov looked pleased with himself. After Burke paid the check, he and Kuznetsov went downstairs to the lobby and got their coats and hats. Then they stepped out into the afternoon gloom. Low clouds still hung over the city, and although it was only two-thirty, daylight was fading.

"Thank you, Andrei Petrovich," Burke said.

"Thank you, Colin. I will walk with you to your car."

Kuznetsov and Burke turned right down the Arbat. "I have been thinking about your questions about Ponomaryov," Kuznetsov said. "I did not want to speak of this indoors."

Burke felt a jolt of excitement. Like a poker player with a pat hand who hears another player make a small bet, he had to encourage Kuznetsov subtly, not overwhelm him with eagerness. So he just nodded. "Oh?"

"What information I have about the general secretary was not given to me for publication. But you know, I believe that it is time to extend the policy of *glasnost* a little further. You must protect me on this, though."

"We'll consider it on deep background," Burke said, trying to control his voice.

"What does that mean?"

"That means I can attribute it to a 'Soviet source,' but I cannot name you or indicate what your position is."

"Agreed. Then I will tell you on deep background, as you say, that the general secretary is indeed ill. He has suffered a stroke. But he is recovering nicely, and running the party from his hospital room in the Politburo clinic at Kuntsevo."

They reached Burke's car. "When did he have this stroke?" Burke asked.

"I do not know. And I cannot stand here and talk with you further, Colin." Kuznetsov extended his hand. Burke shook it.

"Thank you again for lunch," Kuznetsov said. "I hope we will be able to do it again soon." Then he continued on down the Arbat, moving slowly and ponderously along the crowded mall, past a couple of portrait artists trying vainly to persuade people to sit for them in the cold.

Burke got into his car. As soon as Kuznetsov was out of sight, he pounded the steering wheel with an open palm and laughed. Maybe he finally would have a front page of his own to hang on the bureau wall.

Burke called some of the political analysts in the Western embassies. Without naming Kuznetsov, he told them what he had learned. None of them had heard the story. All thought it plausible. On his fourth call, to the political officer at the British embassy, whose name was Douglas Crittenden, he got what he was looking for.

"As it happens, I heard the same thing today, Colin," the Brit said in his tired, precise accent.

"A good source?" Burke asked.

"Of course, I can't say precisely, especially over the phone. But I can tell you he's been absolutely reliable in the past." Crittenden was on his third tour in Moscow, in a career dating back to Khrushchev's time. Burke trusted his judgment.

"So what do you think it means?"

"Clearly, Ponomaryov isn't now the strength that he has been. I think the Rodimenko obituary this morning confirms that."

"Did your source have anything on that? Mine didn't."

"No, he didn't. Odd that yours wouldn't either," Crittenden said.

"Well, we'll have to keep digging."

"Right. Let me know what you hear," Crittenden replied. They thanked one another and hung up.

Burke was excited now, and his story wrote itself in about ten minutes:

Ponomaryov
By COLIN BURKE
Tribune Foreign Service

MOSCOW — General Secretary Vikenty Ponomaryov's hold on power came into question Monday with disclosures that he has suffered a stroke and that one of his allies in the Politburo, Pavel Morozov, has lost his job.

The Soviet leader's health problems were partially acknowledged in the government-controlled press, which printed a statement from Ponomaryov to a group of American scientists visiting Moscow. In it, he said that he was ill with the flu and could not meet them. Ponomaryov, who is 60, has been in generally good health since becoming general secretary six years ago.

But an authoritative Soviet source told the Tribune that in fact, Ponomaryov had suffered a stroke. He is, the source said, conducting business from his bed in the Politburo clinic in Kuntsevo, a wooded area in the northern part of Moscow where Josef Stalin once had a dacha. A well-informed diplomatic source confirmed this account.

The exact date of Ponomaryov's stroke and the details of his condition could not be obtained.

At the same time as it disclosed Ponomaryov's illness, the government-controlled press also disclosed the apparent fall from power of Morozov, 64. Morozov, once the leader of the party organization in Perm, western Siberia, moved to Moscow and became a member of the Politburo a year after his patron, Ponomaryov, became general secretary.

He held the "organizational" portfolio within the secretariat of the Communist Party Central Committee. This gave him the power to appoint party officials to key jobs throughout the country. He used it to make certain that officials loyal to Ponomaryov and his reform policies received promotions.

The causes of Morozov's ouster were not clear. His demise was signaled by an obituary for Marshal Timofei Rodimenko. Every member of the Politburo except Morozov signed. In Soviet practice, such an omission is tantamount to an announcement that a party leader has been fired.

Western observers in Moscow speculated, however, that with Ponomaryov ill, other members of the Politburo might have been able to move against Morozov more easily. Their grievances against him remain obscure.

Morozov's ouster would leave the ruling Politburo with 11 members. Western diplomats believe that Ponomaryov still controls a firm majority of the votes within the ruling group.

ENDIT

As he punched the button that sent the story clicking over the telex toward Washington, Burke thought about the theater. He sent Olga with a note and five rubles to the box office at the Mayakovsky. The note explained that he wished to see *The Dacha* in connection with his work and asked that the ticket be left for him. Shortly after she left, the phone rang.

It was Graves, the *Tribune*'s foreign editor, calling from Washington. He was, as usual, brusque.

"Just got in and read your piece," he said. "Interesting stuff." "Interesting" was about as warm a compliment as Burke had heard from Graves. It was the same word Burke had learned to use when a Russian collective farm director asked how the American journalist liked Russia's pigs.

"This bit about Ponomaryov's stroke is exclusive?"

"As far as I know," Burke said.

"Can't you get an on-the-record source?"

Burke was angry, but tried to stifle it. "I'd like to. I've tried. I was lucky to get the two I have."

"You're sure about them?"

Burke got up and began pacing around the office, carrying the phone in his left hand. He wanted to ask why Graves would think he would use a source he wasn't sure of. He managed not to.

"They've been reliable in the past," Burke said. "And why should the Soviets lie about this? You know the Russians hate to admit their leaders even get colds, let alone strokes."

"Okay, Colin," Graves said. "You're the man on the ground. I'll push it for the lead on page one."

Burke let some air out of his lungs and quieted a quick stab of doubt about Kuznetsov. "Thanks, Ken."

"Of course, we'll want to stay with this, Colin. Sounds like things are breaking."

That was obvious. "I will," Burke said. He said good-bye and hung up.

Burke sat back and silently cursed Graves. His call, and his almost snide lack of confidence, had taken the pleasure out of a front-page exclusive.

The internal politics of the paper, he had come to think, resembled nothing so much as the internal politics of the Kremlin, or the Mafia. Like Politburo members, *Tribune* editors collected protégés and competed to pull their protégés higher up the ladder beneath them. Like Politburo members, *Tribune* editors would piously maintain that there were no factions on the paper, that they were all pulling for the same team. And, like Politburo members and Mafia bosses, *Tribune* editors occasionally tossed bodies over the side as they sailed along.

In Moscow, Burke had the same relationship to the *Tribune* newsroom that a diver had to his boat. He was removed from what went on there, and he did not have to worry about having lunch or playing tennis with the right people. They had to take his word on what was going on in his domain. But, like a diver, he was completely vulnerable to anyone who decided to yank on his air hose. Like Ken Graves.

What he needed was a rabbi in the Washington newsroom. Once, he had had one. Roger Costello, the foreign editor when Burke went to Moscow, had brought Burke into the foreign operation, groomed him to go overseas, and pushed his candidacy when the Moscow bureau vacancy came along. But Roger had somehow lost the inside lane, getting shuffled off to edit the Sunday magazine, an assignment just a notch better than running the obit desk.

Graves came from an entirely different newsroom faction; Burke barely knew him. He was a deskman; Burke was an outside reporter. He was an easterner, from a private school; Burke was a westerner, from a public school. Graves played tennis and wore suspenders under his suits; Burke played poker and favored sport coats. Graves had been assistant city editor before he took over the foreign desk. Not only did he know next to nothing about foreign affairs, but he'd quickly begun yanking incumbent foreign correspondents home and replacing them with his favorites from the city staff. Sometimes, Burke wondered whether Graves had yet told anyone from the city staff to start taking Russian lessons.

Sitting there, alternating between worrying about Graves and scanning the walls for a likely place to hang his front-page exclusive, he almost forgot about the theater.

6

IN Washington that morning, some Iranian Shi'ites, bearing portraits of their late and still-lamented ayatollah, staged a demonstration against the Sunnis who ran the Islamic Center on Massachusetts Avenue. They caught Sergei Korotov by surprise. He had grown accustomed to Iranian demonstrators on Friday mornings, and he had taken to avoiding them by using an alternate route from the Soviet residential compound on Mount Alto to the chancery on Sixteenth Street, downtown. This must be, he thought, some Muslim holiday he didn't know about, and his ignorance had trapped him in traffic that barely moved. Partly, this was due to the cold rain that was falling. Partly, it was due to the occupation of the curb lane by the demonstrators. Mostly it was because the drivers, when they finally drew abreast of the stolid, dark-eyed Iranians and their placards and umbrellas, took a moment to roll down the window and flip them a middle finger, or curse them, or, in a few cases, spit at them.

Earlier during his tour in Washington, this spectacle might have amused Korotov, or at least interested him, because he was a student of American mores. This morning, though, it only made him feel like spitting himself. He had been summoned to the embassy early to read an urgent message. Such a summons came rarely, and he took it seriously.

He was already fretful, due to the news item he had heard on the *Today* show as he dressed. "Vikenty Ponomaryov has called in sick with the flu," the announcer had said, a bit flippantly for Korotov's taste. Korotov respected the better American newspapers. Television news, with a few exceptions, he found unbearably superficial and stupid. He had immediately assumed that if Ponomaryov indeed had the flu, it was the least of his health problems. Any serious journalist would have assumed the same and begun to ponder the consequences.

He finally arrived on Sixteenth Street and squeezed into an illegal parking space in front of the National Geographic Building. Inside the embassy, he went to his office and called the clerk who had summoned him, to let him know he had arrived. Less than a minute later the clerk knocked, entered, and handed him a sealed envelope. It added to his fretfulness. According to the KGB rules of procedure he had memorized long ago, such an envelope, delivered directly into his hands from the embassy code room by a KGB communications specialist, could contain only one thing: a *byez rasproctranyeniya* message. The code clerk could and would unscramble a *byezras* message, in effect filtering out all the electronic garbage added to confuse the National Security Agency's eavesdropping devices. But the clerk could not completely decipher it. He would, according to the rules, destroy all but one copy of the unscrambled, still-encrypted message and convey that one copy into the hands of the KGB *rezidyent*. No one else in the embassy, not even the ambassador, was to see it. Korotov had read that in American embassies, the ambassador oversaw everything that the CIA station chief received and wrote. This struck him as absurd. How would the Americans deal with a treasonous ambassador?

Korotov got up, shut the door to his office, and locked it. Then he opened the combination lock to the secure file along the wall, under the portrait of Lenin. He took from it the cipher book of one-time codes that he had been issued before leaving Moscow. It was the only copy in the embassy. A dedicated computer would have worked much faster, but the KGB's code computers were still very bulky; he could not have hidden one in his office. And his cover required that no one, with the exception of the ambassador and one or two other people in the embassy, be certain of his true role.

Neither Korotov nor his superiors thought they could hide the fact that he worked for the KGB, but that was not their intent. His official role at the embassy was liaison officer for the Institute of International Studies in Moscow; he was the embassy's man in the American academic world, and he arranged the exchange visits between American Sovietologists and Soviet Americanists. He could legitimately claim membership in the latter group. His dissertation, on the role of citizens' lobbies in the American political process, could be found in any decent Soviet library. He was quite proud of it and he often urged his American colleagues to read it. It was among the first Soviet scholarly works to get away from the old ideological drivel that held that only rich capitalists manipulated American politics.

The KGB had recruited him for precisely that reason. Years ago, Yuri Andropov had realized that he needed more sophisticated analysis of the United States than he was getting from the old-line operatives who had survived the Stalin era by hewing closely to the party line in every-thing they wrote and said. He assembled a new cadre of specialists in American studies and began sending them to Washington to run KGB operations there. Early on, however, Moscow had discovered something about its new system.

The Americans, it turned out, generally assumed that anyone in a liaison job with foreigners, such as the one Korotov held, had at least some connection to the KGB, some obligation to report what he learned. They could tolerate and work with someone like that. But once a man became known as the *rezidyent*, as someone who got his hands dirty recruiting and paying spies, he was shunned by everyone in the American government and by the best-connected American academics. His effec-tiveness ended. So Andropov had redesigned the Washington operation to create the semicover that Korotov worked hard to maintain. The actual *rezidyent*'s deputy, usually the head of the embassy's security office, handled virtually all of the administrative chores connected to the KGB operation. He did it just visibly enough to make sure that the FBI noticed him at it. The actual *rezidyent* took part in no operations, as a rule. He edited the reports and analysis sent back to Moscow, making sure that the intelligence product was well informed and unbiased. Andropov's system seemed to work. Once in a while, usually when its budget was up for consideration in Congress, the FBI would engineer the expulsion of the embassy's security chief. Shortly afterward, a leak would appear in a newspaper article or a book to the effect that he had been the *rezidyent*. This state of affairs kept all concerned—the FBI, the American reporters, and the KGB—quite happy.

Korotov opened the envelope and confronted a single sheet of paper covered with numbers. The first five digits were a reference, in a code he had memorized; they told him the appropriate page in his cipher book to use for this message. He tore it from the book and set to work.

Korotov found himself chewing on a fingernail as he worked, a habit he managed to control except when under extreme stress. Thinking about this for a moment, he realized how much he dreaded the prospect that this *byezras* message might involve the nastiest duty he could imagine, conducting a security investigation of a senior embassy official. He liked and respected his colleagues in the foreign service, and they liked him. He was relieved when, ten minutes later, he finished deciphering.

After reminding him that this was a matter of the highest security classification, the message read:

Make contact soonest with senior White House staff. Convey the following points, your authority.

1. Illness of general secretary serious.
2. Regardless of personnel changes that might occur, Soviet leadership united, desires continued good relations with U.S.G.

There was no signature. But Korotov knew that any *byezras* message had to be approved at the highest level within the KGB, if not within the Politburo itself. But if this were a message approved by the Politburo, then Foreign Minister Fyodorov, who was a Politburo member, would have known about it. Fyodorov guarded the Foreign Ministry's prerogatives quite jealously. He would never have agreed to allow the KGB to open a back channel to the White House. Korotov ruled out Politburo approval. But if Andrushin was acting alone, or at least without the full Politburo, what was he up to?

He put the thought out of his mind. His only legitimate concern was to carry out his assignment, which, after all, was not nearly so bad as he had feared. He had already assumed that Ponomaryov's illness was serious, so conveying that message did not bother him. He would not have to investigate one of his friends, as he had feared. There was, he calculated, even a good chance that his message was truthful and the Ponomaryov policy of good relations with the West, which he privately supported, would continue. He looked at his bitten fingernail and smiled.

Korotov thought for a moment. General Forsyth, the president's national security adviser, would be the ideal person to contact. But there were risks. Forsyth worked in the West Wing of the White House, and reporters hung around there. He might be seen going into his office. And the ambassador, if he learned of the meeting, would demand to know why the *rezidyent* was seeing Forsyth without telling him. Setting up a meeting away from the White House might be possible, but it would probably take time. He did not have time. The twin demands for secrecy and urgency compelled him to make contact one level below Forsyth on the National Security Council staff. Korotov burned the small pile of paper with the codes and the message in the ashtray on his desk. He locked his codebook back in the file and put on his coat. Then he left the embassy and walked a block down Sixteenth Street through a cold rain to the Capitol Hilton. From a pay phone near the lobby, he dialed Henry Hoffman's number at the Old Executive Office Building.

Hoffman was, at that moment, staring through his window at the rain falling into the courtyard in the middle of the Old EOB, the great, handsome pile of stone pediments and pilasters next to the White House on Pennsylvania Avenue. In more innocent days for the republic, it had housed all of the State, War, and Navy departments. Now it held just a portion of the president's personal staff. State, War, and Navy had long since ballooned and transmogrified into endless bureaucracies with many buildings of their own.

Had Hoffman been a more senior member of the White House staff, he might have had one of the offices that overlooked the White House, or at least one with a view of the Mall or Pennsylvania Avenue. But he had only eight months' time on the National Security Council staff, where his title was much longer than his job description. The title was Special Assistant to the President for and Senior Director for European and Soviet Affairs. The job was being the house Sovietologist.

With or without a view, the job was a plum, though Hoffman knew he had it for two less-than-gratifying reasons. First, he had done his undergraduate work at Texas A&M. Strictly on educational grounds, that should have been a handicap. A&M's Soviet specialists were little better than crackpots. But the president loved A&M graduates. To him, they embodied the macho, can-do mystique of his adopted state, a spirit he could admire but never quite manage to master. The irony was that Hoffman would actually have preferred to go to an eastern college like the president's own. But as the son of an oil field worker, he had no such luxury; A&M's offer of a full ROTC scholarship had made his decision for him. After his stint as an army intelligence officer, he had gone to Stanford for graduate work and then joined the Stanford faculty. But when he applied to the White House staff, he had taken Graham Barringer's advice and played up his A&M connection.

The second, equally ironic reason was an article he had written three years previously, back at Stanford, for a journal called *International Security*. He had argued that no matter what disproportionate cuts Vikenty Ponomaryov might offer, a conventional-arms agreement in Europe would inevitably work to the disadvantage of the United States. The Soviets simply had too many inherent advantages, particularly land links to the European theater and a social structure better suited to rapid mobilization. At a time of their choosing, he had written, they could and probably would quickly replace whatever they had agreed to cut or withdraw. The West, meanwhile, would have grown irremediably weak and complacent.

The argument, he now knew, seriously erred. At the NSC, with access to daily CIA intelligence reports, he had quickly realized how hollow the Soviet military had become and that *perestroika* was no more able than a Western European economy to remobilize. But the article had caught Graham Barringer's eye. Barringer ran a think tank, the American Freedom Foundation, that specialized in finding bright young conservatives and bringing them to Washington. In due course, Henry Hoffman took a leave from Stanford and joined the foundation. And there he learned how much money American conservatives were prepared to spend to support men able to give an intellectual veneer to their favored policies. He could, he realized, get hold of a chunk of that money and use it to work and live on a level far higher than the Stanford faculty's. The trick would be to distinguish himself at the White House.

On Hoffman's lap lay a copy of the NID, the National Intelligence Daily, a news digest printed by the CIA and distributed each morning to the top hundred or so foreign policy makers in Washington. The NID headlined the Ponomaryov illness and Morozov's apparent ouster, but it offered no more new information than *Pravda*. Occasionally, the Agency kept highly sensitive intelligence out of the NID, and distributed it orally at the White House. But Hoffman had access to that stuff, too, and so he knew that the Agency had no clue about what was going on in the Kremlin. By close of business that day, Hoffman would be preparing a memo for Chuck Forsyth and the president on possible American responses to the situation in Moscow. He hated to recommend doing, in effect, nothing. But without better intelligence, he would be doing precisely that.

His secretary buzzed him.

"Mr. Korotov from the Soviet embassy is on line two," she said.

Hoffman marveled at the way the White House secretaries knew without being told which calls to offer to their bosses and which calls required only a pink message slip. On most days, Korotov would have been a message slip.

"I'll take it," he said, and punched the button.

"Henry," Korotov said cheerily. "How are things?" Korotov had picked up on the American taste for informality.

"Fine, Sergei. You?"

"Personally, I'm fine, too. Not too happy at the news from Moscow. But, anyway . . ."

Perhaps Korotov wanted to find out what the Americans knew. Hoffman wasn't biting. "Uhm," he simply murmured.

After a moment, Korotov went on. "Henry, I realize this is short notice, but are you free for lunch?"

Hoffman considered the question. It might be amusing to let Korotov take him to a place like La Maison Blanche and watch him blow his entire monthly dollar allowance on a single meal. But the suit he was wearing was a cheap, ratty old corduroy, left over from his faculty days at Stanford. He had kept the trim pepper-and-salt beard he had grown as a graduate student because he had decided it was an asset in a White House chronically unsure of its intellectual depth. But he didn't want to appear in a place like the MB wearing a suit that screamed woolly-headed liberal. Someday, he would manage to finish replacing all his old faculty clothes, but it was going to take another year or so.

"Sorry, Sergei. We're crashing on something here. No time for lunch," he said.

"I understand," Korotov said. "Well, could we chat in your office for a moment?"

The Russian was being quite persistent. "Sure," Hoffman said. "How about eleven forty-five?"

Korotov agreed and hung up. Hoffman buzzed his secretary. "Clean the place up for a Russian visitor at eleven forty-five," he said. "And get me Dave Fleming."

Fleming was the NSC's FBI man, assigned to the intelligence directorate. Letting him know about the meeting seemed better than waiting for him to find out about it. In a moment, he was on the line.

"What can I do for you, Hank?"

Hoffman hated being called Hank, but he didn't think Fleming knew that, so he ignored it.

"I've got a meeting here this morning with Sergei Korotov. I've met him a few times, but I don't know much about him. What have you got?"

"Well, he's KGB," Fleming said.

Hoffman had found that to Fleming, all Soviet diplomats were KGB, but he didn't argue.

"Anything special?"

"No," said Fleming. "A typical operative. His job seems to be to scout for targets in academia."

"Send me the file on him, okay?" Hoffman asked. "And have him escorted? Seventeenth Street entrance. Eleven forty-five."

"Sure thing," Fleming said.

An hour later, Korotov walked silently with his escort through the metal detector and turnstile on the ground floor. A White House policeman whose name tag said he was from Alabama logged him in at a computer terminal and gave him a visitor's pass to wear around his neck. They walked down the high-ceilinged hallway, past the circular marble staircase that was one of the gems of the city's architectural history, and stopped at a small elevator. Korotov would have preferred to take the stairs, but he said nothing.

A moment later they were in Hoffman's office. It was an odd, jumbled room, Korotov decided. Quietly tasteful landscapes borrowed from the National Gallery of Art hung on two walls. A paper map of the

Soviet Union and a cheap poster showing the Politburo members hung on another. Hoffman's desk occupied one corner, and a cluster of armchairs, a sofa, and a coffee table occupied another. The upholstery was rich, but the heating pipes visible behind them clanked.

Hoffman greeted him in Russian.

"Zdravstvuitye, Sergei. Khotitye kofe?"

Korotov, judging from the sound of Hoffman's accent, knew he spoke much better English than the American spoke Russian. But if Hoffman wanted to impress him with his erudition, that was all right with Korotov. It suggested a possible line of approach for a difficult conversation.

Replying in Russian, he declined the coffee and took the seat proffered by Hoffman, on the sofa.

"Henry, you know too much about us for me to play any games with you," he said, still in Russian. "That's one reason I came here. I have a message to convey, and it is this. . . . "

He paused and adjusted his weight on the couch and noticed that Hoffman was leaning forward, expectantly. That was a good sign.

7

HAD Anton Chekhov been in the Mayakovsky Theater that night, he might have been amused. He should at least have been flattered. *The Dacha* was a naked imitation, an attempt to transpose Chekhov's *The Cherry Orchard* from the Russia of the late nineteenth century to the Soviet Union of the late twentieth. Chekhov's family of effete Russian aristocrats became a family of poor but proud Communist intellectuals in *The Dacha*. Poverty forced them to sell their only luxury, the small country cottage of the title. The prospective buyer was the handsome, Marlboro-smoking, jeans-wearing, boorish proprietor of an auto repair business, grown wealthy under the individual-enterprise policies of (though his name was not mentioned) Vikenty Ponomaryov. To symbolize the transfer of power, the mechanic seduced the family's honey-haired daughter, played, Colin Burke's program said, by M. B. Makeyeva.

Moscow theaters often sold out. But the Mayakovsky was crammed to its gilded rafters for *The Dacha*. People sat on folding chairs in the aisles, oblivious to fire safety. As was usually the case with a hit play, almost everyone in the audience had already heard from friends the outline of the plot and its denouement. Witnessing a performance was, for them, an occasion for passionate between-the-acts debates about its theses. Wandering through the lobby before the final act, Burke listened to snatches of conversation.

". . . all true," a young man with a pinched face and glasses was saying.

"We could use a little more Philistinism," his companion disagreed.

"I'm amazed Ponomaryov lets it go on," said a third man.

"Especially with Filomenov in it," said a fourth, waving a cigarette. They all laughed.

But by the final act, the politics of *The Dacha* were far from Colin Burke's mind. He squirmed in his seat as he watched the mechanic complete the seduction of Marina's character. He was glad when, in a curious reversion to the puritanical tradition of the pre-*glasnost* state, a discreet blackout concealed the consummation.

Afterward, Burke stood in the cold on Gertzen Street and watched the theater empty. Twenty minutes after the final curtain she came out of an alley at the side of the theater and stepped into the light shining from the front door. She was wearing the same wool skirt Burke had first seen her in. Her face shone from the scrubbing she had given it to remove her makeup. She was frowning.

"I wish I had brought flowers," Burke said. "You were marvelous."

"Like hell," she said.

"No, I really thought you were great. You didn't?"

"I was not bad," she said. "But I wasn't good enough."

They walked up Gertzen Street to Tverskoy Boulevard, where Burke's car was parked. "All right," he said. "You've convinced me. You were lousy."

She stopped and frowned at him. Clearly, she could be as critical of herself as she wanted. He could not.

"Oh, really?"

"Just kidding," Burke said. She kept frowning. "Americans kid a lot," he explained lamely.

"I don't like to be teased," she said. Her face convinced him that for some reason it was indeed very important that he not tease her.

"Okay," he said. "I wish I had brought flowers. You were marvelous."

Marina smiled. "I wish you had brought flowers, too. But I forgive you."

"Thank you very much," he said with elaborate formality.

"Where are we going?" Marina asked.

"It's your town," Burke said. "Pick a place where we can talk."

They went to a café a few blocks away in the park near the Kirovskaya metro station. It was called Tver, after an old Russian city that was now called Kalinin. A rheumy-eyed old man in a soiled blue uniform blocked the entrance.

"We're closing," he told them.

Burke looked at the sign behind the old man. It announced that the café was open until 10:30. He looked at his watch. It said 9:55. "I'm an American," he told the doorman, counting on his accent and his clothes to back up his statement. The cut and fabric of Western clothing were unmistakable in a country where the state sold only polyester suits. "You don't want me to return to the United States thinking of the Tver when I think of Russian hospitality, do you?"

The doorman scowled. The burden of caring for the Motherland's image was indeed a weighty one. "All right," he said, and stepped aside to let them in.

The café consisted of half a dozen scarred, rickety tables and a service window, through which Burke could see a heavyset woman washing cups. A few customers sat smoking and talking. Burke went to the window and persuaded the woman to sell him two cups of coffee. They sat down.

Marina was very direct. "Well, what did you think of the play?" she asked.

"It was fascinating," Burke said. He struggled to remember that he was a reporter and that he was conducting an interview, not out on a date. "I heard someone talking between the acts about Filomenov and Ponomaryov. Why should Ponomaryov care whether Filomenov is in the play?"

Marina hesitated, and Burke instantly regretted asking the question. He wanted to make her laugh and draw closer to him. Instead, he was interrogating her.

"Volodya Filomenov has a relationship with Ponomaryov's daughter. As to why Ponomaryov should care, you would have to ask him," she said.

Burke laughed. "The next time I'm out at his place for the weekend, I will. But I thought his daughter was married."

She looked at him with pain in her face. "Please, Colin."

It was curious. In some respects, *glasnost* had given the Russians an approximation of free speech. Deputies in the Supreme Soviet, when it was in session, could say almost what they pleased about the state and the party. But there still were things one did not speak of. Obviously, Burke realized, the love lives of the general secretary's family were among them.

He changed the subject a little, but the reporter in him kept talking. "I can see why Ponomaryov might not like the play."

She stirred her coffee and shrugged.

He tried to explain himself. "Well, it did seem to be trying to say that good Communists are getting . . ."

He stopped himself. He had been about to say "screwed."

". . . uh, disadvantaged by the reforms."

"Colin, you are not going to write this about us, are you?" Marina was clearly anxious.

"Don't you believe it's true?"

"I'm an actress. I don't concern myself with politics."

Burke put his hand over hers. She did not resist. "All right. I won't. I promise." Looking at her face, he found it impossible to tell whether she believed it. He halfway believed it himself, though, which was curious.

"Anyway," he told her. "You were good. You really made me care about what happened to that girl."

She beamed, and Burke felt better. He realized that he wanted this woman—she seemed almost too young to be called a woman—to like him. He wanted to charm her, to make her laugh. He had gotten out of the habit of wanting that.

The heavyset woman emerged from the kitchen, a mop in her hands. "It's closing time," she announced. "You'll have to go." It was 10:05. But, unlike the old man at the door, the woman did not look like the type who would care what an American might think of Soviet hospitality. She looked like a woman intent on going home. Burke decided not to argue.

They put on their coats and walked out into the park. A bit of moonlight had broken through the clouds and glinted off the snow and ice of the skating pond next to the café. The temperature, Burke guessed, was about twenty-five below.

"There's a cooperative I know that's still open," he said.

"No," she replied. "I don't like cooperatives."

"Why not?"

"They're speculators."

"What do you mean?"

She did not answer immediately. Burke waited.

"If you grow some food, and you sell it to me, and you make a profit, that's one thing," she said. "But these people buy a kilo of meat from the state stores for two rubles and then they cook it and sell it for ten. That's dishonest. They're getting rich, and there's no meat in the stores."

Burke thought about telling her how much the restaurants in New York or Washington marked up their meat, but he didn't.

"Your place?" he asked, partly out of curiosity about what she would reply.

"No," she said. "Yelena will be there. We have only one room."

"How about my place?"

"No, Colin. There are guards there, aren't there? Won't they check my documents?"

"They normally don't if someone comes in my car," Burke said. He shivered slightly at the cold, and at the prospect that the guards might check her papers.

Marina was not persuaded. "It's a beautiful evening," she said. "Let's walk around the park." He wondered if she really feared the document check, or whether she didn't want to go to his apartment.

"Aren't you cold?" Burke asked, hoping she was.

"Not at all." She smiled. Burke could not tell whether she was happy in general, or happy at the thought of the thin-blooded American freezing in the Russian evening.

They walked. Their shoes made squeaky sounds on the cold, dry snow. Burke pulled his tweed cap lower over his ears, drew his wool scarf tighter around his neck, and plunged his hands deeper into the pockets of his parka. Marina was not wearing a hat. Before he could ask another question, she took control of the conversation.

"So you thought our play was about the demise of true Communists?"

"Yes," Burke said. "Maybe we could take a ride in my car."

She moved closer to him and took his arm. "No, Colin. It's a lovely night for a walk."

She was definitely being malicious, Burke thought. Still, in this position, he could smell her hair. He walked on.

"And do you favor the demise of Communists?" she asked, her voice full of innocence. Pleased, he noticed that she had begun using the more intimate *ty* instead of the formal *vy*.

"Do you want the truth?" Burke asked. A little uncertain, he used *vy*.

She stopped and turned toward him. Her face was very close to his. Through all the layers of clothing, he thought he could feel her breasts against his chest. "If I use *ty*, you have to," she said.

Burke could not recall the last time a girl had been so openly, pleasantly flirtatious with him. He felt giddy. "I'm sorry," he said. "I was taught that a foreigner had to wait to be asked to use *ty*."

"You were taught wrong," she said. Then she kissed him. Her lips were warm and pliant. He kissed her back and was surprised to feel his own immediate response. He had not reacted that way to a kiss since his teens.

As Burke began to wonder about the possibility of necking on a Moscow park bench in subzero temperatures, she broke away. She looked straight ahead, walking in the semishuffle that Russians use for navigation in the snow.

"Yes, I want the truth. Always," she said.

He had utterly lost the thread of the conversation. "About what?"

"You asked if I wanted your true opinion about communism," she said.

Burke smiled. "You know, I can't recall ever taking a walk in the moonlight with a beautiful woman and discussing the merits of capitalism and communism," he said.

She smiled back. "It was you who raised the subject," she responded.

They passed a snow-covered band shell. They were halfway around the pond. Burke would have preferred to kiss her again.

"Well," he said. "I like Ponomaryov. I hope *perestroika* succeeds. I don't think it will."

"Why not?"

"It would be suicide for the party, and the party knows it," Burke said.

She nodded.

"What about you?" he said.

"I'll tell you a story," she replied. "Two women are talking. Their grandfathers were Bolsheviks in the Revolution. The first one says: 'Isn't it wonderful? Our grandfathers dreamed of a land without barons oppressing the poor people. And their dream has come true.' 'Speak for yourself,' the second one says. '*My* grandfather dreamed of a land without poor people.' "

Burke smiled. "I thought you didn't concern yourself with politics."

She squeezed his arm. "I don't," she said. "We have a saying: The less you know, the better you sleep."

"Even now?"

She nodded.

"Okay, let's talk about something else."

For a moment she said nothing. He thought it would be nice to tell her about the story he had filed that day, and to ask her to celebrate with him. He didn't. It would only make her nervous.

They simply walked, feet crunching in the snow, past the black hulks of linden trees. Burke forgot, almost, about the cold. He appreciated the deep stillness of the frigid Russian night in a way that he never had before.

"Tell me why you left your wife," she said abruptly.

"How do you know I left her?"

She looked at him sideways and smiled. "What woman could leave you?" There was just enough sincerity in her voice to flatter him, and just enough sarcasm to keep her from sounding foolish.

He snorted. "You'd be surprised."

They were coming around to his car again. "I'll take you home," he said, opening the door.

"Tell me why you're divorced," she said as they drove off. "If it's not too painful."

"No, it's not," he said. "It was a long time ago. We lived together in college. She got pregnant and she wanted to keep the child, so we got married."

"Did you love her?" she asked.

"I thought so. Looking back, she was the first woman in my life who made me feel comfortable. No demands. You do your thing, I'll do mine. Get high. Make love. All that."

"So what happened?"

"After the baby came, things changed, of course. We had known it would, but we both got restless. She was a teacher, but she wanted to be a lawyer. She didn't like the night shifts I was working. I had to work nights. Because I knew she didn't like it, I got more and more difficult to live with. So she left me and went to law school and now she's a lawyer in San Francisco and she has a new husband, who's also a lawyer, and they live in Marin County with my son, their daughter, and a hot tub."

Marina turned slightly and looked squarely at him. "I don't blame her," she said.

Burke, stricken, tried to smile. He imagined it looked lopsided. Seeing this, Marina smiled sweetly.

"Just kidding," she said. "We Russians kid a lot."

Then she told him: "Your wife was a fool."

"No, she wasn't. I wasn't easy to live with. But thank you for saying so."

Burke stopped for a light at Uprising Square. A giant green street sweeper pulled up beside them, idling throatily.

"What's your son's name?"

"Sam. He's almost seventeen."

"Do you see him very often?"

The light changed, and he let the clutch out and moved forward. The car heater kicked in and its warmth made him garrulous.

"Not since I left California. I wanted to, at first. But she could make it so damn difficult. She'd leave him with me when she had exams, but when I missed a visit because of an assignment, she'd mark it down. If she was mad at me for some reason, or just feeling bitchy, she'd tell me I couldn't see him. I'd schedule a vacation and plan to spend it with him, and she'd say it was vital that he stay at home to take some lesson or something. If I wanted to complain to the judge, I had to hire a lawyer. It was free for her. And she'd haul out her old list of complaints. Finally, I got tired of it. And so, when the chance came to go to Washington, I took it. Even though I knew I'd be losing a lot of contact with my son. It was a mistake. I wish I hadn't done it."

"It sounds like you did the best you could," she consoled him.

"No." Burke shook his head. "He hasn't called me 'Dad' since he was ten years old."

"It's tough on a child—to lose a father."

"You did?"

"Yes. I don't think I've ever gotten over it."

They had arrived at her street. She asked him to stop a block away from her building, and he did.

"I don't really know you, but I get this feeling that you're very—" He stopped. The words that came to mind, like "honest" and "truthful," seemed best suited for Girl Scouts. He settled for *otkrovennaya*, a word usually rendered in English as "frank," but one that literally meant "from the blood." "You're very *otkrovennaya*," he said.

She nodded. "I don't pretend."

That seemed fair enough. She didn't pretend.

"I should tell you something, then," he found himself saying. "To be honest about it, my divorce was—is painful."

She leaned over and kissed him lightly. "I know," she told him.

Something occurred to him then, and he couldn't stop himself from asking about it. "This marriage you got into to get a *propiska*. Isn't that pretending?"

She shrugged. "Of course. So is what I do on the stage."

"But they don't count?"

"You really don't know, do you?" she said gently. "If you have to lie on some papers to be able to live where you want to, that's the fault of the system, not yours. So, of course, you lie. Everyone has to, all the time. It's different with the people you know, with your personal life. You have to draw a line around that and say, 'Within this line, no lies.' For self-respect." She paused.

"You don't have the same thing in America?"

"No," he said. "I think maybe in America it's the opposite."

She smiled. "Such a poor country."

He laughed and, over her protests, walked her to the door. He kissed her briefly, and she wrote her telephone number on one of his business cards before she disappeared behind the slatted wood door of the building.

He walked back to the car, feeling somehow graceful. It was not until he was sitting on the cold vinyl seats in the weak glow of the dashboard instruments, waiting for the heater to work and realizing how quickly the air in the car had frozen again, that he began shivering.

He drove back to his quiet, darkened office to check the telex machine and the late wire reports.

Reuters was carrying an account of Ponomaryov's illness, with a paragraph plugged in from Washington citing his story in the *Tribune*. He had three telexes.

The first carried the play message, sent by the foreign desk to all bureaus, listing the stories on the front page of the first edition. It was the correspondents' scoreboard. This one said, "Lead: MOSCOW, Burke, Ponomaryov."

A second, briefer message was a herogram from his old editor, Roger Costello. "Well done. Cheers. Costello." That was nice.

The last message read: "Advise soonest on Ponomaryov folo. Graves."

Graves was such a flatterer, Burke thought. He turned out the lights and drove home.

8

YEARS of dedicated practice had given Andrei Kuznetsov a high tolerance for vodka and a high resistance to hangovers. Nevertheless, this morning his brain felt like a hot, heavy cannonball rolling around loose inside his head. His limbs, never spry, were particularly leaden. His stomach, which normally was leaden, today writhed, ached, and rumbled in a state of incipient mutiny. It had been a long night at Andrei's Table. How many five-hundred-gram vodka carafes had he drunk? He had no idea. He could barely remember getting to the office.

Kuznetsov leaned over his desk, propped his throbbing head in his hands, and rubbed his eyes. He stared morosely at Miss October. He looked at his typewriter and tried to think about writing something. Nothing could stop the churning in his stomach. Nor could writing take his mind off the knowledge that it wasn't really the hangover that was churning his stomach.

He had been only an infant when they came for his grandfather in 1937, during the height of Stalin's terror. Growing up, he had been vaguely aware of a void at the center of the family, of a sadness. But his father and mother never spoke of his grandfather. Then, on a spring evening in 1954, Kuznetsov returned from school to find a bent, wrinkled man, his fingers blackened and split, wearing loose grey clothing, sitting at the kitchen table drinking tea. He remembered seeing this shabby stranger rise, come toward him, and then clutch him in an unexpectedly strong embrace. He remembered the gristly feeling of the old man's cheeks, and the wetness of the tears that the old man shed.

Two days later, he came home to find his grandfather, so recently restored to him, gone.

"Where's Gramps?" he asked his father, who was the only one at home. For a moment, the air in the apartment, or the look of his father, told him that his grandfather was dead. But it was not death.

"He's gone to live in an *internat*, Andrusha," his father had said. He looked steadily at the dingy grey carpet, not at his son.

"Why?" Andrei had demanded. *Internati* were for elderly people who had no relatives to look after them. They were almost as bad as prisons, crowded and riddled with sickness. "Why isn't he staying here?"

"There's no room, Andrusha."

Andrei, for the first time in his life, challenged his father. "You're lying, Poppa," he heard himself say, strangely calm. "He can have my bed. I'll be going to the university in the fall. I can live there."

His father had not reproached him, or denied the accusation. Instead, he walked into the kitchen and sat down at the table. A half-full bottle of vodka was open in front of him, along with an empty glass. "Sit down, Andrusha," his father had said. "Bring a glass."

It was the first time his father had invited him to drink. Flushing now with both anger and pride, he had gone to the speckled sink with the blood-brown stain under the faucet, pulled a glass from the bottom, and taken a seat at the table. His father poured two fingers of vodka into the boy's glass. Silently, they drank.

"Andrusha." His father was looking at him now, but with a look in his eyes that Andrei had not seen before. Their roles were reversed, and his father was looking at him abjectly, fearing judgment. Andrei said nothing.

"Your mother did not want your grandfather to stay here," his father had said. "She feels it is too dangerous."

"Why?" Andrei had asked again, although at that instant he knew everything there was to know. Anger and the vodka made him press his questions further. "Why? He's been rehabilitated by the party! He's an old Bolshevik!"

"Yes, right now he is. Tomorrow, he could be something else. They could decide he's an enemy of the people again."

Andrei had hung his head. "They won't," he said quietly, but there was no conviction in his voice.

His father had placed a hand atop his son's. "Let me tell you what happened the first time they arrested him. Your grandmother's heart was broken; it killed her. You don't even remember her, and that's why. I had to quit the university and take a job as a schoolteacher. I could not join the party. I felt lucky at that." He took his hand off Andrei's. "We can't risk letting that happen again, son. If it were just me, I would take your grandfather in. He's my own father. But I have your mother to think about. I have you to think about. And your grandfather agrees. It's better that he live in the dormitory."

"Fuck them!" Andrei had said. "Fuck them all!"

It was the first time Andrei had used such language at home. Under other circumstances, he would have been punished. Instead, his father poured out two more drinks.

"Don't judge them too hastily, Andrusha," he had said, leaning over the table, his tongue thickening with the vodka.

"They're bastards," Andrei had said, righteously angry.

"Listen to me, Andrusha," his father had replied. "This is your Motherland. You must understand. A country is like any organism. It evolves so slowly, from generation to generation, that it seems never to change. But it is changing. So is our country. And it is evolving in a positive direction. Look how far it has come in less than forty years. We were nothing, Andrei. We were beaten in the war. The Poles invaded us and occupied half the country. Now, we have beaten the Germans, and even the Americans fear us. Now that Stalin is dead, people are being released from the camps. The country is awakening. It will continue to evolve. So don't say, 'Fuck them.' "

"I still want no part of it."

"Yes you do, Andrusha," his father had said, his voice soothing. "You and your generation can achieve things that my generation could not—that I could not. I want you to try, Andrusha. Don't throw your life away."

And Andrei had not. He went to the university and remained a member in good standing of the Komsomol. He determined to get what he could from the system. When the time came to choose a profession, he chose journalism, which placed him in the service of the party. "The press," read the red banner in his journalism classroom, "is the party's mightiest weapon." He began to believe, or at least to hope, that his father had been right: that the country was evolving in a positive direction.

Kuznetsov's head throbbed again. He thought about what he had learned in the twenty hours since he had left Colin Burke at the Praga. From an old friend at the Central Committee, he had heard the story—or at least *a* story—of Pavel Morozov's removal. Boris Zamyatin, the Leningrad party leader, had flown into Moscow for the Politburo meeting. He had, Andrei heard, presented a full dossier of evidence proving that Morozov had a bank account in Zurich with a quarter of a million dollars in it. Zamyatin did not say where he got the evidence, nor was he asked. Igor Andrushin had said nothing. He hadn't had to. In the absence of General Secretary Vikenty Ponomaryov, Morozov's patron, the Politburo voted unanimously for Morozov's removal. On the reliability scale of Moscow rumors, Kuznetsov gave this a B plús. It was too plausible to be completely untrue.

Then, this morning, on the Voice of America and the BBC, Kuznetsov had heard, as he had known he would, the story he had planted with Colin Burke. "The *Washington Tribune* reported today that Soviet Communist Party leader Vikenty Ponomaryov has suffered a stroke. He is, according to the newspaper's sources, expected to recover . . ."

Around the Soviet Union, Kuznetsov knew, party members had heard that broadcast. And they were drawing their own conclusions about the party's future direction—and their own.

So was he. Andrei Kuznetsov had seen five general secretaries lead the party, and he had learned something from watching each of them. Nikita Khrushchev was leading the party when he had joined it, in 1961. Those were anti-Stalinist times, and Andrei Kuznetsov had let his enthusiasm for de-Stalinization show a bit too plainly. He had organized a small celebration for some junior staff members at *Izvestiya* on the night Stalin's remains were removed from the mausoleum on Red Square and buried more modestly in the Kremlin wall. That gathering was noted, he later learned, and remembered in 1964, when Leonid Brezhnev ousted Khrushchev and moved the party back—not all the way to Stalinism, but to a safe remove from Khrushchev's reformism. "There are people who would like to fire you, Andrei," his editor had told him. "I am protecting you. But you had better learn from this."

He did learn. He learned how to project, during business hours at least, the stolid Brezhnev style. He confined his roistering to the evenings. And he learned to be careful, to watch for the signs of a shift in the party line the way a sailor learns to anticipate a shift in the weather. And as the sailor learns to trim his boat for the impending change, Andrei learned to position himself out in front of whatever new political breezes were blowing. In his column, he called for discipline six months before Brezhnev died and Yuri Andropov took his place and initiated a campaign for discipline. Why not? Who could be against discipline? And he had written favorably of economic experimentation when the call for reform was still a seed in the mind of Vikenty Ponomaryov. It was not a difficult trick. One had only to look around to see the needed changes. One had only to wait until a leader was obviously dying before beginning to advocate them.

His head in his hands, Andrei Kuznetsov listened to the rumbling in his insides and wondered whether he had the stomach to sail with the new wind he sensed was coming.

* * *

A mile away, in his office overlooking Dzerzhinsky Square, Igor Andrushin's head was also in his hands, but he was not thinking, directly at
least, about politics. He was studying the report, in *Pravda*, of a chess
game in Zurich between Garry Kasparov, the world champion, and
Anatoly Karpov, the challenger. It was the seventeenth game of their
match, and the fourth match they had played for the championship since
Kasparov had wrested the title from Kărpov in 1985. And finally, after all
those games, the balance of power had begun to shift back to the old
champion. In the seventeenth game, Karpov, playing black, had forced
Kasparov to resign after sixty-two moves. He led the match, three games
to two, with twelve draws. If he could maintain his level of play, he
would regain the championship.

This would please Igor Andrushin, along with millions of other
Russians. It was not, in Andrushin's case, because of prejudice. Karpov
was Russian; Kasparov was the child of a Jewish father and an Armenian
mother who had Russified his name. But Igor Andrushin did not believe
in ethnic superiority. He believed in education.

Nor was it because of the political proclivities of the contestants.
Anatoly Karpov, it was true, steadfastly supported the party and will-
ingly lent his name and support to approved causes, like the Fund for
Peace. Kasparov, on the other hand, was a hotheaded young man who
had once publicly accused the Soviet chess authorities of favoring Karpov. He played as often as possible in Western Europe, and enjoyed the
company of foreign women. Andrushin much preferred Karpov as a
model for Soviet youth, but that was not really why he enjoyed seeing
Karpov gain the upper hand.

Andrushin simply admired the way Karpov played chess. Kasparov
attacked boldly, almost recklessly. Only his genius saved him from
critical mistakes. Karpov played as Igor Andrushin himself aspired to
play. Karpov's brilliance was subtler than Kasparov's. He used what
seemed to be orthodox openings and defenses. He played for incremental
gains, not for major triumphs. To see a Karpov win was to watch small
advantages accumulate and be transformed into crushing superiority. A
long series of Karpov moves might culminate in just the proper position-
ing of a pawn. Playing Karpov at his best, an opponent would seldom feel
threatened. Gradually, his options would narrow and, finally, after
dozens of moves, he would realize that his position was hopeless. But
he would rarely be able to look back on the game and find a particular

move about which he could say, "Ah, there is where I made my mistake."

Andrushin interrupted his study of the chess game for a moment and looked at his watch. It was 11:00 a.m. He buzzed for his secretary. "Yes, Igor Vasilievich," the man answered.

"Ask Comrade Kuznetsov to come by at three this afternoon," Andrushin said.

"Yes, Igor Vasilievich."

Andrushin was, by then, not listening. He was once again bent over *Pravda*, studying the Karpov-Kasparov match, trying to find precisely where Karpov had made his winning moves.

At five minutes before three, the same car and driver appeared at the front door of the *Izvestiya* building for Andrei Kuznetsov. They took the same route through Dzerzhinsky Square, and the same elevator to the office of Igor Andrushin. Andrei Kuznetsov felt the same trepidation in his bowels.

The dull light coming in from the square framed Igor Andrushin's face in a halo of white hair. The two men exchanged greetings, and again Andrushin offered Kuznetsov a Russian *papirosa*. Kuznetsov checked the table before accepting. This time there was an ashtray. He accepted the cigarette, trying to keep his hand steady as he withdrew it from the proffered package.

"Andrei Petrovich," Andrushin began, his face grave. "You did well yesterday."

"Thank you, Igor Vasilievich."

Andrushin gravely waved the thanks away. "You know, of course, that the general secretary's health is rather worse than I was able to tell you yesterday."

Kuznetsov, of course, had not known, and he felt queasy at the sound of the words "rather worse." Andrushin, he noticed, looked quite composed.

Kuznetsov nodded, trying to keep his uneasiness off of his face.

"We are in a difficult period," Andrushin resumed. "I have another favor to ask of you." Andrushin opened the lap drawer on his desk and withdrew a red folder, tied shut with a string. He untied the string and handed it to Kuznetsov.

"Read it," Andrushin said, then added, "Would you join me in a drink?"

Was this some kind of test? Kuznetsov decided that it might be. Rather than take a chance, he declined. "No, thank you, Igor Vasilievich. I've still got work to do today."

"Very well," Andrushin said, smiling slightly. He made no effort to get a drink for himself.

Kuznetsov scanned the papers in the folder. One appeared to be a KGB report on a troop mutiny in a barracks outside Yakutsk. The second was a report on drug use among the troops that had served in Afghanistan. Kuznetsov looked up from the papers to the man who had given them to him. He did not know what to say.

"Well?" Andrushin said. He was not going to prompt Kuznetsov. "What do you think?"

"Very disturbing," Kuznetsov said. He wondered if the offer of a drink was still open.

"Obviously," Andrushin said, once again like a seminar leader prodding a dull student. "I could show you more reports like it. I will, if you need them."

"Need them?" Kuznetsov was genuinely puzzled.

"For your article."

"Article?" Kuznetsov hated to sound and feel stupid in front of the KGB chief and a Politburo member. In fact, he was beginning to understand what Andrushin had in mind. But what the KGB leader apparently wanted him to do was so foreign to his experience as a Soviet journalist that he could not reply.

"Very well, Andrei Petrovich." Andrushin's voice conveyed impatience, but also a touch of condescension. Kuznetsov decided that he definitely did not like this man. What gave a damn Chekist the right to be arrogant?

"Since you don't seem to have the journalistic instincts to understand this," Andrushin continued, "I will spell it out for you. I want you to write an article about the shocking state of discipline among the troops. They are quite clearly not prepared to defend the Motherland."

"The shit would hit the fan," Kuznetsov said. For a moment he wondered if Andrushin would be offended by the profanity.

"The shit needs to hit the fan," Andrushin said. "It needs to be shoveled up and exposed. That's why we have *glasnost*."

"Well, I, don't know—that is, I agree with you, Igor Vasilievich," Kuznetsov said. How could he get out of this? Desperately, he fell back on the traditional Russian response to an uncomfortable choice— bureaucracy. "It will take me a long time to get approval for this—my editors, the Central Committee, the Defense Ministry . . ." He dropped the file on the table in front of him, as if it were diseased.

"That's all taken care of," Andrushin said.

"It is?" Kuznetsov was dumbfounded. An article such as the one Igor Andrushin was proposing he write was like a homemade bomb. It could quite easily destroy both its target and the man who planted it. *Glasnost* had opened many areas to criticism. The state of military preparedness was not one of them.

Quickly, Kuznetsov considered the list of targets the article could be aimed at. There was one obvious possibility—Vyacheslav Kluchevsky, the minister of defense. Publication of an article such as this would be tantamount to an indictment of his stewardship of the military. Beyond that, whom could Andrushin be aiming at? There was only one man beyond Kluchevsky—Vikenty Ponomaryov. Did Andrushin really have such power?

"Yes, it is," he vaguely heard Andrushin say. "You needn't worry about it."

Andrei Kuznetsov felt, more intensely than ever, the knot of fear twisting his stomach. "It would take me a while to write this piece—," he began.

"It must be done by the end of this week," Andrushin said. His tone suggested that there was nothing to be gained from further argument.

Kuznetsov decided that his best course was to agree, for the moment, and look for a way out later. While he was at it, he decided, he ought to do what he could to persuade Andrushin that there was no doubt in his mind about the assignment.

"Very well, Igor Vasilievich. I'm honored that you would choose me."

Andrushin smiled. "I'm glad we're working together, Andrei. You have a lot to contribute."

"Thank you, Igor Vasilievich." Kuznetsov noticed that Andrushin was using his first name only. But he decided to continue using the formal mode of address, with both the first and middle names.

Andrushin once again looked like a kindly professor. His voice was calm, almost soothing. His blue eyes peered directly into Kuznetsov's, but there was not, for the moment, any threat there, nor any coldness, nor any arrogance. "There is an urgent need for your contribution, Andrei, and I don't ask for it lightly. I realize this assignment must seem risky to you. But I can assure you that the real risk is to do nothing. Our country is in terrible shape, Andrei. If we continue on our present course, I do not like to think of what the Americans could do to us."

Kuznetsov nodded.

"I know you are uncomfortable with the word 'discipline,' " Andrushin said, his tone much softer. "I agree. It has terrible connotations. Don't you think I know that?"

Kuznetsov bobbed his head up and down again.

"We will never return to the Terror, Andrei. But we have, unfortunately, tried to move too fast toward democratization, openness. Our people were not ready. How could they be? After a thousand years under tsars? After seventy years under the party? We need to make a very gradual transition. It will take another generation or more. And in the meantime, we must have discipline. We can't have every miner or railway worker thinking he can go on strike. We can't have every little republic demanding independence. Not now. The threats that face us are too grave."

Kuznetsov nodded a third time. He did not believe what Andrushin was telling him. He knew that terror would be the only way to impose Andrushin's kind of discipline again. And he knew that the cost of terror would be far higher than the cost of a few strikes. He also knew he could never persuade Andrushin of that. So he nodded.

"Yes, Igor Vasilievich. I see." Kuznetsov waited a moment. He got up and stepped away from the table. "I'll get to work on it right away. Good-bye."

"Good-bye, Andrei." Andrushin shook Kuznetsov's hand. He waited until Kuznetsov had almost reached the door of his office before he stopped him. "Andrei!"

Kuznetsov stopped as if shot and slowly turned around. The ice was back in Andrushin's eyes. Andrushin gestured toward the red folder, still lying on the table where Kuznetsov had dropped it.

"You forgot something."

"Oh, yes, sorry, Igor Vasilievich," Kuznetsov said. He scurried toward the table and picked up the packet. His face burned with embarrassment. Then, trying simply not to trip and feel stupid, he left, shutting the leather-covered doors behind him.

Igor Andrushin watched him go and then buzzed for his secretary. In a few seconds, the man, whose name was Kuliakov, entered with a notebook in hand. "Monitor Comrade Kuznetsov's telephones," Andrushin told Kuliakov.

"Yes, Igor Vasilievich," Kuliakov answered.

"And I've read the report and proposal on the American correspondent. Go ahead."

"Yes, Igor Vasilievich."

"That will be all."

Andrei Kuznetsov, back in his office, sat down for a moment, pondering his options. He pulled out a bottle from a desk drawer and poured a hundred grams of vodka to help him think. What could he do? To whom could he go? After an hour's reflection, and several hundred more grams, he put his coat back on and, taking the back stairs, went down to the darkening street and into the subway. He got out at the Kiev station and walked over to Kutuzovsky Prospekt. There, in the gathering cold of the winter day, he stood outside a cheerless glass and steel box called Kafe, waiting for Colin Burke.

9

THE morning sky in Moscow was a spectrum of grey, starting with deep black tones in the west and working toward dirty off-white in the south and east, where the sun was putatively shining. By his normal standards, Colin Burke slept in, awakening well after the winter sunrise at eight o'clock. The sound of shovels scraping outside told him that more fresh snow had fallen during the night. He stretched, and decided it had been too long since his last decent workout.

Burke slipped into an old pair of Levi's, a cotton turtleneck, and a sweater. He found some thick woolen socks, put them on, then laced on his ski shoes. At the door to his apartment he added a wool cap, a sleeveless down vest, and some gloves. He grabbed his skis and poles and took the elevator down to the parking lot and the red car.

Burke turned east on Kutuzovsky, where the traffic was light. Instead of taking the bridge over the river toward the Kremlin, he turned right and drove along the embankment road, past the Kiev Station, past a sprawling, buff-colored machine-tool factory, and into the Lenin Hills.

The Lenin Hills were really a ridge crowded up against the river, overlooking Lenin Stadium, Novodevichy Monastery, and central Moscow on the other side. A flat ribbon of parkland lay at the bottom, between the slope and the river. Burke turned into the park, stopped the car, got out, and put on his skis.

Previous skiers had carved four parallel ruts, like inverse railroad tracks, in the snow at the river's edge. This morning they had a frosting of white powder. Burke slipped his skis into two of them and set off. On his left lay the silent, frozen river, covered with a rippling blanket of snow. To his right, the wooded land rose steeply. In the sheltered silence he could hear his skis hissing against the snow. After a few steps he found his rhythm, pushing and gliding, pushing and gliding. He could feel the wind biting his cheeks. He guessed the temperature at about ten degrees.

Burke skied along the river until he felt the first drops of sweat form on his forehead and drip into his eyes. He had covered about two miles. Then he turned around and picked up the pace heading back. By the time he reached the car, he was sweating freely. His limbs felt loose and warm as he drove back into the courtyard, pulled the morning *Pravda* from his mailbox, and headed upstairs for a hot shower.

Downing some instant coffee for breakfast, Burke glanced at the account on page 6 of the Karpov-Kasparov chess match. He was glad they had decided to play in Switzerland, and not in Moscow, where he would have been responsible for covering them. Burke played poker; chess, at their level at least, was beyond his comprehension.

After yesterday's thunderbolts, this morning's *Pravda* was curiously, all too characteristically, empty. There was no mention of Vikenty Ponomaryov's illness, nor of Pavel Morozov. The lead story told how a Siberian milkmaid increased her cows' yields through hard work and diligent application of the latest in dairy technology from Soviet laboratories. Even after several years of Vikenty Ponomaryov's *glasnost* policy, *Pravda* existed in a looking-glass world of its own. An article lauding increased milk production never mentioned the much higher yields that farmers in Europe and North America routinely obtained. The whole paper never hinted that throughout the rest of the world, people were reading and listening to reports about a stroke felling the leader of the party whose organ *Pravda* was.

Burke barely had time to get his coat off before Olga came into his office. She was wringing her hands.

"Colin, the Press Department at the Foreign Ministry called. They have scheduled a briefing this morning at ten with Mr. Grishin. The subject will be Soviet proposals in the START talks."

"Okay," he said. "Anything bothering you?"

"Um, no. They just asked me to be sure you got the message."

He raised his voice a decibel or two over conversational levels, and aimed it directly at the light fixture in the ceiling. "Don't worry. If they interrogate me, I'll never tell that you were my source about Ponomaryov's stroke."

Olga glanced at the light fixture in momentary alarm. Then she looked at him reproachfully, like a mistreated puppy. Burke immediately felt slightly ashamed.

He patted her on the back. "Sorry," he said. "I'll go to their briefing." He looked at his watch. It was already five after ten.

It was twenty after ten by the time he parked in front of the ministry's press building on Zubovsky Boulevard, a white structure built for the 1980 Olympics. Its architect had somehow managed to use lots of glass and at the same time insure that little or no light penetrated its lobby, giving the place a permanently gloomy atmosphere. Burke showed his credentials to the *militioner* at the door and handed his parka to the old woman in the wardrobe.

Someone long ago had decided to decorate the auditorium in orange and brown. The seats were covered in orange upholstery, the carpet and curtains were orange, and the walls were paneled in brown woods with a slightly orange cast. It wasn't pretty, but it was at least different from the usual red and gilt of official decor. Most of the four hundred seats were full and television cameramen blocked the aisles; the same architect who messed up the lobby had neglected to design space for them. Moscow had nowhere near four hundred foreign correspondents, but a lot of the Western embassies routinely sent staff members to monitor Grishin's briefings.

Burke considered Vasily Grishin the best press spokesman he had ever seen, even though he, like most correspondents, generally referred to him by the vaguely homonymous nickname Greaseman. After tours of duty as an *Izvestiya* correspondent in London and Bonn, Grishin had become the Soviet spokesman when *glasnost* was new, and he had helped reshape the Soviet image. He understood the Western media in a way that few Soviets did. He gave them, particularly the television correspondents, precisely what they needed. He was handsome, without being pretty; well dressed, without being effete; capable of turning aside a tough question with an impromptu, ironic phrase that stopped just short of sarcasm. He realized that the novelty of a Soviet spokesman acknowledging fault and error would establish his credibility, so he occasionally acknowledged fault and error. He gave great sound bites—in three languages.

Grishin, dressed in one of the Harris tweed sport coats that appeared in his wardrobe after any major Soviet delegation went to London, was holding forth in Russian on the Soviet position on the elimination of cruise missiles when Burke slipped into a seat at the rear next to Barry Sherman, the bureau chief for AP. He noticed that a few heads swiveled in his direction.

"The man of the hour arrives," Sherman whispered. "Nice piece. We tried to match it with our own sources, but we couldn't. So we ran a piece attributed to you."

"Thanks," Burke whispered. "Have you talked to Doug Crittenden?"

"Yeah, I did. He was very vague. Not with you?"

Burke shrugged and arched his eyebrows. Crittenden, like most good embassy political analysts, preferred to trade information, not hand it out.

"Have I missed anything?" he asked.

"Nope. Same old shit on arms control. The Greaseman's gotta be here to take a question on Ponomaryov."

Burke nodded. He wondered what Grishin would say.

In a few minutes, Grishin wound up his spiel on cruise missiles and opened the floor to questions.

Stu Jorgenson of CNN was the first to get to the microphone and he asked his question in English. "Mr. Grishin, is it true as reported that the general secretary has suffered a stroke, and if you deny it, why has he failed to appear in public for more than a week?"

Grishin turned the corners of his mouth up slightly in a relaxed, indulgent smile, and he responded in English.

"As you know, Mr. Jorgenson, our ground rules say that when a briefing is called to discuss a specific topic, we do not answer questions on other topics." He paused, and the smile flickered across his face again.

"But since you ask, I will tell you that there is nothing to add to what the general secretary himself indicated in the letter published yesterday. He has the flu, like a lot of people at this time of year." The smile disappeared completely, replaced by a condescending twitch of the Russian's eyebrows. "I cannot comment on every speculative report that comes along about the general secretary's health. As to his schedule, as soon as an appropriate occasion arises, I'm sure you will see him."

Serge Burns of the *New York Times* followed Jorgenson. "Is Mr. Morozov still a member of the Politburo?"

"I can see that I made a mistake in allowing Mr. Jorgenson's question," Grishin said in Russian. "This briefing is about strategic-arms control, and I must insist that the questions stick to that topic."

A TASS correspondent loyally jumped up and asked Grishin, "Have opinions of the nonaligned countries been taken into account in the formulation of the Soviet position, and how are they reflected in it?"

Grishin graciously acknowledged that, indeed, the views of the non-aligned world were reflected in the Soviet position, which would undoubtedly free a great deal of money for Third World development if only the stubborn Americans would accept it.

Sherman stood up and pushed past Burke. "I can't stay around for this crap," he said. "I gotta go file." There was always, somewhere in the world, an AP member facing a deadline.

Burke decided to join him. A few of the other correspondents began leaving as well.

Howard Rosenthal of the *Baltimore Sun* caught up with them on the staircase outside the auditorium. "What's the lead, Barry?" he asked. Rosenthal liked to know what his editors would be reading on the AP wire before he filed his own story.

"Soviet spokesman Vasily Grishin said Tuesday that General Secretary Vikenty Ponomaryov has the flu, and branded reports that he has suffered a stroke speculative." Sherman rattled off his response as if he were dictating.

"But if you notice, he didn't really deny that he's had a stroke," Rosenthal said. Burke was glad he was not the only one who'd noticed.

"Yeah, it was classic Grease," Sherman agreed, grabbing his coat and heading toward the door. "But that's in the second graf. You asked me about the lead."

And the absence of an outright denial wouldn't even be on the television news shows, Burke thought. He had to hand it to Grishin. By switching to English, Grishin had delivered the perfect sound bite. His gibe about "speculative reports" would be heard by maybe a billion people. Including, unfortunately, Graves and all the editors at the *Tribune*.

He needed to talk to someone who might have some fresh ideas and some fresh sources. He went back to his office and called Tatiana Kornilova.

"How about if I bring you some sandwiches in a bag for lunch? You must be starving to death," he said.

"I should look like I'm starving. Just bring yourself," she replied.

He opened the drawer of his desk and took out a small treasure he had received in the mail that morning, a reviewer's copy of the new novel by Vasily Aksyonov, the exiled Russian writer who lived in Washington. He put it in his briefcase.

When he entered her apartment he smelled something cooking.

"You've been holding out on me," he said, smiling as he took off his parka. "You can cook."

"Not for everyone," she said over her shoulder, walking slowly and gravely off to the kitchen.

He followed her, and in a moment she was spooning something that looked like cornbread but tasted of oats and honey onto a plate. It was hot and delicious, and he was surprised how hungry he was.

"Not only can you cook, but you're a great cook!" he told her.

"You didn't really think a woman could raise a son and survive here without cooking, did you?" she asked, grey eyebrows raised halfway up her lined forehead.

"So why have you always said you can't?"

"No one takes a woman seriously if she's in the kitchen," she said.

Burke smiled and she smiled back at him, pleased to let him in on her small secret.

"So," she changed the subject. "I heard about your story on the BBC this morning."

He told her about Grishin's statement. "It was a nondenial denial, which interests me," he finished. "If there hadn't been a stroke, and he really had only the flu, I assume Grishin would have denied the stroke unequivocally. Even if they thought he was going to recover quickly from the stroke, they'd deny he'd had one. So my guess is, this means that they're not all that confident he'll recover soon."

"You rule out the possibility Grishin was telling the truth?" Tatiana asked.

"Of course," Burke said.

"Good," she smiled. "It shows you've learned something."

He smiled back. "I didn't have to come here to learn that."

She paused. "Maybe they're afraid he'll show that he's had a stroke," she suggested.

"What do you mean?"

"Well, Brezhnev started slurring his words and walking very slowly as he got older. After he died, they more or less admitted he'd had a couple of strokes."

"Possible," Burke nodded, chewing the last of his food.

"Are you sure you're not reading too much into what Grishin said?"

"Well, I'm speculating, obviously," Burke replied. "But he's a professional. He knew he'd get the question, and he answered it in English to make sure it would get out on TV exactly as he said it; if he speaks in Russian, the reporters paraphrase what he says, and he hates that. I'm sure he and a lot of other people thought about every word."

She nodded.

"Now," he said, "I've got to keep ahead of the story to keep the bastards in Washington off my back."

"I don't understand."

Burke explained, as briefly as he could, the pressure he was under from the newsroom.

Tatiana shook her head. "It's not those bastards you should be worried about," she said. "It's the bastards here."

Burke laughed. "Well, at least the ones here come at you head-on."

"Don't laugh, Colin. *Glasnost* and *perestroika* don't mean the Stalinists have disappeared. They're just keeping quiet."

"Not even that anymore," he said. He told her about the rally on the Arbat.

"And the police did nothing to stop it?"

"No. Just watched."

Tatiana scowled and poured some tea for him. "Find out who let that Ivanov back into Moscow. Then you'll have a story."

He knew he could not spare time for that kind of digging, given all the other projects he was working on. So he only nodded.

"But you be careful. This country . . . ," she began, and shook her head in frustration. "It's like an alcoholic. A strong man—a tsar, a Stalin—is our alcohol. He keeps us from having to deal with our lives ourselves, from being responsible. And even though we have stopped drinking for the last few years, we are still alcoholics. We would dearly love to have just one more drink."

She smiled, sadly. "So what do you do now?"

"Well, I've got to dig up more information. Any suggestions?"

"Have you tried Fyodor Orlov?"

"I kept calling him yesterday. No answer. I'll try again today."

She suggested several other potential sources, all members of the Congress of People's Deputies. They were all already on his list.

He got up to go, and she lumbered to the door and handed him his coat.

"For a man with such troubles, you have some color in your cheeks," she said.

"Thanks," he said. "I went skiing this morning." He grinned. "And I took a long walk last night." He lowered his voice to a whisper and leaned down toward her ear. "With a nice girl, just like you said I should."

"I knew it." She smiled again. "That stupid smile on your face didn't come from some story."

He grinned again. "She's young, she's pretty, she's very . . . I don't know. *Otkrovennaya*. She makes me *otkrovenny*."

Tatiana looked at him reproachfully. "One of ours?" She meant Russian.

He put his finger to his lips. Then he nodded.

"Let me ask you something," he said. She nodded.

"Do you know many people here who are, well, deceitful in their dealings with the state and honest in their personal lives?"

"You mean like someone who joins the party to get ahead at work, and at home at night tells his friends that he doesn't believe in it?"

"Something like that."

Tatiana frowned. "I know lots of people who want to think they are like that. But I don't believe you can be half corrupt. If you start to lie to get along, sooner or later you're lying to everyone."

Burke nodded.

The old woman's face clouded. She lowered her voice. "I take it this has something to do with this girl?"

He nodded.

"I hope it works out for you," she said.

"You don't think it's a good idea?"

"That you met a girl? No. That's fine. But be careful."

"Okay, I'll try," he said. "I've gotta go." He reached into his briefcase and pulled out the book. "I brought you something."

She looked at the book and thanked him. "A lot of people will read this. Aksyonov was a friend of mine before he left, you know."

"I knew," he said.

He kissed her cheek. "Let's go on a double date sometime," he suggested. As he left, he thought he could see her blushing.

10

TO Andrei Kuznetsov, waiting on Kutuzovsky Prospekt, there was no mistaking the tall American. Burke wore a plain rabbit's fur *shapka*, like those of millions of Russians. But Russians shuffled along the street. Burke bounced like an American, picking up his feet with each stride, so that his *shapka* bobbed along atop the tide of pedestrians flowing along the sidewalk, like an ice floe bobbing in the river at the spring thaw. Kuznetsov wished that Burke dressed less conspicuously. He did not want anyone to notice what he was about to do. Still, Kuznetsov could think of no less conspicuous way to make contact. He could not use the phones without risking a tap. He could not walk into the American's office and wait without risking a report. So he had waited on the street, getting colder and colder. It was a little after noon.

He eased his bulk into the flow of walkers alongside Burke, perhaps a foot behind him.

"Good morning, Colin," he said, trying to match his stride to the American's.

Shocked, Burke wheeled toward the voice and began to speak. His stomach sank to somewhere near his knees. Was he being arrested? "Who—"

But before he could even pose the question, Kuznetsov grabbed his arm and propelled him forward. Recognizing the fat Russian, Burke relaxed slightly and allowed himself to be prodded along. If the Soviets wanted to arrest him, he thought, they were unlikely to send Andrei Kuznetsov to do the job.

"Andrei—," Burke began.

"I need to talk to you," Kuznetsov interrupted. He looked straight ahead, not at Burke. They continued to stride along the broad sidewalk, past the toy store. Kuznetsov let his arm drop from Burke's elbow.

Burke tried to think. Was he being set up? It seemed unlikely that Kuznetsov would be involved in a trap. He glanced back, out of the corner of his eye, at the Russian. Kuznetsov's eyes were fixed scrupulously on the sidewalk in front of him. The most likely explanation, Burke decided, was that Kuznetsov was in trouble over the Ponomaryov story and wanted Burke, somehow, to cover for him.

"What's going on?" Burke hissed. He tried to think of anything in his article that Kuznetsov should not have expected or might have found objectionable. He could think of nothing.

"I need to talk to you," Kuznetsov repeated.

"Fine. I was going to call you. Where can we go?" Burke played along with Kuznetsov and stared down at the sidewalk.

"Do you go to the baths?" the Russian asked.

"Sometimes. The Sandunovsky."

Kuznetsov rolled his eyes. "You must read cheap spy novels. The Sandunovsky is full of foreigners and KGB agents. Do you know the Tsentralnaya?"

"No, but I'm sure I could find it."

Kuznetsov nodded. "Good. Tomorrow morning at ten. In the steam room."

"Can't we do it earlier?"

"No," Kuznetsov said. "Tomorrow at ten."

Before Burke could respond, Kuznetsov dropped a step back. Then, cutting to the right behind the American, he descended the stairs into a pedestrian underpass that led to the opposite side of Kutuzovsky Prospekt. He did not look back.

Burke saw only the top of the corpulent Russian's sable *shapka* as he went down the steps, followed by the trail of vapor from his breath. He suppressed an urge to follow and demand an explanation.

The encounter so startled Burke that, without thinking, he walked ten more yards. Then he stopped. He turned around and scanned the sidewalk behind him. There were old women carrying plastic shopping bags, mothers pushing tots in strollers, men in *shapki* hurrying by, their hands in their pockets and their eyes cast down. There was nothing to indicate anyone had seen him with Kuznetsov or heard their brief conversation.

He needed time to think. On his left was an outdoor display board with a copy of today's *Izvestiya*. Burke turned toward the newspaper and pretended to read it. But nothing went past his eyes. His mind was consumed with the question of why Andrei Kuznetsov, once an alternate member of the Central Committee, should make contact with an American correspondent on the street, like a frightened dissident from the 1970s. He turned the possibilities over. Usually, when Soviets tried to set up secret meetings with him, they had a reason. Most often they wanted to see if the American was interested in doing some black-market business. That hardly seemed likely with Andrei Kuznetsov. The most likely possibility, he decided, was that Kuznetsov was frightened, frightened that someone would figure out that he was the source for the *Tribune*'s story about Vikenty Ponomaryov. Burke had assumed that the KGB had recorded their conversation inside the Praga, and that that tape would protect Kuznetsov. He had said nothing in the restaurant. But maybe there was something Burke didn't know about. Maybe Kuznetsov wanted some protection. It would not be hard, Burke thought, to deflect attention from Kuznetsov. A few words at a cocktail party, perhaps, where they would be overheard by the right people. He might suggest that his source had been someone in the Foreign Ministry, or the Institute of USA and Canada Studies. Then, Kuznetsov would owe him a favor. He would probably need to call that favor in as the Ponomaryov story unfolded. In the meantime, he would have to write tomorrow's story without Kuznetsov's help.

Somewhat reassured, Burke walked on down Kutuzovsky toward the Hotel Ukraina, debating with himself. He decided to do what he had left his warm office for in the first place—to call her.

Burke found a pay phone along the massive brick wall of the Ukraina, a Stalin-Gothic cathedral that towered over the boulevard. He held the *dvuchka* in his hand for a long, agonized moment. The last time he had felt this way was in high school. He remembered sitting, staring at the phone for half an hour, trying to work up the nerve to call a girl named Joan and ask for a date. Burke smiled to himself. Feeling like a boy again was better than not feeling at all. He wondered where Joan was.

He dialed Marina's number. She answered on the first ring. He dropped his coin down the slot.

"Marina, this is Colin."

There was a pause, which sounded to him of doubt and uncertainty and reserve. "Hello," she said.

Burke pushed ahead. "How are you?"

"I'm fine."

He wished his Russian were more fluent, that it allowed him to say something subtle and witty and charming. He felt intensely awkward. "I want to see you. If you don't have to be at the theater tonight, will you have dinner with me?"

Another pause. "Where?"

"My place."

"I don't know."

He wondered whether she was reluctant to be alone with him, or simply worried about going to a foreigner's apartment. He searched his mind for something to say to persuade her. The silence hung in the air between them.

Marina broke it. "All right," she said. "Pick me up outside my apartment. Park your car around the corner. What time?"

"How about six-thirty?"

"Fine," she said.

For three hours he worked the phones back at the office, coming up with precious little. Of his six best sources in the Congress of Deputies, three did not answer the phone. Two seemed anxious not to talk to him, and told him they knew nothing. Only Fyodor Orlov, the mathematics professor from a district in southern Moscow, gave him any information.

"I've called the Politburo staff. They say they have no information but what's been in *Pravda*," Orlov told him. "I'm calling deputies to see if they will sign a declaration saying that the Congress should convene and demand an explanation."

"How's that going?" Burke asked.

"Not well, not badly," Orlov said. "But there's no procedure for the deputies to call themselves into session. A lot of them are afraid to act on their own. They say we can wait until the scheduled meeting at the end of next month. Others support the idea, and they've started to call around. If we can get a majority, maybe we can do something. But it will take time." There were more than two thousand deputies.

"Call me and let me know how it's going," Burke said. "It'll be hard to get through to you."

"I will," Orlov said.

At least he had something for a lead. He turned to his computer.

Ponomaryov folo
By COLIN BURKE
Tribune Foreign Service

MOSCOW — Soviet government spokesman Vasily Grishin insisted Tuesday that General Secretary Vikenty Ponomaryov is suffering from the flu. But a dissident member of the Congress of Deputies said he hoped to call the Congress into special session to demand more information about the health of the Soviet leader, who has been out of public view for over a week.

Burke layered in the rest of what he had picked up that day, explaining Grishin's nondenial denial, but quoting his remark about "speculative reports." He decided not to send the piece right away. He would wait to check the late wire service reports and anything that the evening television news might have.

The phone rang, and he picked it up.

"*Washington Tribune.*"

"Mr. Burke, please." The caller spoke English with a heavy accent. Burke did not recognize the voice.

"Speaking."

"This is Shurik."

The name didn't register. There was a moment of silence.

"Vasya's friend," the voice prodded.

"Oh, yeah," Burke remembered. "Thanks for calling."

"If you want to talk, I can meet you in twenty minutes," Shurik said.

The Russians who called his office often asked Burke for immediate meetings. They knew that the KGB, like everything else, was a bureaucracy that worked slowly. Set up a meeting with an American correspondent for the next day, and it would likely be watched. Set it up for twenty minutes later, and the watchers would probably not have time to play their tapes and send someone to the meeting spot. But the video story had slipped several notches on Burke's priority list in the last twenty-four hours. He glanced at his watch. It was after four already.

"Can we put it off for a few days? Maybe till next week?"

"No. I'm going out of town."

Burke grimaced. That was probably a lie. On the other hand, the guy had reason to want to meet quickly. And, on a day when he came up empty on the Ponomaryov story, a feature on underground video might appease Graves. He would squeeze Shurik in.

"Okay, in twenty minutes. Where?"

"You know the Zhiguli bar?"

Burke remembered it, not fondly.

"Okay," he said. "At about five o'clock then." He started to ask how he would recognize Shurik, but the caller had already hung up.

Two *militioneri* and three women occupied the lobby of the Zhiguli. With professional detachment, all five scrutinized Burke as he removed his parka and handed it to the *babushka* behind the counter of the *garderobe*.

She shuffled off, hung the parka on a hook, and gave him a piece of plastic with a number on it. Burke tried to be equally indifferent as he looked over the lobby quintet. The women, tired and worn, looked as if they would have a rough time attracting trade. The *militioneri*, he hoped, were in the lobby just to get warm.

The Zhiguli was a beer hall that filled the basement of one of the large, chevron-shaped buildings that Khrushchev had erected in an overbearing row on Kalinin Prospekt, near the Kremlin. Like most Moscow cafés, the Zhiguli had all the warmth and charm of a junior high school cafeteria. Its grey linoleum floor was overlaid with greasy black dirt tracked in by the patrons, who stood at brown, stomach-high tables under the bright fluorescent lights. Their conversation echoed in the vast room, and the whole place smelled of old beer.

At a service window, Burke bought two glasses and a pitcher of Moskovskoye, which he took to an empty table. It was the only beer available. Sometimes, Burke had found, Moskovskoye was drinkable. But toward the end of each month, as the brewery tried to meet its monthly production quotas, the beer was watered. Judging by the taste of the first glass, the brewery was already far behind its February production schedule.

"I thought Americans drank only Michelob."

Burke looked up. He recognized the voice from the telephone. Standing next to him was a short, slight young man with a hooked nose and close-cropped black hair. He was wearing a navy blue beret, Calvin Klein jeans, and Adidas sneakers. Under his grey cardigan sweater he sported a UCLA tee shirt. He spoke in English.

"You can't always get what you want," Burke said.

"Ah, the Stones," the man replied, showing a yellow-toothed smile. "Shurik," he added, offering his hand.

"Colin Burke," Burke said, and extended his own hand. Shurik had an unexpectedly strong grip.

"You like the Stones?" Shurik said. "I think they're a little passé."

Burke had not deliberately quoted Mick Jagger, but he was amused that Shurik thought he had. "My favorite group," he said.

"I prefer U2," Shurik said.

Burke looked around. The *militioneri* from the lobby were nowhere to be seen. The tables around them were full of tired men nursing their beers, heads down. He looked at Shurik. The shoes, the jeans, and the beret all bespoke a successful *fartsovshchik*, a man who hustled in Moscow's black market. Had Shurik walked up to him unannounced, Burke would have been leery. But Burke had initiated the contact, through Vasya. His general rule was to trust contacts that he himself initiated.

"I like U2, too," he said, and laughed. Shurik didn't look as if he got the pun. Burke fell silent, waiting for Shurik to speak.

After a moment he did. "Vasya tells me you're interested in my business," he said, lowering his voice and moving closer. His breath stank.

"That's right," Burke said. "How did you get into it?"

"I was a student at the Institute of International Languages," Shurik said. "I had a girlfriend whose father was a diplomat in our embassy in Canada. She got me the equipment. I get tapes"—he smiled—"from various places."

Burke took a swallow of beer. "What kind of tapes do you show?"

"Lots of things," Shurik said. "Last week I had a Voody Allen."

Burke decided against correcting Shurik's pronunciation. If the Institute of International Languages couldn't teach him to pronounce a *w*, there was no point in his trying.

"Is it profitable?"

"Very," Shurik said, leaning closer. Burke felt crowded, and leaned away.

"What do you charge?"

"Fifteen rubles," Shurik said. It was more than a day's pay for the average Soviet worker.

"I'd like to come to see a show," Burke said. "I'd keep your name and any other details out of what I wrote."

"You're welcome, of course. But I don't want your money," Shurik said.

Burke had suspected as much. "What do you want?"

"I'd like some tapes to copy."

"I can't do that," Burke said.

"Why not?" Shurik demanded. "You've got them, haven't you?" Burke did have a VCR and some movie tapes.

"It's illegal. If you ever got caught, they'd trace them to me. I can't risk it," he said.

"I don't get caught," Shurik said.

"The story's not worth the risk. That's all there is to it."

Shurik was ready with a fallback position. "You have blank cassettes?"

Burke did. "Yes," he said.

"Give me a blank tape, a U2 album, and a carton of Marlboros, then."

There was nothing illegal, as far as Burke knew, about blank tapes. "All right," he said. "I don't have a U2 album, but the next time I'm in Helsinki, I'll get one for you. And I can get Marlboros."

"Okay," said Shurik, beaming. "I'll be showing a film tonight at eleven-thirty." He gave Burke an address on Trade Union Street, on the outskirts of Moscow. "It's right at Belyayevo metro station," he said. Then he walked away.

Burke waited a few minutes, sipping at his beer. Then he reclaimed his coat. The same two *militioneri* and the same three women were still in the lobby. He ignored them as he left, and headed for the hard-currency store, where he bought a bottle of white Bordeaux, for Marina, and a carton of Marlboros, for Shurik.

11

WALKING home from the Mayakovsky as the winter twilight deepened into darkness, Marina Makeyeva stared down at the packed snow, turned beige, passing beneath her boots. She shook her head. Anger would no longer suffice.

Her performance in the final act the previous night had been inexcusably wooden. Fyodor, the director, had demanded that the actors show up after lunch today, on a scheduled day off. But despite going over the last act again and again, it had been little better.

"Show me something, damn it!" Fyodor had shouted finally. She had felt nothing within her to show.

Until the final act, she was fine. Thinking about it, she understood why. Anger was a good wellspring for the combative encounters she had with Filomenov in the first two acts. But the final act, her seduction, called for something in addition to anger, and she had been unable to summon it. From somewhere within her, she had to bring some warmth, some passion to her embrace of Filomenov.

She thought of her beginning acting classes with old Natalya Borisovna Kondrashova, the Moscow theater's living link to Stanislavsky and the Method. "Your past is your artistic capital, my dears, and while I know you are all good members of the Komsomol," she had told them on the first day, "as artists you must learn to be capitalists. You create characters out of bits and pieces of your past." Marina had laughed nervously at the old woman's remark about capitalism, but the lesson had endured. She was glad for that now. The missing pieces of her role had to be found somewhere in her past.

Searching her mind, oblivious to the pedestrians and the traffic around her, she walked along, thinking about the men in her life. She had not seen her father since she was ten years old. Boris Makeyev had married above himself, to the daughter of an old St. Petersburg family with its roots in the minor tsarist nobility. That, of course, was no longer supposed to mean anything, but it did. Her mother, Olga Andreievna, was an institute graduate, a teacher. There was not supposed to be any distinction between people who worked with their minds and people who worked with their hands, but there was. Boris Makeyev's misfortune was that he had not realized this before he married a well-educated woman from a good family and moved in with his mother-in-law. Once he realized it, he responded in two ways. He drank a lot. And, in 1970, when Marina was four years old, he moved the family to Siberia.

In Siberia they had lived in a raw new town, built to exploit the huge coal deposit that lay under the frozen earth. The town was dominated by the cold and the pit. Boris, although liberated from the disapproval of his mother-in-law, drank all the more. In the winter, it was dark almost all the time and the temperature rarely moved higher than twenty-five degrees below zero. There were lots of companions in Nyerungri for him to drink with. Then, one day, he was gone. Olga Andreievna, by that time the principal of the local grammar school, had no interest in finding him, and she was too proud to return to Leningrad.

Though she had lived with him for the first ten years of her life, Marina had few memories of her father. Most of the time he had not been home. There was, she recalled, a winter picnic when she was nine years old. Her father and some friends had taken her and some other children into the forest. In the freezing cold they had built a huge fire, over which they grilled reindeer meat on skewers. Marina remembered the warmth of the fire and her father taking steaming hot pieces of meat from the skewer with his hand and popping them into her mouth. The warmth she had felt toward him then might be useful to her now, might be part of her artistic capital. Walking past the Garden Ring Road, toward the zoo, she decided to hold on to that memory.

After Boris deserted his family, Marina grew into a tall girl, embarrassed by her height, and shy. When she was fifteen she found two outlets: high jumping for the school athletics team, and acting in school plays. They gave her friends, of a sort. When she was sixteen the rest of her body caught up with her legs and arms. Boys started to notice her, and, in gratitude, she surrendered to one of them, a hurdler named Rodya, one summer evening on the foam rubber high jump landing pit. She was saddened and puzzled, but not entirely surprised, when Rodya stopped talking to her after that.

Because she had always made good grades, and because her mother was a principal, Marina had had her choice of institutes. She chose the Institute of Theatrical Arts in Moscow because she would have been expected to live with her grandmother had she gone to school in Leningrad. At seventeen, she wanted to be independent. During her first year at the institute she had fallen in love with an older student, an aspiring director named Valery. It was her first love, and for three months she was very happy. She all but moved into Valery's room in the men's dormitory. One day, unfortunately, she had walked in and surprised him with another girl. He told her she was prudish to object. She could not believe him.

Still, there had been some good moments, some tender moments, in the beginning with Valery. Waiting for the light to change at the corner of Bolshaya Gruzinskaya Street, she conjured them up and stored them away. Then she thought of Burke, and their stroll in the park, and his telephone call. She did not quite know how to categorize that yet. But those were the memories that would have to suffice. There had been many other men in her life; they had taught her that she was attractive, and that she could get things from some of them. But she had loving memories of none of them.

As she entered her building, the sour smell of old garbage assailed her. Like nearly all Moscow buildings, it had a central garbage disposal chute with an opening on each floor. The city never emptied the garbage bin at the bottom often enough and the stairwell stank of tired, old cabbage. Marina hated the smell, but by now she rarely thought of it. In the dim light, she walked past the phalanx of steel mailboxes and began climbing the stairs. On the fourth floor, she put her key in the lock of No. 12 and opened the dark brown door.

She faced a corridor. On her left was a row of coat hooks with winter boots strewn on the floor. Further down the hall were a bathroom, a kitchen, and four more doors. Four families lived communally in No. 12.

The room she shared with Lena was big enough for a double bed, which was Lena's; a daybed, on which Marina slept; a chest of drawers; and a coffee table. It had a window, facing north, letting in some light from an alley, and a throw rug covering the open patch of parquet floor. Lena paid the city twelve rubles per month for it. She charged Marina ten for her share. Marina stripped off her clothes and laid them on the daybed. She took a blue flannel bathrobe from a hook behind the door and put it on. Then she opened the door and peered down the corridor. It was only 5:45, and none of the other tenants were there. With luck, she could take a hot shower and get back to her room before anyone else got home.

She padded down the corridor and into the bathroom. Inside, she wrinkled her nose in disgust. Anna Matrinko, the fat lady who lived two doors down, had left three pairs of thick stockings hanging from the curtain rod over the bathtub. Marina felt like throwing the stockings into the hallway and telling fat Anna to dry her clothes in her own apartment. But she didn't. Anna had a spiteful streak; she might know about Marina's *propiska* problem. It would not be wise to anger her. Carefully, Marina moved the stockings down to the end of the rod.

The hot water soothed her, and after scrubbing herself down, she lingered under it. It was a mistake. She heard the door slam, and the heavy tread of Semyon Lefortovich, another tenant. Semyon was a lecher. When he heard someone in the shower, he invariably found a reason to hang around in the corridor and watch, in hopes that Marina or Lena would emerge. Marina sighed. There was nothing to do about it. She turned off the water and dried herself as best she could with her threadbare towel. Then she put on her thin flannel robe, wishing it were thicker and longer. She opened the door.

Semyon was standing in the doorway to the kitchen, pretending to be preparing his dinner. When he saw Marina, he beamed. "Good evening, Marina Borisovna," he said, bowing slightly. Marina followed his gaze down to her chest. The robe had molded itself to her damp breasts; her nipples were evident. Blushing angrily, she walked past the kitchen to her own apartment, all too conscious of the fact that Semyon was now leering happily at her ass and legs.

Inside her room again, Marina knelt down beside the daybed and pulled a suitcase from underneath it. She had no closet, and no chest of drawers. She kept her clothes in three vinyl suitcases under the bed. She already knew what she was going to wear. She pulled out her pair of black Lee jeans and her black turtleneck sweater. Black, she felt, was her best color. She stripped, pulled out another suitcase, and glared dolefully at her small collection of underwear. Even her best things had holes in them or looked as if they were made from gunnysacks. She decided not to wear a bra. She pulled on her panties, pants, and the sweater. The material was supposed to look like cashmere, but it was made of polyester, and it felt somehow both oily and abrasive next to her skin.

She took a step across the room to Lena's chest of drawers. There were two perfume bottles on top of the chest, one of them imported from France. But the French perfume was empty. There was only domestic left. Marina knew that it smelled brassy in comparison to the fragrances an American would be used to. She thought for a moment, then reached under her sweater and dabbed a bit of perfume between her breasts. If she decided to take the sweater off, he probably wouldn't notice that the perfume wasn't imported.

The telephone rang just as she finished dressing, and she picked it up.

"Marina?"

"Yes." She recognized the voice. It was Fyodor Brulovsky, her director. He had never called her at home, and she wondered what he could want now.

"This is Fyodor. How are you?"

"I'm fine, Fyodor. I've been thinking about rehearsal. I think I have a way to get what we need in the last act."

"Um, fine. Good. Look, I need to see you. Here at the theater before rehearsal tomorrow. Can you come by at about ten?"

"Yes, I guess I can. What is it about?"

"I'll tell you when I see you," he said. "Until then."

"Good-bye," she said, but he had already hung up.

She felt a tightening in her stomach. What could he want? Extra rehearsal? Perhaps. It couldn't be her. Everyone knew he didn't like women.

It was 6:25. Lena would have made a cup of tea and forced herself to drink it, waiting until at least 6:40 to go downstairs and meet him. Marina did not play games. She was standing on the sidewalk outside the building, slightly annoyed, when Colin Burke arrived five minutes late.

After he said hello and took her arm, she decided that she liked his face. It was lean, in a country where faces were broad. She liked his demeanor. It was quietly self-assured in a country where self-assured men were pompous. She liked his scarf. It was real cashmere in a country of synthetics. And, as they rounded the corner and reached his parking spot, she decided she liked his car, which was solid in a country where few things worked. It was altogether too bad, she decided, that he was an American. Their relationship would always be fenced in by unwritten rules dictating what good citizens did and did not do with Americans.

They said little as he drove along the embankment and onto the Kutuzov Bridge. Across the river, the spires of the Hotel Ukraina towered against a dull, starless sky. Burke drove west of Kutuzovsky until he reached the *razvorot*, made his U-turn, and headed back east toward the entrance to the foreigners' ghetto, and the *militioner* standing watch there.

"Are you worried about the *militioner*?" he asked her. "We'll just drive right by him."

"Okay," she said. She seemed to shrink into the seat and stared straight ahead.

Then Burke was turning right. The *militioner*, peering into the car, saluted as Burke drove past. Marina did not look at him.

They were in a parking lot, driving along a snowy corridor between tightly packed cars. From the street, Burke's building looked much like any other weary Moscow apartment block. Had there been a few addicts sitting on the stoop, it might have been in the South Bronx. But viewed from inside the courtyard it was unmistakably a foreigners' compound. No building for ordinary Russians would have such an array of cars: Saabs and Volvos, an occasional Mercedes. Burke parked, then opened the door and helped her out. This time, she took his arm.

She did not, as some of his Russian visitors did, try to look unimpressed by his apartment; and after he went to the kitchen she walked slowly through it. He had five rooms—as much space, almost, as four families shared in her apartment. She noticed a computer, its cursor blinking steadily from the darkness of one bedroom. A teak bookshelf filled one wall of the living room. She saw a small framed picture of a teenaged boy who had Burke's blue eyes; she hadn't realized Burke's child was that old. She inspected his VCR and mentally cataloged his collection of film cassettes; he seemed to have all of Woody Allen's work. On an adjoining wall she saw a framed page from something called the *Berkeley Barb* and wondered briefly what that was. She examined his stereo; she'd have guessed he'd have a compact disk player. She peered at the titles of his tapes and let her eyes rove over the unfamiliar, Western names: Janis Joplin, Billie Holliday, Ella Fitzgerald, Simon and Garfunkel. She felt as if she were on a private visit to one of the restored homes that were now museums, like Dostoevsky's in Leningrad, examining artifacts to learn about another life, another world.

"Would you like something to drink?"

Burke had walked quietly into the living room. Startled, she jerked upright and spun around, blushing.

He might have said something sarcastic about catching her snooping, or just smiled smugly. Instead, he seemed not to notice. She was grateful.

"Whatever you're having."

"I'm having Jack Daniel's. Would you like some?"

"Please," she said, wondering who, or what, Jack Daniel's was.

He returned in a moment with two glasses, each of which seemed to hold two or three times the normal shot of vodka. Each glass had ice and an amber liquid she assumed was scotch.

He handed her a glass. She hesitated, waiting to see whether an American could toss this huge drink down in one gulp the way a Russian would his vodka.

He did not. He raised his glass toward her, and looked in her eyes. "To you," he said simply. Then he took the smallest of sips. Marina did likewise, and felt the vaguely sweet liquor linger on her tongue before it slid smoothly down. A smile flickered on her lips.

"What is this—*Berkeley Barb*?" she asked, pointing to the framed front page. She knew just enough English to sound out the letters, not enough to understand what they meant.

"It's a newspaper I worked on a long time ago," Burke said. "In California, in a town called Berkeley."

"And why did you frame this page?"

"It's a story I was proud of."

"What is it about?"

"It's about the undercover agents the police used to catch people using and selling marijuana."

Marina took a moment to let that sink in.

"And what happened to you?"

"Nothing."

"Nothing?" She still could not tell if he was telling her a story.

"Nothing happened to anyone. I went on to another newspaper. The chief of the narcotics squad became the police chief; I think he still is. And the people I wrote about are mostly lawyers and stockbrokers now," he said.

She was silent, thinking of what San Francisco capitalists smoking marijuana might look like.

"Freedom of the press," she said. "I envy it."

"It's useful only if you own one," he replied, paraphrasing A. J. Liebling.

She smiled. "You'd make a good Komsomol member."

"Maybe," he said. "But don't kid yourself. Even though you can say anything you want on the stage in America, first you have to find someone with a stage who wants you to."

She shrugged. "Here, even with *glasnost*, it can take months, even a year, to get permission to put on a play."

He nodded. "I know. But we don't have plays that everyone thinks about, and argues about, and takes seriously. A good play or a good book here . . . people really get passionate about it. You know that better than I do."

She nodded. She thought that they were coming too close to talking about the theater, which might help someone reading a transcript of this conversation to identify her. He could see the troubled look on her face, and he changed the subject.

"Would you like to come into the kitchen while I cook?"

Since the picnic in Siberia with her father fourteen years before, no man had cooked for her. She followed him.

He had a pot of water boiling on the stove and some cans and boxes open on the counter. She saw lettuce and tomatoes, and wondered where he had got them in February.

"We're having linguine with clam sauce," he said.

"What's that?"

"It's an Italian dish," he said. He pulled the pasta out of the box and began feeding it into the pot. "This is the linguine." He opened one of the cans. "These are the clams." He used the Russian term, which he had looked up that day in a dictionary: *syedobniye morskiye molyooski.* Literally, "edible sea mollusks."

"We call them 'clams,' " he said, using the English word. She looked at them dubiously.

"Klems," she repeated.

"It's better with fresh clams, I know," he said quickly. "But you can't get them here. I have to get the canned stuff shipped in from Denmark."

She laughed.

"What's the matter? Clams from Denmark aren't good enough for you?"

"No," she said, still smiling. "It's just that I'm not used to seeing a man in the kitchen."

He blushed, and she was afraid she had offended him.

"But I'm glad you are," she added. "I like it. I like being here. I like your klems."

He smiled, and wrinkles crinkled around his blue eyes. "I like your being here, too."

She watched and took another sip of Jack Daniel's as he stirred the pasta and heated butter and oil for the sauce. He let her mince the garlic and chop the *petrushka*, a green Russian herb similar to parsley. Then he drained the linguine and tossed it with the clam sauce.

The long table in the dining room was set with flowers and candles, which Burke lit with a kitchen match. He opened the bottle of white wine and poured two glasses full. Burke held her chair, then sat down.

"I wish," he said, raising a wineglass, "that I could speak Russian well enough to offer the eloquent and charming toast that you deserve. I'm quite witty in English. But in Russian, you're going to have to settle for 'to you,' once again." The candlelight glowed inside his wineglass.

For an instant, Marina thought of Natalya Borisovna and acting class. Whatever else it was, this evening was going to be a valuable part of her artistic capital. Therefore, it would not be a mistake to surrender to it, to let herself think that this was the real world, and she belonged here in the candlelight, talking of San Francisco with an American man who offered flattering toasts and linguine with clam sauce.

"I think you're quite eloquent enough," she said. She touched his glass and met his gaze. The wine was dry and chalky.

Caution circumscribed their conversation. So they talked about him, mainly.

"Why are you a journalist, Colin?" she wanted to know.

"Well, when I went into it, I thought I could do some good. But the longer I'm in it, the more I believe in what someone named Walter Lippmann wrote." He leaned closer and lowered his voice, as if imparting a secret. "We're in it because it appeals to our egos to be able to write the record of what greater men do. We're in it for vanity." He paused. His face was very close to hers. "And why do you do what you do?"

Marina smiled and leaned forward, as if to whisper a secret in his ear. She felt playful, almost giddy. "I never wanted to do any good. It was always vanity," she murmured.

His lips touched hers, and held them. She opened herself to him, nibbling, eager.

He got up, knocking his chair over in his haste. Neither of them noticed. She did not hold back, or hesitate, or protest that it was too soon. She stood, and he measured her body against his, molding her with his hands, kissing her deeply. His hands moved lightly under her sweater, caressing each stiffening nipple in turn. She smiled and ground her hips against his.

He broke the kiss and smiled back at her. "This way," he said. Not taking his hands from her, he walked her into his bedroom. A dim lamp burned beside his double bed. Standing, he kissed her again. Her mouth was hot, and his need was urgent. He pulled her sweater up over her head and off, exposing her small, firm breasts. Bending, he kissed them, moving from nipple to nipple and exploring the pale white skin in between. He began unsnapping the front of her jeans.

"Wait, Colin," she gasped, and stepped away from him. Turning to the lamp, she switched it off, throwing the room into darkness. He heard her zipper and sensed her stepping out of her jeans. He began to strip.

Then, the light came on again. She was standing before him, naked, her breasts thrusting upward. She reached gracefully behind her head and undid her chignon. The hair fell in waves around her face and she shook it lightly. She stepped toward him, and began kissing his chest. Her fingers explored inside his pants. She pushed them down and away.

As he stepped out of the pants, and they fell into each other's arms on the bed, Burke wondered why she had turned out the light. The last thing he saw before her face and her honey-colored hair filled his vision was her panties, puddled on the floor.

They looked as if they were made of burlap, and they were full of holes.

12

"YOU'RE a beautiful woman," he said, running a hand slowly over the parts of her body that proved it. His eyes followed his hand and he could not look long enough at the perfect, faint hairs near her nipples, still stiff, or at the taut, obtuse angles her legs made as she slowly flexed them.

Men had told her she was beautiful before, of course, but always before sex, never after. It sounded better after. She stretched against him, and murmured something appreciative into his neck.

"And you never pretend," he said.

She smiled. "Never."

"Which makes it all the harder for me to go," Burke said. "But I've got some work to do."

She kissed his collarbone and worked her way slowly up to his ear.

"You're not making it any easier, are you?" he said.

"No," she said, still smiling. "It shouldn't be easy for you to leave me."

Burke's resolve wilted as she toyed with his ear and her hand slowly traced concentric circles on his belly. But that was all that wilted. "Well, maybe we could take another twenty minutes," he said.

She smiled and sprang from the bed. "No, I have to go, too," she laughed. Before Burke could respond, she was bending over, slipping her panties and pants on. He lay back watching her for a moment, enjoying the back of her lean legs, the lithe movement of her torso. Then he got up and dressed, remembering to put the blank videotape in his parka pocket.

In the elevator, they kissed. "You don't know how much I've enjoyed this evening," Burke said.

"I'm glad. So did I."

"We'll do it again very soon."

"I hope so."

* * *

They were standing, facing one another, when the elevator doors opened. Victoria Carlson, waiting to take the elevator up, saw them before they saw her. She smiled a formal smile as they got out.

"Hello, Colin," she said.

Burke felt startled, as if he'd been caught at something, then a little pleased that it was she who had caught him. "Hi, Victoria," he said. "Been to the theater?"

"The ballet, actually."

"What did you see?"

"*Spartak.*"

"Good?"

"Excellent. And what have you been up to?"

"We just had dinner."

She cocked one eyebrow. "Good?"

He began to laugh. "Excellent." He tried to say it deadpan.

She smiled back, but it seemed a bit brittle. "Yes, I can tell by that grin on your face."

Burke remembered that an introduction had to be made. "Victoria, this is Marina Makeyeva. Marina, Victoria Carlson." He hoped that it would not be necessary to explain each woman to the other.

Victoria smiled again and offered her hand. Marina took it, noticing the way the full sleeves of the American woman's sable coat fell gracefully from her arm.

"*Ochen priyatno,*" Victoria said.

"*Ochen priyatno,*" Marina replied, wondering what this woman had been saying to Colin in English.

"Have I seen you at the theater? *The Dacha?*" Victoria asked, speaking Russian now.

"Yes," Marina acknowledged, pleased to be recognized.

"You were very good!" Victoria said. Her enthusiasm seemed genuine.

"Thank you," Marina said, beginning to blush.

Victoria hesitated for a moment, considering whether to turn the encounter into a conversation.

"Well, nice to see you, Victoria," Burke said, stepping toward the door.

"Good night, Colin," Victoria replied, getting into the elevator. "Nice to meet you," she said to Marina.

The night had turned bitter cold. Snow was beginning to fall.

Marina took Burke's arm. "Who was she?" she asked as they walked up to the car.

Burke did not reply as he opened her door and helped her in. He waited until he had gotten in and started the engine.

"Victoria is the cultural attaché at the American embassy. She lives on the sixth floor. She's a specialist in Russian literature. She's, um, an interesting woman. Very competent."

He pulled out and began driving slowly through the crowded parking lot, weaving to avoid cars.

"It's rude to use English between you when she speaks Russian," Marina said. She seemed genuinely irritated. He couldn't blame her.

"Sorry," he said. "You're right."

"Are you involved with her?"

Her question flattered him. "Do you care?" he grinned.

She turned to him, eyes and mouth solemn, and waited until he glanced her way and their eyes met. "Yes," she said simply.

"No, I'm not involved with her," Burke said. He decided to be open. "I see her a fair amount at parties and such. I asked her out once and she said no. She's a friend."

Marina's jealousy made him vaguely uncomfortable. He did not need to have a Russian woman feeling possessive of him.

"Do you know she wants you?"

Burke laughed. "What makes you think that?"

"I can tell in her eyes, in the way she shook my hand, in the way her body stiffened. An actor is trained to use such things. She wants you."

Burke considered that. "No. You're wrong. But I can see why you might think that. I once thought I picked up the same signals."

"Maybe she's married."

"No, I don't think so. Maybe she just likes to give out signals."

Victoria Carlson had never been married, as far as Burke knew. She was smart and she was attractive—slim, with blond hair. She dressed well. He had no sense that she disliked men. He had not gotten to know her well enough to know for sure why she was unmarried or why she had politely declined his overture. Maybe she put her career first. Maybe he just didn't appeal to her. But Marina was right. He sensed just the opposite.

"So you think I should make a play for her?" he teased.

She moved closer to him and nibbled his earlobe. "What do you think?" she said, and bit him.

They were approaching Marina's street. "Stop here," she ordered, while the car was still a block away from her building. Burke stopped.

"I'll call you tomorrow," he promised.

"You don't have to make me any promises," she said.

"No, I'll call."

Marina smiled. "Good. I'll be waiting for it." She kissed him quickly, opened the car door, and was gone. Burke watched her disappear into the falling snow. Then he found an alley, turned around, and drove back to his office.

At the office he quickly checked the TASS and Reuters wires. Both were featuring Grishin's statement, but the Reuters account at least pointed out what Grishin hadn't explicitly denied. His colleagues would stand by him, even if he had beaten them on a story. It was one of the things he liked about working in Moscow.

He decided that today's story was as good as it was going to get. He pressed the buttons, and telex tape spewed forth. He took the tape to the telex machine and fed it in. Then he punched in the numbers for the *Tribune* and watched as the story began to click onto the wire. He looked at his watch. It was already past eleven.

The snow was beginning to stick to Aleksei Kosygin Street as Burke drove the Volvo up into the Lenin Hills. His headlights threw out twin cones of light into the swirling snow. He checked in his rearview mirror. No one appeared to be following him. Still, he thought, it was best to be careful. At the Profsoyuznaya metro station, a red *M* was gleaming through the snow. He parked the car in front of an apartment building, took the cigarettes from under the front seat of the car, then walked back to the metro station and went downstairs.

Stalin and Nikita Khrushchev had built the metro stations in the center of Moscow as showcases to impress the proletarians who would use them, palaces of communal transport for the new world Russia was building. They were lit with chandeliers, and heroic bas-relief statues adorned their marble walls. But Profsoyuznaya was on the outskirts of the city, where tourists seldom went, and it reflected a less hopeful era when proletarian merged with utilitarian. Fluorescent lights glared harshly off cold, bare tile walls. A drunk lolled on a bench. Burke stepped to the edge of the platform and looked at the clock hanging over the train tunnel: 2:33, it said, giving the time in minutes and seconds since the last train had left the station. There was never supposed to be more than a four-minute gap between trains. Burke wondered whether, this late at night, that was still true.

The clock read 3:47 when the blue train clattered into the station. New Yorkers, Burke thought, really had no excuse for their subways.

Then he got on the train; it was almost empty. A boy and a girl, who looked to be about eighteen, sat opposite him, oblivious of all but themselves. An old woman, sitting a few meters further away, stared openly at him, frowning. Burke wondered whether he should have put on Russian clothing.

Belyayevo, Shurik's stop, was the end of the line. Burke walked as quickly as he could away from the old woman, hoping that she would not see the direction he took when he left the station. Outside, he walked a hundred meters down the street, past a bus stop, before pausing to get his bearings.

Belyayevo was row after row of white six-story apartment buildings, all the same. It was raw, with no colors. One squat building said GROCERY. It was closed. Burke knew there would be a liquor store in another squat building, and perhaps a school, and a clinic somewhere, and a patch of bare ground that served as a soccer field in summer and a hockey rink in winter. In the gloom, Burke saw No. 98, Shurik's address. He walked toward it. The fresh snow brushed his ankles and seeped into his boots. He looked over his shoulder. No one was there.

Shurik opened the door carrying a tumbler full of vodka. He stepped out onto the landing, closing the door behind him.

"*Salyut*," he said, smiling. Then he lowered his voice. "Listen. The guys inside won't be too comfortable with an American correspondent around. I am going to introduce you as an Estonian. Your accent sounds sort of Estonian."

Burke nodded.

Shurik opened the door and Burke followed him inside. They stopped in a corridor, where Burke hung up his coat and silently handed Shurik the cigarettes and the videotape. Then they went inside.

The only light in the next room came from the image flickering on the small color television screen. Burke had to look at it twice before he could recognize it. On a badly copied, grainy tape, Linda Lovelace in a nurse's uniform was beginning to undress a male actor. The film was *Deep Throat*.

"Guys, this is Valdis, from Tallinn," Shurik said softly.

Burke looked around the room. Two men and a woman sat on a daybed across from the television, each with a tumbler of vodka. The woman looked at him and smiled. Her eyelids were blackened with too much makeup. Two other men sat in chairs, drinking and staring at the scene on the TV. They nodded slightly, acknowledging the introduction.

"What happened to Voody Allen?" Burke whispered to Shurik.

He was only slightly surprised to see pornography. One of the newspaper accounts that had prompted him to research this story had mentioned it among the vices that were infecting the Soviet Union thanks to video technology. Seeing it here, though, was unexpected, and the unexpected made him uneasy. But the writer in him was already spinning leads: "In a dimly lit Moscow living room, a small, clandestine circle of Russians met this week to taste a choice morsel of Western decadence—Linda Lovelace in *Deep Throat*." He looked at the screen again, wondering if this was an uncensored version. Apparently it was.

"This is called *Big Throat*," Shurik whispered. "It's very popular right now." Burke wondered whether Shurik meant the film or the act being performed on the screen. Burke had nothing against pornography. But with Marina's scent still fresh in his nostrils, it seemed particularly joyless. He began looking around the room, making notes in his mind. There was a door that seemed to lead to a kitchen. The walls were red; a beer poster showing a buxom German barmaid was pasted to one of them. On another, Burke saw a cabinet with a stereo and two U2 albums. Shurik pressed a glass into his hand. Burke took a sip of vodka.

"Is this about the normal size of your audience?" he asked.

"No," Shurik said. "Most times, I have about ten people. This time less."

"Why?" Burke asked.

Shurik shrugged. "Would you like to meet the girl?" he asked, leering. "Very nice."

Burke began to wonder what Shurik did for a living besides show films. He decided he didn't want to find out.

"No, thanks," he said. He had seen enough to get some color for his story; he didn't need to write a review of the film. "I've got to run."

Shurik nodded. "I'll get your coat," he said, and walked away toward the hall. Burke heard a switch flip, and the hall light came on.

There was a rap at the door, a thump, then a tearing sound as the door to Shurik's apartment was pushed violently out of its frame.

"*Militia!*" someone shouted. Burke froze.

Two *militioneri* in grey greatcoats, two men in black leather coats, and a photographer burst into the room. The photographer stood in front of Burke. The flash exploded twice in his face.

The flash produced something akin to shock, and Burke, numbed, watched the raid unfold with detachment. One *militioner*, the burlier of the two, stood guard in the shattered doorway so no one could get out. The second, a thin man with a hooked nose, stalked about the room, followed by the photographer. He watched the movie, still flickering, for a few seconds and shook his head in graphic disgust. Then he switched the television off and pulled the cassette out of the VCR. He scooped up the blank videocassette and the carton of Marlboros from the shelf where Shurik had left them. The photographer followed in his tracks, his flash popping. Shurik and the others just sat, heads bowed.

The pair in black leather coats stood silently and watched the proceedings. They wore red armbands with gold letters that said DRU-ZHINNIKI. *Druzhinniki* were a kind of police auxiliary whose members walked the streets to help keep order. But Burke had seen similar silent men in similar black leather coats before. They were always present at political demonstrations. He had seen them watching at the airport when friends and relatives came to bid farewell to a refusenik who had finally gotten permission to emigrate. They were KGB. Their presence, and that of the photographer, told Burke beyond question that this was no bust by the local vice squad. It was a setup, and he had walked into it with his eyes wide open, like a turkey waddling into the slaughterhouse.

Thoughts swirled through his mind. He felt the shame of a twelve-year-old caught reading *Playboy* by his mother. The policemen were looking at him as if he had been molesting children.

Then the shame left him, and was replaced by anger. He had, after all, done nothing wrong, despite the cops' dirty looks. Only by the perverse standards of the Soviet Union had he sinned. Sometimes it was hard to remember that the Soviet state morality was evil, and not the people who flouted it.

Then he felt a different kind of shame—shame at his own stupidity. He had been recklessly overconfident. Now, he stood in danger of being expelled from the country on morality charges.

Back against the wall, Burke watched the *militioneri* go through the charade of a search. The photographer was still shooting, his flash attachment bursting brightly in the dim room. The other moviegoers and Shurik sat looking penitent. Burke wondered where the KGB had found them—in an acting school?

He considered the reasons the KGB might have for setting him up. Years ago, they had done this kind of thing to American correspondents just for the exercise, on general principles. But that was before the Soviets had learned the value of a benign image. This kind of thing didn't happen in the *glasnost* era. It could only be connected to his story on Ponomaryov's health. It had to be vengeance for what he had written.

But so quickly? He counted back and decided that perhaps thirty hours had passed since the story had clicked over the telex machine. Was that time enough to plan and carry out an operation like this? If it was, the KGB was more efficient than he had given it credit for. He remembered, too late, what Tatiana had said. "The Stalinists haven't disappeared. They're just keeping quiet." Their silence had certainly lulled him into overconfidence.

Finally, the hook-nosed cop felt he had searched enough. He stood in the middle of the room. "Who owns this place?" he demanded.

Shurik stood up slowly. "Me."

"Follow me," said the hook-nosed cop, and went into an adjoining room Burke assumed was the kitchen. Shurik followed. The door shut.

Burke wanted to knock on the door and tell them that the show had gone on long enough, and they should simply do whatever it was they planned to do with him. No doubt, he thought, this interlude was written into the script to give him a chance to think about his situation. And he did. No one, he knew, was going to advise him that he had the right to remain silent and the right to a lawyer. There would be no dime, no phone call. Even if he had a chance to call a lawyer, it would do him no good. The lawyers in the Soviet system worked for the same people the cops did. He might very well spend at least a night in jail before the police called the American embassy and arranged for his release—if they did. As a journalist, Burke knew, he had no immunity from prosecution, as diplomats did. He could be arrested, he could be tried, he could be sentenced. As a practical matter, he knew that the Soviets had often expelled American journalists on trumped-up charges. They had never held one for more than two weeks, which was the amount of time Nick Daniloff of *U.S. News & World Report* had spent in jail in the summer of 1986. So there was little chance of his actually doing time—but there was a chance. A hoary old dissidents' joke flashed through his mind:

Q. What's the tallest building in any Soviet city?

A. KGB headquarters. Even from the basement, you can see all the way to Siberia.

The hook-nosed cop came out of the kitchen, with Shurik on his heels. Burke tried to catch Shurik's eye. Shurik avoided him.

"You," the cop said, pointing at Burke. "Inside."

Burke followed the *militioner* into the kitchen. The cop shut the door and sat down at a small kitchen table that was strewn with papers and two videocassettes—the blank that Burke had brought and the *Deep Throat* tape.

"Sit down," he said, not looking up. He was scribbling on a piece of paper. "Documents."

Burke did not sit down. He handed his blue U.S. passport to the man. The cop looked at the cover. He opened it, looked at the photo, and looked briefly at Burke's face. "American," the cop said. He did not bother to try to look surprised.

There was no point in cooperating further. "Yes, I'm an American," Burke said in English. "I don't speak Russian and I want an interpreter."

"Sit down," the *militioner* said again, this time in flawless English. "You will not need an interpreter. It happens that I speak English." He looked at Burke with a small, tight smile. Then he began copying Burke's name and passport number onto the document in front of him. He looked again at the photo in the passport, then at Burke, then back at the photo. He resumed writing. Burke remained standing.

"Interesting, Mr. Burke," the cop said, still in English and not looking up. "Comrade Stukachov says you speak Russian quite well." He paused. "Well enough to pass yourself off as a Soviet citizen from Estonia."

Burke felt as if he had been punched in the stomach. Was there a law against impersonating an Estonian? Probably. Would it make any difference if he told this cop that he had never passed himself off as an Estonian, that Shurik had done the passing? Probably not. He kept silent.

"Sit down, Mr. Burke," the *militioner* said again, more harshly this time. Burke sat down. The man continued writing.

"So when are you going to read me my rights?" said Burke.

The *militioner*'s brow furrowed. "Excuse me?"

"You know. I have the right to remain silent and to consult an attorney and anything I say can be used against me and all that. Like the Miranda warning in the U.S. It's probably printed on a card in your wallet and you forgot about it."

"You're not in a good position to be joking, Mr. Burke," the cop said, looking up from his papers.

"Well, sorry," Burke said. "I only know what I read in *Pravda*." The cop said nothing.

"I'd like to consult with the United States embassy," Burke said.

The cop raised his eyes and stopped writing. "Do you work for the United States government, Mr. Burke? Are you claiming diplomatic immunity? Your visa says you are a journalist."

"Well, that's right, but I still would like to consult with a member of the embassy staff."

"In due time, Mr. Burke. And, when our investigation is completed, you know that the state will provide you with a lawyer free of charge."

Burke refrained from expressing his opinion of Soviet lawyers.

The *militioner* finished writing. He handed the paper to Burke. It was in Russian, and Burke, glancing at it, could see that it was a confession.

"Sign this," the *militioner* said.

"Sign it? I can't read it," Burke lied. He tossed the paper back on the *militioner*'s side of the table.

"Very well, Mr. Burke. I shall translate it for you," the cop said, excessively courteous.

"Item One: You entered this place falsely claiming to be a Soviet citizen.

"Item Two: You brought with you several items of contraband: imported cigarettes, a copy of a pornographic American film, and a blank cassette to make another copy of the film.

"Item Three: You supplied these to the tenant in this apartment, Aleksandr Stukachov, in return for a share of the proceeds from his illegal video business."

"I guess I've become quite an item," Burke said.

"I don't understand," the cop said, for the first time looking a bit uncertain of himself.

"I guess you're not a very good translator," Burke said, and the man scowled. "It's a common English expression. All the more reason why I won't sign."

The *militioner* glowered at him again. "This is not a confession, Mr. Burke. It's merely an investigative report. These points summarize what Comrade Stukachov told us. If you disagree, that can be noted."

The tiny kitchen seemed to be getting smaller all the time, till there was room only for the small table, the harsh white overhead light, the scowling *militioner*, and Burke. It was like a closet. Burke felt nauseous. Still, he decided that being stubborn was his only option. "I'm not telling you anything and I'm not signing anything."

To Burke's relief, the *militioner* got up without a word and went into the other room. Burke was tempted to read the statement still sitting on the table. He decided against it. The room might well have a hidden camera. He did not want to be caught reading Russian. He smiled to himself. With all the other things, real and imagined, that the KGB had on him as a result of this evening, he had no reason to worry about being caught in a lie like that. He could see the headline: "Correspondent Expelled for Secret Knowledge of Russian!"

Burke's mind moved on to the consequences of what he was facing. He would very likely be expelled from the country. That would have many negative repercussions. His long preparation, the difficult resuscitation of the Russian he had learned at Berkeley, would be largely wasted. He might never be able to work in Russia again. The *Tribune*, of course, would publicly defend him and denounce the Soviets. But the paper would also be privately annoyed. Moscow coverage would be cut off at a critical time. Graves would no doubt take pleasure in finding a replacement, but for Burke the outcome was likely to be a stint covering the board of education in Prince George's County—maybe a permanent stint. And for what? A story about an illicit video business? The ideal, for a Moscow correspondent, was like the ideal for a test pilot. You were supposed to test the outer limits of Soviet tolerance, just as a test pilot was supposed to push his plane to its limits. But the pilot wasn't supposed to crash and a correspondent wasn't supposed to be expelled.

That was assuming that expulsion would be his punishment. What if they prosecuted him? He had no doubt that Shurik and his friends would say whatever the KGB wanted them to say. Shurik, Burke guessed, might well have been partly real. He might have been an illicit video operator discovered by the police. He might have been given a chance to get off if he would cooperate in snaring an American. On the other hand, he might have been a full-time KGB man. It made little difference. If they pursued the case, they could, Burke realized, do whatever they wanted. It was not a comforting thought. His stomach began to churn.

The kitchen door opened and the *militioner* returned. No doubt he had been consulting one of the men in the black leather coats and had received his instructions. Burke turned and stood up.

"You are free to go, Mr. Burke," the cop said. "This investigation will continue. You will hear from us." He stepped aside and let Burke pass into the living room. Shurik, the woman, and the four men were gone. So was the photographer. The two men in black leather coats were smoking in a corner, and the burly cop still stood guard at the ruined door. The apartment was getting cold.

With an effort, Burke held his head up. Silently, he found his parka, put it on, and walked outside. He gulped in great drafts of the freezing night air. His legs were trembling. He looked at his watch. It was 12:15. The whole episode had taken only forty-five minutes. Less than an hour to throw his life into turmoil.

He wondered why they were letting him go. Probably they wouldn't expel him immediately. Booting him right after the Ponomaryov story would only make their motive obvious. Maybe they'd "investigate" for a month or two, until the Ponomaryov story had blown over. Then they'd nail him.

As he walked toward the metro station, Burke pondered the missteps he had taken. He had trusted Shurik because he had trusted Vasya. He had trusted Vasya because he had been the one who initiated the relationship. His rule for judging people's reliability had failed him. Then another, more disturbing thought struck him.

Vasya had betrayed him. Vasya had also introduced him to Marina.

13

. . . I refused to sign. Whereupon they let me go. Am now waiting for the next hobnail boot to drop. Obviously, this was a setup, presumably because they are pissed off about the Ponomaryov story. I think, however, that we should not write about it until we find out their next move. Our response should be to keep doing exactly what we've been doing. Will keep you posted. Regards. Burke.

Burke reread his message, then sent it. He hated to let Graves know he was in trouble. But he had no choice. He had to tell the KGB he was not cowed. He could not call them up, or knock on their door to deliver the message. But the KGB read all the outgoing telex transmissions from Moscow. It would read his. And it would learn from it that Burke was prepared, if prosecuted or harassed, to tell the world that he had been framed because he had told the truth about Vikenty Ponomaryov's illness. It was not much of a defense, but he could count on his colleagues in the press corps to write about it. It would damage, in some small way, the carefully nurtured Soviet image. Maybe they would think twice.

How long, he wondered, would he be in Moscow? Normally, when they expelled a correspondent, the Soviets allowed him a couple of weeks to pack his things and say his good-byes. Would they be so considerate of someone accused of disseminating pornography? Not likely.

Burke pondered his next move. He thought about going to the American embassy and asking them to lodge a protest, then rejected the idea. He felt ashamed that he had even asked the *militioner* at Shurik's for an embassy translator. The fact that he had been desperate did not excuse it. He had spent a year trying to uphold the principle that one difference between the U.S. and the USSR was that American journalists were not part of their government. He would not go running to that government now that he was in trouble. The best thing to do, he decided, was to ignore what had happened last night and get back to work. And work, this morning, meant getting together with Andrei Kuznetsov. He looked at his watch. It was nine-thirty. Time to get going.

Before he could rise, the telephone rang. Burke found that his stomach involuntarily turned at the sound. He picked up the receiver.

"*Gospodin* Burke?"

"Yes."

"This is Skorov, Press Department, MFA."

"Yes."

"I wonder if you could meet me here today."

So that was it. They were going to hand him his expulsion notice and tell him to shut the door behind him.

"You guys work fast," Burke snapped.

"I'm sorry. I don't understand, *Gospodin*."

There was no point in berating Skorov. He was just doing as he was told.

"All right," Burke said. "What time would suit you?"

"Perhaps one o'clock?"

"See you at one," Burke said. Without waiting for an answer, he hung up. He glanced at his watch. He was going to have to hurry to meet Kuznetsov at ten.

Burke strode to the door, pulling on his parka. "Back this afternoon," he called to Olga.

Outside, he hurried to the car and started it. He pulled out into the drive and moved toward the exit. A black taxicab quickly pulled out in front of him, then stopped. Burke could see the driver hunched over the ignition key. Apparently, the cab had stalled.

Burke fumed, looking at his watch. The last thing he needed was another obstacle.

"Move your ass," he muttered, drumming his fingers against the steering wheel. He was about to get out and offer to help push the cab aside when it started moving again, rolling slowly out toward Kutuzovsky Prospekt. Burke followed.

At the street, the cab hesitated, pulled out into the right-hand lane, and moved slowly west. Burke glanced at the traffic, saw an opening, and pulled out one lane closer to the center. Pressing the accelerator toward the floor, he pulled past the cab and looked quickly to his right. If the cabbie was looking, he would flash him a finger.

But the cabbie was not looking. He was talking into the transmitter of a two-way radio.

Burke had seen the inside of a lot of Soviet taxis. He had never seen one with a radio.

He checked his rearview mirror. Behind him was the usual assortment of red and green Zhigulis, two dump trucks, and a lumbering orange bus. Then he saw a white Volga sedan rush up to within two cars of him, slow down, and pull in behind a green Zhiguli; its driver was wearing a sable *shapka*. The Volga sedan was the standard issue car for midlevel Soviet functionaries—and for the KGB? Had the cabdriver been a lookout whose job was to stall him, then radio for the surveillance car to get started?

Burke decided to find out. He turned on his left turn signal and swung into the left lane. He checked the mirror; the white Volga did the same. Ahead of him, at the corner of Kutuzovsky and Dunayevskogo, was the *razvorot* where he normally made his U-turn before heading into central Moscow. A line of cars was forming in the left lane, waiting for the green arrow that would permit them to turn. Just before he got to the back of the line, Burke veered right and accelerated, heading through the intersection. He checked his mirror again. The white Volga had duplicated his move. Now they knew that he knew he was being followed.

Traffic was light heading west, out of the city, and Burke had a chance to think. He had been tailed once, at least as far as he knew. It was during his first month in Moscow. The tail, like this one, had been blatant. Burke had reacted by simply giving up on the meeting he was going to and returning to the office. There was no reason to risk compromising a source. There was then no point in trying to evade the tail. That would only have aroused the KGB's curiosity.

That was then. In the past twelve hours he had moved beyond worries about provoking the watchers. There might never be another chance to find out what Andrei Kuznetsov wanted to tell him.

Burke slammed on the brakes and swerved to the curb, tires screeching, at the Kutuzovskaya metro station. He jumped out of the car and ran toward the entrance, hoping that the KGB man—was there only one?—would be slow to react. Thrusting a hand into his pocket, he prayed that he had the right change. He did. Running full tilt down the stairs, thinking as he ran, he lunged past startled, plodding Muscovites for the metro turnstile, thrust his five kopecks into the coin slot, and kept running.

By this time, Burke calculated, the KGB man would have parked and come running after him. He bolted down the long escalator, slowing down just enough to avoid being collared by the dour policewoman who stood guard at the bottom, on the platform level, ever vigilant against hooliganism.

Reaching the platform, he glanced at the electric clock at the end of the station, which showed the elapsed time since the last train—2:45. Half running, half walking, Burke hurried down the long ribbon of concrete, bumping into strangers as he went. He was in luck. Kutuzovskaya was one of the older metro stations, with the baroque Khrushchevian decor. The wall on his right was punctuated by small alcoves, each of which held a hideous brass light fixture. He ducked into an alcove and pressed himself against the wall. The lamplight blazed in his eyes and a trickle of sweat began to fall from beneath his *shapka*. But the alcove was deep enough to hide him from the view of anyone scanning the platform from the bottom of the escalator. His pursuer would have to search the length of the platform to find him. If the trains were running on schedule, there would not be time to do it.

Burke waited, the seconds ticking by, his heartbeat keeping time. He could imagine the KGB man making his way down the platform, looking for the tall American in the blue parka. Then he saw a glint of light playing along the rail and felt the rumble of an approaching train. With a roar and clatter, the train pulled into the station, headed for the western edge of the city. On the platform, people moved forward, preparing to board. The sweat dripped into Burke's eyes, stinging. The train doors opened.

An old woman, getting off, stared for a moment at the sight in front of her—a tall man in Western clothes pressed up against the wall of the station, his head cocked to one side of a light fixture. Surely, Burke thought, she could tell he was hiding. Surely she would cry out. But the woman, after a moment, lowered her head and trudged toward the escalators.

"Careful, the doors are closing. Next stop, Fili," he heard the conductor say over the train's gravelly loudspeaker. The doors shut. The train began to roll past, picking up speed. Burke studied the heads behind the train's windows, which glowed like gold in the dim station light. He thought he saw the sable *shapka*, but he could not be sure.

When the train was gone, Burke leaned forward and peered down the platform. He expected to see the KGB man standing a few feet away, grinning at the foolish American like a cat about to pounce on a mouse.

But the platform was empty. Burke's legs felt rubbery and his head light as he walked to the escalator, went up, and crossed over to catch the downtown train.

* * *

The Tsentralnaya Baths, on a crumbling block in the center of the city, were a relic of another Russia. In the old Russia of villages and towns, each neighborhood had its *banya*, or bathhouse. It was a windowless hut near the village's well or stream, with a stove for heating the interior and the bathwater. Everyone used it—assuming he had no religious scruples against bathing, which some variants of Russian Orthodoxy did. As Russia became an empire and cities were built, the baths became grander. The Sandunovsky Baths, which Burke occasionally used, were Moscow's grandest, with walls paneled in dark wood and lockers the size of first-class train compartments. The Tsentralnaya had never aspired to such luxury. The changing rooms were austere and grey, with pegs on the wall instead of lockers. But the *banshchik*, for a moderate tip, could be induced to deliver anything from a dried sturgeon to a cold bottle of vodka, the steam was just as hot, and the regulars preferred it the way it was.

Coming out of the subway, Burke kept his eyes straight ahead, unwilling to know what he might see if he turned around. Outside the block-long facade of the *banya*, an old *babushka*, sitting on an upturned crate, was selling bundles of green birch branches, an essential element of a proper Russian steam bath. Burke handed her a ruble. While she searched for change, he glanced up and down the street. He saw nothing except the normal flow of pedestrians. That, he knew, meant nothing. If he really had evaded a tail by jumping into the metro, the next shadows assigned to him would be more careful about being seen.

Birch branches in hand, Burke entered the building and walked up a dimly lit staircase to a cashier's window. He paid his ruble and got a ticket. Through a door on the left he entered the dressing room.

The *banya*, Burke knew, was no longer a necessity in Moscow life. The last of the wooden houses had disappeared years ago, leaving a city of thousands of drab apartment blocks which, whatever their shortcomings, at least had indoor plumbing. Respectable Muscovites bathed at home. The *banya* survived because, in a country whose taverns were scarce and squalid, men wanted a congenial place to drink together. The dressing room was full of men doing precisely that. It was a large room that smelled of sweat and alcohol and birch leaves. Groups of men sat, some naked, some wrapped in white sheets, talking and passing a bottle among themselves. They came to the *banya* to sweat out old hangovers and start new ones.

Burke handed his ticket to the *banshchik* and received a white sheet and a small bag in return. He put his wallet in the bag and handed it to the thin, pimply-faced man for safekeeping.

The *banshchik* looked at Burke, and at his eel-skin wallet, which he had picked up in Korea. "Want to change some currency?" he asked quietly.

Burke smiled. "No, thanks."

"Very good rate," the *banshchik* said. The official exchange rate was six rubles for one dollar. On the black market, Russians anxious to have some Western currency would pay three or four times that much.

Burke smiled again. He had troubles enough without getting involved in the currency black market. "I'm sure it is. Not today."

The *banshchik* shrugged and led Burke to an empty bench in the middle of the room. "Number seventy-eight," he said, gesturing to a hook mounted over the bench. "Need anything else?"

"No, thanks." Burke began to undress. The *banshchik* hung around just long enough to know that there would be no tip.

Naked, birch branches in hand, Burke left the changing room through a metal door and entered the bathing room. Faded, cracked tiles lined the walls, punctuated by soapstone sinks. Rows and rows of marble benches lay before him, occupied by heavy Russian men. The bathers took careful, mincing little steps on the slippery floors, their bellies preceding them.

There were two smaller rooms off the main bathing room. One contained a large tiled pool of slightly green, frigid water. Burke headed toward the second room, the steam room, and stepped through the door.

He entered a dark, gloomy room. The heat of the place seared his nostrils, mixing with the smell of birch leaves. Underfoot he could feel the slimy residue of countless leaves, ground to a viscous pulp. As his eyes adjusted to the darkness, he could see before him a steep, broad wooden staircase leading up to a platform close to the ceiling. A few men sat at various levels of the staircase, acclimating themselves to the heat.

Burke began to sweat heavily. He climbed the first two steps, feeling the air get hotter as he ascended. He could see the platform now. It held perhaps a dozen men, mostly middle-aged, all naked, all sweating, sitting on simple wooden benches against the wall. Some were swatting themselves with their bound birch branches, their motions heavy and slow. Others swatted their companions' backs. In the far corner, sitting alone, swathed in his own fat, sat Andrei Kuznetsov.

As he reached the platform, Burke felt the heat of the room at its most intense, in the air trapped against the ceiling. His lungs burned. He crossed the platform to Kuznetsov's corner and sank gratefully to the bench beside him.

"Sorry I'm late." Burke decided not to tell the Russian about the taxicab, the white car, and the man in the sable hat.

Kuznetsov said nothing for a moment. Then he looked at the bundle in Burke's hand. "You brought birch branches," he said, with a slight nod. "Let me show you what to do with them." With a jiggle and a tremble, Kuznetsov stood up. He puffed for a moment from the exertion in the hot air, like a steam locomotive getting under way. Then he took a bundle of birch from the bench beside him and held the branches under his chin. "Hold them like this," he said, throwing his shoulders back. He looked like a fat man pretending to be a bride smelling her bouquet.

Burke wondered whether he was supposed to laugh. But Kuznetsov's brow knitted together in the attitude of a patient teacher. Burke got to his feet; his head entered the hottest layer of air again. He stood facing Kuznetsov, birch branches in front of his chest.

"Now, inhale," Kuznetsov said. He sniffed deeply, and the branches rose on his gleaming, sweaty chest. Burke did the same. The smell of hot birch vapors filled his head and lungs.

"Good for the sinuses," Kuznetsov explained between breaths. "It will keep you from catching colds."

"I'll bet," Burke replied. The smell reminded him of the stuff his mother used to rub on his chest after he *had* caught cold.

Burke wondered whether Kuznetsov was going to ask him to swat his broad back with the branches. He hoped not. There were few things he wouldn't do for a story. Flogging a naked fat man in a Russian steam bath, however, was one of them.

To his relief, Kuznetsov sat down again. Raising one plump leg, he carefully worked from thigh to calf, beating himself with the birch branches. "Good for the circulation," he grunted. His leg did seem to be turning pinker.

Burke sat down and gave his own legs a couple of token swats on the thigh.

Kuznetsov shifted legs. Swat. "You know that story I gave you about Ponomaryov's stroke?" he asked quietly.

"Yes?" Burke leaned closer to hear precisely what Kuznetsov was saying. He could see the individual beads of sweat dribbling down the Russian's puffy cheeks.

Swat. "I don't think it was true."

"What?" Burke almost shouted. Hearing his own voice, he glanced around. No one appeared to be paying attention.

"What?" he said again, hissing.

Kuznetsov leaned back. Swat. "It probably wasn't true," he said dully.

Burke felt a little dizzy. His head was throbbing.

"He hasn't had a stroke?"

"No," Kuznetsov said. "I mean, yes, he has had a stroke." He paused. "At least I think he has."

"So what did you tell me that wasn't true?" Burke wanted to punch him.

"That he's recovering."

"He's not recovering?"

"I don't think so."

"You don't think so?" Burke, for a moment, could only sputter. "What do you mean, you don't think so?"

"Not so loud." Kuznetsov was hissing now.

"You got me to publish a lie and you want me not to be loud?"

"If you calm down, I'll tell you what I know."

Burke clenched and unclenched his sweating hands.

"All right," he said. "Tell me the truth."

Kuznetsov sighed. "A couple of days ago, I was summoned and told to give you the information I gave you on the street outside the Praga."

"By whom?"

Kuznetsov could not bring himself to say the name. "By someone at the highest level of government."

"Who?" Burke demanded.

"Igor Andrushin."

Burke felt nauseous.

"Why?"

"I don't know. I only know that he was in his office with Marshal Petrusevich. They were talking about discipline problems in the army. He told me what to tell you. I believe he was telling the truth about the stroke. I do not think he was telling the truth when he said Ponomaryov was recovering."

Burke forgot his anger for a moment. The implications of what Kuznetsov had said began percolating through his brain.

"Is that the truth?"

"Yes. I think so." Kuznetsov looked sincere, but Burke had never been good at spotting a lie.

"But I had another source confirm it," Burke said.

Kuznetsov looked interested.

"Who?"

Burke considered, briefly, the possibility that Kuznetsov had arranged this meeting as a ruse to learn who his source was. It didn't seem likely, assuming his phone call to Crittenden had been recorded.

Still, he could tell Kuznetsov nothing. "I can't say," he said.

"A diplomat?"

Burke nodded.

"Someone you talk to regularly?"

Burke nodded again.

Kuznetsov merely shrugged, as if the matter of the KGB planting the same story with one of Burke's sources were too simple to be worthy of explanation.

"Why would they want to plant a story with me?" Burke demanded.

On the lowest, entry level of the steam room, a naked *banshchik* took a ladle full of water from a bucket, opened the steel door to what looked like an incinerator, and tossed the water on the hot coals inside. Steam hissed, and the room got hotter. Kuznetsov leaned forward.

"I think that he and Petrusevich are maneuvering to get a majority on the Politburo. That is why Morozov was removed. I don't think Morozov would have been removed if Ponomaryov was conscious and could fight. And now Andrushin and Petrusevich are going after the defense minister. They have asked me to write a story that will be very damaging to him. If they can remove him, and make Petrusevich the defense minister, the Politburo would see where the power was flowing. Andrushin might get a majority. But if the Politburo learns too soon that Ponomaryov is not recovering, the members could insist on electing a new general secretary, someone who would follow Ponomaryov's line. So he needed to put out a story, through you, to explain Ponomaryov's illness but not cause a new election."

"How can the Politburo not know?" Burke struggled to keep his voice down.

Kuznetsov spread his palms and shrugged again. "I don't know. But it doesn't surprise me. The Politburo doctors all work for the KGB."

Burke felt only suspicion. "Why are you telling me this? Why should I believe you now?" he hissed.

Kuznetsov looked directly in Burke's eyes. "Because I don't want Andrushin to succeed. If you publish the truth, the BBC and the Voice of America will broadcast it back into the country. Maybe the rest of the Politburo can stop Andrushin."

Burke wanted to believe him. He needed, at that moment, to believe in something.

"How do you know Andrushin wasn't telling you a complete lie?" Kuznetsov smiled slightly.

"I don't."

Kuznetsov slowly, almost gracefully, rose to his feet.

"There's one thing more," he said. "This story about the Defense Ministry—it has a deadline. The end of this week. So please . . ." Kuznetsov smiled slightly. ". . . Work quickly."

Burke put his face in his hands and rubbed his eyes. When he looked up, Kuznetsov was still smiling slightly, as if to acknowledge the futility of their situation.

"Good-bye, Colin," he said. "Wait a few moments before you leave, please." He waddled off down the staircase.

Burke sat on the bench and watched the Russian's buttocks disappear. More sweat dripped down into his eyes. Then he beat himself, as hard as he could, with his birch branches.

The penultimate part of a proper morning at the *banya* was the cold pool. Burke, with his thin American blood, had always skipped that part of the ritual, as well as the final segment, the shared bottle of vodka. But this was a morning for penitence; had Burke owned a hair shirt, he would have put it on. He walked out of the steam room dripping sweat. Without stopping, he waded into the freezing water. His breath turned to sharp gasps, and his testicles jumped toward his stomach, but he forced himself onward until he was chest deep in the icy, turbid water. Then he took a deep breath and lowered his head under. The effect, he discovered, was exhilarating. His pores closed and his skin tingled. As his head cooled, his mind began to function; it was like jump-starting his brain. And the first thought that popped into his mind was a sad one: discovering small pleasures like this one in the bleak vastness of Russia was a satisfaction he was not likely to have again. After his meeting with Skorov, he was probably going to have to pack and leave.

He poked his head above the water and stood still. As his anger subsided, Burke began to analyze what Andrei Kuznetsov had told him. Obviously, Kuznetsov had been lying. But had he lied outside the restaurant or in the steam room? Or both? Probably not both times, Burke thought. The KGB was not above planting a false story just to damage the credibility of an American reporter. But it was hard to believe that Andrushin would plant two false stories, both of them damaging to Vikenty Ponomaryov, just to toy with Colin Burke and the *Washington Tribune*. It was more likely that one of the stories Kuznetsov had told him was true. But which one? His instinct told him that if

Kuznetsov had wanted simply to plant a lie, he would have done it cleanly at the Praga. The meeting this morning would have been superfluous. But his experience also told him that Kuznetsov had fooled him at least once.

The cold water could not soothe the guilt that throbbed in his conscience like a headache. He should have sat on Kuznetsov's original tip until he had gotten another Soviet source to confirm it, not just a diplomat. So eager had he been to break the story that he had broken faith with his readers, and himself. Then he had compounded that error by stupidly allowing himself to be set up at Shurik's. If they booted him, he would get no second chance at the Ponomaryov story.

Shivering now, Burke felt he had had enough—enough cold water, enough of Russia. He climbed out of the pool and put on his clothes. As he recovered his wallet and counted his money, the *banshchik* tried again. "Twenty rubles per dollar," he said softly.

Burke made it a practice never to curse in Russian. Someone had told him that the nuances of Russian profanity were unwritten, and too subtle for a foreigner to grasp. The moment seemed, however, to require an exception.

"*Yob tvoyu mat*," Burke said to the *banshchik*, and walked out.

14

THE digital clock on the dashboard read 5:28 a.m. when Henry Hoffman crossed Key Bridge and turned right on M Street. He was going to have to hurry. When Forsyth said he would start running at 5:30, he began at 5:30. If you weren't there, you had to catch up. Hoffman had heard stories about NSC staffers who had arrived a minute or two late, sprinted into the darkness after Forsyth, and were so breathless by the time they caught him that they couldn't talk.

And the chance to talk to Chuck Forsyth was the only thing that could make Henry Hoffman rise at 5:00 a.m. in Alexandria, pull on running clothes, kiss his sleepy wife good-bye, throw his work clothes in the car, and drive into Georgetown. He disliked sports in general, jogging more than most. It made his knees ache, and he hated the way members of the jogging cult blathered about their training schedules, their mileage, their podiatrists. At Stanford he had kept himself in reasonable enough shape by watching his diet and walking to the campus. If his department chairman had suggested running at five in the morning, he would have laughed in his face.

But that was Stanford, and this was the NSC. Chuck Forsyth jogged and played tennis. Chuck Forsyth liked his staffers lean and fit, just as he had liked his junior officers lean and fit. He didn't order an NSC staffer to exercise. But he could and did make himself available for extended conversations in only two places: the tennis court and the C&O Canal towpath. The staffers who wanted his ear joined him at one place or the other, and Henry Hoffman had realized it was too late in life to become a decent tennis player. So he ran three days a week, begrudging every step, to be ready for the mornings when Forsyth asked for his company on his daily four miles. The fact that Susan, his wife, smiled smugly when he got out of bed did not make it any easier. But she was still teaching. She could be smug now, but she would not have the kind of career her husband wanted.

M Street was deserted except for a few homeless men making their way to another dumpster. Hoffman checked the rearview mirror and ran the red light to the right of the bridge, then ran another light as he turned down Thirty-first Street. At the foot of Thirty-first he barely paused before turning right, under the shadowy girders of the Whitehurst Freeway, back underneath Key Bridge. He saw Forsyth's black, government-issue Chrysler parked opposite the Potomac Boat Club, engine idling. A Secret Service driver sat behind the wheel, reading the morning *Post* by the dome light. Hoffman squealed to a stop beside him.

"Morning, Dr. Hoffman," the driver said, amiably warm and lazy.

"Have they started yet?" Hoffman asked, jumping out.

"Nope. You'll make it."

Hoffman scrambled up the slope in front of the cars. At least it wasn't too cold. Jogging was bad enough. But jogging when it was cold enough to freeze the water in the canal was even worse.

Brig. Gen. Charles Montgomery Forsyth, dressed in a plain grey sweat suit, was carefully stretching a hamstring, propping his left foot atop the brown pillar of towpath milepost No. 1 and bending until his forehead almost touched his left knee. He was one of those officers who take great care to stay lean and fit into middle age. Ten years older than Hoffman, he looked younger. He was six feet tall, tanned, blue eyed. Only the deep pilot's wrinkles around his eyes kept him from looking too pretty.

A second Secret Service agent, also dressed in running clothes, stood next to him, jogging in place, ready to go. The agent's breath frosted lightly in front of him.

"Morning, Hank," Forsyth said pleasantly. Forsyth pulled his foot from the milepost. "Ready to go?"

Running without warming up was going to be his punishment for failing to arrive early.

"My only regret," Hoffman said, nodding, "is that I have but two legs to give for my country."

Forsyth nodded, but didn't smile. They set off, the agent first, then Hoffman and Forsyth, side by side. Streetlamps from Canal Road and the general glow from the city cast a little light. Hoffman could make out the towpath of packed clay and gravel, the shadows of bare-branched trees overhead, and blackness to their right, where the canal was. The canal had long since stopped carrying cargo barges pulled by mules, but the towpath remained, stretching 180 miles to the west, giving pleasure to joggers, hikers, and cyclers. Hoffman, who had a sense of history, appreciated that, if someone had to jog, there were few better places for it. His legs felt stiff and sore, but he was beginning to feel a rhythm, and he knew they would loosen up. At least Forsyth wasn't pushing the pace, the way he sometimes did with staffers he was unhappy with.

"Tell me what's going on in Moscow," Forsyth said, breathing easily, arms pumping steadily.

"Looks like Korotov was telling it straight." Sergei Korotov, the KGB emissary from the Soviet embassy, was Hoffman's contribution to what little the White House knew about the situation in Moscow. Hoffman wanted him to be right.

"The first part or the second?"

"Both." He kept his sentences short.

The sound of their footfalls changed as they pounded over a wooden footbridge that spanned a spillway that bled canal water down toward the Potomac, on their left.

"Why would they send a message like that?" Forsyth asked.

"Probably because if the people who sent it take over, they don't want us to hit their economy. And make it hard for them," Hoffman explained. "Stopping joint ventures or grain sales."

Forsyth said nothing, so Hoffman elaborated. "Let's assume Ponomaryov is really sick. The *Tribune* may have it right. Maybe it's a stroke. He's the right age."

"Always been healthy," Forsyth objected, but not strongly.

"Always a first time," Hoffman rebutted. "I think the best bet is that what we hear is right. That he's not getting better. That there's going to be a leadership change."

"All right. Who's gonna take over?"

"My bet would be a collective leadership. But much more conservative."

"Why?"

"Because they squeezed Morozov out. Because Korotov came to us," Hoffman explained. "He's KGB. If the whole leadership were sending the message, they'd have used the ambassador. If Fyodorov were on board with whoever sent the message, they'd have used the ambassador. But Fyodorov's the biggest Ponomaryov man in the Politburo. We can assume he's not on board. Still, the KGB feels like it can open a back channel. The conservatives must be pretty confident."

"And if the conservatives take over?" Forsyth said. He economized his breath, letting Hoffman talk.

Hoffman normally looked anxiously for each milepost when he ran the towpath with Forsyth, for each sign that he was making progress toward stopping. But this morning he was focused so tightly on his subject that it was as if his head had detached itself from his body. His brain and his mouth were working on one level, talking about the situation in Moscow. His legs and his lungs were operating somewhere below him, like a machine.

"The reaction around the world would be near panic," Hoffman said. "People worship Ponomaryov. They think he's the greatest peace-maker since Gandhi. If he goes, they'll think it's back to the Cold War."

"But you don't," Forsyth said.

"No."

"Why not?"

"What choice do they have? They'd crack down domestically. Hard. We'd have problems with them on human rights issues again. But they'd still have to get soap to the coal miners, just like Ponomaryov does. They can't do that and run an arms race."

"They tried before Ponomaryov," Forsyth said.

"That generation is dead."

They passed milepost No. 2. Hoffman decided to try out the riskier part of his analysis. Officially, he knew, the president wanted *perestroika* to succeed and wished Ponomaryov well.

"There could be some real advantages for us," Hoffman said.

Forsyth said nothing, so Hoffman plunged ahead.

"We get no competition for the high ground in public opinion. We control the agenda. Up on the Hill, people stop writing defense budgets as if there's no threat out there."

Forsyth neither agreed nor disagreed.

"So what should we do?" Forsyth asked. "The Boss is such a nice guy—he wants to send him a get-well card."

Hoffman knew he had to present all the possible options to Forsyth if he wanted to retain his credibility. "First, if we want to help the reformers," he said. Forsyth said nothing again.

"We can have State let their ambassador know quietly that Korotov saw me and what he said." Hoffman had told only Forsyth about the Korotov meeting. Forsyth, as far as he knew, had told only the president.

"That would tip the liberals off that something's going on," Forsyth said.

"Right," Hoffman said. "But I don't think we should do anything right now. Let him send a get-well card. Don't phone him and actually ask to speak to him. And let's not tell anyone about Korotov. Least of all the ambassador. I think we ought to let nature take its course on this one. If he recovers, we have the status quo. If he goes, we might get, maybe, Molotsky, or someone who's proreform." He puffed a bit. "He'd still have to prove he's got Ponomaryov's charisma. More likely we get conservatives, maybe Lizachevsky, with Andrushin the power behind the throne. But not conservatives who want to cause us any trouble. There's no downside variant. I think we should sit tight. There's not much we can do about it, anyway. The main thing is to avoid doing something that would hurt the conservatives."

Forsyth nodded. "Okay. But I want better intelligence. I want you to draft a list of questions we need the Agency to answer. They're not giving us squat, and I'm tired of finding out what's going on over there from the newspapers. We have to tell the Boss we're doing something."

"Sure," Hoffman said. He could not remember Forsyth using the pronoun "we" with him before, and it pleased him to hear it.

They reached milepost No. 3 and turned around. Heading back toward the city, Hoffman saw the sky in the east was beginning to brighten.

15

VALENTIN Skorov looked at the dossier on the desk in front of him with the enthusiasm of a man contemplating a dead rat in his kitchen. It had been a long time since he had been required to deal with a matter of this sort. But not long enough.

In his undergraduate days at the Institute of International Relations, he had heard about dossiers like this one. He had learned that they often landed on the desk he occupied, the American desk in the Press Department of the Ministry of Foreign Affairs. That was one reason why the Press Department was traditionally a ministry personnel dumping ground, like the African Affairs Department. It was a nasty assignment that led nowhere.

And that was why Valentin Skorov had resisted the job when it was offered to him after his first tour in Washington. He had wanted to work in the arms control section. Then he had received a call from a friend in the foreign service, a man who, though only in his mid-thirties, was already occupying a major desk in the international department at the Central Committee.

"Valentin, why don't you want the Press Department?" his friend had asked, sounding annoyed.

"If the party wants me to take it, of course I'll take it," Skorov had answered, quite surprised that the Central Committee even cared who filled the job.

"Don't look at it that way, Valentin," his friend had said. "You should be happy to get it. Maybe you've been abroad too long and you don't quite realize how things have changed."

"What do you mean?" Skorov had asked. He was flattered, but still suspicious.

"I mean that we are no longer in the days when guys with baggy suits and bad tempers handled press relations," his friend had said. "I mean that if you show you can handle American correspondents, appear on their TV shows occasionally, you can do yourself a lot of good." He paused. "Frankly, I'm surprised you hadn't figured that out." He laughed. "*Glasnost* arrived several years ago."

Skorov had felt stupid, and he rushed to cover up that fact. "Well, of course I realize that. It's just that I've spent a lot of time on arms control. I'd've liked to keep on doing it." This was true. Working on arms control made Valentin Skorov feel that there was more to his career than collecting trips abroad, although he had nothing against them.

"If you do a good job handling the American press, you will be working on arms control, because you will be influencing American public opinion in a favorable direction," his friend had said, and Skorov had believed him. And for a year he had found the work interesting, and at times rewarding. He was a handsome man, with blue eyes and a thatch of sandy hair. He dressed in tweeds and precise suits he had bought in Washington. When Vasily Grishin was out of town, he had shown that he could make a favorable impression on American TV. He had begun to think that if and when Grishin moved on to an even higher job, he might become the ministry's spokesman. Press work had begun to appeal to him.

Until this morning. When he arrived at work, the Burke dossier was on his desk, along with a covering note of instructions from Roldunov, the first deputy chief of the department—the KGB's representative.

The dossier and the letter, he noted with distaste, could serve as a textbook example of press relations of the old style, a style that Valentin Skorov had allowed himself to believe would not be seen again in Moscow. Burke had been set up. And now he, Skorov, was supposed to apply the squeeze. Skorov had no personal feelings toward Colin Burke. He was one of the more competent Americans in the press corps. They had dealt with each other over the red tape of an American correspondent's life—visas and accreditation. He occasionally answered Burke's routine questions. They had never really gotten to know one another. That was fortunate, because Skorov disliked the tactics he would have to employ. It would have been even more difficult with someone he liked.

The telephone rang, and he picked it up. "Skorov."

"Valentin Nikolayevich. This is the front desk. Mr. Burke is here to see you."

"Have him wait. I'll be right down."

Skorov sighed. There was nothing to do but handle the assignment as professionally as possible. That was the lot of the foreign service officer in any country—cleaning up messes for the politicians.

He took the elevator down to the second floor and a staircase down to the lobby.

The American correspondent was leaning against the counter of the almost empty coat check area, his eyes fixed on the policeman guarding the front door. Burke was wearing a trench coat, rumpled corduroy pants, and no tie. Skorov noticed that his lips were sealed in a tight line across his face, and his chin jutted out under his mouth like the prow of a boat. It was about the expression Skorov had expected. The American turned around as Skorov approached.

"Good afternoon, Mr. Burke," Skorov said, extending his hand. "Thank you for coming on short notice."

The American looked dubiously at the Russian's hand for a moment. His lips curled upward, amused. Skorov was afraid he would not shake his hand, causing a scene. Finally, Burke extended his hand. "So we're going to do this in a civil fashion," he said. "All right." They shook.

"And when have we ever not been civil with you, Mr. Burke?" Skorov said, arching his eyebrows.

The American smiled again. "Let's cut the crap, all right?" he said in English.

"Very well," Skorov replied, switching to English. "We shall, as you say, cut the crap. We have serious things to discuss. But there is no reason not to discuss them civilly."

The American hesitated. "Lead on," he said, smiling thinly.

Skorov took that for assent. "I was wondering if you've had lunch yet."

Burke seemed genuinely startled. "No, I haven't."

"Well," Skorov said, "there are two choices. We can eat here, but the restaurant here isn't very good. Or, we can go to the Dom Zhurnalistov."

The American snorted. "A hearty last meal?"

"Don't jump to conclusions, Mr. Burke."

Burke looked at the Russian skeptically. But Skorov thought he read some hope in Burke's eyes, and he was pleased in that professional sector of his mind that was devoted to fulfilling his assignment. As had been anticipated, Burke was anxious to avoid expulsion. That would make his task easier.

"All right," Burke said. "Dom Zhurnalistov. But how can you get us in?"

Dom Zhurnalistov was the headquarters for the Soviet Journalists' Union—in formal terms, a union hall. In reality, though, it was one of the best restaurants and bars in Moscow, a private club for that segment of the Soviet elite that controlled the media. It admitted no foreign journalists, especially not Americans.

"While we work in the press section here, we can use it. We are like honorary members," Skorov smiled.

"Let's go," Burke said. They walked outside.

A black Volga, parked outside the front door, rolled toward them in response to Skorov's wave. They got in, and Skorov told the driver where to go. Burke said nothing, staring out the window on the right. They turned right on Kropotkinskaya, past the Serbsky Institute, a mental hospital where dissidents, in the old days under Brezhnev and Andropov, received a Thorazine cure for their political neuroses. They turned left, up Gogolevskaya, and over Burke's shoulder Skorov saw the vapors rising from Moscow's heated outdoor swimming pool. The pool looked like a giant hot spring bubbling up in central Moscow, but it was actually a construction error. Stalin had razed the colossal Church of the Holy Innocents from the site, intending to build a massive hall for Communist Party meetings. But the construction pit, which was close to the Moscow River, kept flooding, and the best Soviet engineers had failed to stop the seepage of the waters. When Khrushchev heard that the citizens of Moscow were interpreting this as a sign of God's displeasure, he ordered that the site be turned into a swimming pool. And it was.

"Do you know the story of that pool?" Skorov asked.

Burke had heard the story. And he had heard one too many Soviet officials try to establish his reform credentials by telling a story about Stalin. He was in no mood for another.

"I've heard it often," he said.

Skorov nodded.

The Volga pulled up outside the graceful, ocher-colored Dom Zhurnalistov and stopped. Skorov and Burke, without exchanging a word, got out of the car and walked inside, past a doorman in a greasy serge suit, who nodded to Skorov as they passed.

The journalists' club, Skorov thought, was by far the best restaurant in Moscow. He had chosen to bring Burke there for precisely that reason. To their right was a dimly lit barroom with heavy wooden tables and leather chairs. Beyond that were the dining rooms, sunlit, painted a cheerful pale green with white accents. A plump, smiling woman with her blond hair tied back in girlish bunches greeted them.

"Valentin Nikolayevich! It's a pleasure to see you."

Skorov bowed slightly. "Can you give us a table for two?"

"Of course," the woman said, and led them to a table under a window. It had a white tablecloth and real linen napkins instead of the small scraps of thin white paper that were normal in Moscow.

"It's not quite up to Washington standards yet, but it's close," Skorov said, with a small smile. "It's not absolutely true that when communism triumphs, we must spare a few capitalists to teach us to run a decent restaurant."

The American turned pale and stared quizzically at Skorov, but did not reply.

Skorov wondered what had disconcerted Burke. Perhaps the American was simply nervous. If so, that was good. It would make his task easier. He picked up the small mimeographed menu. "I recommend you try the *tsyplyata tabaka*," he said. "The cook here is Georgian, and he does it very well."

"Fine," the American said, and flipped the white sheet of paper onto the table. There was a moment's silence.

"It's chicken cooked in a beef and garlic sauce," Skorov said.

"I know," the American said.

Skorov decided there was nothing further to be gained by being charming; the American was clearly not receptive. So he began.

"You know," he said, trying to assume an air of friendly regret, "I've been getting a lot of complaints about you."

"Good," said Burke.

Skorov had always found Americans to be grossly arrogant, considering the nature of their country. Burke's answer typified that arrogance, and Skorov began genuinely to dislike him.

"It's not good, Mr. Burke, not good for you, not good for the Foreign Ministry. We don't like getting reports of correspondents in serious trouble."

Skorov beckoned for the waiter, letting his last phrase hang in the air. He ordered two *tsyplyati tabaka*.

Burke waited for the waiter to leave. He leaned back in his chair and folded his arms across his chest.

"Exactly what complaints have you been getting?"

Skorov permitted himself to smile. He was, as the Americans said, in the driver's seat.

"First, you composed an absolutely groundless story about the leader of the Soviet Union. Then you got caught in a vice squad raid. I've got people in the ministry and in the Central Committee telling me you should be expelled. I've got people at the Ministry of Internal Affairs telling me you should be prosecuted." Skorov shrugged his shoulders, as if to say that he, as a man of the world, was indifferent to whatever perversion Burke was guilty of; he merely wanted to deal with his bureaucratic problem. "What should I tell them?"

Burke leaned forward. His facade of superiority, Skorov noted with some satisfaction, seemed to be cracking a little. There was anger and tension in his voice. "Tell them that if the leader of this country is sick, in any country with a free press, that's news. It's my job to report the news. And tell them to stop setting up correspondents."

Skorov took a sip of water and sighed loudly. "Please, Mr. Burke," he said. "I am rather tired of hearing Americans talk about the so-called free press. We both know there is no such thing. You are no more free to write what you want than any Soviet correspondent. You can only write what your publisher wants to print."

Burke said nothing. He was leaning back again, arms still folded, but his face was flushed. Skorov took this as an encouraging sign.

"Now," he said, leaning forward across the white napery. "Let me be plain. You are in danger of being prosecuted for serious crimes. I need not remind you that correspondents have no diplomatic immunity. We in the Foreign Ministry . . ." He paused and pretended to search for the right words. "Some of us in the Foreign Ministry," he corrected himself, "see no purpose to be served by such a prosecution. We know it would cause problems with your government. It would not help our image. But the police, I can assure you, are insisting that you be treated no differently from any other criminal."

Skorov waited for a reply. When none came, he decided that he had done the best he could to prepare the American for what he had to say.

"Mr. Burke, when I was a student at the Institute for International Relations, do you know what I wrote my dissertation on?"

"No."

"Watergate."

"Oh."

"And I remember reading in one of your newspapers an account of a press conference by Senator Ervin from South Carolina. Do you remember him?"

"He was from North Carolina," Burke said in clipped words. "And, yes, I remember him."

"He used an expression in talking of the situation your President Nixon was in vis-à-vis the committee. 'We have him where the hair is short,' he said. Have I quoted that expression correctly?"

"Close enough," the American said, scowling. "So what?"

"Mr. Burke, I believe you are in an analogous position. You are caught where your hair is short."

The American was laughing. "You mean, by the short hairs."

Skorov blushed, angry at himself. There had been no need to flaunt a command of colloquial English. By trying to do so and failing, he sensed he had given up the offensive.

"Whether I quoted the expression correctly or not, Mr. Burke, the situation remains the same. I must tell you that our ability to prevent a prosecution will depend on your behavior. If you were to write another article suggesting that the leader of the Soviet Union is seriously ill, I don't think we could protect you any longer."

Skorov looked at the American, who remained without expression for a moment. Then Burke unfolded his arms, and leaned forward so that their faces were only a couple of feet apart. Skorov looked into his unblinking blue eyes. The proximity made him slightly uneasy.

"Well then," Burke said slowly, "let's hope he gets well soon."

Skorov drew back to his own side of the table.

"Mr. Burke," he said, still smiling thinly, "I assure you that you do not realize the gravity of your situation. I am told the criminal charges you could be facing carry a cumulative penalty of thirty years in prison."

Skorov paused to let the number sink in, and took a sip of water. "Let me give you a few words of advice. Perhaps you have heard the old Russian proverb: Don't butt into a strange—"

"—monastery with your own prayer book," Burke finished for him. "I've heard it."

Burke paused and seemed to be thinking. Skorov waited and watched Burke's jaw, looking for it to protrude in another expression of contempt or defiance. He was not prepared for what he thought he saw next on Burke's face, which was sadness.

"You know, I heard a story," Burke said. "During the Stalin years, a man in Moscow is heard on the street saying, 'We're all screwed up because of one man.' They arrest him, and he's taken to an interrogation room."

Skorov did not like the turn the conversation had taken, but Burke gave him no opportunity to interrupt.

"The interrogator looks at him sternly and says, 'All right, comrade. Why don't you just make it easy and tell us who you were blaming for screwing up our society.' The prisoner says, 'Why, Hitler, of course.' The interrogator, surprised, has no choice but to let the man go. But as he's leaving, the man turns to the interrogator and says, 'And just who were *you* thinking of, comrade?' "

Burke smiled thinly. Skorov didn't.

"I don't find that funny, Mr. Burke," Skorov said.

"Neither did the interrogator," Burke said.

Before Skorov could reply, Burke rose and walked from the room. The man from the Ministry of Foreign Affairs watched his back disappear from sight. He did and said nothing to indicate that the American's departure was not exactly what he had expected to happen. He was wondering what he would do with two plates of *tsyplyata tabaka* when they arrived. And whether, in his report, he would say that Burke would or would not heed the warning he had been given.

16

IT was only a little past one when Burke returned to his office. He tossed his coat on the floor and sat down behind his desk. Outside the window, the grey snow was turning black from the dirt in the air. He stared for a while at the steel and glass cube next door with the sign that said KAFE. If he got hungrier, the Kafe's fatty sausage was the only thing around for a quick lunch. Burke decided to brood on an empty stomach.

Skorov's warning puzzled him. After the raid at Shurik's, he had expected the ministry to wait a couple of weeks, then expel him. When Skorov had called so quickly, he had allowed himself to hope, implausibly, that they might tell him the security types had gotten out of hand and the matter was being dropped. Either that or an immediate expulsion. He had not expected to be kept dangling.

Why warn him off pursuing the Ponomaryov story? Only one explanation seemed plausible. Kuznetsov had been telling him the truth in the *banya*. Whoever was behind this wanted the first story out, and he had obliged them. They didn't want the real story out. And they had put the squeeze on him to keep him from pursuing it, perhaps to warn the rest of the press corps not to pursue it.

With a light tap on the door, Olga came in. Burke wondered if she would rub her breasts on his shoulders again. But there were no papers in her hand, and she stopped a step away from his desk. He was disappointed.

"Mr. McIntire from your embassy called," she said. "He would like you to call him back." Burke grunted but said nothing. She paused. "He said as soon as possible," she added, apparently embarrassed about prodding him. Burke decided there was no use being rude to her.

"Thank you, Olga," he said, raising his eyes and meeting hers for the first time. He thought he saw something sharp and probing there.

"Christ," he exploded. "Not you, too!"

Olga stepped back, hands crossed against her chest as if warding off a blow. Now he thought he saw fear. She said nothing.

"I'm sorry," he said, embarrassed. He tried to grin at her. "It hasn't been a good day."

Now Olga disconcerted him further. She smiled sweetly. "It's all right, Colin," she said softly, and left the room.

Burke watched her go. He sighed and decided to return J. Porter McIntire's urgent phone call.

He dialed McIntire's number. "Press and Culture," a woman answered.

"Press, please. Not culture."

"I'm sorry?" the secretary said.

"Mr. McIntire, please."

"I'm sorry, he's in a meeting right now. Can I take a message?"

"This is Colin Burke. I'm returning his call. Tell him I won't be available for quite a while after this."

"Oh, yes, Mr. Burke," the secretary said, suddenly deferential. "I'll see if I can break in. Please hold on."

There was a moment's pause. A man came on.

"Colin," McIntire said. "Thanks for getting back."

"Not at all. What can I do for you?"

"Well, I think we'd better not talk about it over the phone. Can you come in?"

"When?" Burke had a pretty good idea what it would be about.

"The sooner the better, Colin. How about right now?"

"All right," Burke said. "See you in fifteen minutes."

"Fine, Colin. Bye."

The new American embassy office building was twelve years old. It was also empty. Empty it would remain as long as congressmen could get their faces on the evening news complaining about it. One subcommittee insisted that the building could not be occupied because of bugs. Another subcommittee insisted there was not enough money to pay for tearing the building down and starting over. Meanwhile, the embassy continued to function in its tired old building on Tchaikovsky Street. The old building had been thoroughly bugged for decades.

The marine guard at the embassy entrance, who had been watching Burke come and go at least once a week for a year, sternly asked him for his building pass. Burke fumbled inside his wallet looking for it and spilled his credit cards. The marine did not help pick them up.

"Keep that security tight, Ace," Burke said to the marine when he straightened up. "Don't let any spies in here disguised as me."

The marine said nothing.

Burke walked down a corridor to a single elevator, entered it, and rode to the top floor, the ninth. When he got out he waited behind a glass door until another marine guard, standing watch at the entry point to the supposedly secure areas of the embassy, pressed a button. An unseen bolt slid back and Burke entered a small reception area. Pictures of the president, the secretary of state, and former American ambassadors hung on the walls. The president looked delighted with something. It was not clear why.

J. Porter McIntire was waiting. He was a short, bald man with a fringe of grey hair and a pair of reading glasses sitting on the tip of his nose. They gave him the look of a well-fed accountant. He loved nothing more, he had once told Burke, than Japanese art, a passion he indulged by leaving Moscow for Japan whenever an opportunity presented itself. He dreamed of becoming consul general in Kyoto.

"Thank you for coming on short notice, Colin," McIntire said, shaking hands.

"I wish the circumstances were more pleasant," Burke replied.

"Yes." An expression of distaste flickered over McIntire's face for a second, but only for a moment. A look of professional good cheer quickly replaced it, rather like the look of a doctor facing a patient with an unpleasant, but curable, illness. "We're anxious to hear about the circumstances—from you. We already got a call from your friend Skorov."

"Such a nice man," Burke said.

Usually, when Burke visited an embassy official, they walked from the guard post to an inside staircase and down to an office on the eighth or seventh floor, the working levels of the embassy. But this time McIntire opened another door and gestured for Burke to enter. Burke found himself in a white-walled corridor. Judging from the pitch of the ceiling, it was directly under the roof. McIntire walked ahead and opened another door on the left side of the corridor. Burke walked through it.

He entered a large, unfinished attic room. In the center of the room, wedged underneath the roof, stood what looked like a huge Plexiglas shoe box. It was seven feet high, twenty feet long, and perhaps ten feet wide, with a door at one end. Curtains hanging on the inside of the box concealed its contents.

"Welcome to The Bubble," said J. Porter McIntire. "We thought we'd better have this meeting someplace where you could speak freely."

McIntire threw a switch on the wall. Burke heard a hum; he guessed it was some kind of white noise. The glass box made it impossible to conceal a microphone in the walls. The white noise was supposed to foil any microphones the Soviets aimed at the roof from outside.

Inside The Bubble it was as quiet as a coffin. He saw a table and chairs, made of the same Plexiglas as the walls. Sitting at the far end were two men and a woman. Pete Tolliver, the ambassador's deputy and one of the foreign service's foremost linguists, sat in the chairman's spot. Burke had once heard him, at a dinner, deliver the same toast in English, Norwegian, Russian, and Latvian. Tolliver sat at the head of the table, looking genial and a trifle bemused. On his right was a man Burke barely knew, Frank McCardle. He had arrived in Moscow a month earlier to be the embassy's new security officer. He came from the FBI, and the foreign service officers on the embassy staff roundly detested him. But that was normally the case between foreign service officers and embassy gumshoes. It was the person on Tolliver's left who engaged Burke's attention: Victoria Carlson. Why was she there?

"I believe you know everyone, Colin," Tolliver said. "Why don't you sit down?" Burke sat down, one seat removed from McCardle, across the table from Victoria. She was wearing a silk blouse of eggshell white and a scarf. She smiled warmly at him.

In the State Department, Burke knew, you could tell a lot by who showed up at meetings. If Fyodorov, for instance, met with an American delegation that included someone from the Department of Energy and someone from the Bureau of Near East and South Asian Affairs, it was a good bet that the meeting was about nuclear weapons proliferation in the Middle East. The key was knowing that the Department of Energy, not the Pentagon, controlled bomb building for the United States.

So why were the people at this meeting invited? McIntire was obvious. His responsibilities included the American correspondents in Moscow. So was McCardle, who had to worry about anything that might breach embassy security. Presumably, he would want to know whether Burke had been compromised badly enough that he might start working for the Russians. And Tolliver was there to represent the ambassador. That left one interested agency, and one person, Victoria Carlson, unaccounted for. It was not something Burke would have guessed before. But it didn't seem likely that she was there to compile material about pornography for the cultural affairs office.

The names of the CIA's representatives in Moscow were secret. They held jobs just like everyone else on the embassy staff. Occasionally, Burke came across someone who spoke fluent Russian, was an expert on one or another Soviet minority, and held a menial job in the library or the embassy store. Such persons, he assumed, were CIA. But until today, he had never suspected Victoria.

"Port, why don't you begin?" Tolliver said.

"Of course," the press attaché said. He opened a fresh manila file folder on the table in front of him and extracted a page of yellow legal note paper. "I received a call from Mr. Skorov at the Foreign Ministry press office this morning."

"So did I," Burke said. "What did he say to you?"

"He told me about an incident last night," McIntire said. Looking up from the page, he peered at Burke over his half-moon spectacles. "He told me you were arrested in a pornography raid."

Burke felt heat rise in his cheeks. He forced himself to smile. "Well, I'm not sure that I was arrested. Raided is certainly true. I don't think there have been any charges filed."

McIntire frowned. Perhaps he had been hoping that Burke could plausibly deny the whole story. "No, but Skorov said there might be."

Tolliver broke in. "Well, Colin. I'm sure there's more to this than Mr. Skorov cared to convey," he said genially. "Why don't you tell us what happened?"

Burke recounted most of what had happened. He told them he had been working on a story about underground video operations. Without naming Vasya, he told them how he had made contact with Shurik Stukachov. He told them of the rendezvous at Shurik's apartment, Linda Lovelace on the tiny black-and-white video, the arrival of the police, and the interrogation.

McCardle took up the questioning. "Did Shurik ask for anything in return for letting you in?"

Burke blushed again. "He wanted to copy some of my videos."

"And did you let him?"

"No. We settled on a blank videocassette and a carton of Marlboros," Burke said. He felt, again, like a schoolboy in the principal's office.

"And you gave them to him?"

"Afraid I did."

McCardle rolled his eyes. "You can be damn sure that blank has something juicy on it now," he said. "Along with your fingerprints." Burke got the impression that McCardle was more than a bit pleased with the situation.

McCardle confirmed it. He turned to Tolliver. "We should all take a lesson from this," he said.

The embassy's Sovietologists and gumshoes, Burke knew, argued constantly. The security rules required the Sovietologists to report each contact with an unknown Soviet citizen and get advance permission for meetings. When they did get permission to talk to someone, they went only in pairs. The Sovietologists complained bitterly that the rules hampered their ability to find out what was going on in Moscow. Burke's case would help McCardle argue that the rules were necessary.

While McCardle droned on, doing just that, Burke looked at Victoria. Through the glass tabletop he could see that her legs were crossed in front of her and one polished black pump was dangling from the front of her foot. She was writing notes of some kind on a yellow legal pad, face neutral. Seeming to sense his eyes on her, she looked up and caught his glance. Her expression softened at the edges, and she gave him a small, sympathetic smile as McCardle finished his oration about Burke's carelessness.

". . . shows what the KGB can do if you allow unsupervised, unaccompanied contacts," McCardle finished.

"Least I could do for you," Burke said, smiling. No one smiled back.

"All right, Colin," Tolliver said. "Let's get serious. Is there anything else you should tell us?"

Burke thought about the parts of the story he had left out. "No," he replied. "I just got overconfident. You know, you operate here for a year or so, nothing bad happens, and you start to think nothing can."

Tolliver considered that in silence for a moment. To Burke, it seemed that they all thought he was lying.

Tolliver spoke again. "Well, do you have any idea why they should pick you out for a setup?"

Victoria spoke up. "I think it's obvious, Pete," she said. "He got a good story. It embarrassed them. They saw a chance to set him up, teach the press corps a lesson. They took it."

Burke nodded. It was not the whole truth, but it was close enough. To tell them what he really thought, he would have to tell what Kuznetsov had said in the *banya*. And he wasn't about to do that.

He looked around the tiny room. Tolliver was blandly playing with a pipe. McCardle stared at him with the undisguised hostility most cops feel for reporters. McIntire was writing something on his own yellow pad. They didn't look as if they bought Victoria's explanation. Only Victoria met his eyes evenly.

"I had lunch with Skorov today. He as much as told me," Burke said.

"What did he say?" Tolliver asked.

"He told me that if I wanted to avoid prosecution, I should stay away from any more stories describing the general secretary's health."

"And what did you say to that?" Tolliver was interested again.

"I told him an *anekdot* about Stalinism and walked out on him."

There was silence for a while as the diplomats considered this conduct.

Victoria spoke. "Did he tell you your Ponomaryov story was not true?"

"No," Burke said, smiling wanly. "He called it groundless, but he didn't say it was not true."

No one smiled back.

Finally, Tolliver spoke. "Have you thought about taking his advice?"

"You mean not writing any more about Ponomaryov's health?"

"Yes."

Burke thought about saying something snide. He decided against it. "No. I haven't. I can't," he replied levelly.

Tolliver smiled his warmest smile at Burke. It was a smile that said, "I'm on your side. I've got your best interests at heart." It made Burke feel like patting his coat pocket to check on his wallet.

"Well, Colin, you're in an unenviable position. I know you've got professional responsibilities and ethics, and I wouldn't try to tell you how to do your job."

"Sure, Pete," Burke said.

Tolliver plunged on.

"Normally, when a correspondent is threatened the Soviets know we can use the weapon of reciprocity. We tell them we'll retaliate. They throw one of ours out, we throw one—maybe two—of their correspondents in Washington out. Sometimes it deters them."

There was a "but" coming, Burke knew. He squirmed in his Plexiglas chair.

"But in this case, we can't threaten reciprocity. If they arrest you, we can't fabricate a case against one of their people. We can kick a couple of them out, but that's not the same as putting them on trial. So you see what I mean when I say you've gotten yourself into an unenviable position."

Tolliver paused.

"I should think the Russians got him into it, Pete," McIntire piped up.

"I take your point, Port," Tolliver replied. Burke wondered whether he was listening to a rehearsed bit of dialogue.

"But the fact remains, Colin," Tolliver said, turning back to Burke, "that we can't do much to protect you."

Burke grunted.

"So, while I wouldn't want to tell you how to do your job—which, by the way, you do brilliantly—I would think about Skorov's advice if I were you."

Burke gazed silently at Tolliver until the genial corners of the man's mouth turned downward.

"Well, I appreciate your letting me know where you stand, Pete," Burke said finally.

"Don't get the wrong impression, Colin," Tolliver said hastily. "We know you're the good guy and we know who the bad guys are. I just don't want you to have any misunderstanding about how helpful we can be."

"And I just wanted you to know I appreciated that," Burke repeated, voice flat.

Tolliver pushed his chair back from the table. His lips flexed back into their genial position. "Right," he said. "Well, gentlemen—and you, Victoria—I guess that takes care of our agenda. Thank you for coming."

Tolliver stood up and leaned forward, offering his hand. Burke took it, shook briefly, nodded to the others, and left The Bubble. He heard the hum of the white noise machine as he left.

Victoria caught him at the elevator. She touched his arm. He caught a whiff of a familiar perfume and remembered what Marina had said about her.

"Don't think too badly of us, Colin," she said when the elevator doors had closed.

"Why should I think badly of you?"

She grimaced, then smiled sweetly at him. "I can think of a lot of reasons, unfortunately." Her teeth were bright white. "But don't be angry."

"I'm not angry."

"Yes you are. I can see it in your face. Your jaws are grinding together."

Burke felt himself flush. He was tired of women telling him what he felt, or what someone else felt about him. He did not reply. The elevator stopped.

"Let me buy you a cup of coffee?"

It was the first time she had asked for his company. He was tempted to refuse. His curiosity told him not to. "Sure," he said.

Instead of going down a corridor and out the front door of the embassy, they turned in the opposite direction and walked out into a courtyard. She let go of his arm. They walked quickly through the cold air toward the "new" embassy compound. Next to the hulk of the empty office building, Burke saw the long row of two-story brick townhouses for the senior embassy staff. It always reminded him of an American urban renewal project dropped by mistake into the middle of Russia. They turned a corner and were about to descend into the complex's underground arcade when Victoria spoke again.

"We work so hard trying to develop good relations with the Soviets," she said. "There's a natural tendency to wish that something like your case would just go away. But that doesn't mean we blame you, or we don't sympathize with you."

"Thanks, Victoria. I feel much, much better."

She touched his arm again. "Don't be sarcastic. It doesn't become you."

Burke had never trusted women who reached out to men's forearms; it was a gesture of feigned intimacy. But Victoria came close to carrying it off. He felt some warmth in it. He admired her skill.

"All right," he smiled. "I'll try."

Burke opened the door and held it for her.

"Thank you," she said, and she smiled at him as she passed.

They walked downstairs, past the swimming pool, and the grocery store, and the barber shop, all of which the United States government had installed so its emissaries to Moscow would have to brush against Soviet life as little as possible.

That was the spirit of Uncle Sam's, the embassy snack bar. It looked like a new, upscale McDonald's, with counter service, green plants in the windows, and blond wood fixtures. A handful of people were finishing their lunches. Burke let Victoria buy the coffee, and they sat down. He sipped while she put saccharin in her cup and stirred it, waiting for her to get to the point.

"You'll probably think I'm saying this just to make you feel better, but they're also jealous," she began.

"Who's jealous?"

"Tolliver and company," she said.

"Why?"

"Because you're doing the reporting they should be doing," she said. She sipped her coffee, but her gaze never left his face. He could see her eyes over the rim of her cup. "Because you seem to have sources they don't."

He let that sentence hang for a moment. He was right about her.

"You're right," he said. "I think you're saying that just to make me feel better." Then he smiled. "But I do appreciate it."

She smiled back. "It's true. I can't imagine it's pleasant to get a cable from Washington saying, 'We understand from the *Washington Tribune* that Ponomaryov has had a stroke.'"

He looked directly at her. "No, I imagine it wasn't pleasant," he said.

She stiffened just a little and her eyes narrowed. Burke knew that she knew that he had guessed. That was all right. At least they understood each other. She said nothing, and after a moment, sipped her coffee again.

"I just don't want you to feel that we're the enemy here," she said, carefully choosing her words. "We're not. We might be able to help."

"Thanks," Burke said. "I need all the friends I can get."

17

HE had expected no sympathy from Graves for the raid at Shurik's. Graves did not surprise him. Less than forty-eight hours had gone by since the telex printer was glowing with congratulations. It might as well have been forty-eight days.

> To: Burke, Moscow
> From: Graves, Foreign
> Re: Ponomaryov folo
>
> Skedding folo on Ponomaryov illness for tomorrow. What are your sources saying about jockeying in the Politburo as a result of his stroke? Any rumblings from the military? Any thought being given to the overall problem of replacing aged or infirm leaders? Does the man in the street know about this? Who are the likely candidates to succeed Ponomaryov if his health deteriorates further?
>
> Also, please advise whether situation there requires an extra hand due to news crush, your legal problems. Have potential short-term relief pitcher, Russian speaker Jennifer Shorenstein, here on Metro staff. Should we apply for a visa for her?
>
> Advise soonest. Regards.

Burke needed this like the Moscow River needed cabanas. But to keep control of the situation, he had to come up with a better story than the last one. It had been a real soufflé—nine-tenths hot air. The next one needed meat. And to get it, Burke needed a second source.

If an American president had had a stroke, the press's problem would have been sifting through the avalanche of available information. The president's doctors would give press conferences. So would surgeons who only wished they were his doctors. *Time* and *Newsweek* would publish maps of the lobes of the great man's brain. Twice daily, the cameras would catch the First Lady bravely waving at the entrance to Bethesda Naval Hospital.

In Moscow, there was only official silence and an unofficial threat, delivered over lunch at the Dom Zhurnalistov.

There was a subtext to Graves's message, another reason for restlessness in Washington. No one had matched Burke's story, although a few seemed to have picked up hints from Douglas Crittenden or his colleagues in the diplomatic corps that something was wrong with the general secretary. Graves was no doubt scanning the rival papers for catch-up stories on Ponomaryov's stroke. Burke wished there had been some. Nothing was better than breaking a story and watching the competition catch up. Nothing was worse than breaking a sensational story that remained exclusive forever.

Burke took the final bite from his standard lunch for one, a sandwich made from the canned Danish ham he always kept in the office refrigerator. He dropped the paper plate and bread crusts into the trash. He went into his office, where his computer's cursor winked greenly in the gathering afternoon gloaming, sat down, and began pecking at the keyboard in the message jargon still favored by foreign desks, a holdover from the era when telegraph companies charged correspondents per word of copy filed.

What could he tell Graves? Not about Skorov's threat. If Graves could show the *Tribune*'s editors that the Russians had compromised Burke's independence, Jennifer Shorenstein, whoever she was, would need warm clothes fast. They would pull him out. They would agree that he had been framed because of displeasure at the Ponomaryov story and pat him on the back. Then they would put him to work in whatever department needed a body while he waited for another chance to go overseas.

Nor would he tell them about his conversation in the *banya* with Andrei Kuznetsov. He did not want the KGB to know what he knew, or who his source was. Nor was he yet ready to tell the *Tribune* that a part of his story, the part about Ponomaryov's recovery, might have been disinformation. He would do what he should have done the first time, and confirm what Kuznetsov had told him from a second source. Then he would decide how to tell them. There was no point in informing Washington that their correspondent was groping.

For now, he would tell Washington very little:

To: Graves, Foreign
From: Burke, Moscow
Re: Ponomaryov advisory

Advise offholding Ponomaryov folo. Need more reporting time. New leads.

Regards.

That might hold him for a day. Maybe two.

Under the circumstances, Burke could not use the office phones. He pulled a pocketful of *dvuchki* from the stash in his desk, put them into his pocket, checked to make sure he had his address book, slipped into his parka, and walked out into the evening. On Kutuzovsky Prospekt he turned east, toward the river, and walked until he was clear of the foreigners' compound. There was a pay phone against the wall of an apartment building. He began dialing

An hour later Burke tallied up his score. He had tried to reach twenty people. He had hit roughly fifty wrong numbers. Six lines had been consistently busy. Nine had never answered. Of the five sources he had managed to talk to, no one had agreed to meet him. Three told him regretfully—and, it seemed, truthfully—that they knew nothing about Ponomaryov's health but what they had read in the newspapers and heard on the BBC. Two told him they simply preferred not to talk about it. His fingers were getting numb, and he thought that the traffic cop, standing out in the middle of Kutuzovsky, had noticed him and was getting curious.

He had only one idea left. He readied his coin and dialed the number Marina had given him. On the first ring, a woman answered. He did not recognize her voice. He assumed she was Lena, the roommate.

"Marina, if you would be so kind," Burke said in his most formal Russian.

"Just a second," the woman answered. "I'll see if she's here."

This, Burke realized, had to be a lie. In a one-room communal apartment, how could there be any doubt whether Marina was there?

"Marina," he heard through muffling fingers. "It's the American." For the thousandth time Burke wished he could speak Russian without such a conspicuous accent. There was a moment of silence.

"She's not here," the woman said.

Burke felt weak and cold. "She's not?" was all he could manage to say.

"No. Good-bye," the woman said, and abruptly hung up.

Burke stood for a moment, staring at the phone. Why should Marina refuse to talk to him? He thought about their last meeting. He had promised to call, and she had promised to wait for it.

Burke turned around and walked a few paces back toward his apartment. The gloomy spire of the Hotel Ukraina loomed across

Kutuzovsky Prospekt. He could think of no reason why she should shun him.

After a moment, he returned to the pay phone and dialed again. This time he recognized Marina's voice.

"Marina, it's Colin," he said, trying to sound more confident than he felt. "Why didn't you want to talk to me?"

There was silence on the other end. Finally she spoke. "It's just better not to," she said. Her voice was tired, flat.

"That's not a reason," he pressed.

He heard her sigh. "Colin, it's complicated. It's about the theater, and my job . . . and everything."

"Someone's gotten to you about me?"

She said nothing.

"Why can't we talk about it?"

"It wouldn't do any good," she said.

"How do you know?" he said, trying to keep her talking.

"I just know."

"Maybe I can help you," Burke said. He had no idea how, but he was getting desperate.

"It's not likely." He thought he heard a softer note in her voice. "But it's nice of you to offer."

"At least tell me what's wrong."

"I don't think so." She was wavering.

"Tell me. You've got a problem at the theater?"

"I can't talk about it over the phone."

That was an opening. "Well then, we'll talk about it face-to-face."

Suddenly she was irritated. "You think this is America, don't you?" she said sharply. "That we'll talk about it and work it out."

"No, Marina," he said levelly. Maybe he could appeal to her pride. "I know this is Russia. And I also know you're not the type of woman to just cut things off like this."

The cold was seeping up through the soles of his shoes and into his feet. He stamped against the concrete while he waited for her response.

"All right," she said. "When?"

Burke was ready for that. "Tomorrow morning at ten," he said. "Do you have skis?"

"Lena has some," she said. "Why?"

"Bring them," Burke said. "I'll meet you on the corner where I dropped you off."

She seemed bemused. "All right," she said. "Until then."

Burke hung up. His fingers, he found, had stiffened in the cold like a claw around the receiver, and he plunged them deep into his pockets as he walked home.

18

SHE was waiting at the appointed hour, dressed again in the black jeans. The borrowed skis stood beside her. The sun was shining and her skin glowed. She did not look happy.

He stopped the car and got out. "Hi," he said. "Beautiful day, isn't it?"

She looked up at the unusual sight of a blue sky over the city and chuckled slightly. "Yeah." She stepped toward him suddenly and hugged him, pressing her cheek against his shoulder.

He waited until she lifted her head and looked at him, then smiled at her. He hoped it was reassuring.

She smiled a tentative smile. "How are you?" she said. Burke felt foolishly relieved to hear her use *ty*.

He took her skis and stuck them inside the car, on top of his own. He pushed the tails through the little hole behind the backseat armrest and into the trunk. The front ends lay in the middle of the front seat, their curved tips like question marks between them.

"Where are we going?" she asked, as they pulled away from the curb.

"To Peredelkino," he replied.

She said nothing for a moment. "Colin—," she began, but he put a finger to her lips and silenced her.

"We'll talk when we get there," he said.

Marina's eyes widened slightly, but she accepted his admonition and said nothing. Burke hoped she was not too frightened. But, given the circumstances, it would be stupid not to be frightened.

He looked in the rearview mirror and saw only the usual array of muddy Zhigulis, ancient trucks, and lumbering yellow buses. He had seen no surveillance all morning. But that might only mean they were being a little more skillful about their work. Burke also did not know whether his car was bugged. Where they were going, it would not matter.

He was driving along the inner ring road, and now he turned west on Kalinin Prospekt, heading out of town. They passed the Ukraina's towers, and the foreigners' ghetto. The *militioneri* stood impassively in the middle of the road, and Burke wondered whether they noticed, or cared about, the Russian girl in the American correspondent's Volvo.

Traffic was sparse, mostly trucks headed toward Minsk or Kiev. Burke accelerated. Sprawling housing projects sped past the car windows, one white twelve-story building after another, dwarfing the pedestrians who trudged stolidly through the snow, their fur-framed faces staring at the slippery ground. Marina seemed to chafe at the imposed quiet, sitting with her hands twisting in her lap. He turned on the tape player. The cassette was by a singer he knew named Carol Sloane, doing mostly Cole Porter. She had a good trio backing her up, and the music sounded sinuous and bright.

Burke glanced at Marina. The tape seemed to be softening her a trifle, but if she understood the words, she did not show it.

Responding to the rhythm, Burke pressed the pedal down, and the car sped over the bridge that spanned Moscow's outer ring highway. Abruptly, the city ended and the countryside began. On their left were open, snow-covered fields. On the right were villages, clusters of one-story wood cottages painted red, green, and blue. Their roofs seemed to sag under the snow and smoke curled from their stovepipes.

A few miles past the outer ring highway there was a sign over the road, with an arrow pointing left: PEREDELKINO. ZONE OF REST. As Burke turned, he looked in the rearview mirror. He saw nothing.

They were on a narrow, well-ploughed blacktop road, framed on each side by towering pine trees. Through the trees, occasionally, they could see a wooden fence enclosing a compound, and behind the fence the roofs of two or three cottages. Peredelkino was a writers' colony. The trade unions for novelists, playwrights, and journalists owned most of the village's dachas and parceled them out to favored members. Once, they had been strictly summer cottages. But with the advent of the automobile, Peredelkino had become a kind of suburb. Writers favored with dachas lived there all year. They kept their Moscow apartments for their mistresses, if that was their wont, or sublet them, if it was not.

"It's my favorite place in Russia," Burke said, waving at the scenery. "Have you been here before?"

Marina simply nodded.

"You like it?"

She nodded again. He wanted to tell her it was all right to speak now, at least about Peredelkino, out of range of Moscow's listening devices. He had heard that the KGB bugged cars with short-range radios that transmitted to a receiver in a tall building overlooking Kutuzovsky Prospekt and the American embassy. It should be safe to talk this far outside the city. But raising the subject of the silence he had asked for would only have reminded both of them of Moscow and their troubles there, and he did not want to do that any sooner than necessary. He sensed, as he had with her before, that she wanted to squeeze everything else out, and to know only this place, this time. Or was that his desire, projected onto her?

"Have you seen Pasternak's house?" he asked.

She shook her head no.

"Would you like to?"

She nodded solemnly.

The road led over an earthen dam that enclosed a pond. It was frozen, and they could see dark figures sitting on the ice, fishing. He turned right between two more files of pine trees, then left down a narrow, snow-covered road. On their left was a row of dachas. To the right was a rolling, snow-covered field, and beyond it glinted the golden, onion-shaped domes of the village church, the Cathedral of the Transfiguration.

He stopped the car beside a gate, on which hung a hand-lettered cardboard sign: THERE WILL BE A MUSEUM HERE. Pasternak's children had hung on to the house for years after he died in disgrace in 1960. They lived in it, keeping his study as he had left it, showing visitors around, and resisting, with the help of sympathetic friends, the periodic efforts of the Writers' Union to evict them and assign the dacha to someone else. Finally, shortly after Vikenty Ponomaryov became general secretary, Pasternak was officially forgiven for writing *Doctor Zhivago* and winning the Nobel Prize. A proposal to make the house a museum was accepted.

But then, nothing happened. Just as unseen liberal forces somewhere in the party hierarchy had helped keep the house in the Pasternak family, unseen conservatives seemed to be blocking the creation of the museum.

"I have a file on this house, and the rumors about why the museum has never opened," he told her. "But I've never been able to figure out who's behind the delay, or why, so I've never written the story."

She nodded, still silent.

Burke opened the gate. Marina took his arm again, as she had that night at the pond. He felt her body's firmness against him. Pasternak's house loomed in front of them, a two-story, brown-shingled structure with a silvery tin roof. Facing them was a rounded wing that always reminded Burke of the stern of a steamship. Its windows looked out over the field to the church in the distance. Burke walked up to the tiny front porch door and knocked loudly. No one answered. He tried the door-knob. It was locked.

"There's always been a caretaker here to let people in," he said, turning to Marina. "I'm sorry. I guess we can't go in."

She smiled. "It's enough just to see the house," she said. She turned to gaze at the view Pasternak had commanded from his study on the second floor, at the rounded end of the house. Then she began to recite.

"Here I am with you in the lodge.
No one walks through the woods these days.
As in the old song, undergrowth
Has almost hidden the forest ways.

"We shall sit down from one till three,
You with embroidery, I deep
In a book, and at dawn shall not see
When we kiss each other to sleep."

"Pasternak?" he asked.

"Yes," she replied. "It's a poem he wrote to his lover one autumn when they lived here."

"I didn't know you liked poetry."

"I'm Russian," she said.

"You're a romantic, too," he said, and turned toward her. He took her gloved hand.

Her blue eyes locked onto his for a moment. Then she lowered them. "Don't forget," she said. "We have to memorize all sorts of poetry in school."

He let go of her hand. "Let's go skiing."

She nodded, silent again, and they returned to the car. He saw his camera bag in the backseat.

"May I take your picture?" he asked.

She thought for a second, then nodded her head. She posed, first grave, then smiling, in front of Pasternak's house. Then she wanted to take his picture, so he showed her the button to press and he posed in front of the house, gravely. "Smile!" she said, but he would not, until she walked up to him, wrapped her arms around his neck, and kissed him deeply. "Now, smile," she said, breaking off the kiss. He smiled.

They got into the car and he retraced their route for about a mile. On the pond, the fishermen were gone. It was almost lunchtime.

Burke stopped the car and parked at an indentation in a grove of pines a few hundred yards past the pond. He pulled the skis out and they slipped into them.

Two ski tracks led into the woods from the end of the little parking area, four parallel grooves of packed snow. Burke shuffled forward, pushing one ski deliberately in front of the other, seeking his rhythm. Marina breezed past him. She had the knack of canting her skis slightly to one side, getting some traction, pushing off and gliding, like an ice skater gathering speed. He watched her open a lead of twenty yards. Her legs seemed very long in her black jeans.

She turned to see what was keeping him, smiled, and slowed down. In a moment they were abreast again, she gliding easily and Burke trying hard to keep her pace. The path led them through a grove of spruce trees that towered above them like cathedral spires. Where the sunlight pierced the forest cover, the white snow on the green boughs glinted brightly. For a while, the only sound was the rhythmic hiss of their skis on the trail.

"You're a good skier," he said between breaths.

She laughed and her teeth glistened in the reflected sunlight. "Not really. It's just something else we learn in school."

They came to another pond. Most of it was frozen, but at one end running water burbled over a small dam. A few picnic tables and some children's swings stood buried in the snow at the edge of the pond. The ski tracks led over an arched footbridge. Burke stopped short of the bridge. She stopped alongside. There could not, he assumed, possibly be any bugs nearby.

"So," he said. "What's the problem at the theater?"

She frowned, and hesitated, as if she were debating whether to tell him. Then she began.

"I went to see Fyodor Maximovich yesterday," she said, and her voice trailed off. She brushed some snow off her shoe with the tip of her ski pole.

"Your director?" he prompted.

"Yes. He asked me to come in to talk. I asked him when he could make me a regular member of the company."

"And what did he say?"

"Well, he knows my situation. But he just sort of squirmed around in his chair . . ." Marina began twitching as Fyodor Maximovich had done. "And he said . . ." She lowered her voice and tucked her chin into her neck. " 'I'm sorry, Marina Borisovna, but we have no prospects for that. In fact, I think we are going to have to close *The Dacha* a little earlier than we had planned.' "

She was into repeating the scene for him now, and needed no prompting. She straightened slightly, becoming herself again.

" 'Why?' I asked. 'It's doing very well.' "

The chin went back into the neck. " 'Yes, I know,' he said. Then he pointed toward the ceiling. 'But they want to replace it with something else. Something by Chekhov. Maybe the real *Cherry Orchard*.'

" 'Everyone in Russia has seen *The Cherry Orchard*. That's the last thing we need,' I told him.

" 'Even if I agreed with you, I couldn't do anything about it,' he said."

"So why can't he find you a permanent place?" Burke interrupted.

"I asked him that," Marina said. "I was angry. 'You've told me how well I've been doing, Fyodor,' I said. He looked at the ceiling again. 'I know,' he said."

She was getting angry all over again. "He knows! I said, 'So give me a job!' He shook his head and looked very sad. 'I can't,' he said." She shook her head sadly in imitation of the director, then straightened up again to resume playing herself.

" 'Why not?' " she quoted herself. "I was going to make him tell me."

She looked at Burke then, and she was back at the pond addressing him, no longer re-creating the scene in the director's office. But the anger and grief were still playing in her eyes. "Connections." She spit out the word. "That's all he would tell me: 'Your connections.' "

"I was afraid of that," he said.

"When I asked him to explain, he refused and asked me to leave the office."

Burke wondered if she would cry. But on her face he saw only anger and a stoic acceptance.

He broached the uncomfortable. "And by 'Your connections,' you're sure he meant me."

She looked at him. For a moment he thought she was going to say yes. But she did not. "I don't know," she said. "It could be a lot of people. It could mean that I don't have connections, or at least not the right ones." She shook her head. "I don't know."

Suddenly she pushed off on her ski and ascended the front half of the footbridge, then schussed smoothly down the other side. Burke labored up behind her, grabbing the handrails. He plunged down the other side, unable to stop until he had gone a few feet past her. He turned and clomped awkwardly back toward her, until they were facing each other, standing quite close, skis going in opposite directions.

"If I'm the problem," he said, "I'm sorry. I should have known better."

She had the grace to smile at him. "You didn't do anything wrong," she said. "And I didn't. They did."

"What are you going to do?"

She shook her head. "I don't know. Try to catch on at another theater, I guess."

"Your husband still wants you to live with him?"

Marina shuddered. "Yes."

They skied around the far bank of the frozen pond and then into a stand of slender birch trees. The brook that fed the pond gurgled beside them. Burke's cheeks were tingling. He remembered his glib offer to help her. It embarrassed him. So he concentrated on the trail, and the rhythm of the skis, and the ghostly white birch trees.

She broke into his reverie. "And how are you?"

He looked at her carefully for a moment, seeking some sign in her face that she knew something of what had happened to him in the thirty-six hours since they had separated. He saw nothing. If she was playing a role, she was too good for him to catch her at it.

So he told her almost everything, starting with the story about Ponomaryov's health, the raid at Shurik's, and ending with the meeting at the American embassy. He did not tell her about the second meeting with Kuznetsov, nor what he thought he had learned about Victoria. There were a few things he could not tell anybody yet. "The people at the embassy told me I ought to think about taking Skorov's advice and not write any more about Ponomaryov's health," he concluded.

"And will you?" she asked.

"What do you think?"

"I think you won't, because you know what will happen if you do," she said.

"What's that?" he asked.

"Then they will tell you not to write about something else, and something else, and it would never stop. You would not put yourself in that position."

She said it matter-of-factly, confidently, as if it were the most obvious thing in the world to anyone who knew him. He wanted to believe her.

He nodded. A moment went by.

"So what will you do?" she asked.

He looked at her again, and she returned his look, calmly and levelly.

There was, he thought, no good reason to trust her. He had a feeling of certainty about her. But he was still objective enough—barely—to realize how easy it would be for her to manipulate those feelings.

It came down to this: He could stop fighting, sit back, and let himself be intimidated. It all might blow over. But Graves would still be sharpening his knife. And the Soviets would not stop pushing once they had moved him. She was right about that.

"What the hell," he said softly. "If I'm going to crash this plane, I might as well do it nose first."

"What did you say?" she asked, puzzled.

"Nothing," he told her. "But I may need a favor from you."

"Tell me," she said.

"No," he said, wavering. "It wouldn't be a good idea." But as he said it, he was aware that his tone told her he was willing to be persuaded otherwise.

"Tell me," she said again, in mock severity.

"Well . . . ," he said.

"Tell me, or I'll ski off and leave you alone in the woods," she smiled, playing the game.

"All right," he said. "But only because you're threatening me."

"I am," she affirmed, nodding solemnly.

"I want you to introduce me to Volodya Filomenov."

She said nothing for a moment. Her face told him that if he had asked her to strip off her clothes and roll around in the snow, she would have been less reluctant.

"Why?" she finally asked.

"You know why."

She lowered her head. "You want to ask him about . . ." She could not bring herself to name Ponomaryov.

"That's right."

"What do you expect him to tell you?" she demanded.

"I'm not sure," Burke said. "Whether he's getting better or not."

"He would know," she agreed. "But won't your bosses want to know why you said he was recovering if he's not?"

"I'm afraid so," he said. His stomach spasmed at the thought.

"What will you say?"

"I don't know. I suppose I'll have to tell them that my source changed his original story. I'll have to write that. It won't be pleasant," he said. That much, at least, he knew.

Marina thought for a while. "And what will they do to you for publishing this story?"

"Which they? My bosses?"

"No," she said. "My bosses."

He was afraid if he frightened her further, he would surely lose her help. "They won't be happy about it, I'm sure," he said.

"Will they expel you?"

"It's possible."

"Do you want to leave? Would your bosses be happy if you had to leave?"

"No and no," he said. He touched her red cheek with his gloved hand. "I want to stay."

She said nothing.

"Not just because of you," he said. "But you're important to me."

She smiled and seemed a little braver. "Why else?"

"I like Ponomaryov. I like what he's been trying to do for this country. I don't like the people who are against him. And I think they're the ones trying to keep this secret," he said. "I don't want to let them."

Marina abruptly began skiing again, silently. The trail bent to the right, away from the brook and into a small meadow dominated by a broad, lone oak tree standing like a bull in the middle of the field. He couldn't tell whether she was thinking, or just angry. Pushing off, he kept pace.

"What happens to me if they find out I helped you?" she asked, continuing to ski.

She was willing to be talked into it. He felt both pleased and frightened. He plunged ahead.

"They won't find out."

"So you say."

"Marina, I give you my word. I will never tell anyone you helped me. I protect sources."

"They could find out anyway."

"Look," he argued. "I asked you to talk to me about the theater, right? Then I asked you to introduce me to Filomenov. I never told you why I wanted to talk to him. No one can prove otherwise."

They skied farther. Suddenly she stopped.

"All right," she said. "I'll do it."

"I'm glad," he said. "Thank you."
"But there is one condition," she added.
"What's that?"
"Marry me."

19

LOOKING back on that moment, Burke sometimes thought he should have lied. He could have told her what she wanted to hear, gotten to Filomenov, gotten his story, and gotten out of town.

But he didn't. He didn't lie and say yes. He didn't say no. He stood on his skis in the snow, trying to think of something to say at all.

The silence scraped against her ego like ground glass. She broke it.

"Colin, dear!" she said, a little too brightly. "I've frightened you. I don't mean really to marry me. It will be only another piece of paper." She put her hand on his forearm, the gesture of a reassuring friend.

It seemed to him that a piece of paper was not everything Marina had originally had in mind. But maybe that was his own vanity. Maybe that was just romance. It was much easier to go along with the idea of a piece of paper.

"So you can get a *propiska*," he suggested.

"Possibly," she said. "But not just that. If I help you, they may find out. I'll be in worse trouble. If I'm married to you, I can get an American passport and just leave. Go to the West."

For the second time, silence was all he could offer. To an American, "go to the West" meant nothing. A vacation trip to the Grand Canyon or Disneyland. Buy the ticket and go. To a Russian, the words meant something entirely different. To "go to the West" still meant crossing a political and social gulf and burning your boat on the far shore. *Perestroika* allowed Jews and Armenians to emigrate, but very few Russians. For them, emigration meant cutting a life off at the roots and leaving Russia behind, perhaps forever. And Marina knew that.

She broke the silence again. "Being out here," she said, gesturing with her ski pole in the general direction of Pasternak's house, "it's become clear to me." She looked at the middle distance, speaking more to herself than to Burke. "My place here is worse than nothing. I'm not going to catch on with another theater. I'm going to have to have that man's baby or go back to Nyerungri. I will not do either one. I'm still young enough to make a life in the West." She paused. "Isn't that right?"

"I suppose so," Burke managed to say.

She looked at him. "As soon as we got to the West we would get divorced, of course. You would never have to see me again."

Burke wanted to reply: "Don't sell yourself short." But he didn't know the Russian. So he simply said: "I wouldn't like that." And fell silent again, wondering whether she thought he meant "I wouldn't like marrying you" or "I wouldn't like never seeing you again."

"Well," she said finally, with another brittle smile. "What do you say?"

"Well," he began. "It's not exactly what I had in mind for a second marriage."

She looked gravely at him. "Nor I," she said, and began to laugh.

For a moment he joined her. They stood in the middle of the snow-covered woods, within earshot of the gurgling stream, laughing at themselves.

"Marina . . . ," he began.

"Yes?" she prompted him.

In his brain, he began the process of translating his thought into Russian. "I'll marry you, but it must be a real marriage" was what he was thinking about saying. But before the words could come out of his mouth, a second, more pragmatic thought crowded into his consciousness. With a rush of something that felt a little like sadness and a little like relief, Burke remembered suddenly why marrying this woman was not an option, at least not now, regardless of his feelings. He was off the hook.

"We can't," he said.

"Why?" she asked, and her brows furrowed in suspicion. "Are you really divorced?"

He laughed again. Briefly. "Definitely. But the paperwork for a Soviet getting a divorce and marrying a foreigner takes weeks. I've got to file this story within a few days. And I've got to do it from outside the country."

She was puzzled. "Why?"

"Because I'm not certain how the *vlasti* will react to it," he said, using a Russian word that meant "authorities" but usually referred to the KGB. "Badly, I suspect. I can't be in Moscow when they do. I'm going to have to file the story from Finland and wait and see what happens before I come back."

"And they might not let you back," Marina said. Her lips formed a straight, angry line.

"No," he admitted.

"Damn them," she said, and skied off.

The trail caught up to the winding stream again and accompanied it into a stand of spruce trees. Marina did not slow herself to accommodate the American, but he had learned from watching her, and he managed to stay only a stride or two behind. In the middle of a glade she stopped again, leaning on her ski poles, head down.

"I'm sorry," he said, catching up. For a moment she said nothing, simply stood there, head down, staring at her skis and the snow.

"Don't be," she finally said. She straightened up. "I'll do it anyway. I'll talk to him this evening and you can meet him after the performance."

Now that he had what he wanted, Burke felt no elation, only a vague sense of fear and guilt.

"Why?" he asked.

"Why not?" she shrugged.

"That's no reason."

She laughed at him. "Are you trying to talk me out of it?"

He had to smile at himself. "No. I'd just like to understand why you want to help me."

She looked quite levelly at him and her voice was serious. Her lips turned upward in the suggestion of a smile. "Because I like you better than I like them."

He wanted to kiss her then, but he felt that if he leaned over, he would fall off his skis and onto his face.

Instead, he told her something brash. "I think I can still help you get out to the West."

"You don't have to," she said, still gazing steadily at him, smiling slightly.

"I want to," he said, and meant it.

"How?"

"I can't tell you that now."

She did not reply. He hoped she believed him.

They said almost nothing as they skied back to his car. As he opened her door, she smiled, kissed him briefly and lightly on the lips, then held a finger to her own, repeating his gesture of the morning. As they drove away from the "zone of rest," the skies clouded over and became dull grey again. A black Volga appeared in the rearview mirror, and Burke watched it fretfully all the way back to Moscow.

20

THEY met again at the theater, twenty minutes after the final curtain. He stood in the lobby amid the chattering throngs who were getting their coats and leaving. He tried to look like someone waiting, bored, for a wife who was taking an inordinately long time in the ladies' room.

She came out of an unmarked door that led backstage, wearing the wool skirt she had on when he first met her at Vasya's. Her face was flat, opaque.

"Is everything all right?" he whispered.

She nodded. "We're meeting him at his place. He's gone ahead. We're supposed to walk. He doesn't want your car outside his flat."

Burke nodded. "You know where it is?"

"Yes. Let's go."

She took him through the unmarked door and down a narrow corridor, painted bilious green, barely lit by a naked bulb. He had a sense that they were approaching the wings to the left of the stage. Then she turned, opened another unmarked door, and they were in an alley behind the theater. Papers and trash littered an ice-covered pavement.

She did not take his arm, so he took hers as they walked into the night on Gertzen Street. She didn't pull away, but she didn't draw closer, either. There was a stiffness to her body which he had not sensed before.

"Is something wrong?" he asked.

"No," she said.

"Where are we going?" he tried again.

"You'll see," was all she would say.

He had learned, by then, that when she preferred to remain silent, she would not be drawn out, and he knew better than to try. They walked briskly down Gertzen Street about five blocks to Marx Prospekt and turned left, past the ocher buildings of Moscow State University's central campus and the baroque facade of the National Hotel. She turned down the stairs and into the pedestrian underpass that led toward Red Square. The people walking past them in the white-tiled tunnel had their eyes to the ground, intent on getting home. They ascended again and walked into Red Square. The cupolas of Saint Basil's Cathedral loomed before them, bold swatches of color bequeathed by the distant past to the drab present.

It was almost eleven o'clock, when the bells in Spassky Tower would resonate. From across the square Burke heard the rhythmic slapping of boots on the cobblestones. Two soldiers, escorted by a sergeant, were goose-stepping in tight, precise formation from a gate in the Kremlin walls to the entrance to Lenin's tomb for the hourly changing of the guard. Even at this hour, a few spectators were gathered to watch. But Marina was clearly not interested in stopping. They hurried past Saint Basil's and out of the square, down past the Rossiya Hotel and onto the riverside walk. Across the dull slate of the frozen river stood an old electric generating plant. One of Lenin's less successful prophecies had once been spelled out atop its roof in light bulbs: "Communism is Soviet power plus the electrification of the whole country." Russia had had Soviet power for almost seventy-five years, and electricity for almost as long. It was still waiting for communism, and the promised withering away of the state that went with it. Under Vikenty Ponomaryov, the sign had been quietly removed.

The night air was quickly getting colder. Burke was about to ask how much farther they had to go when Marina turned off the sidewalk toward the entrance of yet another Stalin Gothic tower, in the same enormous style as the Hotel Ukraina, the Foreign Ministry, and the Lenin Hills campus of Moscow State University. Without hesitating, she led him through an arched entry into a rear courtyard, and up to the wooden door marked ENTRANCE NO. 3. Burke had the sense she had been there before. A few Zhigulis were parked haphazardly around the open space. There was no one afoot outside, and no crone in the entrance hall to note their arrival. Stalin's architects had tried to design a grand foyer. A sad coat of glossy blue-green paint and dozens of years of muddy bootprints on the grimy tile floor had destroyed whatever splendor their design created. But at least there was no smell of old cabbage. They got into the elevator and closed the steel mesh door behind them. Marina pressed the button marked 12, and the elevator, with a pitiful shudder, began slowly to ascend.

On the twelfth floor he saw three doors covered in brown leather. Again, Marina did not hesitate. She pressed the buzzer on the center door. After a minute or two, the door opened.

Burke saw an entrance hall like millions of others in Russia, with coats hanging from pegs on the walls and boots and slippers strewn on the floor.

"Hello," said their host in a loud whisper, and beckoned them inside. He gave Marina a quick kiss—not on the cheek, Burke noticed, but on the neck, just below her earlobe. Marina stiffened.

Filomenov turned to Burke. He was tall—at least six four, Burke decided—and broad shouldered. His jet black hair drooped over his left eye, and in contrast to the blocky face that so many Russians have, he had high cheekbones and a long neck. He was wearing a carefully faded pair of Wranglers, slippers, and a silk dressing gown open almost to his waist. But for the network of tiny red veins that marked his nose and eyes and for the layer of fat around his belly, Filomenov might have been the handsomest Russian man Burke had met.

"Filomenov," he said, extending his hand and bowing slightly.

Burke paused in the act of taking off his coat. "Colin Burke," he said, and shook hands.

Beyond the entrance hall was a small living room. Burke had expected an actor with Filomenov's connections to have a bigger place. Brezhnev's in-laws certainly had, if the legends about their lavish lifestyles were even partly true. So had his daughter's lovers. Apparently, the stories about Vikenty Ponomaryov's abstemious personal standards were not exaggerated. The only visible signs that the room belonged to a member of the Soviet elite were the Sony television, the VCR, and the furniture, made of blond Finnish wood. It included a coffee table, and atop the table was a bottle of vodka, three-quarters full. Alongside it were two shot glasses.

"Sit down, please," Filomenov said to Burke, gesturing toward the sofa behind the table. Burke sat down, and Filomenov took the end opposite him. Marina, ignored, stood in a corner of the room.

The actor turned his head halfway in her direction. "Marina, there are *zakuski* in the kitchen."

Burke found himself irritated at the way Russian men treated women like servants. But as Marina submissively and silently disappeared into the kitchen, he reminded himself not to show it.

Filomenov turned to him and grinned. It was the cocky grin of a crocodile. "I have heard that American journalists are good drinkers, Mr. Burke. Is that true?"

Some Russian men, upon meeting an American, seemed to think that a drinking contest was the best way to determine which superpower was hardier. Filomenov seemed to be one of them. To avoid having to drink with them, Burke had taken to telling such men that he was a recovering alcoholic. But that tended to put a damper on conversation. So he played along.

He remembered some of the grey-haired men with bottles in their desk drawers that he had known years ago in Oakland. Then he thought of the *Washington Tribune* staff, which seemed to be composed equally of joggers and racquetball players. The news business, like his neighborhood on Capitol Hill, had been gentrified. "They used to be," he said.

"But not now?"

"Less so."

"Ah, too bad," Filomenov said. "I was hoping it would still be like it was in *The Front Page*. You know the film?"

Some Russian men, upon meeting an American, liked to show that they knew more about American jazz saxophonists, or Hollywood movies, than the American did. It was not endearing, but it was better than drinking bouts.

"Yes," Burke said cautiously.

"Which version did you like best?"

Best to play the game. "Uhmm," Burke said. "I think it had Jack Lemmon in it."

"Ah, the recent one," said Filomenov, smiling triumphantly. He seemed to savor the sound of his voice saying "ah." "I actually prefer the second version, with Rosalind Russell and Cary Grant. Of course, it was not called *The Front Page*. It was *His Girl Friday*." He used English for the title, pronouncing it "Hees Gee-r-rl F-r-riday."

"Most of your critics agree with me that that was the best," Filomenov added when Burke said nothing.

"I'm sure," Burke said.

"At any rate, let's assume you are a hard-drinking American reporter like the ones in *The Front Page*," Filomenov said, pouring vodka into the two shot glasses. He raised his glass. Burke did the same.

"To Ben Hecht and Charles MacArthur," Filomenov said.

"To Ben Hecht and Charles MacArthur," Burke repeated.

Filomenov tossed back his head, opened his mouth, and poured the vodka directly down his throat in one rapid motion. He set the glass back on the table and looked expectantly at Burke.

Burke had found this was the best way to drink vodka. Sipping only prolonged the acrid moment when the alcohol, nearly raw, lay upon the tongue and in the nostrils. He threw back his head and tossed the vodka back in one motion, as Filomenov had done. He felt the warmth in his stomach. In a few moments, he knew, there would be a lightness in his head.

Filomenov looked pleased. "Good," he said, still grinning like a crocodile. He refilled the glasses and raised his.

"To friendship," he said solemnly. He drained his glass again.

"To friendship," Burke replied, and drained his. The warmth in his stomach turned to heat, and his upper lip seemed to be growing numb.

Filomenov filled the glasses again, but before he could propose another toast Marina arrived with a platter of *zakuski*—slices of bread slathered with butter and topped with sausage. Burke could almost see grease dripping from them. But, he remembered from somewhere in the distant past, coating the stomach with fat or oil helped slow the ingestion of alcohol into the system. Marina said nothing as she set the platter down, but her eyes seemed to be telling him to eat something. He did, and the numbness in his upper lip disappeared as he chewed.

Filomenov suddenly jumped to his feet, shaking the table enough that a bit of the vodka spilled out of Burke's glass. Standing, Filomenov refilled it. Burke noticed that he seemed to be having some trouble hitting the glass.

"To the beautiful actress whose brilliance illuminates *The Dacha*. To Marina Borisovna!" Filomenov proclaimed.

Burke got to his feet, trying to be more graceful than Filomenov had been. "To Marina!" he agreed.

This time he tried to sip the vodka, but Filomenov was watching.

"All of it, Mr. Burke. To the bottom. Or else you will besmirch the honor of this splendid woman," Filomenov said loudly. His grin was getting lopsided.

Burke complied. They sat down.

"Thank you, gentlemen," Marina said curtly, then turned her back on them and walked into the kitchen.

Filomenov shrugged. "Women . . . ," he said, and his voice trailed off. Burke could tell what was coming. Filomenov filled the glasses again.

"To women!" he declaimed.

"Yes!" Burke agreed.

Filomenov tossed the shot back. His head did not snap back as quickly as it had a few toasts ago, but seemed to wobble from his neck like a loose tooth for a second before he slowly, deliberately drew it erect.

Burke felt obliged to toss down his shot in the approved fashion. Somewhere within him a voice could be heard telling him to get to the point immediately.

"Tell me about the women in your life," he managed to say.

"Ah," said Filomenov, his eyes narrowing. Suddenly he seemed to Burke very close to sober. "Subtly, cleverly, the American journalist begins to extract information."

"Please," Burke said. "I'm doing the best I can under the circumstances. If you wanted real subtlety, you shouldn't have asked me to drink."

"S'all right," said Filomenov, slurring his words for the first time. He blinked and peered at Burke, as if trying to size him up for the first time. "Why do you give a fuck?"

Burke reached for a piece of bread and sausage, hoping to clear his head a little. He bit down on the sausage while Filomenov peered intently at him. He could mention that when the leader of the Soviet Union disappeared for a week or two, people around the world naturally got curious. That was not, he thought, what Filomenov wanted to hear.

"It's my job," he said finally.

If it was not what Filomenov had wanted to hear, at least it kept the conversation going. Filomenov poured himself another shot, draining the bottle. He picked up the glass and offered it to Burke. With a relieved wave of his hand, Burke declined. He hoped there were no other bottles left in the apartment. Quickly, Filomenov drained his glass. A small rivulet of vodka dribbled down his cleft chin. With the back of his shirtsleeve, he wiped it off. Burke calculated that Filomenov, with his head start, had consumed two-thirds of the bottle.

"And who tells you that this is your job?" he wanted to know.

"No one, directly. I know what I'm supposed to do."

"If the newspaper owner didn't trust you, he wouldn't send you here, right?"

"More or less."

Burke had heard the line Filomenov was developing before.

"So how can you say you have a free press?" Filomenov continued, right out of the textbook. "You are as obligated to your owner as our reporters are to the party. They write what the party wants, you write what your owner wants."

Burke sympathized with the argument, but not in the crude terms that Filomenov used. "The difference is, that we have lots of owners. Some of them dislike the government. You have only one owner, and it is the government." As soon as the words were out of his mouth, he regretted them, regretted drinking so much he had been unable to refrain from saying them.

But Filomenov only smiled, lopsidedly again, leaned toward Burke, and cupped his hand over the American's ear. "I think you're right," he said in a loud whisper. "But don't tell anyone." Then he giggled, and his head fell onto Burke's shoulder. He seemed about to pass out.

Burke tried hard to nurture Filomenov's sodden feeling of bonhomie. He put his arm around the Russian's shoulder. Filomenov's breath stank.

"So as long as I have to write what my owner wants," he whispered into the man's ear, "how's Oksana's father?"

Filomenov chuckled and turned to Burke. Their bloodshot eyes were inches apart. With an expression of great earnestness, he said: "He's a fucking corpse. She doesn't know how the hell they keep him alive." Then he giggled again, and sprang from the couch, reeling halfway across the room before he found his balance.

"Marina!" he called. "Bring Mr. Burke his coat. He's leaving."

Marina appeared from the kitchen. The look on her face was sepulchral. She got Burke's coat as he struggled to rise.

"How long has he been this way?" Burke asked the actor. "Ponomaryov, I mean."

Filomenov shook his head and put a finger to his lips. He was through talking. Burke looked at Marina. She was not moving toward her coat.

"You're not coming?" Burke was having trouble comprehending the situation.

She cut him off with a sharp shake of her head. "No," she said. Filomenov lumbered across the room and put his arm around her. His hand came around her back and squeezed her right breast. Filomenov grinned at Burke, then began licking her neck.

"Good night, Colin," she said, through lips drawn like parallel lines across her face. She thrust his coat into his arms.

Finally Burke understood the price she had paid to get him his interview with Filomenov, his corroborating source. A wave of nausea broke in his stomach.

"Good night," she said again, and opened the door for him.

Foggily, Burke weighed his options. He could take a swing at Filomenov and drag Marina from the apartment. But the likely outcome of that would be a fight, and the police. And Burke could imagine how well he would fare in a Soviet court right now.

He could also leave. Staggering slightly, he did. He made it to the elevator, to the lobby, through the courtyard, and across the street. For a long time he stared at the ice of the Moscow River, inhaling the biting cold air like a tonic.

21

THE arrival of the embassy mail pouch from Helsinki made a bad day worse for Victoria Carlson. There was already another hectoring cable on her desk from Langley, saying that the White House demanded fresher, better information about Ponomaryov. The mail added a letter from her mother in Manhattan; along with it came a wedding invitation. They were as welcome as the depressing grey clouds that hung over the city.

"Helene the Intrepid is doing it again! Wedding day is March 22!" her mother began. Mother's perpetual cheerfulness could be grating. This would be Helene's third marriage, for God's sake. And she was not yet forty. What was so great about that?

"Your father and I think (well, we hope) that this time, your sister's found the right man. He's a stockbroker from Larchmont. Princeton and the Dartmouth business school. Father of a seven-year-old boy from his first marriage." Mother had never believed in complete sentences. "So, with Helene's two girls, they'll have quite a family!"

A glance at the invitation revealed that prospective brother-in-law No. 3 was no one she had ever met. A reception would follow at her father's club, the Union League. Why did they continue to treat Helene to formal weddings? They could afford them, of course. But by the third time, it would be more tasteful to do things quietly. She guessed, from the fact that Helene had not written her, that she would not be asked this time to be a member of the wedding. It was just as well. She would have been inclined to refuse.

"So, we trust you'll be here on March 22," her mother concluded. "Perhaps you can take a couple of weeks and have a good, long visit." Victoria sighed. With all the pressure she was under from Langley, she had already backed out of her usual spring ski trip to Klosters with old friends from the service. She had no spare time, certainly not for yet another of her sister's weddings.

Still, she owed it to her mother. It was ironic, she thought. Her mother, true to her generation, had thrown all her talents into being a proper wife. To show for it, she had a detached husband on the verge of retirement and two daughters whose lives denied all her family values. Helene's only talent seemed to be entering and leaving marriages. Victoria had never managed to get married.

Not that she couldn't have. Throughout her school years, throughout her three boring years teaching Russian literature, there had always been lots of boys and men. So many, that it seemed the supply would never run out. Even after she joined the Agency there had been men. But there had always been something—a dissertation, a new job, a promotion to an overseas assignment—that seemed to matter more at the time. And then, in her late thirties, she had looked up and discovered that her career was flourishing and all the men she knew were married.

She found herself chewing on a pencil. Exasperated with herself, she set it down. She would have to stop pitying herself and find some more constructive channel for her anxiety. Grimly she turned to her word processor.

There, glowing green from the screen, was the problem she had to concentrate on—today's report on the health of Vikenty Ponomaryov. Or, at least, the beginnings of a report. She had composed a couple of paragraphs summarizing the public record—a history of robust health, followed by, at this point, ten days out of public view. Then she mentioned the news item in *Pravda* about the flu, the report by Colin Burke in the *Washington Tribune*, Grishin's curious press conference, and the rumors rampant in Moscow. Then she had stopped.

So much of the Soviet Union was transparent to the CIA. What orbiting cameras didn't see from the heavens, the inspectors monitoring arms control treaties often saw on the ground. Satellites picked up virtually every telephone conversation in the country and fed the signals into massive computers, which sorted through those billions of words and found the ones that would interest American intelligence. Sometimes, the CIA's sister agency, the NSA, knew what Far Eastern military commanders were telling their superiors in Moscow before the Politburo did. But when it came to something as simple, and as vital, as the health of Vikenty Ponomaryov, the Kremlin still knew how to keep its secrets. On more than one occasion during the days of Ponomaryov's absence, Victoria Carlson had sent her people out to stand along Kalinin Prospekt, watching the limousines go by on the way to the Kremlin and straining to see whether Ponomaryov was in one of them. But the limousine windows were of treated glass. Unless the sun shone directly through them, they remained opaque. A convoy of two black ZILs with Volga escorts continued to roar down Kalinin Prospekt to the Kremlin every morning. But whether Ponomaryov was in one of them, the CIA could not tell.

She had stopped typing because she had nothing specific to report to her superiors about the only question that would interest them: Where was Vikenty Ponomaryov? And she hated to transmit a report that was not precise and knowledgeable. Hated it so much she started doing things like chewing pencils.

The ringing of the telephone was an almost welcome distraction. She picked it up.

"This is Victoria Carlson."

"Hello, Victoria. This is Colin."

"Good morning, Colin. How are you?" she said.

She could feel a slow flush spreading up her neck to her cheeks.

"I'm fine," Burke said. "I need to see you this morning, Victoria."

Normally, she would have declined. Any meeting with a reporter required filing a security form acknowledging a contact with a journalist. The counterintelligence people used those forms to compile suspect lists whenever they investigated leaks. So Victoria met with journalists only as much as a cultural attaché had to be seen doing.

But under the circumstances, she had little choice. Burke seemed to have a source or sources no one else had. A second thought flitted through her mind. He could be writing something totally irresponsible— like his deductions about her position at the embassy. No. That didn't seem like him.

"All right," she said, trying to keep her tone calm and neutral. "What time?"

"Ten-thirty?"

She glanced at her watch. It was a few minutes after ten.

"Fine. See you then."

"Thanks," he said, and hung up.

She was not prepared for the way he looked when she arrived at the ninth-floor security post to meet him. Burke was standing against the wall where photos of former American ambassadors hung. He was midway between the grim George Kennan and the dapper Arthur Hartman. The way he looked, he might have slept there. His eyes were red. Beneath the normal Moscow winter pallor, his face was sallow, almost yellow. Victoria had always assumed that she was a year or two older than Burke; he had always seemed to move so vitally. Now he looked older. His shoulders sagged and his jacket was rumpled. She found herself feeling sad about that.

"Colin," she said. "Are you all right?"

He smiled and looked normal again. "I feel like shit," he said. "But not as bad as I probably look."

The marine guard was watching, and she said nothing. She opened the door to the ninth-floor corridor and beckoned him through. When the door closed behind them, she put three fingers lightly behind his elbow and led him down the hallway.

"Another wild night with a Russian actress?" she asked.

"A wild Russian actor, I'm afraid. And a vodka bottle."

"An actor?" She smiled. "I would never have suspected, Colin."

"Don't. He definitely preferred the bottle."

"How could he resist such big, bloodshot eyes?"

"I guess he was blind drunk," Burke replied.

"Was he the only one?"

Burke said nothing.

"Did I touch a nerve? I'm sorry," Victoria said.

"It's not that," Burke said. "We reporters are foolishly macho about the amount we drink, you know. It's just that this headache is making it a bit difficult for me to carry my end of this witty repartee."

"Well, I'm sorry your head hurts," she said, smiling at him.

They had reached the door to the attic room that contained The Bubble. She opened it and turned on a light.

The plastic room was empty. Victoria flipped another switch. Machinery began to hum quietly.

"Directly to The Bubble?" he asked.

"It seems best," she replied.

Burke didn't argue. Victoria opened the transparent door and held it for him. Ducking his head slightly, he went inside and sat down at the plastic table. She followed, seating herself across from him. He propped his chin in one hand.

She glanced at her skirt, which buttoned down the front. Under the transparent table it had opened and fallen from her legs, revealing half her thighs. With one hand, she flipped the fabric over her knees. Then she glanced at him to see if he had noticed. He had.

"So," she began. "What can I do for you?"

He sat up in his chair. "I want to trade a couple of favors."

"What do you mean?"

"I have some information. I need a big favor in return for it."

She didn't bother to tell him he should be talking to one of the embassy's political officers and not to a cultural attaché. He knew too much and she was in too much of a hurry.

"What's your information?"

"It's about Ponomaryov's health. Do I get the favor?"

"It depends on the information and the favor."

"I want a commitment."

"No commitments."

Burke grinned. "That's the story of my life. Women who won't make a commitment."

She did not laugh. "Before I can talk about any favors, I have to know your information. And I have to know your sources."

Burke's smile disappeared and his jaw set.

"You know I can't do that, Victoria."

"Why not?"

"It's bad enough I'm willing to tell you things before I've published them. But I can't tell you my sources. You know why."

She felt stubborn. "No, I don't."

He poked his jaw forward and she could suddenly feel his intensity. "Because I protect my sources." His voice was low.

"That's very noble of you, Colin, but I have to know sources." She folded her arms and tried to look at his retinas.

He sat quietly for a moment, returning her gaze. Then he stood up. "Nice talking to you, Victoria," he said, and without a backward glance opened the door of The Bubble and stepped out.

He turned then, and looked at her. "Don't the security rules require you to escort me out?"

For an instant she thought about escorting him to the door and seeing if he would give in. Then she decided he was not bluffing. She had overplayed her hand. "Come back in," she said. "Maybe we can work something out."

Burke looked at her for a moment, shrugged his shoulders, and ducked back inside the transparent room. She bit her lip and looked at him. His face showed no sign that he knew he had won—no emotion at all.

"Either you're a very good poker player or you make a habit of walking out of unpleasant situations," she said. She could almost feel her anger and humiliation curling about her like smoke from a cigarette.

"Excuse me?"

"You walked out on Skorov the other day. You walk out on me. Do you ever face things?"

Burke started to flush with anger. She was losing control of this situation and she did not like it.

"Sorry," she said hastily. "That wasn't fair."

Burke surprised her. He was sad and silent for a moment, his eyes as mournful as those of a small boy. "Nothing to forgive," he said. "I tend to do that. I'm sorry."

"No, I'm sorry."

"Okay," he grinned. "We're both sorry."

"Are you a good poker player?" she said, forcing a small smile.

"You'd have to play to find out," he replied. "There's a game every Sunday night."

"I'll pass," she said. "I don't gamble against people who know more than I do."

He grinned. "Then you'll never find out how good you can be."

She let it go. "Now then," she said, "I have to be able to evaluate the sources of any information I get. It's best to know their names. But if that's not possible, I've got to be able to assess their reliability. Can we work on that basis?"

"Maybe." His jaw set itself firmly again.

"Well, can you tell me whether their information is firsthand, secondhand, or what?"

Burke thought for a moment. "One source gets his information from a member of the Politburo," he said. "The other gets it from the family."

"How are they in a position to do that?"

Burke shook his head. The jaw jutted. "If I told you that, you might figure out who they are."

She tried again. "Well, on a scale of one to five, how reliable and well informed is each source?"

He thought again. "One is a three and the other a four."

"I'm glad you didn't try to tell me they were both fives," she said. "It shows some objectivity."

"Thank you."

"Have you used these people as sources before?"

Burke shifted slightly in his chair. "That's as much as I'm going to tell you, Victoria."

She sensed it would be futile to try to push him further. "All right, we'll let that go for the time being. So what's the information?"

Burke took a breath. "Ponomaryov's had a serious stroke."

"You've already published that, Colin," she said.

"This is new information." He hesitated. "And different."

"Why haven't you put it in the *Tribune*?"

"I can't send it from here. I'm going to have to leave the country to publish it."

She looked at him closely. Potential sources always overdramatized the dangers they faced while they were negotiating the price for their information. But the stillness of Burke's hands persuaded her. When most people lied, they tried to keep a straight face, and you could see the effort in their hands. People who kept their hands still struck her as credible. Burke's rested quietly on the table.

"Permanently?" she asked.

He shrugged. "Maybe. I'll have to see what the reaction is here. I'm not in a good position to take risks."

"Yes. You have to be careful." She wanted to tell him she would be sorry if he left, but that would have given him a bit more power in this situation than he already had. She didn't.

Burke sat back and folded his arms. "So. Are you interested?"

"I have to know more before I can tell you."

It was Burke's turn to be silent. She heard the quiet hum of the air-conditioning.

He sat up again, his decision made. He leaned toward her. "Okay," he said. "Ponomaryov has had a stroke, but he's not recovering. He's a vegetable—in a coma. One of my sources thinks that Andrushin and Petrusevich are keeping him under wraps until they can purge enough of his people from the Politburo to take control. They've gotten Morozov. They want to get the defense minister next. Then they'll let him die."

Victoria felt a surge of excitement; she struggled not to show it. Could he be putting her on? No, she thought, his red-rimmed eyes were earnest. If Burke was right, he was telling her about a sort of slow-motion Stalinist coup d'état by the KGB and the army. She wanted to believe him. The story fit with her own analysis of Kremlin politics and where the country was headed.

Could she trust him? If she got this right, if she got it quickly, she could be the next national intelligence officer for the Soviet Union and Europe. If she botched it, she could be looking for a job teaching Russian literature at a second-rate college. There were two ways to botch it. She could report it and then find it was not true. She could sit on it, then be embarrassed as the newspapers broke the story.

"Could you go over that again?" she asked him. She fished into a purse for a notebook and began jotting notes as Burke repeated his story. There was no way to verify what he was telling her, except for the way he told it. He was clearly telling her the truth as he saw it.

"There's one thing I should add," he said as he completed his recapitulation. "One of my sources thinks things are moving quickly. He mentioned the end of this week as a deadline."

"That's very interesting, and it makes sense," she murmured. "But there's one thing I can't figure out. Your article said Ponomaryov was recovering."

For the first time that morning, she saw Burke's hands move. He even blushed slightly.

"Yeah," he said. "I know."

"Well," she demanded. "Which is it?"

He laid his hands palms up on the table. "I'm not going to bullshit you, Victoria," he said. "In the first story I got taken in."

"How?"

"By a source who told me a story that was partly true. A couple of days later, he contacted me—very, um, discreetly. He told me he'd been assigned to plant the first story so that Andrushin and Petrusevich would have a way to explain Ponomaryov's absence without raising the question of replacing him before they've got control of the Politburo."

"You didn't have a second source?"

Burke grimaced. "I did. But apparently they planted the same story with him, knowing that I talk to him. And I took what he said as confirmation. Actually, thinking back on it, he only said he'd heard the same story and it sounded plausible."

Victoria nodded. "So why do you think this source of yours is telling the truth this time?"

"Because after I talked to him I did what I should've done the first time. I checked it out with someone who's in a real position to know."

"The one with connections to the family?"

He nodded.

"How can Andrushin and Petrusevich control Ponomaryov's medical care?"

"I assume the KGB runs the Fourth Chief Directorate," Burke said, referring to the branch of the Ministry of Health that ran the Kremlin clinic and other medical facilities for the privileged.

"They do," she agreed. "But why put the story out through you?"

"It gets broadcast back into the country by the BBC and the VOA," he said. "When you think about it, there's no Soviet equivalent to the unauthorized leak. If someone wants to put out a story unofficially about a touchy subject like Ponomaryov's health, he can't whisper it to *Pravda*.

He's got to use the foreign press. The people he wants to reach know how to interpret what they hear."

"All right," she said, tentatively. "But how do you know they're not just running a disinformation operation against you?"

He grimaced. "Look," he said. "I'm risking my career two ways with this story. I could get barred from coming back to the country for publishing it. And I'm not going to look very goddamn good when it is published, because people at the *Tribune* are going to want to know why I didn't get the story right in the first place. What's more, I've already compromised myself by telling you about it before I publish it." His voice rose slightly. "You think I'd do all that for a story I wasn't sure of?"

"I don't know," she said. But she believed he was right.

After a long silence he spoke again. "Now here's what I need from you." He glanced at her, seeking assent to go ahead.

"Yes." She nodded.

He reached into his coat pocket and pulled out a roll of Kodak film. It clicked as he placed it on the table. "I need an American passport and a Soviet exit visa," he said. "You can get the pictures from that roll of film."

She had expected him to ask for information of some kind. "For whom?" she asked.

"You met her," Burke said. "Marina Makeyeva."

Victoria felt the small hairs on her back stand up. "Oh, Jesus, Colin. Her?"

Across the table, Burke stiffened. "Yes," he said. "Her."

"Why?"

"Because I promised her that if she helped me with this story, I'd help her get out of the country."

"Colin, that's insane," Victoria said. She checked herself. Was she jealous? Yes, she admitted to herself. She was, a little. But that was not all. No. There were lots of good reasons against an American correspondent's smuggling a young Russian actress over the border. She started with the most obvious.

"What do you really know about her?"

He shrugged. "Not all that much. Enough."

"Where did you meet her?"

"With the guy who set me up with the porn mogul," he admitted. "Look, I know what you're going to say next. She could be setting me up, too. Believe me, I've thought about that." He paused. "I've decided to go ahead."

"Let me tell you something else about her that maybe you don't know," Victoria said. "Did you know that the Mayakovsky has always been notorious for its ties to the KGB?"

Burke blinked. "No. What do you mean, ties?"

"I mean that over the years, we've heard that some of the actors and directors from the Mayakovsky have been on their payroll. Fyodor Brulovsky is notorious. He's gay, and they've used that to control him for years. It's their way of keeping track of the theater crowd."

Burke sagged a bit. "She talked with him recently," he said. Then he turned stubborn. "Look, I know it's a risk. It's just something I've made up my mind to do." He shrugged.

She pressed the argument, leaning across the table toward him. "Even if she is what she says she is, she's using you."

"I don't think so. You don't know the details. I think I've been using her."

She reached out and put her hand on top of his, surprised a bit by her own gesture. It was not something she generally did.

"Colin, I admire you for keeping your promises," she said. "I even admire you for wanting to take this kind of risk for a . . ." She searched for the word.

"Bimbo," he offered.

"No," she said sharply. Her voice softened. "For a lover. God knows, I'd be tempted to do it myself if the situation came along. Or, at least, I hope I would. Or that someone would do it for me. I envy you a little. I envy her . . ." She stopped, unwilling to go further.

Burke only looked at her levelly.

"But I'm telling you as a friend. This is too dangerous. Even if she's not setting you up, she could panic and you could get caught. Even if she's been honest, they could pull her in, squeeze her, and turn her anytime they want to. And if you do get caught—" She looked directly into his eyes. "—You're on your own."

He put his other hand on top of hers. "Thanks, Victoria. I appreciate your concern."

She stiffened a little and drew away.

"I mean it," he said.

"But you want to go ahead with this?"

He nodded. "It surprises me, too. I'm a little old to be romantic. I just know that I've made a commitment to her and I have to keep it. It's partly ethics. It's partly . . ." The right word wouldn't come. "Personal," he finally said.

"How could you have that kind of commitment so soon?"

"It's funny," he said. "I think I got involved with her because I didn't think there could really be any commitment. It felt safe, emotionally. You know, she's a Russian, I'm a foreigner. I'm in control. I can always let the *militioneri* keep some distance between us."

He looked at her. She nodded.

"Then things snowballed. And here I am." He shrugged again and tried to smile. "I don't think I have any choice."

"I hope you're right and I don't regret this," Victoria said.

"I hope so, too."

"I'll see what I can do," Victoria said.

22

THERE was a false spring in Washington, as sometimes happens in February. Temperatures rose into the sixties and a soft, caressing breeze blew. Men took off their overcoats and secretaries sat on benches in Lafayette Park, across the street from the White House, eating yogurt for lunch and thinking of summer.

Inside the White House compound, Brig. Gen. Charles Montgomery Forsyth and Dr. Henry Hoffman were walking along the colonnade between the residence and the West Wing. Forsyth wore a grey pinstriped suit, nipped subtly at the waist. Hoffman also wore a grey pinstripe, but his was a Brooks Brothers bag.

Forsyth stopped in the middle of the colonnade and looked out over the Rose Garden. It was still bare, but the shoots of some crocuses were pushing through the earth. Beyond it, the South Lawn, green and precisely trimmed, imparted a reassuring sense of order as it rolled gently toward the Washington Monument and the Jefferson Memorial.

"Tennis weather soon, Hank," Forsyth said, sniffing the morning air. "Best time of year in Washington. You play?"

"No," Hoffman said, then added a small lie. "I used to, but I had to give it up. Shoulder problem." Maybe Forsyth would think he had once been good.

"Too bad," Forsyth said. He pointed to a cluster of trees and low mounds that hid the tennis court from public view. "Got the court right there. The president's always looking for doubles partners."

"Sorry," Hoffman said. The president was reputed to play very well. A game with him would be more embarrassing than one with Forsyth. Forsyth said nothing, and Hoffman seized the chance to bring up business.

"What are we going to do about Moscow?" he asked.

"Let's talk about that in my office," Forsyth said. They walked through a set of french doors into the West Wing, past a guard's desk and through the visitors' lobby, with its antique furniture and portrait of James K. Polk. Then they swung right, away from the Oval Office and into Forsyth's corner of the West Wing. Three secretaries sat squeezed into a small outer office, typing in front of CRT screens.

The national security adviser's office had a working fireplace, an original Morris Louis painting borrowed from the National Gallery of Art, and windows that looked out on Pennsylvania Avenue and the Old Executive Office Building. Forsyth walked around behind his desk and stooped down over his computer terminal, reading the messages left for him on the NSC's internal system. Hoffman noticed that on Forsyth's desk was a copy of the *Washington Tribune*, open to the personalities column. There was a picture of General Forsyth with an actress, dancing at a Kennedy Center gala. Hoffman was inclined to think that if he were divorced, like Chuck Forsyth, and dated the kind of public women Forsyth dated, he would not let any colleagues catch him reading his own notices. But he was neither of those. And, perhaps, he ought to learn a bit about self-promotion and image from Chuck Forsyth. Forsyth had been the deputy director of the NSC staff until a year ago, an air force officer seconded from the Pentagon to keep the NSC's paper flow orderly. But Forsyth made sure the president knew that he had been an ace in Vietnam, that he had a master's degree in business administration, that he spent time in the company of beautiful women. He projected an image irresistible to a president who admired the military, free enterprise, and beautiful women in about that order. And he had become national security adviser.

Forsyth touched a button and his computer screen went blank, except for the winking cursor. He looked at his watch.

"We've got a few minutes blocked out with the Boss. You're coming with me. I think we have to brief him on this beforehand, see how he reacts, get him involved early, rather than run it through the SIAG and pop it on him. More than likely, he'll say he wants to hear what the SIAG thinks."

Hoffman felt a surge of adrenaline. Forsyth rarely invited staff members to brief the president. He usually handled that himself.

On the other hand, he told himself, it might just mean that Forsyth regarded his idea as so risky that he wanted someone else to bear the responsibility.

"Okay, great," he told Forsyth.

The general checked his watch again, then picked up a manila folder with a red stripe at the top. "Let's go," he said.

They walked down a short corridor, carpeted in thick, beige pile, to the Oval Office. The president's personal secretary, Amanda Clark, smiled at Forsyth. "Go right in, General. He's expecting you."

Forsyth opened the door and Hoffman walked in. He had been in the Oval Office before and had never been able to describe it to his wife afterward. This time, he thought to look around. But he registered only the rug on the floor, with the presidential seal, and the dozen or so photographs of members of the president's large and exuberant family on the credenza behind his desk. Then the president commanded all of his attention as soon as he got up from his desk to greet them.

"Chuck. Henry," he said cheerily. "Nice to see you." Hoffman was flattered, as always, that the president, who barely knew him, nevertheless knew better than to call him Hank. That kind of thoughtfulness with people helped distinguish a real leader from a Forsyth, Hoffman thought.

The president beckoned them to sit on the sofa in the far corner of the office. He took the armchair that made certain he was a few inches above his interlocutors.

Ever gracious, the president offered to ring for coffee. Politely, they declined.

Then Forsyth began. "Mr. President, you've seen the reports from State and the Agency on Ponomaryov's health."

The president nodded.

"Something new has been tossed into the pot," Forsyth went on. "Hank is on top of it." He turned to Hoffman.

Hoffman cleared his throat. How much time would he have? The president was due to have lunch with the Senate leadership to discuss budget problems. He couldn't spare much time for background information.

"There was a kind of a footnote to the Agency's report, which I picked out of the cable traffic," Hoffman said.

"What was that?" The president seemed interested.

"The Moscow station chief apparently got some information from an American reporter with good sources," Hoffman said.

"The *Tribune* guy?"

"Yeah. This guy wants something in return: a passport for his Russian girlfriend, so he can take her with him when he files the story."

"He doesn't want to file it from Moscow, eh? Why not? What's the story?"

"It's not entirely clear from the cables, sir. It has to do with Ponomaryov's health. I think he's afraid the Soviets will retaliate in some way."

The president nodded again, smiling a little. "So much for *glasnost*."

"Yes, sir," Hoffman continued. "The station chief is recommending that the reporter get what he wants." Hoffman paused and looked at Forsyth. Forsyth was looking at the president. Hoffman plunged on.

"It's my feeling that we should stop this if we can."

"Why?"

"If he gets out and files this story, it could be a major factor in the succession struggle over there."

"To whose benefit?"

"The reformers."

The president nodded. "Tell me why I shouldn't want to help them," he said, a bit tartly. "I believe our policy is to wish them well."

Hoffman gulped. He sensed he was getting onto shaky ground. But how much could the president really care about internal reforms in Russia?

"Basically for this reason, Mr. President. No matter who gets in there, the economy is going to force them to continue with Ponomaryov's policies on arms control, defense spending, Afghanistan. Their foreign profile will stay low. But if the conservatives come in and start knocking heads together, that blows their cover in public opinion, especially in Germany. The people talking about a neutral Germany will look stupid." Hoffman chose not to mention some details that he knew were all too well known to the president, like the polls that showed Ponomaryov and the Soviet reformers more popular in Western Europe than he was.

"Would we be doing anything the Soviets could use against us?"

"No sir," Hoffman said. He refrained from adding an explanation, remembering what Forsyth always said about the president and details.

"What's the risk that Ponomaryov gets better and finds out we've tried to screw his side?" the president asked.

"I would say none, sir," Hoffman answered.

The president rose and turned to Forsyth. "Well, I don't know. My instincts say to be very careful in this. We could have a shit storm. But you can bring it up in more detail with the SIAG. I want to hear what they say."

Forsyth nodded. "The meeting's not on your schedule, sir. Will you be coming?"

"I know," the president replied. He took out a small white card from the breast pocket of his jacket and peered at it for a second. "I've got some folks coming over from the Hill to have lunch and talk about the budget. But I'll squeeze in ten minutes. Bring it up when I get down there."

"Yes sir," Forsyth said.

As he left the Oval Office, Hoffman tried to read Forsyth's reaction, but the general's face remained impassive as they walked back to his office in the West Wing.

"It doesn't look good, I guess," he said after Forsyth had shut the door behind them.

"Not good?" Forsyth looked at him sharply.

"Well, he didn't sound enthused to me," Hoffman said.

Forsyth chuckled. "He's like the girl who says she'll go to Inspiration Point, but only to look at the view. He wants to be persuaded."

Hoffman still wasn't sure. "He did remind us of the stated policy."

"Yeah, and the last thing he asked about was whether he could get caught."

"True," Hoffman said.

"It could go either way," Forsyth continued. "You're going to have to persuade the SIAG. If you do, the Boss'll go along."

Hoffman nodded, and felt a little sweat dripping from his armpits. He wondered if it would show through his shirt.

The SIAG, or Special Inter-Agency Group, formally consisted of the heads of all the government agencies involved with foreign policy and intelligence. But when intelligence matters were on the agenda, the cabinet secretaries rarely came, sending their deputies instead. It was not that they weren't interested. They were, and their deputies briefed them on anything they needed to know about. It was simply that cabinet secretaries were always facing questions on the Hill, testifying in open session. Their deputies rarely had to. It was much better all around if the cabinet member could tell an inquisitive congressman that he had not been involved in a given matter. On a big snafu, like the Iran-contra mess, of course that little cover didn't suffice. But on a lot of lesser snafus, Congress and the press would assume that if the secretary of state wasn't involved, nothing must have happened.

The attendance list Forsyth's secretary handed them for the SIAG lunch showed only deputies, except for the director of central intelligence, Saul Blumenthal.

"I'm going to let you take the point again," Forsyth told Hoffman. "Harwood maybe we'll be able to lean on. But not Blumenthal. He's the lead agency in this, and you know how tough he is. You've got to convince him. I think it's doable, though. Blumenthal hates the Russians, and he's a player. He loves to have the Agency take initiatives. Let's go."

"Okay," Hoffman said.

Forsyth gathered up his folders and led the way out the door, down a staircase, and into the West Wing basement. Hoffman followed. He wished for a moment that Forsyth had not left the argument up to him. Forsyth liked his idea, or so he had said. Why was Forsyth still hedging his bet? Well, maybe after twenty-five years in various government bureaucracies, Forsyth had learned never to leave his ass completely exposed. Hoffman would play it bolder. When the plan worked, he'd get more of the credit, at least when the memoirs of this administration began to come out.

In contrast to the studied Early American atmosphere on the first floor of the West Wing, the room they entered in the basement could have been a meeting room in any Holiday Inn in America. The paneled walls were bare. They had to be because, when the occasion warranted, they slid away to reveal maps. There was a plain brown conference table, set for lunch with eight places. The State Department, Pentagon, and CIA were already there. Hoffman and Forsyth moved through the room quickly, shaking hands. Two stewards in white jackets came in with bowls of clam chowder.

"Why don't we sit down?" Forsyth asked. He took the place at the left corner of the table, near the door, leaving the chair at the head of the table empty.

"You're not in the chair today, Chuck?" Blumenthal asked.

"I will be, but the president said he may drop in briefly," Forsyth explained.

Hoffman sat at Forsyth's right and squeezed a yellow legal pad into the space between him and Hoyt Harwood, the deputy secretary of state. Harwood shifted his chair a few inches to the right. He was an affable, white-haired, and slightly paunchy investment banker from Chicago, recruited by Secretary of State Michael Pratt primarily to handle the department's budget and personnel headaches. Next to him sat his political aide, a foreign service officer named Anthony Simonson.

Across the table on the left sat Tommy Fortunato, the deputy secretary of defense. His second was a navy captain named Bradshaw.

A CIA man who mumbled his name so that Hoffman couldn't catch it sat next to Bradshaw, assisting the Agency's director. Blumenthal sat at the end of the table opposite the empty chair. Forsyth began going over the agenda, starting with a proposal from State to put money for a new consulate in Kiev into next year's budget. There were murmurs of assent amid the clicking of spoons against bowls.

After finishing his soup, Blumenthal waved off the steward carrying sandwiches and lit up a cigar only slightly smaller than a baseball bat. It was a Davidoff, and Blumenthal enjoyed the occasional public speculation about how the DCI happened to smoke Havana's best cigars. He left the impression, in a vague sort of way, that they came directly from Cuba, via an Agency asset. Actually, they were gifts from his friend, the Saudi ambassador to Washington.

Harwood, who hated smoke, glared at Blumenthal as the first cloud of it drifted toward his end of the table.

"You don't mind if I smoke, do you, Hoyt?" Blumenthal asked, gravely solicitous.

"They're your lungs," Harwood said. His thick lips pursed upward, making him look like a fish trying to smile, and he laughed—heh, heh, heh. It sounded uncertain instead of amused. Harwood wished he had the rank or the stature or the ties to the president to tell Blumenthal to stuff the cigar up his ass. He didn't.

The door to the room opened, and the president came in. Silverware clinked against plates and chair legs scraped against the carpet as the diners rose silently.

"Gentlemen," the president said, waving them down into their seats again. "Nice to see you all."

"Glad you could make it, sir," Forsyth said.

The president sat down. "Okay, let's talk about Moscow," he said.

Forsyth turned to Hoffman. "Hank?"

He was on again. He felt as nervous as the day he defended his dissertation. He took a breath and reminded himself to make eye contact with everyone, particularly Saul Blumenthal and the president.

"You've had a chance to read the Agency's report on the Ponomaryov situation," he began. "I think there's an opportunity here that will be lost unless we overrule the Moscow station chief."

Blumenthal blew a smoke ring and stared back at him.

"A big opportunity," Hoffman said.

Blumenthal knocked a bit of ash into his soup bowl and leaned back. "How do you figure that?" he asked. His tone was neutral, but Hoffman knew Blumenthal would not react kindly to criticism of his shop, especially delivered in front of the president.

"Well, let's assume that the information this reporter has given the Agency is correct. Moscow station seems to think it is. It recommends we give the documents to him in return for the tip. Alternatively, it suggests we turn him down. In either case, we blow it."

"Blow what?" Fortunato asked.

"Again, assuming that the information is accurate, what we have is an effort by the Stalinist wing of the party, led by the KGB and the army, to capitalize on Ponomaryov's terminal illness and take the country back from the reformers. What I suggest we do is think about which side we'd like to win."

Blumenthal perked up. "You're suggesting we should favor the Stalinists."

"Exactly." Hoffman could sense Blumenthal's interest. He could feel the CIA chief coming his way.

"Why, for heaven's sake?" Harwood entered the conversation for the first time.

Hoffman glanced quickly at the president. He was sitting back, hands steepled on his chest. Hoffman thought he looked as if he welcomed Harwood's question. His answer would have to be good.

"Two reasons," Hoffman replied. "First, I suggest that we're much better off if the Soviets don't reform. So far, the reforms haven't produced much economic growth. There's been a lot of grumbling. You know—prices are higher, there's no soap in the stores. But in another year or so, the reforms might start to work. The standard of living will start to rise. So will their whole economy. Then, it'll be too late. Even the Stalinists will realize the reforms are working. They won't want to turn back. The reforms will be locked in, and down the road we'll be looking at a much richer, more capable enemy. But if, say, Andrushin comes in now, not only will the reforms be cut off but he'll try to crack down, tighten discipline. People will have two reasons to grumble about the party. And the economy will stay stuck in the same bog.

"Second, propaganda. I don't have to tell you how successful Ponomaryov has been at persuading the Western Europeans that the Russians ain't comin' no more. Andrushin and his friends wouldn't be able to peddle that line. We might even start getting the Hill to pay attention to defense again. I can tell you this. If nothing changes, we're going to be looking at a neutral, reunified Germany inside of two years. NATO will go to hell, and we'll be looking at 1914 all over again. Or 1939."

Harwood shook his head slightly and bit into his sandwich. Blumenthal said nothing. He puffed on his cigar and blew a stream of smoke toward the ceiling.

"Fine," Fortunato said. "How do you propose doing it?"

"Well, neither of the options Moscow station is offering is very helpful," Hoffman replied. "If we give this Burke the passport, he takes his girlfriend out of the country, writes the story, and everyone in

Moscow learns what shape Ponomaryov is in and what's going on. If we don't give him the passport, the odds are that he dumps the girl, leaves the country, and writes the story. We're no better off."

"Get to the point," Harwood said.

Hoffman plunged ahead. "What I suggest is that we make sure there is no story, and that events in Moscow take their course. I suggest we arrange for Burke to get caught trying to smuggle the girl out."

There was a long moment of silence. Hoffman saw the corners of Blumenthal's lips start to curl upward in a smile. Harwood stopped chewing for a moment, his mouth open.

The president broke the silence. "How, Henry?"

"I don't know precisely, but I assume it can be arranged. Maybe the Agency phones in an anonymous tip to the KGB. Maybe they do something else. That's up to them."

"Let me get this straight," Harwood said, putting his sandwich down. "We're going to arrange for an American reporter to get caught trying to smuggle a Soviet citizen out? We're going to deliberately touch off a crisis with the Russians? That's . . ." Harwood paused, searching for the most derogatory adjective he could find.

". . . an interesting idea," Blumenthal broke in, finishing the sentence. He looked at Hoffman. "What do you think the Soviets would do?"

"They'd go ballistic for a few days," Hoffman said. "But they'd get over it. They have no other choice."

Blumenthal nodded.

"What'll they do with the *Tribune* man?" Harwood demanded.

"I'm sure he'll be in the Lubyanka for a while. It won't be a vacation for him. But remember what happened to that guy Daniloff back in '86. He was in for a couple of weeks, but then we got him out, and suddenly his lecture fee was fifteen grand. He wrote a book. He was set for life. He was a hero. We've got a couple of Soviet assets doing time we could swap for Burke. He'll be a hero, too."

Blumenthal put his cigar down on the soup plate and carefully trimmed the ash.

"I agree with you up to a point, Hank. I think you're right about what the Soviets would do and right that the reporter would thank us in the end. But what if he and the *Tribune* go public? Or what if the Russians put the screws on him and he tells them? How do we keep ourselves out of it?"

Hoffman was ready for that question. "I think we can manage that. First, we get him to promise that if he gets caught, he's on his own. He doesn't know us. That's not much insurance. But in this case, I think it'll help. Here's why. Reporters hate even a rumor that any of them work for the Agency. If Burke or his paper want to go public with this, the first thing they'll have to talk about is what he was doing bringing information to the Moscow station in return for the girl's passport. I think they'll decide it's not worth it. But even if they do decide to talk about it, we can handle it. Publicly, of course, we say we don't comment on intelligence matters. Privately, we point out to a few people that the woods are full of gunrunners and other sleazeballs who get caught red-handed and then claim they were working with the CIA. We just suggest Burke falls into that category. If the Soviets make the accusation, we deny it and tell them that. They've got no credibility."

"Well, I think it's outrageous," Harwood sputtered, having finally found the appropriate adjective. "We're in business to protect Americans abroad, not get them in trouble with the Russians. And we don't need a crisis there."

Blumenthal exhaled some cigar smoke and looked at Harwood. Before becoming the president's campaign manager, he had been a trial lawyer. He regarded investment bankers as grossly overpaid accountants, and he enjoyed making Harwood suffer.

"We're in business, Hoyt, to protect and further the interests of the United States," he said coldly. "And we're paid to handle whatever unpleasantness that entails. As for this reporter, he's the one who wants to violate the law. He's getting himself into this."

Blumenthal blew a little more smoke. "I think we have to decide this on one basis, and one basis alone. Would the United States be better off if Andrushin or someone on his side came to power? And I think we would."

Harwood said nothing.

"Tommy?" the president queried the Pentagon.

Fortunato's mouth was full of corned beef. He nodded and pointed in Blumenthal's direction. This was not the Pentagon's problem. And help with the P.R. for the defense budget would, of course, be gratefully accepted.

"Can it be done technically without leaving fingerprints?" the president asked Blumenthal.

"Certainly," Blumenthal said. "I'm not sure we'd use Dr. Hoffman's anonymous phone call, but there are ways."

The president turned to Harwood, the last holdout.

"Hoyt, can we reach a consensus here?"

"Well," Harwood hemmed. "Um, Tony, any thoughts?"

The foreign service officer was sitting with his fingers curled around his lips. He thought for a moment about what to say.

"Well, I would suggest caution here," he said. "There may be angles to this that we haven't thought of. I'd like to run it past our Soviet affairs people."

The suggestion to delay action and allow the bureaucracy to weigh in galvanized Blumenthal. In his oft-expressed opinion, Western civilization would be delivered to hell by bureaucrats fiddling with papers.

"Gentlemen, this train is not going to wait for the State Department's Soviet affairs experts," Blumenthal said, jabbing the cigar toward Simonson and Harwood. "If this reporter doesn't get what he wants from us now, he's very likely to publish his story and worry about his girlfriend later. If we want to move, we have to move now." Blumenthal paused, looking for arguments the way a lion might look at smaller animals gathered around a kill. "I suggest we adopt Dr. Hoffman's suggestion, on the condition that we can satisfy ourselves that there won't be a way to trace it to us."

The president looked again at Harwood. Harwood looked at the ceiling.

"All right," the State Department's man said. "On that condition, we'd go along."

The president sat quietly for a moment, apparently thinking. He turned to Forsyth. "All right. Go ahead. But remember, no tracks."

He turned to the larger group. "Gentlemen, thanks for your input. I'm sorry I've got to run. Enjoy your lunch."

They began to rise. "Don't get up," the president said, and then he was gone.

Hoffman picked up his corned beef sandwich and held it up to his mouth, trying to hide the smile that was threatening to force its way onto his face. It had been so easy!

A short time later, in a black Chrysler heading back to Foggy Bottom, Simonson turned to Harwood. "We're going to pull some long hours cleaning up the mess this is going to make in Moscow."

"I know," Harwood said, shaking his head. "I wish we could have stopped it. But, you know, these kinds of machinations rarely amount to much in the long run. And we're going to be back at the NSC next month on getting the Soviets into the IMF and the World Bank. That will matter in the long run. If we had fought on this, we wouldn't have any green stamps left for that." He looked at Simonson, who appeared to nod.

"The whole idea for the State Department, Tony," said Harwood, settling back against the seat, "is to be smart, to pick our fights carefully, and not to let anyone consistently out-tough us. We can't be seen as wimps."

23

WORK, Burke decided, might make the time pass faster. Washington was eight hours behind Moscow and Victoria couldn't possibly get an answer until early evening. He had to wait. Work might produce something that would keep Graves off his back for another day. Work might keep him from thinking of all the things that could go wrong. Work might reassure anyone watching him that everything was normal. So Burke went to the office and tried to work.

He fumbled at the pile of newspaper articles that Olga had clipped for him the day before, but couldn't summon the concentration required to turn Russian into English. If he was going to get anything done, it would have to be with a person. He should call someone and learn something. But he couldn't face going out into the cold to find a pay phone that worked.

Then the phone rang, and it was Tatiana Kornilova. She sounded odd, as if someone had his hands around her neck and was squeezing.

"Can you come by?" she asked.

"Sure," he said, glad for an excuse to get out of the office and do something. "Are you all right?"

There was a long pause. "Yes," she finally said. "When will you be here?"

Worried, he was there in ten minutes. He did not see anyone following him. But, on this trip, he didn't much care.

Tatiana looked the same, perhaps a shade paler, and so did her apartment, except that she had cleaned her desk. She greeted him somberly.

They sat on the couch. "I have something for you, and I want you to pass it along to the other correspondents," she said, proffering a paper.

Burke nodded. In American cities, reporters competed. In Moscow, the rules were different. Since the 1970s, American reporters had shared news from dissidents. If everyone wrote the same stories about them, the authorities couldn't single out any one correspondent for being too friendly with them. Post-*glasnost*, it was also a way of reducing the time devoted to a segment of Soviet society that seemed, to most of their editors at least, to be increasingly less interesting and relevant.

The paper was a flyer, shredded in places where the glue had fastened it to a wall. The big black print at the top said:

"Comrades! Russians!

"How much longer must we let the stinking Jews have all the soft places in Russia? How much longer must we put up with their whining and treason? When will Russia be for Russians again?"

There were a few more sentences in the same vein, and at the bottom a signature:

"The D.Y. Organization."

"What's 'D.Y.'?" he asked her.

"Death to Yids," Tatiana said.

"Charming," Burke said.

"These were pasted all over the door of the Jewish Cultural Association two nights ago."

Burke began copying the text into his notebook.

"I assume the police got right on the case?"

"As you'd expect. 'The investigation is continuing.' They may have done it themselves," she said, scowling. Tatiana's memories of the Soviet police were long and not particularly warm.

"Do you know anything else about this D.Y. Organization?"

She did not. No one in the Moscow Jewish community had heard of it before, knew how many people were in it, or what their intentions were.

"We know only one thing. They have access to a printing press."

"Do you think it's Pamyat?"

"Maybe. Or some of the same people."

"The pattern is what strikes you, isn't it?" Burke said. "First, Ivanov comes back. Then the Pamyat rally. Now this."

She nodded. "You should know something else. This Ivanov . . . I can't prove it . . . but I've heard that a couple of weeks ago he was called to the KGB office for the district in Siberia where he was living. They told him he could go back to Moscow."

"It fits," Burke said. "So what do you think is going to happen?"

"I don't know," she said. "This flyer—why put it on our door? To recruit us?" She laughed harshly.

"To frighten you, obviously," Burke said.

"That. But something else, I think."

"What?"

"Publicity."

Burke was puzzled.

"What do you mean?"

"They wanted us to find it. They wanted us to tell you about it."

It made sense, except for the underlying motive. "Why?" Burke asked her.

She shook her head. "I don't know."

"It could be a cute cover," he speculated. "Let's assume that the hard-liners are maneuvering to take over and crack down. They've got to be worried about world opinion. But if they seem to be cracking down first against fascists and anti-Semites, then the world is going to be a lot more tolerant. So they let these goons out of their cages. And now this."

"You could be right," she said.

"In which case, you might be helping them by publicizing this."

She nodded gravely. "I don't care. This kind of thing cannot be ignored. It's too dangerous. It smells of a pogrom. The only defense we have is publicity."

Burke nodded, and slipped the flyer into his jacket pocket.

"There's one more thing I wanted to tell you," she said. She seemed to be holding herself together with great difficulty. He could see her lower lip tremble.

"What's that?"

"I'm leaving," she said, and her eyes were moist and glassy. It was the first time he could remember seeing her come close to losing her composure.

"Leaving? For where?"

"I'm going to live with Anton in America."

"I don't know whether to cry or congratulate you," he said.

Then she was crying, and he put an arm around her shoulder and gave her what comfort he could. After a minute, she sniffed, pulled a handkerchief from her pocket, and dried her eyes.

Burke tried to be cheerful. "So are you taking this man of yours with you?"

She looked at him sadly, though she had regained her composure. "There is no man."

Burke did not understand. "But you said—"

She interrupted.

"I said there was a man because I didn't want to emigrate when Anton left."

She looked refreshed, like a sinner unburdening herself of a terrible secret. Burke was intrigued.

"Why not?"

She was silent for a moment, thinking.

"You know, Colin, it seems odd to say this, but I'm a Communist."

Burke smiled. "You're probably the first one I've met in this country."

A real Communist, she told him, had had to be a dissident in the Stalin years, or the Brezhnev years. So she had dissented, and then, with Anton, applied to emigrate. Then came Vikenty Ponomaryov.

"When they gave us permission to emigrate, it was like your American novel—*Catch-22?*"

Burke nodded.

"You wait all your life for the party—for the country, really—to be what you read when you were a girl. Then, when it does, of course, it gives you permission to leave so you can't be part of it. I wanted to stay. But I couldn't say publicly that everything was fine. It wasn't fine. They didn't deserve an endorsement. It just seemed like it might get better and keep getting better. So I made up a story."

"And now?" Burke prompted her.

"Now . . ." She stopped.

"If you had lived in this country all your life," she finally said, "you would have a sense of what I feel. It's maybe the way you know a storm is coming on the steppe even before the wind blows or the sky gets cloudy."

"And you think it's coming?"

She nodded.

"I'm afraid. Ponomaryov is sick. That flyer. Pamyat. The pendulum is swinging back. And this time, I am too old to stay here and fight it."

There were tears in her eyes again. She rubbed them with the back of one hand, angry at herself for showing weakness.

Burke tried to cheer her up. He told her she would like New York, and he described Lincoln Center and Broadway and the half-price ticket vendor in Times Square.

"And you'll be with Anton," he said.

"Yes," she said, smiling a bit. "I'll be with Anton."

"I'll miss you," he said.

She cried again.

He thought of telling her that he might soon be back in the States himself, but he didn't want to get into a conversation like that in her apartment. It was too hard to remember what he had to avoid saying in case someone was recording his words.

So he left, promising to spread the word and join the group that would see her off at the airport in the next week. She, he thought, would surely understand if he didn't show.

Back at the office, Burke found that this one was easy to write:

Anti-Semitism
By COLIN BURKE
Tribune Foreign Service

MOSCOW—New manifestations of Russian anti-Semitism have appeared in Moscow, causing fears of a pogrom like the ones that terrorized Russian Jews early in this century.

One prominent Jewish dissident, Tatiana Kornilova, disclosed this week that she planned to emigrate to America, where a son lives. She said she feared the political climate was growing worse for Soviet Jews.

Kornilova said that a flyer from an organization calling itself "D.Y." was found this week, pasted to the door of the Jewish Cultural Association's headquarters. D.Y., she said, stands for "Death to Yids."

The flyer, addressed to ethnic Russians, alleged that Soviet Jews have a disproportionate share of the better jobs in Soviet society and promised that Russia would soon be for Russians again.

Kornilova said that the Moscow police had promised to investigate the anti-Semitic flyer, but had produced no suspects.

Another cause of concern to Moscow's Jews is the reemergence of Pamyat, the association whose name means "Memory." Pamyat first appeared in the early 1980s as a group ostensibly concerned with preserving churches, icons, and other relics of Russian culture.

But the group faded under official disfavor after its members began displaying open anti-Semitic and fascist tendencies. Its leader, Ivan Ivanov, was banished from Moscow for failure to have the required residence permit.

Ivanov was back in Moscow this week, addressing a Pamyat rally on Moscow's Arbat. About two thousand people heard him repeat the same "Russia for the Russians" theme found in the flyer on the door of the Jewish Cultural Association.

He also called for the removal of Yuri Milstein, a Communist Party official blamed by Pamyat for pushing plans to divert water from Russian rivers to the parched farms of central Asia, flooding some old Russian churches in the process. Milstein is ethnically Jewish, according to one party source.

Police looked on, but did not interfere with the demonstration.

Ethnic conflict has a long history in Russia. In addition to Jews, other minorities, including Ukrainians, Lithuanians, Latvians, Estonians, and other groups, have been suppressed at various times by the Russians, who now constitute a bare majority of the Soviet Union's population.

Official government policy opposes violence or discrimination against the ethnic minorities. Officially, anti-Semitism is an evil of tsarist times that has been eliminated by the Communist Party. But that policy has often been ignored. Stalin, for instance, sought to make Jews a pretext for another wide-scale purge just before he died in 1953.

Burke cut the telex tape and fed it into the transmitter. Then he stuffed a carbon into his pocket and headed to the AP office, on the other side of Kutuzovsky Prospekt. It might be the last story he would ever file from Moscow. He wondered if it really would serve the purposes of the KGB. No matter. It was truthful, as best he could make it. He could think of worse efforts to quit on.

24

IN his dream, some things were clear and others happened so fast that he could not be sure what he had seen. It was an auto race, certainly. He could see, from a great height, the grandstand full of people and the cars coming down the track, their engines roaring like a million machine guns. He was driving one of them. That was also clear. It was a red car, like his boxy little Zhiguli, but it was keeping pace with the low, sharklike racing machines, all grey and black. On the straightaway, in front of the crowd, he suddenly, inexplicably, swerved toward the wall. Was he trying to pass, trying to avoid some other car, trying to immolate himself? Or had someone bumped him? He did not know. He could feel pressure, but no sharp thud.

Then the car was against the wall. With a shriek, the metal tore away from the frame. He could see a tire arching lazily up from the wreckage against a blue sky and hanging in the air for a long instant like a rocket soaring up in a fireworks display. Then, as it fell to earth, the car exploded in a ball of fire.

Shuddering and sweating, Andrei Kuznetsov woke up. He took inventory. He had been dreaming. The beginnings of pale February daylight were showing at the window. It was morning. He was in his underwear, and the bedclothes were mostly on the floor. Motionless, he absorbed these data for a moment. His mouth tasted like old vomit. He shook his head to see if it would hurt. It did.

Where had he ever seen an auto race? There were no automobile manufacturers seeking publicity in the Soviet Union, and therefore no Grand Prix to watch. There had been an American movie about a race driver, *Bobby Deerfield*. He had seen it. It was about the suicidal choices facing the American working class. Maybe the images had stuck in his mind. He knew dreams were supposed to reflect the subconscious mind. He wondered what this dream showed about his subconscious. Perhaps he was suicidal. Perhaps the dream was a premonition, a true glimpse of the future, and someone was planning to bump him against a wall and kill him. He would have liked to talk about it with a psychoanalyst, a Freudian. But in Moscow there were no Freudians, and no one in his right mind would voluntarily go to a psychiatrist anyway. Kuznetsov giggled at his insight.

He turned on the shortwave radio on his bedside table and managed to get the Voice of America newscast. There was no story citing a *Washington Tribune* dispatch from Moscow on Ponomaryov. Nor had there been one the previous day. Obviously, he had failed to persuade Colin Burke that he was telling the truth. And for that, he could hardly blame the American. Now, to do anything to stop Andrushin he would have to act himself. And that meant he was a certain loser. If Andrushin won this power struggle, he would learn of Kuznetsov's betrayal. Even if Andrushin lost, the winners would learn how he had let the KGB chief use him.

Kuznetsov slowly and carefully got out of bed, threw on a dressing gown, and went to the kitchen. There was no bread. He looked at a piece of fatty sausage and his stomach turned. He thought briefly about making tea. It would take a long time and a lot of bother. He settled for a shot of vodka from the half-full bottle in the fridge. Then he got under the shower and stayed there for a long time. The telephone rang. He did not answer it.

When he went outside, his red Zhiguli reminded him of his dream again, and he drove to work like a Grand Prix driver, twisting and turning around the slower cars and the lumbering trucks as the great masses of people on Gorky Street walked by, unappreciative of his skill and daring. He settled at his desk and looked at Miss October with fresh respect for her obvious zest for life.

Within two minutes, the phone rang.

He let it ring. He opened the morning paper. He knew what would be in it; he had, after all, been present at yesterday's editorial meeting. Still, he scanned the grey columns, looking for some little item that might have been placed there late last night. Maybe a paragraph about a meeting in the Central Committee building where the right names were present and the wrong ones mysteriously absent. But, no, there was nothing there but the same stuff he had heard about the day before.

He turned to the big Japanese shortwave radio—it was a JVC, of course—which he kept on a bookshelf. He switched it on and began searching the band for a foreign radio broadcast—VOA, BBC, Deutsche

Welle. It wasn't important which one. He'd take Radio Israel. It was futile, he knew. If the *Washington Tribune* had published his story last night, it would have been on the newscast he'd listened to in bed. Still, maybe the VOA was unaccountably slow today.

But all he could pick up were whistles, static, and Radio Moscow. Were they jamming again? No. He would have heard about that. He must not be tuning properly. It hurt to force his eyes to focus on the radio band, but he squinted at it and carefully, slowly, began turning the tuning knob again.

There was a knock on the door. "Andrei Petrovich!" a voice from the hallway said. "Andrei Petrovich, are you in there?"

Kuznetsov froze. Dear God, they were coming because of the radio! He snapped it off, grabbed it from the shelf, and began looking for a place to hide it. Then he shook his head. What was happening to him? Not since the war had it been illegal to have a radio. He remembered when they were all taken away, so that people wouldn't be tempted to listen to propaganda from the German fascists.

There was another knock. "Andrei Petrovich, are you there?"

Kuznetsov took a deep breath to calm himself. He looked at the radio in his hands, reminded himself of how it got there, and set it back on the bookshelf. He stood up and ran his hands over his hair to smooth it out. Then he opened the door.

A pretty young woman stood in the hallway. He recognized her. She was Dmitriev's assistant from down the hall. Her name was Tatiana. Why had he expected a policeman?

With the door open, Tatiana did not quite know what to say. Kuznetsov could not help her. He simply looked at her. She was a pretty girl, he thought, but her breasts were small. He liked large breasts.

"Andrei Petrovich . . .," she began hesitantly. He forced himself to try to look into her eyes and not at her sweater. Her eyes were brown. "Andrei Petrovich, well, um . . . ."

"Please. Come in," Kuznetsov said. He bowed slightly from the waist and turned ninety degrees, opening the door wide and gesturing for her to come past him.

"No!" she said sharply, and suddenly, very acutely, he could see her shrink away from him and could sense her awkwardness.

"Andrei Petrovich . . . ," she said again. "There's a call for you on Comrade Dmitriev's phone. They, uh, they said they had rung you, but that no one answered." She looked at him intently. He thought he saw suspicion in her eyes.

"Well, um, I'm sorry," Kuznetsov said. He was picking up her case of nerves. "I'm not feeling well." That was getting truer every second. "I must have dozed off."

"Would you like to take it in Comrade Dmitriev's office?" she said, brightening. "They're holding for you."

Kuznetsov did not want to know who "they" were. "That's all right," he said. "Have them call me again, would you please?"

"Yes, of course, Andrei Petrovich," she said, and again he thought she was peering at him suspiciously from underneath eyelashes caked in mascara that Dmitriev had probably bought for her on his trip to London last month. She turned around and walked off down the hall, and he saw that she had a nice rear end even if her breasts were small, and he wondered how he could be paying attention to that at a time like this. He closed the door.

Kuznetsov discovered that his head was clear and his pulse seemed slow. He knew he had only a moment until the phone rang, and that this time he would have to answer it. Just to be sure that he wasn't fantasizing about what was happening, he looked out his window to the courtyard below. As he had expected, he saw a black Volga idling down there.

The phone rang. This time, he picked up the receiver.

"I'm listening," he said.

"Andrei Petrovich." It was the smooth, dull voice of Andrushin's male secretary.

"Yes."

"Are you all right? We were told you were not feeling well."

Kuznetsov could manage only monosyllables. "That's right," he said.

"I hope it's nothing serious."

"No," said Kuznetsov. The silence on the other end suggested that Andrushin's secretary was waiting for some further explanation of Kuznetsov's illness. His mind sluggishly refused to come up with one. "It's not," he finally said. He felt he was croaking. Could the secretary hear what he thought he heard in his own voice?

"Well, good," the secretary said, suggesting nothing. "Could you come over, then, please? A car is waiting for you."

Kuznetsov hung up. "I know," he said to the dead receiver.

Immediately he knew that he could not get into that car. He thought about what he would do instead. He could call the Ministry of Defense and demand to see Kluchevsky immediately. There was, he calculated, about a 50 percent chance that he would get in. But there was a 90 percent certainty that if one of Kluchevsky's drones instead offered him an appointment tomorrow or the next day, Andrushin would intercept him before he could keep it.

Then he knew exactly what he would do instead. As in the dream that had awakened him that morning, he had a sense of being detached from himself, of watching himself from somewhere on high. He was pleasantly surprised by his own calmness, by the clarity of his purpose.

He put on his coat and his *shapka* and carefully covered his throat with a scarf. He checked to make sure his briefcase had some paper in it, then tucked it under his arm. Quietly, he left his office and walked down the long corridor, past the offices of his colleagues, to the elevator. But instead of getting out of the elevator at the ground floor lobby, he pushed the button for the basement, got out, and walked through a dim concrete passage to a staircase that led upward to a back exit, in an alley behind the building. Then he walked around the corner onto Chekhov Street, past the broad steel marquee of the Rossiya movie theater, and into Pushkin Square. Strangely, he felt no pressure to hurry. He knew, or thought he knew, exactly how much time he would have before someone began looking for him. He walked slowly past the rows of snow-covered benches, savoring the snap in the frosty air. As always, there were a few flowers on the plinth of Pushkin's statue. Kuznetsov paused for a moment to look at the poet's curly-haired image. Unbidden, a couple of Pushkin's verses jumped into his mind:

> I want to live
> My way, serve no one but myself and please no other,
> Not bending my mind, my honor or my knee.

It was stupidly romantic, he thought, all the marvelous poems Pushkin had written in his brief life, all the quiet pleasure he had given to their countrymen. He considered removing his hat in a farewell tribute, then dismissed the idea as uncharacteristically mawkish. Besides, the cold was starting to bite. He turned and walked slowly to the metro entrance on Gorky Street.

He took the train headed for Rechnoi Vokzal, but only for a couple of stops, until he reached the Byelorussia station. There, he switched to the circular line that traveled around and around central Moscow, linking the radial lines that stretched from the hub of the Kremlin to the far reaches of the city. At midday, the train was not crowded, and he took a seat. He pulled the sheets of plain white paper from his briefcase and took a pen from his coat pocket. Then, as the train moved smoothly from one station to the next, he propped the briefcase on his pudgy thighs and composed a letter to Vyacheslav Kluchevsky.

He found that he knew exactly what he wanted to say and that the words came easily to him. Sometimes when he wrote quickly his work felt sloppy. But this time each word looked and felt right as it appeared on the paper. He wrote of his meeting with Andrushin and Marshal Petrusevich and what they had told him, of his two meetings with Colin Burke. He described his second meeting with Andrushin and the commission he had been given. He did not bother telling Kluchevsky that he had not written the article. He assumed the minister of defense would figure that out for himself.

The letter complete, he folded it and wrote Kluchevsky's name on the blank side. He gave a little thought to where he should deliver it. He could take it to the Ministry of Defense, but there it would most probably be read by a military aide to Kluchevsky who reported through Petrusevich, and he did not feel he could trust any officer. At party headquarters, it might find the eyes of a more sympathetic functionary and actually make its way to the minister. He looked up and waited patiently until the next station appeared in the windows. It was Taganskaya. He had spent some happy hours at the theater there, he remembered. He waited one more stop, got out at Kursk station, and caught the inbound train to Nogina Square. He got out, and again noticed how serene he felt. He walked the block from Nogina Square to Old Square, where the Central Committee headquarters was, and walked in the front door.

He had entered the Central Committee's lobby of grey, featureless granite dozens of times before, but always as a man with connections, as a journalist who knew the right people. Now he realized how the occasional foolhardy dissident felt entering the sanctum and demanding to pass his petition into the hands of a party elder. Though the entrance hall was larger and grander than most in the Soviet Union, it had one thing in common with the lobby of every government building in the country. On the right was a desk, and behind the desk sat a uniformed *militioner*. His eyes were a flat, pale blue.

"What do you want?" the *militioner* said. His voice was vaguely hostile, disinterested. Kuznetsov was mildly surprised that he was not recognized.

"I have a letter for Comrade Kluchevsky," he said politely. "May I deliver it to his office?"

The *militioner* looked sullenly at the piece of paper in Kuznetsov's extended hand. After a moment of inspection, he took it and turned it over once in his broad hands like a piece of old meat, to make certain there was nothing overtly wrong with it. Then he set it down on the desk.

"No," he said, without looking up at Kuznetsov. "I'll see that it gets there."

Kuznetsov gauged the chances of Kluchevsky's actually reading the note at one in three. He considered identifying himself and trying to persuade the guard to let him carry the letter personally to Kluchevsky's office. He decided not to. He had done his part. If the system did not get the letter to Kluchevsky, then perhaps the system deserved its fate. He was tired of fighting it.

There was nothing more to say or do. He left the lobby and crossed the street again to the metro station, went down the stairs, and got on the first train that entered the station. To his surprise, it reached Pushkin Square in only two stops. Then he remembered.

"You took the long way to the Central Committee," he said to himself, and smiled. He got out of the train.

His car was where he had left it that morning, on Chekhov Street. No one seemed to be watching for him, so he got in and started the engine.

He turned right on Gorky Street, heading out of the city. He concentrated on his driving—slow, but not too slow, steady, stay to the right, don't attract attention. He passed the Byelorussia Station and got onto Leningrad Prospekt.

A *militioner* peered at the passing traffic near Dynamo Stadium. Kuznetsov tried to shrink into his seat. After passing, he watched the *militioner* in his rearview mirror. He saw the man walk off the pavement and into the glass and steel observation post that stood, on a pedestal, in the median strip. Was he calling in, reporting that he had sighted Kuznetsov? Or was he trying to get warm?

The boulevard forked and Kuznetsov took the side that led toward Sheremetyevo Airport. If this were an American film, he thought, he would dash to the airport, buy a ticket, and fly to another country. It was not.

He looked again in the rearview mirror. An orange Zhiguli with three men inside had pulled in behind him. He looked closely at them. Their stolid faces gave no clue to their purpose.

Kuznetsov accelerated. The orange car receded a bit. He led it out the Leningrad Highway, past the River Station, past the yellow dock cranes, to where the Moscow River looped along the northern border of the city. There was an exit for the Soyuz Hotel on the right. Kuznetsov pulled off and stopped his car. The orange car went past, its occupants staring straight ahead.

Sitting behind the wheel, he felt a twinge of disappointment. Being arrested would have taken the decision out of his hands. Now he had to complete his plan.

He got out of the car and walked up onto the high bridge over the frozen river. The wind, freed of any restraints, blew through his coat and chilled him. At the apex of the bridge he stood and looked out over the clean white river perhaps fifty meters below. The snow was pockmarked with the footprints of ice fishermen. He could see a couple of them sitting on crates in the distance. The sky was grey and glinted with the fading afternoon light. It was not the most beautiful view in Russia, but it would have to do. Closing his eyes, holding the image of the ice fishermen in his mind, he propped a pudgy thigh on the top of the guardrail and leaned over it, letting his head lead the rest of his weight to the other side. He felt his *shapka* fly off as he fell and the cold wind in his hair as his body, like the tire in his dream that morning, fell slowly to the ice below.

25

BURKE stepped on the piece of white paper when he opened the door to his apartment. It was plain note paper, but it had heft and texture. He picked it up and read the message, in blue ink that ran with the moisture from his shoes, like tear-stained mascara:

> Colin,
> Please drop by when you get home.
>   Victoria

He walked down the four flights to Victoria's apartment and rang the bell. He heard her footsteps and then the door opened. She was wearing faded jeans and a tee shirt that said FRIENDS OF THE NATIONAL ZOO. Her hair was tied back in bunches, her feet were in wool socks, and her breasts swayed underneath the cotton. It was the first time he had seen her without makeup.

"Come into the kitchen," she invited him, and he followed her in there.

Victoria's kitchen was tiny, but it had a small table with two chairs, next to the refrigerator. "Sit down," she said, and she closed the door behind him.

Burke sat.

"I'm having tea," she said. "Would you like some? Or something stronger?"

"Tea is fine," he said. He normally didn't drink tea after 6:00 p.m., but he had the feeling that this was not the time to start drinking scotch. His body still vaguely hurt from the evening with Filomenov.

He could smell her as she moved around the small room, pouring hot water from a bright yellow kettle into a porcelain teapot. She smelled like freshly washed denim and old, faint perfume. She produced a cup and saucer that matched the teapot and poured him a cup.

"If we're going to talk," she said, "we'll have to go out on the landing. And we need to talk."

"Maybe I'll take something stronger then," he said.

"Help yourself," she replied. "The liquor is in the pantry." Burke followed her out of the kitchen. She stopped by the front door and slipped a coat over her shoulders. He opened the pantry door, found a glass and a bottle of Jack Daniel's, and poured three fingers, neat. They went outside.

The landing was cold and dank. The walls were painted a bright institutional blue. Stairs led up and down. The elevator shaft, enclosed in wire mesh, gaped in the middle. Across the concrete floor there was the door to another apartment. Victoria sat on the bottom step of the up staircase. Burke sat beside her. She sipped her tea. He sipped some whiskey. It burnt slightly as it went down, taking the chill off the landing.

"Nice place you've got here," he said.

She did not respond. After a moment of silence, he said: "You called the meeting, Victoria."

"Yes, I did," she said, and looked into her teacup. "It's hard to start."

He waited for her.

"Look," she said abruptly. "You know you're probably being set up again," she said.

He shook his head. "I've thought about that. I don't think so."

"What makes you think she's not?"

"Well, lots of reasons. What makes you believe anybody? Lots of little signals and things that you're not even aware of."

"Such as?"

He offered a bland example. "Well, the morning I met her, no one knew where I was going. She couldn't have been sent there in advance."

"She could have been turned since then. Didn't you say she needs a *propiska?*"

"I know. But I don't think they did."

"Why? You think you know her that well?"

"Yeah," he said. "I think I know her."

"Okay," Victoria said. "Why not just have someone in the States invite her for a visit? People do get out for visits nowadays."

"Well," he said, "I thought about that. But once they find out she's helped me, she's not going anywhere. And they'll find out."

"If they're smart enough to find that out, why don't you think they're smart enough to know already? They could be following you. They could be following her. If they are, they'll catch you."

"I'll have to try to spot it if they are."

"But why risk so much for her? If they were to catch you, you'd be in trouble a lot worse than that porn raid."

"I know," he said. "But I promised her I'd help her if she helped me. She did." He remembered Filomenov. "It cost her."

Victoria simply nodded and said nothing. "Well," she broke the silence, "I'm sorry I can't talk you out of it."

"You can't," he agreed.

Down below, they heard the elevator door open and the clank of the floor as someone got in. Victoria fell silent again. The motor whirred noisily and the car ascended past them, to perhaps the tenth floor. They heard the elevator door open, another clank from the floor, some voices, and the sound of an apartment door opening and closing. After all the sound had subsided, Victoria turned to him again.

"But I have something that will persuade you." She got up and went back to the apartment. Burke sipped his whiskey, wondering what she had in mind. In a moment she came back, carrying a manila envelope. She dropped it in his lap.

"Open it," she said.

He tore the seal on the envelope and saw a blue American passport, glinting dully in the light. He opened it and saw Marina's picture. "Tatiana Burke," it called her. The passport was supposed to be two years old. Riffling through it, he saw that it already had visa stamps from Heathrow, Charles de Gaulle, and reentry stamps from Dulles. Tucked between the last page and the back cover was a green Soviet multiple-entry-and-exit visa.

"She's my wife?" he asked.

"Yes. She emigrated to the United States in 1979 and married you in 1986."

"Okay," he said. "Anything else I should know?"

She looked squarely at him. "Yes. Don't use it."

"Thanks for being concerned, Victoria, but I've made up my mind."

"All right," she said. "I'll tell you why you shouldn't use it. But I have to have your word you'll never repeat this."

Burke wondered what she could tell him that she hadn't already said. Did they know something about Marina?

"Okay. I won't repeat it."

"The visa's no good."

Burke didn't follow. "What do you mean, no good?"

"I mean she'll get caught if you try to use it."

Burke looked at Marina's exit visa. It looked exactly like the one in his passport.

"Why? It looks good to me."

Victoria sighed. "Did you ever go to a disco or something where you paid a cover charge and they stamped your hand with some ink that showed up under an ultraviolet light?"

"Yeah. What's that got to do with it?"

"Well, in a more sophisticated way, the Soviets put an invisible seal on their visas. You can't see it. But the passport security checkpoint at the airport has a special light. They run the visa under that light, and if the seal doesn't show up, they know it's a phony."

It took a while for what she was telling him to register. "I don't get it. Why are you giving me something that's not going to work?"

Victoria flushed. "It's no good because it was designed to be no good. I don't know exactly why . . ."

"Who wants to set me up?"

She was silent for a moment. "I can't tell you any more, Colin. Please don't ask me. I've said a lot more than I should have."

"My own government is trying to set me up?"

She stared down at the stairs and said nothing.

"Why the hell would they want to do that?"

Victoria did not move.

"Shit," Burke said quietly.

Victoria looked at him again. Her eyes testified either to true pain or to true acting talent. Burke couldn't decide.

"Colin, please believe me that I had no idea they were going to do this until they did it. It wasn't what I wanted."

"Are they trying to create a crisis for some reason?"

"I'm not even sure what their motives are. All I know is if you try to go through passport control at Sheremetyevo with that visa, you're going to get busted."

Burke drained the whiskey.

"Why are you telling me this?" he asked her.

She turned away slightly, so that she saw only the floor between her feet. When she spoke, her voice was flat and low. It was as if the effort of pronouncing the words drained all her strength.

"Two reasons, I guess. Because I want you to file your story. I think it's important. I don't want to see all the good things that have happened in this country go down the tubes."

"But someone in Washington does?"

She shrugged, then continued. "And because I decided I won't be involved in setting you up."

They sat in silence for a minute or so. Finally, Burke rose.

"What are you going to do?" she asked, still sitting.

He started up the stairs, holding the tainted passport. "I don't know," he said. "I guess I'll have to make a new plan, won't I?"

"Colin, you have only one choice. You have to leave her here, leave the country, and file your story."

"Maybe," he said.

"What else can you do?"

"I don't know yet," he said. "But I have to try something."

"Why? Why do you have to?"

"Do you mean filing the story or taking her with me?"

"Both."

He tried to swig from the glass, forgetting it was empty.

"Well, the story . . . I could tell you that it's my duty to my readers to report what I know, and that would be true. I could tell you I care what happens here, too, because I do. But, to be honest with you, it's mostly because I'm mad. They used me. They compromised me. And now they think they're controlling me. It pisses me off."

She nodded. "Fine, I can see that. But the girl—do you love her? Or is it just . . ." She hesitated.

". . . one of the more elaborate mid-life crises of the late twentieth century?" he finished for her.

She smiled faintly and nodded. "Yes."

"Well," said Burke, "she's got a great sense of humor, makes her own clothes, and all the girls like her."

"Be serious, please."

"I am serious," Burke said. "I'd do it for any twenty-two-year-old with a great body."

"I'm tempted to believe you."

"Okay," he said. "I don't know. I think the last time I was certain I was in love was September 15, 1968, on the beach in Santa Cruz, California, with a girl named Rebecca. Since then, life's gotten . . . shall we say, ambiguous?"

Victoria nodded, still bemused. "Yes. Ambiguous I think is a good word for it."

"Anyway, all I can tell you is that being with her makes me feel good. It surprises me a little I can still feel that way. I like it."

He stopped. She was looking intently at him, chin cupped in her hand, elbow propped on her knee. She said nothing.

"And I'm ready to settle for that," he said.

"Well," Victoria said, "I was kind of hoping you'd say you were really in love with her." She smiled at him. "But I guess I'll have to settle, too."

He punched the button for the elevator. She rose and put her hand on his shoulder. "As long as we're being honest," she said, "there's one other thing I should tell you."

"What's that?"

"I wish that things could have been, well, otherwise between us. But I thought I couldn't let anything happen, because of my, uh, job." She pursed her lips in a tight line, embarrassed.

"I know," he said. "Thanks."

She stepped back. "For a man in as much trouble as you are, you're awfully cocky."

"It's just a facade," he said. "If you weren't here, I think I'd curl up in the corner and suck my thumb."

The elevator came, and the door opened. Stepping very quickly, she kissed him on the mouth. The scent of her hair filled his nostrils. Before he could respond, she pulled away.

"Be careful," she said. "They're not going to fool around with you."

"Yeah," he said, stepping into the elevator. "I figured that out."

26

IT was not much of a plan, but it was the best he could think of in the time he had, which consisted primarily of the sleepless hours between midnight and dawn. Maybe simplicity would be an advantage.

As the first dull light struck his bedroom window, Burke got up and went to the kitchen. For breakfast, he made some coffee and sliced some black bread. He had trouble swallowing the bread in his mouth, and the coffee lay in his stomach like battery acid.

He got into the shower and stood under the hot water, thinking about the timing, lulled, until he realized how much there was to do. He got out, toweled off quickly, and got dressed.

Burke took the clanking elevator downstairs, walked out through the courtyard and onto Kutuzovsky Prospekt, turning east, toward the river. He walked past the edge of the foreigners' ghetto, then past the first cluster of pay phones, and up to the second. He dialed Marina's number, hoping that she, rather than her roommate, would answer. She did.

"Marina, it's Colin. Did I wake you?"

"Colin! No. I couldn't sleep very much. I was afraid you wouldn't call." She sounded a little breathless.

"Why?"

"Because you didn't call yesterday."

"I didn't have anything to tell you."

"Forgive me, then, darling," she said. "I should have known you'd call when the time came. It's just hard for me to get used to relying on someone."

"Sure."

"You understand?"

"Yes," he said, wishing he felt more reliable. "Meet me two blocks from your building—where I parked that first night—in fifteen minutes?"

"All right," she said, without hesitating.

"Okay," he told her, and hung up.

He looked around. Everything on the sidewalk seemed ordinary. At the curbside taxi stand, a couple of cabs were idling. A few *babushki* were about, pushing baby carriages or leading toddlers by the hand. If someone was watching, Burke could not detect it. Even so, he decided against driving. Instead of going back to the courtyard for his car, he cut north through a small park and headed quickly over to the metro at the Kiev Station. Trying to act casually, he cast an occasional glance back over his shoulder. No one stopped. No one looked like a tail.

It was still rush hour, the metro station was jammed, and the trains were frequent. The clock at the end of the platform read 0:47 when the train rumbled in and Burke squeezed on. If someone were following, he would have to be quick.

He got out at the Krasnaya Presnya station, looking around as he rode the long escalator to the surface, across the street from the tiny, decrepit old Moscow Zoo. He saw schoolgirls, their hair done up in white ribbons, chattering on their way to school. He saw army officers on their way to work. He saw women, their shoulders bent, carrying shopping bags. He didn't see anyone who reminded him of the men in the sable *shapki* who had followed him three days before. He had three blocks to walk to the corner she had agreed to be on. He looked at his watch. He would be a couple of minutes late.

She was standing where she was supposed to be, staring into the window of a fabric store at bolts of polyester cloth. He tapped her on the shoulder. When she turned around, he was surprised at how haggard she looked. Her eyes were black rimmed and her cheeks were sallow and sunken. With a quick step, she fell into his arms and kissed him. He held her for a second, then gently pushed her away. They could not afford to attract attention.

"Let's walk," he said, and they set off down the sidewalk, side by side, not touching. He kept his gaze straight ahead.

She looked at him with wide eyes. "What is it?"

"Nothing," he said. "But this will have to be brief. I'm leaving for Helsinki today. I think there's a way to take you with me. If you want to try it, you'll have to take the train to Leningrad tonight. Be hitchhiking on the road to Vyborg at four o'clock tomorrow afternoon. I'll pick you up. Wear the warmest clothes you've got. Don't take any luggage. Okay?"

"What are we going to do?" she said, her voice so low she was almost whispering.

"I'll tell you then," he said.

She did not hesitate. "All right," she said. "I'll be there."

"Good," he said. "Now I've got to go." He touched her cheek and tried to smile. He didn't know whether he had carried it off.

She smiled back. "I'll see you tomorrow."

"At four," he reminded her.

"At four," she repeated.

"How long has it been since you've eaten?" he asked.

"A while," she said.

"Eat something."

His concern seemed to please her. "All right," she said, still smiling. "I will."

He started to walk away, then had a second thought.

"Marina," he said.

She stopped. "Yes?"

"There's a chance that something will happen and I won't be there. If I'm not, it'll be because I can't be, not because I don't want to."

The smile vanished and she nodded solemnly. "I understand."

"And you know this could be very risky for you."

She nodded again.

"Okay," he said. "Now 'bye."

" 'Bye," she said. She turned and walked back toward her apartment, head down. He watched her go for a moment, remembered the look of trust in her eyes, and tried to put it out of his mind. Then he headed in the opposite direction, toward the metro.

Back at his apartment, Burke tossed some clothes into an overnight bag, then added a small flashlight. Scrounging in the refrigerator, he found some apples, a couple of cans of Coke, and enough ham for a sandwich. He made the sandwich, then packed the food in a plastic shopping sack, along with a thermos bottle. Maybe his appetite would return, and there was no McDonald's on the road he would be traveling. Looking around the apartment, he considered for a moment taking his photographs and a few other things that made the place slightly more personal than a hotel room. He decided not to. It would have to look precisely like a weekend trip to Finland. If he couldn't come back, he would just have to rely on the next *Tribune* correspondent to make sure his stuff was packed and shipped out to wherever he wound up.

He took the two bags and his skis and poles down to the car. He put the bags in the backseat and the skis and poles in the trunk. They poked through the ski-hole in the backseat and almost to the gearshift.

He drove out of the courtyard, nodding to the *militioner*, and made the correct turns—east on Kutuzovsky to the river, a U-turn under the bridge, and back, west, to his office. He politely stayed out of the center lane. A check in the rearview mirror showed nothing he could spot. But what did he know?

At the office, Olga, surprisingly, was there, and the coffeepot was full.

"Since when do you work Saturdays?" he asked.

She looked embarrassed. "Well," she said, "with Ponomaryov ill, I thought I should come in. And I had a lot of filing to catch up on."

Burke could think of several reasons why she might be in the office, but voluntarily working overtime was not one of them. Maybe she was supposed to let someone in to look for something. Maybe she was just supposed to keep an eye out for him. It didn't matter. What he was going to do would have to be done in plain sight anyway.

Burke checked the telex machine. The play message said his story on anti-Semitism had been buried on page 16. There was no other word from Washington.

He sat down and wrote out a list of things he still needed. He got his camera bag and the portable, laptop computer from the closet. From the locked drawer in his desk he pulled out his passport, his visa, his last customs entry form, and all the petty cash in the office, which came to $220. He checked to make sure that his address book was in his jacket pocket and that he had enough gasoline coupons. When everything on the list had been checked off, save one item, he walked into the translator's room. She was sitting at her desk, scissors in hand, reading *Sovietskaya Rossiya*.

"Olga, I've decided to go up to Helsinki this weekend instead of next month. The car needs a tune-up and I need a couple of days off," he announced. "Would you fill up my thermos with coffee and call Intourist and make a reservation at the Astoriya?"

If his statement surprised her, she did not show it. "All right, Colin," she said. "When will you be back?"

"Tuesday, probably," he lied. "Why don't you take Monday off?"

"Thank you," she said. "But there's something else I'd like?"

"What's that?"

"Could you please buy me some pantyhose and laundry detergent and take it out of my salary? I'll write down the size."

Burke laughed. He knew she was watching him. She probably knew he knew. But nothing could stand in the way of a chance to get some soap powder and stockings. He couldn't even be angry with her. Petty acquisitiveness seemed so beguilingly innocent.

"It'll be a gift," he said. "How many pair do you want?"

"Oh, thank you," she said, her eyes lighting up. "Well, just a few." She scribbled her order and handed it to him. She wanted one taupe pair, one white pair, two neutral pair, and one black pair (with pattern).

"Fine," he said, and slipped the paper into his shirt pocket. He owed her at least a few pair of pantyhose for her pillowing-breasts trick.

There was one thing left to do in the office. He sat down at the computer and batted out the obligatory message that correspondents had to send whenever they wanted to travel outside the Moscow area.

To: Ministry of Foreign Affairs, Press Department
Att: Skorov
From: Burke, Washington Tribune
I will be driving to Helsinki today via Leningrad. Overnight at the Astoriya. Intend to return Tuesday or Wednesday depending on how long it takes to get the car serviced. Will notify you of exact return travel plans. Thanks and regards.

He punched the button and watched the perforated tape spew forth. Then he sent the tape clacking through the machine.

Olga, very solicitous now with her pantyhose in sight, came in with another cup of coffee and read the telex message.

"The Astoriya is all set," she said. "But don't you have to give forty-eight hours' notice when you travel?"

"Those were the old rules. They loosened them up last year," Burke said. "And it's a good thing."

"You bet your ass," she said, proud of her new English phrase.

"Yeah," Burke said. "I bet my ass."

The last item on his list was a compass, and he figured he would get it on Gorky Street, on the way out of town. There was a sporting goods store there with a sign that proclaimed the availability of supplies for the Pioneers, the local version of the Boy Scouts.

Just before lunchtime, the store was still full of mothers shopping for their sons and grandsons. What they were trying to buy, Burke found hard to imagine. There were a few flimsy red backpacks and some soccer balls on the green metal shelves. He saw nothing that looked like a compass.

Burke sighed. Failure to spot a compass on a shelf was going to require at least one additional conversation with one of the salesgirls. He pushed between a couple of hefty women toward the counter. They scowled as he went past. There were two girls behind the counter in brown store smocks. One, a blonde, was desultorily dealing with customers. The other, a brunette, was doing some paperwork and studiously avoiding eye contact with the phalanx of people who crowded around her counter, waiting hopefully for her attention.

"Excuse me," Burke said.

The girl did not look up.

"Uh, miss," he tried again.

She continued to write.

He reached over the counter and took the pen from her fingers.

The brunette's head snapped up and her small eyes widened in outrage. "Hooligan!" she snapped. "Just who do you think you are, comrade?"

"I'm not your comrade, I'm an American," Burke said. "I'm a reporter for the *Washington Tribune*. We're doing a story about the lousy service in Soviet stores and we'd like to feature you in it."

The girl glared at him for a moment, taking in his clothing, considering his accent. "What do you want?" she asked, sullenly.

"A compass."

"I think we're out," she said. She did not sound unhappy about it. "Now give me back my pen."

Burke withheld the pen. "Why don't you look?"

"I don't have time. I have other things to do," the girl scowled.

"How did you say you spelled your name?"

The girl glared at him again, turned on her heel, and disappeared into a back room. A few minutes later she returned with a flimsy cardboard box and slammed it on the counter.

"Careful, you might break it," Burke said mildly. He opened the box and saw a serviceable compass in a black metal case. "How much is it?"

"Three rubles, ten kopecks," the girl said.

Burke handed her the pen. He walked to another counter where another woman in a smock operated a cash register. He paid her three rubles and ten kopecks, got a receipt, and walked back to the first counter, where he exchanged the receipt for the compass.

"Pleasure doing business with you," he smiled. The girl did not respond.

He turned to go. An old woman in a kerchief touched his arm. Burke stopped.

"American," the woman hissed.

"Yes?" he said.

"Before you write that story, there are a couple of stores in my neighborhood you should go to," the woman said. "Department store No. 23 on Panfilovsky Street is just horrible. You have to bribe them to get anything there."

"Okay, I'll remember that," Burke said. "No. 23."

Another woman, standing within hearing range, chimed in. "The dry cleaner on Vavilova Street steals your clothes and laughs at you when you complain," she confided.

"Okay," Burke said. "I'll remember that."

"Good luck," the first old woman said.

"Thanks," Burke said, turning for the exit. "I'll need it."

Past the Byelorussia Station, the street signs disclosed that Gorky Street had become the Leningrad Highway. Burke glanced at his watch. It was a few minutes before noon. He was getting out of Moscow just in time. He pulled into the center lane to get around a slow green truck and accelerated.

A few hundred meters outside the city limit, he passed the first GAI checkpoint. The GAI—Gosudarstvennaya Avtomobilnaya Inspectsiya—controlled traffic, and its men were stationed in steel and glass observation towers placed fifteen or twenty kilometers apart on the side of the road all the way to the border. Burke saw the man on duty inside the checkpoint peering at his Volvo as he approached. As he passed, the man was jotting something down with a pencil. And in the rearview mirror as he went on, he could see the man pick up a phone.

Past Moscow and Sheremetyevo Airport, the six-lane boulevard narrowed to four lanes, and then two. He was in the country. Villages hugged the side of the road like beads on a string, each consisting of a couple of dozen weather-beaten green cottages with gaily carved lintels and white lace curtains. Burke wondered why anyone would prefer to live in a standard, dreary Soviet apartment building rather than out in the countryside. Then he noticed an old woman walking from a well on a path of beaten snow. Across her shoulders was a pole, and hanging from the pole were two oaken buckets full of water. Maybe when indoor plumbing came to the countryside, people would stop trying to move to Moscow and return to the villages.

A couple of miles from the town of Klin, he saw a grizzled man in muddy boots hitchhiking on the side of the road. He needed to establish, for the benefit of anyone watching, that he intended to give people rides on this trip. So he stopped. The man got into the car delicately, trying not to get mud on the carpet. He wore a greasy *shapka*, a black overcoat, and a stubbly growth on his lined chin. He had not bathed, Burke calculated, in at least two weeks.

"Thank you," the man said. He pressed his back into the upholstery and looked around with a pleased smile. "This is my first time in a foreign car. It's Swedish, right?"

"That's right," Burke said.

"Are you Swedish?"

"No. American."

"Oh." The man smiled as broadly as he could. "Tourist?"

"No. Correspondent."

"A correspondent!" The rider was silent for a while.

"I'm Colin Burke."

"Vitaly. Very pleased to meet you."

"What do you do, Vitaly?"

"I work in a furniture factory in Kalinin. I'm a lathe operator. That's where I'm going."

"I'm headed that way," Burke said. "I'll drop you."

"So," Vitaly said, with that business out of the way. "How do you like it here?"

"Well," Burke said, trying to be judicious, "it's very interesting."

"Who lives better—us or you?"

"Hmm. I'm afraid I'd have to say Americans do."

"How can you say that?" Vitaly seemed genuinely shocked. "You have unemployment and we don't."

"Most people aren't unemployed, Vitaly."

"Well, yes, but your workers are exploited."

In the countryside, there were still true believers, their minds untouched by *glasnost* or anything else since Stalin's death.

"Vitaly, how old are you?"

Vitaly confessed to fifty-six years.

"And how long have you been working?"

"Since I got out of the army."

"And you're still hitchhiking. My exploiting capitalist boss gives me this car."

Vitaly said nothing for a moment. Then he resumed the debate. "But don't you think we have more freedom than you do?"

"No."

"Why not?"

"Well, suppose you wanted to move to Moscow. You couldn't unless you could get a permit."

"But if they needed me in Moscow, they'd give me a permit."

"Well, I'd prefer to be able to move whether they thought they needed me or not."

"But that would be . . ." Vitaly searched for the right word. "Anarchy!"

"Maybe so," Burke laughed.

Ahead of them, a sign announced a fork in the road. Leningrad traffic and "foreigners" were directed to the left. Kalinin traffic went right. Burke took the right fork, past a GAI outpost.

Within seconds, blue lights were flashing in his rearview mirror. Burke pulled over and rolled down his window. Vitaly shrunk into his seat.

The GAI man walked up to the car on Burke's side and snapped off a salute. "Good afternoon, sir," he said.

"Good afternoon, officer," Burke replied. "Was I speeding?"

"No. Didn't you read the sign? Foreigners are forbidden on this road."

"Why? Something secret in Kalinin?"

The GAI man flushed. Vitaly cowered. "That's not my affair, or yours," the cop said. "You'll have to turn around and go the other way."

"But I promised Vitaly, here, that I'd drop him in Kalinin."

The GAI man seemed on the verge of an anxiety attack. The cords on his thick neck began to tremble.

"I told you. It's forbidden."

"Well, all right," Burke said. "Vitaly, it's been nice meeting you."

A pale Vitaly was already scrambling out of the car. "I can walk from here," he said loudly, and set off, very quickly, intent on doing just that.

"Sorry to trouble you, officer," Burke said.

"Wait a moment," the cop said. "I'll escort you to the right road." And, blue lights flashing, he did.

In Moscow, off Dzerzhinsky Square, the afternoon watch officer in the quarters of the Second Chief Directorate of the KGB knocked on the door of Maj. Svyatoslav Nachalkov, who was concentrating on a desk that contained both weekly expense reports and a worn copy of *Crime and*

Punishment. "Come in," the major barked. He did not like drawing weekend evening duty, and his temper showed it.

"Sir," the watch officer said, stiffened by Nachalkov's tone. "There are some movements by the *Washington Tribune* correspondent I thought you should be aware of." He proffered the file folder in his hand, but Nachalkov did not take it. Both men knew that the *Washington Tribune* correspondent was the subject of a current special operation.

"This morning, sir, he sent a telex to the Press Department at the Foreign Ministry announcing he was going to Leningrad and Helsinki for maintenance on his car," the watch officer said.

"So?" Nachalkov seemed uninterested.

"Well, he then went to the Pioneer store on Gorky Street and made quite a fuss over buying a compass."

"A compass? For geometry?"

"No, sir. A field compass, for finding direction."

"Hmm. Anything else?"

"A little while ago, we got a report from GAI. The correspondent tried to take the closed road to Kalinin. He said he had promised to drop a hitchhiker there."

"And what happened?"

"He was stopped and taken back to the through road. The hitchhiker was questioned and turned out to be a resident of Kalinin with no connection to the correspondent as far as we know now."

"Where did this hitchhiker work?"

"In a furniture factory."

"Anything else?"

"Well, sir, the file indicates that this correspondent has a habit of picking up hitchhikers."

"I know. I've read the damn file. Anything else that isn't in the file?" The watch officer was cowed. "No, sir."

"All right," Nachalkov decided. "Tell GAI if he's late getting to any of their checkpoints, we're to be notified immediately. Have him watched in Leningrad. Let him see it."

27

THE water from the tap in the Astoriya ran brown the next morning. To brush his teeth, Burke had to buy bottled water from the bulky, glum *dezhurnaya* who sat at a desk in the corridor, dispensed keys, and kept track of everyone's exits and entrances. It would be nice to get to Finland and check into a hotel where the water ran clear and the corridors were empty. He stripped the white bottom sheet from the mattress, tore three holes in it, and stuffed it into an outside pocket of his suitcase before he left.

In the hotel dining room, he was almost alone. In late February, casual tourists stayed away from Leningrad. The breakfast buffet featured fatty sausage. Burke passed and instead took a bowl of kasha, the bland peasant's porridge. The front page of the morning edition of *Pravda* was as dull as the kasha. Vikenty Ponomaryov's name did not appear.

But Andrei Kuznetsov's name did, in a small black box on page 3:

A. P. Kuznetsov, journalist and political commentator for *Izvestiya*, died suddenly on February 23. He was a member of the CPSU since 1958 and was elected an alternate member of the Central Committee at the XXVI Party Congress. In his work and life, he was a faithful supporter of the party and the Motherland. His bright memory will live forever in our hearts.

Burke read and reread the lone paragraph. The signatures underneath the obit were the ones he would expect for a person of Kuznetsov's rank—party propagandists and journalists. What did "died suddenly" mean? *Pravda* obituaries followed two rigid but unwritten formulae in giving the cause of death. People died "after a prolonged illness." Or they died "after a difficult illness." He had never seen one about someone dying "suddenly."

Could Kuznetsov have been arrested and executed? No. Even in Stalin's time the process took a few days. Maybe his heart had failed. That would be understandable, given the way he ate and drank and his present state of anxiety. But then, why no mention of illness? A third possibility occurred to him—suicide. Could Kuznetsov have killed himself?

He had an urge to call Tatiana to ask for her analysis of the obit. But he stifled it. Beyond doubt, either her phone or his phone in the hotel would be bugged. He could not risk alerting anyone to his interest in Kuznetsov right now.

Burke ground his jaws together, thinking. If Kuznetsov had killed himself, why? What was he afraid of? The exposure of their conversation in the *banya*? What else could it be? And if Kuznetsov was that frightened, how frightened should he be?

He had all the right questions, and no way of getting any answers. The image of Andrei Kuznetsov in the steam room, inhaling birch fumes, filled his mind. He could smell, for a moment, the sweet birch aroma. Then he thought he could see Kuznetsov's great, lifeless body, and smell the flesh moldering. Burke felt no particular grief. The man had lied to him, compromised him. Presumably, he was trying, in their second meeting, to right things somehow. In God's eyes that might excuse the first lie. Not in Burke's. The first lie hadn't threatened God's credibility. Burke felt a dribble of sweat rise in his armpit and trickle down his side. Death was something he never permitted himself to contemplate, but he could sense it now. Kuznetsov and he had become partners of sorts. And now Kuznetsov was dead.

Burke pushed the kasha away, unable even to look at it. He rose and walked stiffly out of the dining room, leaving his newspaper at the table. He could give up, leave Marina waiting on the Vyborg road, and drive back to Moscow. Or he could stick to his plan. Flimsy as it was, the plan and Marina still seemed a better alternative than Moscow, where Andrei Kuznetsov lay dead. If only he could banish the smell of moldering flesh from his nostrils.

According to the plan, he had to waste most of the daylight hours, creatively and plausibly. He went to the Intourist desk in the hotel lobby. Another plump woman, who might have been the sister of the *dezhurnaya* on his floor, actually smiled as he approached.

"Good morning, *Gospodin*. May we help you?"

"Yes," Burke said. "Say that again a few times. It sounds pleasant."

The woman frowned. "I don't understand, *Gospodin*."

"Sorry," Burke said. "No reason you should."

The woman nodded dubiously. She could never figure out foreigners.

"I'd like a map of the city, please."

"Of course," she said, and handed him a folding map. "Would you like a car, or a guide?"

"No, thanks."

It was another grey day, cold. The clouds seemed heavy with snow and the air had a tang of salt in it. Burke walked out of the hotel across a snow-covered park to Saint Isaac's Cathedral. Some bureaucrat had chosen the malachite and gilt splendor of its nave to house a science demonstration, a replica of Foucault's pendulum. The pendulum swung from the apex of the domed roof and periodically knocked blocks of wood skittering across the floor, proving to visiting schoolchildren that the earth rotated. Presumably, its location in a church made a point about science superseding religion. Burke wasn't sure exactly.

He went to the car, opened the hood, and very carefully checked the oil. Then he closed the hood and drove to the colonnaded Kazan Cathedral, on Nevsky Prospekt. He had read that it had once contained a state museum devoted to atheism. Pictures of cavemen and bishops lined one side of the erstwhile church, the side devoted to the age of superstition. Quotations from Marx and Lenin on the other side marked the dawn of enlightenment. Now, however, a sign informed him that the museum was closed for renovation. He wondered whether God would be rehabilitated when it reopened.

A black Volga pulled in behind him as he left the cathedral. He could see two men with thick faces and fur *shapki* sitting in its front seat. Burke made a quick right turn. The Volga followed. He turned again, this time illegally. The Volga stayed ten yards behind him.

He drove through the canal district of the city to the Dostoevsky house, a four-story brick building at 5 Kuznyechy Lane, and parked. The Volga eased into a spot two cars behind him and waited, engine idling.

Fyodor Dostoevsky had spent the final years of his life, it turned out, in a perfectly bourgeois apartment with floral wallpaper, a white stove, and a tidy desk where he wrote *The Brothers Karamazov*. His quarters had become the domain of a platoon of iron-haired lovers of literature. One stood guard at the coatrack in the basement, dispensing plastic tags with numbers on them. Others sat on folding chairs, quiet and stern as librarians, in each of the four rooms, lest anyone touch the furniture. Others gave tours, and, yes, that clock on the mantel was stopped at precisely the hour at which Dostoevsky passed away, 9:18 on a Sunday morning. Burke was afraid of breaking something.

He asked one of the iron-haired women if Raskolnikov's house was nearby.

"Not far," she answered.

"Really?"

"Of course, *Gospodin*. It still exists. Near the old Hay Square. Stolyarny Place. Fifth floor."

"Is it a museum?"

"No. A house."

"People live there?"

"Yes."

"In Raskolnikov's garret?"

"Well, of course, it was not his apartment. But in the place described in the book."

"Do people go see it?"

"You would not be the first, *Gospodin*."

He got directions.

He drove to Raskolnikov's building, which was a dirty yellow and had dented garbage cans next to the door. He climbed the stairs, as Dostoevsky must have done, imagining that the tsar's police were closing in. Shadows lengthened and disappeared under the occasional bare light bulbs. At the top of the stairs he saw an unmarked white door. He pressed the buzzer. No one answered.

Burke heard footfalls coming quickly up the stairs and for a moment he felt like Raskolnikov, stuck in this vast, impermeable cell of a country, waiting for the police to find him, certain that the police would find him, just hoping they would get it over with and end the waiting. He looked at his watch. It was 3:45. He turned around and walked back down. On the third floor he almost ran into one of the thick-faced men from the black car. The man stepped to one side, let Burke pass, then followed him out to the street, saying nothing. Darkness was closing in and there was still a promise of snow in the clouds. The black Volga was parked directly behind his Volvo.

He walked past his own car and up to the Volga. The driver was smoking inside. An open pack of Marlboros lay on the dash. Burke tapped on the driver's window. The driver stared straight ahead. Burke tapped again. The driver, after a moment, shrugged and rolled down the window.

"I think you're too late," Burke said.

The driver considered this for a second, frowning and puffing at his cigarette. "Too late?"

"Yeah," Burke said as he turned and walked back to the Volvo. "Raskolnikov seems to have gotten away."

The snow began falling as he crossed the Neva River heading northwest, small flakes that promised a long night's storm. Snowplows, fixed to lumbering orange tank trucks, hit the streets a few moments later. Driving would be no problem unless the snow turned to ice.

When he got onto the Vyborg road, Marina was waiting exactly where he had told her to be, in an allée of bare, spiky linden trees, waving her arm, as Russian hitchhikers do. He stopped. She peered into the car for a second, then got in. With the palm of his hand pressed against her chest, he stopped her from leaning over to kiss him. Her eyes got wider. He pressed a finger to his lips and, with his eyebrows, directed her attention out the back.

She glanced quickly over her shoulder.

The black car had stopped fifty meters behind him. As he pulled back onto the road, it followed.

Marina turned and looked at its headlights through the rear window. She understood immediately.

"Thank you for picking me up," she said.

"You're welcome," he said, feeling rather foolish. "Glad to have company. My name's Colin Burke."

"Marina," she replied.

They rode in silence through the snow for a while, sharing the road only with an occasional plow. As the city faded into countryside, Burke looked back in the mirror. The trailing headlights had disappeared.

"Well," he said. "Looks like they turned around at the city line."

"We can talk?" she asked.

"Quickly," he said. "If they've bugged the car, they're not using the car battery for power. I checked for wires. So any bug has a small battery and they'll need someone close to pick up the transmission. We can talk unless the boys from the next county pick us up."

"What are we going to do?" she asked.

"If they keep following us, I drop you off at the station in Vyborg, you take the train back to Moscow, and we proceed to plan C," Burke said. "But I'm hoping that they don't."

"What was plan A?"

"Don't ask."

"What's plan C?"

"I'll let you know when I figure it out."

"Oh. Well, it's nice to see you, darling."

"You, too."

In fact, it was nice to see her. Her cheeks were flushed from standing in the cold, making the fine bones of her face stand out, and she filled the car with the faint smell of old perfume and freshly washed hair.

"So," he said. "Where you headed?"

"Colin," she answered. "Please. Be serious for once."

"Okay," he said. "Hitchhike much?"

She laughed. "Just when I need a man."

She swiveled around in her seat and watched the lights of Leningrad disappear.

"Sad?" he asked her.

"My mother was from an old Peterbourg family," she said. "I was born there."

"I thought you told me you were from Siberia."

"I am. My father moved us there when I was five."

"Do you remember anything about . . ." He started to say "Leningrad," then remembered that she had used the prerevolutionary French name for St. Petersburg. ". . . Peterbourg?"

"When I was ten my mother took me back for a summer to live with my grandparents. I went to the Kirov twice." She smiled at the memory. "It was instant love."

He felt awkward in the silence.

"You'll see it again," he told her. "Things are changing. Émigrés sometimes come back."

"Perhaps," she said. She did not sound as if she believed it.

Despite the snow, he found he could make a steady forty miles per hour. To their right, in the deepening darkness, they could see the occasional hulks of cottages. To their left lay the Gulf of Finland, perfectly dark. They entered the deserted seaside resort of Zelenogorsk, the route twisting and turning through the town.

As soon as they were out on the darkened highway again, he pulled over, stopped, and yanked the lever under the dash that popped the trunk open.

"Hop out and get in the trunk," he said.

She stiffened. "Why?"

"I'll tell you when you're in there," he said. "Now hurry."

"But they'll search the trunk!"

"I know," he said. "You won't be in it. Now please, hurry."

Casting a last doubtful glance at him, she got out and walked to the back of the car. He walked around from the other side. She fit in the trunk easily, curled into a fetal position. He reached over her and pushed his skis further up through the hole into the passenger compartment. He squeezed her hand.

"Reach up and close the trunk," he said.

There were possible handholds in the trunk lid, where the car's outer skin separated from the metal internal skeleton. She managed to grab one, bending an elbow awkwardly out toward the road, and pulled the lid down.

"Good," he said, lifting it open again. "But you'll have to slam it so it latches. Try again."

She pulled down harder and the latch caught with a dull click.

"Great!" he said. He ran back to the front of the car, got in, and pulled away.

"Colin!" Marina hissed from the rear.

"Yes?"

"What am I doing here?"

"This is how you're going to get through the first border checkpoint."

"But they'll search the car!"

Her voice, coming through the ski hole in the backseat, was muffled and anxious. It was hard to concentrate on the road and still make out what she was saying.

"Not at the first checkpoint."

"How do you know?"

"Because I've been through the border here before. At the first checkpoint, they just look at the driver's documents. They search the car at the second checkpoint, the customshouse."

"They'll find me then!"

"No, they won't. You won't be in the car then."

"Where will I be? Walking? The border zone is closed!"

"No, you'll go around the customshouse. After that, there's about one kilometer of road until the last checkpoint, at the actual border. At the last checkpoint, it's like the first. They just look in the window and check my documents. There's a bend in the road halfway between the customshouse and the border checkpoints. It's out of the line of sight of both. You'll get there, and I'll slow down and open the trunk. You'll hop in and close it again. We'll go through the border gate. That's another document check."

"But how will I get around the customshouse?"

"On skis. I've got a compass for you."

"Oh, great!" she said. "They have dogs!"

"They won't take the dogs out on a night like this unless they think there's someone out there. They won't."

"Don't they have sensors that tell them?"

"Yeah. Wires buried in the ground. They pick up the vibrations when your feet hit. But you'll be on skis. They'll spread your weight out. You won't make any more impact than a cat."

She was silent for a couple of minutes. The snowfall thickened, and Burke felt as if he were driving into the mouth of a white funnel.

"It's too simple," she said.

"Ingeniously simple," he corrected her. He knew it wasn't, but she would have to think so to give it any chance to work.

"If it's so easy, why haven't other people done it?"

"Maybe other people haven't been the skier that you are. Maybe they haven't had someone driving over the border to help them. Maybe they have and *Pravda* didn't think you needed to know about it."

She was silent for another long minute. "I'm afraid, Colin."

"I know you are," he said. "That's natural."

"I'm afraid something will go wrong and I'm afraid of what will happen to us if they catch me."

"That just shows you're intelligent. I can't guarantee you that this will work."

"But you think it will?"

"I think it's got a very good chance," he replied. "But I have to tell you: the risk is a lot higher for you."

They were entering Vyborg, and he slowed down. Once, it had been the easternmost town in Finland; now it was the last Soviet town before the border zone. In the dark, he couldn't tell whether the three- and four-story stone buildings that lined the streets were any prettier for once having been Finnish. The snow seemed to be letting up, and he peered out into the night for road signs.

"We're in Vyborg," he announced. "This is it, kid. The railroad station is just ahead." He slowed down further.

She felt the car slowing down. It made up her mind for her.

"Don't stop," she said firmly. "I want to try."

"Okay," Burke said. "Let's go for it." He winced. He hated clichés.

* * *

On Dzerzhinsky Square, Major Nachalkov, his expense reports complete, was a hundred pages into his rereading of *Crime and Punishment* when the desk officer knocked.

"Come in," he said, a little less harshly than the night before.

"Sir, we have a report from Leningrad on the correspondent," the desk officer said, still wary of catching his superior in a bad mood.

"And?"

"Well, he visited some normal tourist sites today," the deskman said, reading from notes. "Saint Isaac's Cathedral. Kazan Cathedral. And you might find this interesting, sir. He went to the Dostoevsky house. Apparently he's not a completely uncultured man." The desk officer gestured almost imperceptibly to Nachalkov's copy of *Crime and Punishment*.

Nachalkov, who felt vaguely guilty about reading on duty—though heaven knew there were worse abuses committed all the time!—did not like the presumption in the junior man's gesture.

"So?" he growled.

The deskman assumed an appropriately cowed look. "Well, sir, then he did something a little, er, unusual."

"I'll evaluate his actions. You just report them."

"Yes, sir. Well, he went to Stolyarny Place."

Nachalkov felt a chill. He had just been reading a scene set on Stolyarny Place.

"To Raskolnikov's?"

"Yes, sir. That house."

"What did he do there?"

"Well, he went inside. After a minute, one of our guys followed him in. They met on the staircase. And the American told him he was too late, that Raskolnikov was gone."

"Raskolnikov was gone?"

"Yes, sir."

"*Yob tvoyu mat*," he swore. "What the hell was he doing?"

The desk officer's left eye began to twitch. "We don't know, sir. He left Leningrad about four o'clock, heading toward Helsinki. He picked up another hitchhiker."

Nachalkov's stomach began to growl, a sure sign, his wife had told him, of stress. Or maybe the sausage he'd had for dinner didn't agree with him. Or both. Was the correspondent up to something? Could he be trying to send a message? To whom? And could it be a coincidence that he'd been reading *Crime and Punishment?*

"Have the men go back to Stolyarny Place and take a look around—a thorough look. Have them do it tonight," Nachalkov ordered.

"Yes, sir," the deskman said. "And the American? Should we let him go?"

"What are we supposed to do?" Nachalkov grumbled. "Arrest him for visiting a literary shrine? For being a smart-ass and sassing his tail? The American press would love that." It was damned exasperating. Still, he ought to cover himself.

"I'm going to check and see if anyone upstairs wants to arrest him on the pornography charges," Nachalkov told the deskman.

"Yes, sir," the deskman said, and turned to go.

"Just a minute," Nachalkov stopped him. "Make sure this bastard is checked thoroughly at the border."

"Yes, sir," the deskman said.

"Very thoroughly," Nachalkov told him.

28

OUTSIDE of Vyborg, the buildings and lights disappeared and the snow stopped falling. The sky remained low and black. At least there was no moonlight.

Plows had not touched the road ahead of him, and Burke had to slow down and concentrate on driving, steering the car down the center of a white path outlined by banks of piled snow. He welcomed the difficulty. It meant he did not have to dwell on what was ahead.

When he finally saw the lights of the first checkpoint, he glanced at the clock on the dashboard. It said 7:45. He was surprised that so much time had passed. Strangely, he felt something like relief. At least the waiting was over.

"We're coming up to the first checkpoint," he said to the silent presence in the trunk. He was whispering, though he realized there was no reason to. "I'll just have to show them my passport and visa. You'll just stay still. You okay?"

"Yes," she hissed back. Burke doubted that, but he had decided not to burden her with his fears, and if she had made a similar decision, that was all right with him.

A black-and-white-striped turnpike blocked the road ahead. Instead of slowly braking, Burke jabbed at the pedal, and the car fishtailed. Ponderously, it slid toward the deep snow on the shoulder of the road. A vision of tow trucks, flashing lights, and the trunk popping open appeared in his mind. The car seemed to be moving in slow motion, sickeningly sideways, and he felt like a passenger. He had no control.

He forced his right foot into the floor to keep it from jabbing at the brake again and tried to steer with the skid. Underneath, he felt the tires begin to grip something. With agonizing slowness the car stopped skidding, and he touched the brakes, as lightly as he could, to stop it. He was thirty yards from the striped barrier, his rear end almost off the road, his headlights pointed off to the left side, at the border guards' hut.

"Skidded a bit," he said to the trunk. "It's all right." He felt a drop of sweat roll down his cheek. He wiped it off. She said nothing.

Gingerly, he pressed the gas pedal and headed toward the turnpike, straightening the car as he went. A border guard appeared next to the barrier, a white and black baton in his hand. Burke managed to stop the car without running into him. He rolled down the window.

The border guard was dressed in the usual greatcoat, *shapka*, and black felt boots. He stepped up to Burke's window and gestured vaguely toward his forehead in salute as Burke rolled the window down.

"Good evening," the guard said, peering intently at Burke. "Documents." He held out his hand.

Burke fished his passport out of his coat pocket and handed it over. He tried to remember how he had felt and acted the first time he had passed this checkpoint, when he had nothing to hide. Superior, he remembered. Glad he did not live in a country that felt obliged to guard its borders so carefully. A little nervous all the same. He tried to persuade himself that he felt the same way now.

"A little slippery," he said to the guard. "Don't they plow this road?"

The guard looked up from his intent study of Burke's exit visa.

"Soon," he replied, and lowered his eyes to the passport again.

Burke found himself drumming his fingers on the steering wheel, and wondering whether he would have done that the last time. He decided it was a symptom of impatience, not guilt. He kept doing it for a moment. Then, self-conscious, he stopped.

"Turn toward me," the guard said. Burke did. Carefully, the guard compared Burke's face to the picture in the passport.

"All right," the guard said, closing the passport and handing it back. "Customs is six kilometers up this road. It is forbidden to stop or to leave the road. Drive directly there."

Burke nodded.

"And be careful," the guard added solicitously. "No more than twenty-five kilometers an hour."

"Yes, sir," Burke said. "And thank you."

"Not at all," the guard replied. "Have a good trip and a nice time in Helsinki." He looked almost wistful.

"Thank you," Burke said again. He pressed the button on the trip odometer, setting the numbers at zero. The striped turnpike rose into the air, and he headed west.

"See?" he said to the trunk. "Easy."

* * *

No one lived in the border zone, a forbidden strip of land about five miles wide that defined the perimeter of the Soviet Union. Burke saw no houses, no lights. There was only the white road, the shadows of birch trees off to the side, and the cones of light from the car.

He was glad Marina could not see the way civilization seemed to have disappeared, because the blackness only accentuated his own fear. It occurred to him that, for the first time on this trip, he was now in violation of the law. He assumed it was legal to give someone a ride, even in the trunk. By driving her into this black hole, he was violating the law, probably in a dozen ways. He could imagine the cop in Shurik's apartment, fat jowled and pig eyed, slowly reading each of the charges, savoring them, adding up the sentences in his head.

He thought about stopping and going back. The road was wide enough for a three-point turn, and with care, he could brake without skidding. He could tell the border guard that he had left something in a restaurant in Vyborg.

But what could he tell Marina? That he was breaking his promise? That he'd lost his courage? She, after all, was the Soviet citizen. She was risking more than he was. Assuming she was sincere.

But he had to assume that.

His plan saved him from the paralysis of his doubts. The plan demanded that when the odometer hit three kilometers, he stop. And as he struggled with the road and his fears, one eye watched the numbers roll: 2.7, 2.8, 2.9, 3.0. Obedient to the plan's decisiveness, Burke stopped the car. He opened the glove compartment and pulled out a flashlight. He reached into the backseat, unzipped the pocket of his overnight bag, and pulled out the torn sheet. Then he pulled the lever that opened the trunk, pulled his scarf up over his ears, and got out of the car.

The first thing he did was inhale through his nose. He had found that when the temperature dropped below zero (Fahrenheit, not Celsius; he understood Celsius, but he did not think in it), his nostrils got a frosty tingle with one inhalation. But there was no tingle. He judged the temperature to be about ten degrees above zero, which was about as warm as he could expect. He walked around to the back of the car.

She was slowly emerging from the trunk, one leg out and one leg in. He helped her out.

"Show time," he said. She smiled a little.

He waited while she stretched each limb slowly and deliberately.

"We need to hurry," he said. "I don't want to risk a plow or a border guard coming past while you're here."

He pulled out his ski shoes and gave them to her. She sat on the lip of the trunk and put them on.

"They're too big," she complained, handing the first shoe back to him.

Burke tore a small piece off the sheet and tore it into two pieces. He stuffed them into the toes.

"Try it now."

She laced up the shoes and took a few steps, sliding her foot into the ground. "All right," she said.

"Come here," he said, and she stood in front of him.

He gave her the compass and the flashlight. She put them in her coat pocket. Then he slipped the white sheet over her and maneuvered the torn hole over her head. It settled on her shoulders. "Now you'll be harder to see," he said.

She smiled. He kissed her lightly.

"How long does it take you to ski ten kilometers?"

She shrugged. "Half an hour, maybe. It depends on the trail."

"Well, there won't be a trail."

"Maybe forty-five minutes."

"Go slow. Take an hour. The border is to the west. Use the compass. Go north about three kilometers. Go west about three and a half. Then go south. You'll see the customshouse lights. They're one kilometer from the actual border. You have to hit this road almost exactly half a kilometer to the west of the customshouse. There's a bend in the road there; it's not visible either from the customshouse or the border gate. It should be about nine o'clock when I get there. When I do, I'll slow down almost to a stop and pop the trunk open. Wait till you see the trunk light go on. Leave the skis and hop into the trunk and close it. Then we'll cross the border. The last checkpoint is just like the first one."

"Easy," she said, but she looked dubious.

"You can do it," he said. He thought he sounded like a bad high school football coach. Maybe she wouldn't notice.

"Good-bye, Colin," she said, and kissed him again. This time, she put her arms around him and got her tongue into it.

"See you soon," he smiled. "You're going to love Helsinki."

She smiled back. "Yes. I know."

He reached into the trunk and got out the skis and poles. "Put the skis on out there," he said, and pointed north, into the night.

She took the skis and poles without another word and trudged off the road about twenty meters. By the dim light from the trunk and the inside of the car, he could barely see her as she stooped to put them on. She looked ghostly as she straightened up and waved, then skied off out of sight, using the same skating stride he remembered from Peredelkino.

He waved back. Then he took the brush that he used in the mornings to clean snow from the windshield and tried quickly to brush away the footprints that led off the road. He hurled the shoes she had been wearing as far as he could into the blackness to the south. Around the car, he tried to make sure his own footprints covered all of hers. He walked to the front of the car, where the hood latch was, opened it, and smeared some grease from the block on his fingers. If anyone noticed the tracks and challenged him, he would say the engine had sounded funny, and he had stopped briefly to look at it before moving on.

Burke had traveled barely one hundred meters farther before he saw a flashing yellow light and two headlights approaching from the west. He slowed down. The yellow and blue police car, a Zhiguli, passed him, slowed, then made a U-turn, skidding in the snow, and came up close behind him. Its beams hit Burke's rearview mirror and nearly blinded him. He stopped.

A burly border guard got out of the passenger side of the Zhiguli and walked slowly toward the Volvo. In the rearview mirror, Burke thought he wobbled a little. He rolled down the window.

The border guard dispensed with the usual salute. He stuck his hand in the window. "Documents," he demanded.

Burke produced his passport and visa. The guard looked at them briefly and handed them back. "Follow us," he said, and walked back to his car.

"It's him," Burke heard the guard say before he rolled the window up again. He looked at his watch. Stopping to let Marina out had taken no more than five minutes. That was all the slack they had allowed before they sent someone out to look for him.

The border guards pulled past him. At least the high beams were lighting his way instead of reflecting into his eyes. Burke followed, and in a few minutes he saw the lights of the customshouse on the right side of the road. It had a towerlike cupola for a second story, and Burke assumed that there was an observation post in the tower.

The guards' car pulled up an incline to a portico in front of the brick building. Burke pulled in behind them. One of the guards, a thinner one with a mustache and wisps of greasy hair dangling from under his hat, got out of the car and stood next to what looked like a trench running lengthwise in the driveway. It was about two feet wide and ten feet long. He motioned until Burke lined the Volvo up behind the trench, then beckoned him forward, with the tires straddling its length. When the car was over the trench he put a palm in the air, and Burke stopped.

The second guard, the beefy one who had checked his documents, opened Burke's door. "Get out and follow me," he said. Burke thought he heard him hiccup.

The beefy guard had a pimple-scarred face, almost no neck, and a shaven scalp. Burke took the car registration papers out of the glove compartment and followed him into the building.

They were in a customs hall. To the left, he saw a few rows of low steel inspection tables gleaming dully under the dim, cold fluorescent light. No one was manning them. To the right was an open counter marked PASSPORT CONTROL.

"Stand there and fill out one of these forms," the guard ordered. He shoved a stack of customs declaration blanks at Burke, then pushed through a swinging door in the counter and disappeared into a back room.

Burke had filled out the form a dozen times before. He opened his wallet and counted his money, then wrote "$409" in the blank for currency being taken out of the USSR. He fished a bank receipt for $500 out of his wallet so he could show that he came by the money legally. He wrote "none" in the blanks for art objects, firearms, jewelry, and narcotics he proposed to take with him over the border.

He tried again to think of how he normally felt when crossing the border into Finland. He remembered a feeling of pleasant anticipation that had always balanced the grimness of the customs process and he tried to pretend he felt it now. But there was only tension, even when he reminded himself that no matter how they might search him here, they would find nothing.

The door to the back room opened and a tall, broad-shouldered man emerged, followed by the thick, pimply-faced guard. The insignia on the tall man's epaulets said he was a lieutenant.

The lieutenant snapped off a credible salute. "Good evening, *Gospodin* Burke. I am Lieutenant Fursenko. Your passport, please."

Burke wondered for a moment how Fursenko knew his name before reading his passport. Obviously, they were expecting him. He handed over the passport, the customs form, and all the other papers he had assembled. Fursenko looked them over quickly.

"And you're going to Helsinki for . . . ?"

Burke thought of telling Fursenko it was none of his business. But why annoy him?

"To have the car serviced. And to do some shopping."

"Don't they have a Volvo service facility in Moscow?"

"Yes, but I prefer to go to Helsinki."

Fursenko raised an eyebrow. "They don't do a good job in Moscow?"

"As a matter of fact, no. But even if they did, I'd go to Helsinki. I told you I want to do some shopping."

"Ah, yes." Fursenko nodded. Burke hoped he was satisfied.

He wasn't.

"You spent last night in Leningrad?"

"Yes."

"What hotel?"

"The Astoriya."

"It took you a long time to arrive here."

"I wanted to see a little bit of Leningrad."

"You are going to arrive in Helsinki quite late."

Burke didn't want to talk any further about his itinerary. He could think of only one way to try to close the conversation.

"Helsinki stays open late," he told Fursenko. "Ever been there?"

He assumed that Fursenko had never crossed the border he guarded, but that he would have liked to very much.

The lieutenant looked coldly at him. "No," he said.

"Too bad," Burke said, as airily as he could.

Fursenko gathered the papers, tapped them on the counter to straighten them, and handed them back.

"I assume you have no objections if we search your car."

"None," Burke replied.

The lieutenant turned to the guard. "Borya," he said. "You and Volodya take a look at *Gospodin* Burke's car."

Outside, Borya and the mustachioed guard began the search. The thinner man put on coveralls, turned on a flashlight, and climbed down a ladder into the trench. He walked slowly under the car, examining it from the bottom.

Borya headed for the trunk. "Open it," he said to Burke.

Even in the cold night air, Burke caught a whiff of vodka and stale sweat as he stood next to Borya and opened the trunk with the key.

The trunk contained one overnight bag and the spare tire. Burke looked quickly for signs of Marina. There were none, though he thought he could smell her for an instant. Borya took the bag and placed it on the asphalt next to the car.

"That's all?" he demanded.

"That's all," Burke said.

With thick, grimy fingers, Borya pulled the spare tire from the well at the side of the trunk. "We'll have to have a look inside this," he said. He leered at Burke for a moment, showing off a steel front tooth.

"How?" Burke asked.

Borya reached into his pocket and pulled out a long knife. "With this," he said.

"That'll ruin the tire," Burke objected.

Borya shrugged. "You can leave it," he said. "We'll send it to headquarters in Vyborg. They'll find someone to take it off the hub and inspect it. Takes about a week or ten days." Again Burke saw the steel tooth between the pimply flesh.

"But I'll be coming back in only three or four days."

"Too bad." Borya shrugged again.

Burke was tempted to tell him to cut it open. If he was going to lose his spare tire, he was damned if he would give it to Borya to sell in the *na levo* market for car parts. Then he reminded himself not to annoy these people.

"What'll I do for a spare tire?"

"Your tires look good," Borya said, almost reproachfully.

"All right," Burke told him. "Take it. I'll come back for it someday."

Borya nodded solemnly, but his eyes, Burke thought, reflected piggish greed. Maybe they always did. He put the tire under his arm and waddled around to the side of the building with it. Underneath the car, the second guard was hammering against the muffler. Burke hoped they wouldn't take that, too. He looked at his watch. He might have to kill ten minutes to give her time to get to the road.

Skiing was rhythm, and it took a while for Marina to find hers. She had grown accustomed to skiing on broken trails in the daylight. This was fresh snow, broken only by the tracks of small animals that she hoped were not guard dogs. But at least it was fairly firm snow, and after five minutes her body remembered the knack of staying near the top of it and pushing through it, and she started to glide, peering intently through the darkness for the shadows of rocks and small bushes. The cold did not bother her. As her eyes grew more accustomed to the dark she could see she was in an open, gently rolling field, broken by clumps of birch trees.

All she could control was maintaining direction and pace. She thought for a moment of what would happen if she were caught. She felt panic rise from her stomach into her brain, and she fought to push the thought out of her mind, staring straight ahead at her ski tips as they broke through the snow.

Direction and pace. She estimated that it would take fifteen minutes to ski the first three kilometers, twenty for the next three and a half, and, allowing for fatigue, twenty for the final three. That would bring her back to the road with five minutes to spare. She squatted down, her back turned to where she thought the customshouse was. Holding the compass and the flashlight under the white sheet, she checked her direction. She was still headed north. She glided on.

It would have been easier if the skiing had been harder, because now that her body was handling the skiing automatically, her mind was free to wander back to her arrest and interrogation. If they caught her, she decided, she would wait a few hours, then tell the truth. By that time, Colin would be over the border, and the only person she could hurt would be Filomenov. It would be a pleasure to take that bastard down with her.

She tried to think of something more hopeful, and she remembered an American film called *Tootsie*. Her first boyfriend at the institute, Valery, had taken her to see it. One of the characters was an actress, played by Jessica Lange. She was not a famous actress, just a regular in some daytime television show. But she had a big apartment and a beautiful child. Maybe she could find such roles.

Then she thought of all the problems she would have to face: learning English, learning it without an accent, learning the American acting style. It would be impossible. She felt her legs slowing down at the thought. Angrily, she pumped them harder.

Anger would work. She focused her mind on it. She had lots to be angry about: her drunken father, the men who had used her, the system that had forced her to this place. She glided on faster.

Lieutenant Fursenko emerged from the customs hall just as Borya returned and the second guard climbed out of the trench empty-handed.

"Come with me, please," he said to Burke.

Burke and Borya followed him back inside. He walked through the swinging door in the passport control counter and beckoned Burke to follow.

This had not happened the first time Burke passed though, and he felt his heartbeat surge and his right leg involuntarily begin to tremble. Had they found Marina? Was he being arrested?

They were in a staff room with grimy linoleum floors, bare fluorescent lights, and a couple of battered desks. Burke could see an iron staircase, like a ship's ladder, leading through an opening to the second floor. Looking upward, he got a partial look at another uniformed man, wearing earphones and staring at some kind of screen. There did not seem to be any kind of alert on.

Fursenko turned right and stopped in front of an unmarked door. "You will not object to a personal search, I hope," he told Burke.

"Do I have a choice?"

Fursenko did not smile. "You may enter an objection for the record," he said.

"But I still get searched."

"Yes."

Burke glanced at his watch. It said 8:25. "I guess I have time," he said.

Fursenko's lips turned slightly upward. "Good," he said. He turned to Borya. "Corporal. Proceed."

The examining room was about the size of a bathroom, windowless, with bare beige walls and a wooden bench. When the door closed, Borya's fetid odor filled Burke's nostrils. He smelled like an outhouse.

"Take your clothes off," Borya said.

Burke shrugged off his *shapka*, parka, then his sport coat. As he did, he almost froze. Her fake passport was next to his billfold in the coat's inside pocket.

He was standing three feet away from the bulky guard, facing him. There was no way to evade detection. Reaching into the coat pocket, he handed Borya the billfold. The guard took it and began to inspect each of Burke's credit cards. Burke dropped the coat on the bench next to the parka.

Burke took off his shirt. Borya was suspiciously looking at the hologram on his Visa card. Burke took off his pants and felt the coins in his pocket jingle. He fished them out and handed them to Borya.

"It is okay to take these coins across?"

Borya looked at the jumble of kopecks in Burke's hand. Not enough to bother with.

"Okay," he said.

Burke was standing in underwear, shoes, and socks. "The rest of it," Borya said. He laid the wallet on the bench.

"All of it?" Burke asked.

"Yeah." It was hard to tell whether Borya looked bored or interested. His face was a flat, doughy cipher. The combination of alcohol and sour food on his breath was beginning to fill the small room.

Burke sat down, took off his shoes and socks, and stood up. He was wearing only underwear. Borya waited expectantly. Burke shrugged and pulled down the underwear. He stood naked in front of the guard, shivering slightly though it was warm in the little room. His penis felt small and shriveled.

"Turn around, bend over, and spread your cheeks," Borya said.

Jesus. He wanted to check his rectum for secret messages. Burke did as he was told.

He thought he felt Borya's warm breath on his balls as he made his inspection.

The words leaped from his lips, unvetted by the reflective half of his mind.

"Kind of like looking in a mirror, isn't it, Borya?" Burke asked.

It took a few seconds for Borya to figure out the insult. Then Burke heard a rustle. He turned around and Borya was standing up, a thin, lopsided grin on his fleshy face.

"Stay bent over, American. I haven't finished," he ordered.

Borya reached for his pistol and drew it out. It looked like a .45 with a long, thin barrel. Still grinning, he spat on the barrel.

"I said, bend over, motherfucker." Borya seemed exceedingly calm and focused.

Burke decided that of all the options he had, bending over posed the least threat to his health and longevity.

He bent. A second or two later he felt the cold metal of the gun barrel shoved up his rectum.

29

A DULL gleam of light on the horizon ahead and to her left told Marina she was coming close to the customshouse. Her legs hurt. Pushing through unbroken snow proved twice the work of skiing a packed trail like the one at Peredelkino. She stopped behind a clump of birch trees to rest, and she noticed that her legs were trembling. She wondered if it was fatigue or fear that made them do that. Some of both, probably.

Pushing off, her left ski jammed against a tree root hidden in the snow. Her foot twisted off the ski and she fell. The flashlight tucked under her belt hit the ground first, with her hip right on top of it. She felt her knee wrench painfully, and she cried out. She lay on her side with her right arm supporting her and keeping her face off the snow. She found that she was crying.

But there was no one to hear her in the darkness, and no place to go. Grimacing, she got up, bracing on her ski poles, feeling the strain in her arms. Pain from her twisted knee stabbed her. Her hip ached where the flashlight had bruised it. Nothing seemed broken. Still sobbing slightly, she pushed on.

On the second floor of the customshouse, a sergeant named Novikov was sitting at a table, monitoring the surveillance equipment. He wore earphones; they were connected to microphones scattered in the trees around the border zone. In front of him a screen glowed; blips appeared on it when one of the underground sensor wires detected something passing above.

Not very distinctly, Novikov heard a voice cry out in his earphones. He listened carefully for a couple of minutes, but heard nothing else.

"Lieutenant," he called out. "Can you come up here a minute?"

Fursenko's head soon rose through the hole in the floor.

"What is it, Novikov?"

"Heard a voice, sir."

Fursenko climbed the rest of the way up the steel stairs and stood next to the sergeant.

"A voice?"

"Yes, sir."

"What did it say?"

"Nothing, sir. Just a cry—like 'Ouch.' "

"Could it have been an animal?"

"Don't think so, sir."

Fursenko pondered for a moment. Novikov had been on the job for only a few months, but he seemed sober and had never made a false report.

"Get anything on the scope?"

"Not really, sir. A few little things, but nothing bigger than a fox."

Fursenko peered out the window into the gloom. He saw nothing. Was it worth a full-scale search? He would have to call to Vyborg for more men, and he still had the American to worry about. It was not.

"Well, let's get a snowmobile out along the fence," Fursenko said.

"Yes, sir," Novikov said.

"I'll call. Let me know if you hear anything else," Fursenko said. He stepped onto the stairs and began to descend.

"Yes, sir," Novikov said.

Downstairs, Fursenko picked up the phone on his desk and called the guard post, one kilometer down the road. This post guarded the gate that was the last bastion of Soviet authority before Finland. From it, border guards patrolled a fifteen-kilometer stretch of twin, six-meter, electrified wire fences that ran along the boundary. The ground between the two fences was carefully raked in summer and closely watched in winter.

"Get two men in a snowmobile out along the fence," he told the border guard who answered his call. "Novikov thinks he's heard something."

The first thing Burke did after Borya left him was put on his clothes and cover his nakedness. Then he sat for a couple of minutes. Although the room was cool, he was sweating. The physical sensation of violation quickly faded to a small, raw pain. He checked and saw no blood underneath him. An image flitted through his mind of himself with some kind of hand-held cannon, laying waste the building and all the guards in it, then blasting his way over the border. He shook it off. He would have to think realistically. Getting out was the only revenge he could realistically hope for. And realistically, time was getting terribly short. He looked at his watch: 8:52. He tried to will his hand to stop shaking. It did not, quite, but the shakes slowed down to a minor tremble. As he slipped on his jacket, he stifled an impulse to pat the pocket where the phony passport still sat, undetected by Borya's inspection. There might be a camera hidden in the wall, keeping an eye on him. He put on his parka and went outside.

In the staff room, Lieutenant Fursenko had just finished his telephone call to the guard post at the fence. He looked up when Burke emerged from the inspection room. If he knew what Borya had done, his face gave no sign of it.

"*Gospodin* Burke," he said, curtly and formally. "Your papers are in order. You may proceed to the border." He held out Burke's passport in his right hand.

"Thank you, Lieutenant," Burke said, taking the passport. Fursenko escorted him through the door to the customs hall. Borya and the second guard were waiting, sitting on two inspection tables. Borya leered at him, then pursed his lips as if kissing the air. He was enjoying this. It was not every day he got a chance to humiliate an American.

"Escort *Gospodin* Burke to the border," Fursenko told Borya. Then he turned and went back into the staff room, shutting the door behind him.

When Marina heard the whine of the snowmobile engine, she was almost relieved. At least it wasn't dogs. She feared dogs, particularly the kind she imagined the border guards would have, big, ravenous German shepherds like wolves. She could not see the snowmobile, but she could tell it was on her right, and she changed her bearing a little to the left, trying to stay in between the gleam of light from the customshouse and the sound of the engine. Her knee throbbed.

She was only a few meters from the pavement when she first saw the road, and she immediately dropped into a crouch. Staying as low as possible, she took her skis off. She thought of burying them in the snow. Then she decided that if Burke did not pick her up, she might have to try to ski back toward Vyborg. So she clasped the skis in her left hand and the poles in her right and carried them. She could not see her watch and she dared not turn on the flashlight to look at it. The last time she checked it had been 8:48, and she judged that to be somewhere between five and ten minutes ago.

Where was the bend in the road he had spoken of? She could see the customshouse light. She could not see a light from the guardhouse at the fence. So she moved slowly west, staying low, backing off a few meters from the edge of the road. In a minute, she saw that the road curved away from her and the ground sloped downward a bit. The light from the customshouse was no longer visible. She still could not see a light from the guardhouse. This had to be it. Still carrying her skis, she crawled toward the edge of the road. She reached the bank of snow pushed up on the roadside by plows. She sprawled in the snow behind it, shivering and waiting.

Burke cursed himself again. No one had stripped him for a body search the first time he had crossed the border here, but why had he assumed they never would? Worse, why had he assumed they would always let him drive alone to the border? Just because they had done it that way the last time?

He started his car. Ahead of him, Borya and his companion started theirs. The yellow light atop the car began revolving. They were waiting for him to pull out.

Burke tried to make himself think calmly. With the cops on his tail, he could not stop to put Marina back in the trunk. But suppose she jumped out and waved at him? They'd both be arrested. He wouldn't be able to file his story, and that would probably be the least of his problems. He had to hope she would have sense enough to know the yellow lights meant the pickup was off.

Even if she did, so what? He'd probably make it through the border into Finland. But the chances that she could make it back to Vyborg through the border zone undetected were slight. Once they arrested her, it would be only a matter of hours before they knew about him. If he tried to return to Moscow from Finland, he'd be risking arrest.

Burke pulled past the border guards' car and onto the road. The yellow lights followed him. He had to try, somehow, to lose the tail. There was no other way. The only idea that came to him was delay. Still driving slowly, he reached for his scarf, pulled it from around his neck, and stuffed it under the front seat as far back as he could. Then he hit the brakes and carefully stopped his car.

The police car skidded behind him and glided to a halt ten inches from his rear bumper. Burke thought he saw a bottle glint in Borya's hand. It disappeared. Then, the hulking guard once again got out from the passenger's side and lumbered up to Burke's window.

"What's going on?" he demanded.

"I seem to have lost my new scarf," Burke told him. The lie seemed very flimsy, and he wondered if any of the scarf was visible on the floor of the car. He stifled the urge to glance down at the floor and check.

"So?" Borya seemed relieved, somehow. Maybe he was worried that Burke wanted to report his trick with the pistol barrel to Lieutenant Fursenko.

"Well, it's cashmere, and it was a gift from my mother. I've got to go back and look for it." Burke's mother had been dead for six years, but there was nothing about that on his papers.

Borya shook his heavy, thick head, but in resignation, not denial.

"All right," he said. He walked back to the yellow and blue car and got in. In a moment, the yellow lights began to back away. Putting the car in reverse, and peering out the rear window, Burke drove back to the customshouse.

Marina lay prone in the snow, knee throbbing, the cold seeping up into her bones. Her toes were numb, and her fingers were getting stiff. She was too tired and frightened to cry. A thought forced its way into her consciousness. Sometime, playing a role that demanded that she project true despair, she would remember her feeling at this moment and use it. She laughed at herself, so far from any stage, at the sheer bravado of her thoughts, and felt a little better.

When she saw the headlights piercing the night sky and moving toward her, she almost leapt up. If her knee were not aching, she might have. But getting up required a conscious effort not to put weight on the bad leg, and by the time she had figured out how to do that, she saw the yellow lights flashing and realized something was wrong.

She could not quite see the two cars from where she lay, fifty meters ahead, at the bend in the road. But she could hear the engines and even thought she could smell their oily exhaust in the freezing air. She heard a couple of voices, and thought one of them was Colin's, but she could not quite make out what they were saying. Then she saw the headlights and the blinking yellow lights recede, back toward the customshouse.

She could not understand why Colin would go back, or why the police were following him, but it was plain that his plan had fallen apart. She thought about interrogation and prison. She thought about the fence and the snowmobile to her right and the distance she would have to ski back to Vyborg to her left. It would be so much easier just to turn herself in.

* * *

Burke walked into the staff room, followed by Borya and the second guard. Lieutenant Fursenko was sitting at his desk, doing some paperwork. "Lost my scarf. It's got to be around here someplace," Burke told him with as much rueful sincerity as he could manage. "I know I had it on today."

Fursenko scowled, nodded abruptly, and went back to his paperwork.

"Most likely it's in here," Burke said, and he walked into the small room where Borya conducted his inspections. Borya followed, a few paces behind, swaggering a little. He could not understand why this American would delay his arrival in Finland for the sake of a scarf, but he relished the chance to toy with him.

"So," the guard said, too softly for Fursenko to hear. "You want some more, asshole?"

Burke did not look at him. He tried to keep his voice level.

"Just my scarf."

It was hard to pretend to be making a thorough search. The little room had only a bench for furniture. Burke did the best he could, turning the bench upside down and peering carefully into all the corners.

"Damn," he said, coming out of the room. "Not there." Borya looked at him with an expression of deepening irritation.

Guard No. 2 was leaning against the wall on the far side of the room, next to a table that contained a battered steel samovar, some glass tea mugs, a sugar bowl, and a small pile of paper napkins.

Burke decided to test the power of suggestion. He walked across the room to the samovar.

"Mind if I have a bit of tea?" he asked No. 2. "It's been a cold drive."

No. 2 looked tentatively at Fursenko. Fursenko nodded.

No. 2 handed Burke a glass frosted with old dust. Burke took a napkin, wiped out the insides, and turned the tap on the samovar. Dark, steaming tea filled the glass and burned his fingers.

He sipped and smiled at No. 2. "Good! Thanks!" He put the glass down.

No. 2 looked at the glass and the samovar, then reached for a second glass and poured himself one. Tea in hand, he sat down behind the second desk and unbuttoned his coat.

One down, Burke thought. One to go. He turned toward Borya, hoping he, too, would have some tea. But the massive guard only stood there, frowning, waiting for Burke to start looking for his scarf again.

Come on, Borya, Burke thought. Have some tea. Relax. Take your shoes off. But Borya, apparently, was not a tea drinker.

Burke walked out of the staff room into the customs hall and began looking around the inspection tables. Borya stood in the doorway, still watching.

"I don't think it's here," the guard said impatiently.

Prolonging the search might only make them more suspicious, Burke decided. So he agreed.

"I guess you're right," he told Borya abruptly. He walked toward the door without saying good-bye.

He went out into the cold, climbed into the car, and tried to get started as fast as he could. He looked in the rearview mirror, hoping to see no one. But Borya, alone this time, came out of the building. By the time Burke had pulled out of the customshouse driveway, the yellow lights were blinking and Borya was on his tail again. He saw the bottle glint once more.

Inside his mind, only one of the many images whirling around stopped and clarified itself: a sullen, bearded man with hooded eyes named Wilmer Oates. Years ago, he had covered Oates's trial for killing a California highway patrolman with a tire iron. He could still see the man on the stand, shrugging as his lawyer tried vainly to get him to testify that his crime was not premeditated.

"Simple," Oates had shrugged. "It was bust him or get busted."

That was where he was. He stopped the car at the bend in the road and opened the trunk.

This time Borya, with the exaggerated caution of the experienced drunk driver, stopped ten feet behind him.

Burke got out and headed straight for the trunk. As he did, he peered over the roof of the car. He saw her, spread-eagled behind the snowbank, starting to get up. Carefully, he looked away.

The trunk light was on, bathing the contents in light. Before Borya could get out of his car, Burke leaned into the trunk and rummaged around. He found the jack handle and palmed it. The bar fit snugly against the blue sleeve of his parka, running up his forearm to the elbow.

The fumes from Borya's breath reached Burke before the heavy hand on his shoulder spun him around.

"What is it this time, asshole?" Borya's *s*'s were slurred. His pockmarked face was flushed, his eyes bloodshot, and his jaw was a little slack. The vapor poured out of his open mouth and seemed to hang in front of his head for a moment in the cold night air before it dissipated.

Burke held his right arm stiff at his side, trying to keep the jack handle out of sight.

"Something's loose and rattling. Sounded like it might be in the trunk," he said.

"Shit," Borya grumbled. He leaned over and looked in the trunk, turning his back.

Burke focused on the grey fur at the back of Borya's *shapka*. This was the moment and that was the target. If he wanted to knock him out, but not kill him, how hard should he hit him? He had no idea. He hesitated.

His moment passed.

Borya straightened up. "Fucking nothing in there," he growled, turning back to Burke.

Burke's arm was extended, at an awkward, forty-five-degree angle from his body. The jack handle was clenched in his fist, now clearly visible.

Borya seemed to stare at it for a moment, not comprehending. Burke could see first understanding, and an instant later rage, fill those eyes. Then Borya stepped back and reached for his gun.

The loud sob from the side of the road startled them both. Both turned. Burke could see Marina, her face taut and red, the tears streaming from her eyes, trying clumsily to get up.

Borya reacted. He stepped toward Marina, pulling the gun out of its holster.

Burke's right arm seemed to move of its own volition. He saw the black tire iron describe a short arc that intersected with the crown of Borya's skull. He sensed solid contact, like hitting a fastball with the sweet, heavy part of a bat. And he saw the guard collapse in stages, starting with the knees, and crumple until he lay huge and still in the snow at the side of the road.

The trembling was back in Burke's arms and in his legs. His breath was coming in short gasps. He wanted to hit the prone figure in front of him again, and again, until he had driven that skull into the pavement like a stake into the ground.

She stopped him.

"Colin, no! Don't kill him!"

He stopped, the jack handle suspended in midair. She hobbled up to the hulk on the road and knelt beside it. Burke saw the hulk stir.

"He's breathing," she hissed. "Let's leave him that way."

Burke nodded. He helped her into the trunk and shut the lid. Then he drove on, trying not to hurry, wanting to hurry, watching the yellow light from the police car until it disappeared from his mirror, obscured by the last curve in the road before the border fence.

The gate was open, with only the white-and-black turnpike blocking the way. Floodlights lit up the gate area. Burke could see a red Soviet flag hanging limply on his side of the fence, and, a few meters further down the road, a white and blue Finnish flag. Burke looked for the guard, fearful that he would have his gun pulled.

He didn't. Looking bored, the guard strolled up to Burke's window. He saluted. Burke held the steering wheel as tightly as he could, trying to stop the palsy in his hands.

"Documents?"

Burke handed him his passport. The guard looked casually at the page with the visa stamp.

"Okay," he said, and handed the passport back. He turned and walked toward his hut, at the left gatepost. Burke waited for the sound of an alarm, or a siren, or a telephone ringing. There was only the quiet grumble of the Volvo's engine. The turnpike rose slowly, and he drove through the gate, almost afraid to breathe.

At the Finnish customshouse, a kilometer down the road, four guards were in a back room playing cards.

"Hello?" Burke called. Marina clung to his side, gently flexing her knee.

Smiling sheepishly, a towheaded kid wearing a ski sweater over his pastel blue uniform trousers emerged. He took their passports.

"Hi," he said in English. "Welcome to Finland." He stamped visas in both.

"You have insurance for the car?" he asked Burke.

"Yeah," Burke said.

"Okay. Have a nice stay." He stamped the passports with a tool that went *kerchunk* and handed them back.

They walked back out into the little parking lot.

"That's all we have to do?" Marina whispered.

"That's all."

He opened the door on the right side of the car and she got in. She slid across the front seat and clung to his arm when he got in. He kissed her and tears ran down her cheeks.

30

AFTER a while Marina fell asleep, nestled against his arm, and he drove through the dark Finnish night to Helsinki. He wished it were light, so she could see what he had seen the first time he had driven on this road: the tidy, red-painted little family farmhouses, the Saabs and Volvos parked next to them, the civilization of the other side of the divide.

The best hotel he knew of in Helsinki was the Kalistajatorppa, on a Baltic bay at the edge of the city. The name meant "fisherman's hut." The night clerk let them in and he was glad there was a room available.

When they got to the room she kissed him, without tears, and he wanted to stay with her. But Helsinki was seven hours ahead of Washington and there was still time to file his story. "I've got to go do some work, darling," he told her. She objected drowsily, then kissed him again and let him go.

The night clerk let him sit up with his laptop at a table in the darkened bar. He worked by the glow of light from the lobby and from the small screen in front of him. It didn't matter. He had no notes to read, and the dimness allowed him to remember with utter clarity what he had learned over the last three days. He thought of phoning the office first, but he decided to write the article first. He did not trust himself to tell Graves what he knew over the phone. There was too much that he didn't want him to know.

Ponomaryov
By COLIN BURKE
Tribune Foreign Service

MOSCOW—

He stopped. He was not in Moscow. The dateline was supposed to be the point from which he filed the story. Reporters frequently fudged.

If they had been in a city while they worked on a story, they went ahead and used it as a dateline even if they filed from somewhere else. But Burke did not want to fudge anything on this piece. The desk might change it back to Moscow, but he wouldn't. He started again.

Ponomaryov
By COLIN BURKE
Tribune Foreign Service

HELSINKI—General Secretary Vikenty Ponomaryov, leader of the Soviet Union, has fallen into a coma after suffering a stroke and is no longer capable of running the country, the Tribune has learned from Soviet sources.

KGB chairman Igor Andrushin is taking advantage of Ponomaryov's incapacity by maneuvering against the general secretary's Politburo allies, one source said. Andrushin hopes to take power for himself and reverse Ponomaryov's reform policies, the source charged.

Burke stopped and reread the second paragraph. It was too strong. He had only one source for it, and that source was dead. His troubles had all started because he neglected to get a second source for the first Ponomaryov story. Tapping on the key marked DEL he excised it.

HELSINKI—General Secretary Vikenty Ponomaryov, leader of the Soviet Union, has fallen into a coma after suffering a stroke and is no longer capable of running the country, the Tribune has learned from Soviet sources who wished to remain anonymous.

Ponomaryov's prognosis could not be determined. While he has been ill, however, his political position has deteriorated, with the removal of his ally, Pavel Morozov, from the Politburo.

That fit the facts. The *Tribune*'s readers would have to draw their own conclusions about who was behind Morozov's ouster. But maybe he could help them.

The general secretary's illness comes at a critical juncture for his reform program. While he is pushing Soviet society toward a more Western, democratic form of government, new manifestations of Stalinism have appeared in Moscow. One Western diplomat suggested that the military and the KGB may be unhappy with the depth of Ponomaryov's reforms and are maneuvering against him while he is incapacitated.

That much was true. Victoria could reasonably be called a "Western diplomat."

He realized that he would have to say more about his sources to support his story. He was willing. Kuznetsov was beyond his protection. Filomenov hadn't asked for it. Besides, Filomenov had already taken payment for his information. Burke owed him nothing. So he wrote two sentences he would normally never have written.

> The information about Ponomaryov's coma comes from a journalist
> and ranking Communist Party member who earlier had disclosed the
> general secretary's stroke, but said he was recovering. It was confirmed
> by a source close to the general secretary's immediate family.

That was as close as he wanted to come to admitting that the first story on Ponomaryov's health was partly wrong, and explaining how it had happened. It was as close as he needed to come.

The rest was boilerplate: the time since Ponomaryov's last public appearance, a recapitulation of the story about the "flu" in *Pravda*, mention of the fact that Ponomaryov's next scheduled appearance would be March 8, at the Bolshoi Theater ceremony marking International Women's Day. He would have to make sure Marina got flowers that day.

The story was tight, but that was all right. It was getting late to put a long story into the paper. He walked back to the night clerk's station. The clerk was studying a medical textbook by the intense light of a single lamp.

"Mind if I use your phone to call the U.S.?" Burke asked. "It's a credit card call."

The clerk closed the book and looked doubtful.

"My friend's asleep upstairs and I don't want to wake her," he added.

"For sure," the clerk said, smiling. He opened the door to the manager's office and gave Burke the desk.

Burke plugged the computer into the telephone and dialed the *Tribune*'s computer. He heard the high-pitched whine the machine emitted, entered the "send" commands, and waited.

Nothing happened.

"Sonofabitch!" he muttered.

He tried again. Dial. Whine. Send. Nothing.

"Goddamn it to hell!"

He looked carefully at the machine. The little switch on the side was set at ACL for sending with acoustic couplers instead of DIR for direct transmission. He flipped it.

WASHTRIB225900056, the machine said.

Burke waited.

SEND MSG.

Burke entered the "send" command.

MSG UPLOADING, the machine replied, satisfied at last.

And that was it. The rest would be up to the *Tribune*. And to the Soviets. He felt a calm. Maybe it was just exhaustion.

He needed to call Graves, but he wanted to give him time to read the piece before he did. He walked through the lobby to the lounge, slipped under the bar, and found a bottle of Jack Daniel's. The clerk walked in on him.

"Sir, that's illegal."

"I know. We won't tell anyone. Put it on my bill," Burke said, and brushed past before the clerk could stop him.

Coatless, he walked outside into the cold, along a path through the woods by the sea. He took a swallow of whiskey and silently toasted himself. In the summertime, he'd be aware that the woods were full of houses, but in the darkness of February his solitude seemed complete. He walked down the path until he started to shiver, then came back again.

The clerk was waiting for him. "There has been a call for you from Washington," he said, sounding impressed. "A Mr. Graves. Please call him as soon as you may."

"As soon as you can," Burke corrected him. Then he sat down and dialed Washington.

"Graves," the foreign editor said.

"Ken, Colin Burke. You get my piece?"

"Yes. Just read it." Graves's tone said he was reserving judgment.

"Good," Burke said, waiting for Graves to start picking at it.

"Not only that," Graves went on. "I got a couple of strange calls asking about you. One from the public affairs director at the CIA. One from a guy named Hoffman at the NSC."

Burke tried to sound casual. "What'd they want?"

"Just to know where you were. Hoffman wanted to know if you'd filed a story and what it said."

"And?"

"And I told him where the nearest vending box was. He can read it with everyone else."

"Good for you," Burke said.

"I was wondering why they'd suddenly want to know all this," Graves said. "Then I got your piece. They must've known what you were working on somehow."

"Quite possible," Burke said. "I ran it past someone at the embassy for reaction."

Two thoughts coupled in his mind and, for a second, he wanted to tell Graves about the setup with the phony visa. This Hoffman must have known about it. But he held back. Getting into that subject would require him to tell Graves too many things he couldn't afford to let Graves know—about Marina, Victoria, and deals that correspondents weren't supposed to make.

Burke did not know Hoffman, but he immediately respected the man's mind. He had designed a game in which he could not lose. The only people who might hurt Hoffman were Victoria and Burke himself. Victoria couldn't tell without risking her career. Neither could he. Maybe, someday down the road, there would be a time when Hoffman would be vulnerable on something else, and Burke would be the reporter to nail him. But for now, at least, Hoffman and his friends could sit in the White House, read the morning paper, and cluck, "Oh, well. Better luck next time."

"That explains Hoffman, then," Graves said. "But why the Agency? Did you talk to the spooks?"

"Who knows?" Burke replied. "They don't wear numbers and they don't sell programs."

"I guess," Graves said.

"And they didn't say anything else?"

"No," Graves said. "Hoffman didn't sound too happy, though."

"I bet," Burke said.

"Story's got some problems," Graves went on.

"How can I help?" Burke tried to sound more confident than he felt.

"First of all, why the Helsinki dateline?"

" 'Cause I'm in Helsinki."

"I know that, Colin," said Graves, sounding exasperated. "Why?"

"I was warned by the Foreign Ministry not to write again about Ponomaryov's health. So I thought it would be better to file here and see what happens before I go back." He hoped he didn't sound too paranoid.

"Well, we'll change it to Moscow."

Burke didn't argue.

"The second thing. First we said he was recovering. Now we say he's in a coma. If I'm to go up front and tell 'em to get this on the front page of tomorrow's paper, I have to know who your sources are and why they're more reliable this time."

"Okay," Burke said. "In the first place, I tried, but couldn't find out how long he's been in a coma. That's why the piece is vague on the time element. So I'm not certain that he wasn't recovering at first and then went into the coma." It was not exactly a lie, but it wasn't the whole truth, either.

Graves bought it. "Okay. I need to know the sources." Burke had never disclosed his sources to an editor before. No one had ever asked. He had an obligation to tell the *Tribune* if he wanted it to publish the story. Normally, though, he would never have mentioned the names over the telephone. Too many people listened in to international calls. But there was no time to send a letter.

Burke took a breath. "Andrei Kuznetsov was the first. Once an alternate member of the Central Committee. *Izvestiya* columnist. TV commentator. Very well connected." Corpse, but Burke didn't say so. He doubted Kuznetsov's death had made the wire services. Graves wouldn't know about it and there was no need to tell him.

"And the family member?"

"Source close to the family," Burke corrected him.

"Right. Who was it?"

"Vladimir Filomenov. He's an actor. Sleeps with Ponomaryov's daughter."

Graves laughed. Editors loved to hear stories about the illicit trysts of the rich and famous. They could rarely print them, but they made great dinner party conversation.

"How'd you find out about him?"

"Through a theater person I know."

Graves sounded only slightly reassured.

"Can we go into any more detail about this maneuvering against Ponomaryov?"

"Not and be absolutely confident about it," Burke said. "Kuznetsov spoke with Andrushin, and he has . . . Well, he told me a lot of theories about what Andrushin is up to and how he plans to do it. But I can't confirm it."

"Damn," Graves said. "I wish we could get that stuff. Can't you talk to someone in the Supreme Soviet?"

"I have," Burke said. "They're more in the dark than we are."

Graves was reproachfully silent, no doubt thinking that Jennifer Whatshername would have been on top of the story.

"A lot of their politics is open now," Burke said. "But the Politburo is still as closed as it ever was. It's like watching a fight from outside a saloon. You know something's going on because the walls shake and some blood seeps under the door. Every now and then a body comes flying out. But you can't tell who's punching whom inside."

If Graves appreciated Burke's disquisition on Kremlinology, he refrained from expressing it.

"Okay," he said. "I'll see if I can get it in the paper."

Then, to show he was a good guy: "Get a little rest, why don't you? We'll see how much shit hits the fan and talk in a couple of days."

"Thanks, Ken." Burke hung up. He thanked the desk clerk, apologized for expropriating his whiskey, and went upstairs. Marina was asleep, and he did not wake her. He lay on the bed in the dark for an hour before exhaustion finally overcame him.

In the morning, when they awoke, it was still dark. She needed everything, starting with clothes. So he drove her into the center of the city, down the boulevard called Mannerheimintie. He pointed out the places he knew—the concert hall, the Olympic Stadium, the Hesperia Hotel, the national theater. She glanced quickly at them, but she was watching the people they passed, so many blond heads and blue eyes, hurrying through the morning gloam to work.

"Is this the way people dress in America?" she asked.

"Well, they don't bundle up the same way, because it's warmer," he told her. "And Finnish women have a peculiar tendency to wear white socks and black shoes. But apart from that, yes."

She nodded.

They came to Stockmann's, and he parked at a taxi stand.

"This is a department store, like GUM, except . . . Well, you'll see," he said. He took her past the candy and magazine and perfume departments to the elevators, and up to the seventh floor. She stared openly at what she saw.

Stockmann's had a special office for foreign customers, especially the diplomats, journalists, and businessmen who lived in Moscow and came to Helsinki to shop. Burke introduced himself and "my friend, Miss Makeyeva, who needs some things." If the clerk was surprised, she did not show it. He gave the woman his American Express card, and in a few minutes Marina had a piece of paper authorizing her to charge whatever she liked and have it sent to the Kalistajatorppa.

Burke felt like an Arab prince.

"This is a dream, Colin," she said. "But how will I tell them what I want?"

"The clerks here speak almost everything. They have little flags on their name tags to tell you their languages, so you look for a red flag." He laughed. "If that doesn't work, show 'em the note and point."

He gave her some cash. "When you're done, take a cab back to the hotel." He suspected it would be a while before she had had enough shopping. He drove back to the Kalistajatorppa and took a swim in the indoor pool, turning laps until his arms got tired. Then he sat in a sauna as long as he could stand it, trying to sweat the feel of Borya out of his body. Then, cleansed, he slept.

He awoke when Marina came into the room. She was wearing a camel's hair coat with a brown fur collar that looked like beaver, a tweed skirt, a sweater that looked like cashmere, sheer stockings, and brown alligator pumps. Someone had done her hair; it was up in the chignon he had first seen her in, but shinier. Somehow, she had naturally elegant taste. Burke told her so. She smiled broadly and pirouetted. She looked like a model.

"Thank you, darling," she said, and shrugged off the coat and walked over to him and kissed him. He put his arms around her, but she pulled away.

"I have something else to show you," she said, smiling serenely.

She walked into the bathroom, picking up a small shopping bag along the way.

When she came out, a minute later, her hair was down on her shoulders and she was wearing something made of polished ivory silk, cut low on the sides so he could see the swell of her breasts, which swayed slightly behind the silk as she walked toward him, smiling. She pirouetted again, showing him how the silk cupped her from behind, above her long, slender legs.

"I think you like it," she said proudly, watching his reaction.

"Almost as much as I'm going to like taking it off you," he said.

She came to him then, eagerly, all lips and tongue and grasping hands. He could smell something subtle and French.

"Let's be slow," he told her after a long minute. "No one is watching, and we have all the time we want."

She rose up from his ear and neck, which she had been devouring with gusto, and smiled into his eyes.

"Yes, darling, we do, don't we?" She kissed him, then lingered, looking into his eyes and smiling.

He found a little silk bow on the side, near her hip, pulled the string, and untied it.

"Let's not be all that slow," he told her.

"Whatever you say, dear."

* * *

Midway through the next afternoon, Marina was lying, nude, on the top shelf of the sauna, murmuring appreciation as Burke slowly and gently massaged her tender knee. Her body gleamed with perspiration in the shaded golden light of the sauna.

"There's something I want to ask you," she said, reflectively.

"Anything," he said, still rubbing.

"Why did you trust me?"

Burke laughed. "The look in your big eyes," he said.

"Really?" she said. "I could have fooled you, you know."

"I know," he said. "Well, when you suggested marrying, I figured that was not something you would have needed to do to set me up."

"But when I asked you, you had already asked me to help you get to Filomenov. You had committed yourself," she pointed out.

"That's true," Burke sighed in mock sadness. "Well, since you force me to tell you, I will."

"I'm forcing you," she agreed.

"It was your underwear."

"What?"

He rubbed a little higher. "That's right."

"How?"

"Well, I figured that if you'd have been sent to seduce me, you'd have been given, shall we say, the appropriate lingerie."

She laughed. "You were right." Then, "I'm glad."

He rubbed higher on her thigh, and she shifted on the shelf to accommodate him.

The attendant, a blond young woman, knocked twice and stuck her head in the door. Burke jerked his hand away and tried to cover himself with a towel. Then he grinned. "I'm glad I hadn't gotten any higher," he told the girl.

"I'm sorry, Mr. Burke," the Finnish girl said, showing no sign of embarrassment. "There's an urgent phone call for you from the U.S. You can take it right out here."

Burke fastened the towel around himself and walked out of the sauna into a lounge with wicker chairs and a picture window overlooking the grey Baltic. A telephone sat on an end table, the receiver off the hook. The Finnish girl pointed to it, and Burke sat down and picked it up.

"Burke."

"Hey, hero. Helluva time finding you." It was Graves, but a cheerier, bubblier Graves than Burke had ever heard before.

"Shit," Burke said. "I thought you were going to leave me alone for a couple of days."

Graves's voice rose in mock angst. "I call him a hero and all he says is, 'Shit, leave me alone.' I should know better than to give a bastard like you a compliment."

"Well, thanks, Ken. Story went over, huh?"

"Went over?" Graves was exultant. "It may have brought down the government!"

Burke felt dumb.

"What?" he finally asked.

"You haven't heard?"

"Can't read the Finnish papers, Ken," Burke said. "Didn't have time to pack my radio."

"Your friend Andrushin has come flying through the saloon window. So's Petrus—Petrusetsky?"

"Petrusevich," Burke offered. "What do you mean?" It was hard to believe what Graves was telling him.

"They're both out. The Central Committee is meeting and the wires are saying they're going to pick a new general secretary. And everyone in the world is quoting us!"

Burke felt like a boy in the woods whose little campfire got out of hand and burned down the whole forest. "Jesus," was all he could say.

"So when's the next plane?" Graves was asking.

"Next plane?"

"Yeah, to Moscow."

"I don't know. I think there's a night flight."

"Catch it," Graves said. "The boss wants to stay right on top of this one. He likes beating the world."

"How were Andrushin and Petrusevich announced?"

"Little notices in the papers today about their successors."

"Well, if our story came out Monday morning in Washington, that means the Soviets might have heard it Monday afternoon in Moscow. It doesn't seem likely that they could react fast enough to get rid of Andrushin and Petrusevich, pick new people, and put an announcement in the papers by Tuesday morning."

"So?" Graves asked.

"I'm just saying something else must have happened. They must have found out what was going on before our story came out," Burke said.

"So what?"

"So we didn't bring down the government."

"Maybe," Graves said. "But that's not what the world thinks."

"Well, let's not claim any credit, all right?"

"Okay," Graves said. "But why do you care?"

"Let's just say that when I go back, I don't need the KGB blaming me for anything I didn't do."

"Yeah, I can see that," Graves said.

"By the way," Burke said, trying to sound casual. "You haven't seen anything about me on the wires, have you?"

"No," Graves said. "Why?"

"Little altercation I had with customs at the border on the way up here," Burke said.

"Oh. No, nothing about that. But you got through all right?"

"Yeah," Burke said. "I got through all right."

"Good," Graves said. "Get your ass back there. Give us a call as soon as you get in."

"Okay, Ken," Burke said. "Take care."

"Take care yourself. Good show, Colin." Coming from Graves, that was like the Pulitzer Prize. Burke calculated it might be at least a month before the editor started thinking about replacing him again.

"Thanks," Burke said, and hung up.

Over the sea, he could see the sky darkening. There wasn't much time to get to the airport.

She had covered herself with a towel and moved to the lower level of the sauna, where the heat was less intense. She looked intently at him as he opened the thick wooden door, came in, and sat down, facing her.

"Marina, I have to go back to Moscow," he said.

She lowered her head. For a moment, he thought she looked like a little girl, very small.

"Why?"

"Things are happening there. They're about to elect a new general secretary. I've got to be there."

She raised her eyes. A drop of water was running down her cheek, but he couldn't tell whether it was a tear or a bead of sweat. "But you hit that guard! They'll arrest you."

"I don't think so," he said. "The Soviets apparently haven't said anything about it. The guy was drunk. He shouldn't have followed me by himself. He let an unarmed man get the drop on him. He let you escape. My guess is he got up, saw we were gone, and kept his mouth shut."

She nodded gravely.

"Did your story have anything to do with this election?"

He told her what Graves had told him.

"You must feel very happy," she said, but she was not smiling.

He shook his head. "I got one story wrong and one story right. Nothing to be happy about. And if they hadn't picked me out for a setup, I wouldn't have gotten anything."

She was silent for a moment. "What about me?"

"Well, you can't go back right now, obviously." Burke was making it up as he went along. "I think you should stay here for a week or so till I can fly back. Then we'll find you an apartment. You can live here and take English lessons."

"And how often would I see you?"

"As many weekends as I could get up here," he said. "Most of them," he promised.

She nodded.

"It'll work," he said.

She nodded again.

They threw on robes and went back upstairs so he could pack his things.

"Colin, I'm not going to stay," she said.

He stopped stuffing socks into his bag.

"You're not?"

"No. There's nothing for me to do in Helsinki."

He looked at her. "Are you afraid I wouldn't come back for you?"

"No. You would," she said. "But you'd always leave me again, wouldn't you? For some story."

He took her in his arms. He kissed her and her lips were as warm as ever. "You're focused on the leaving. I'm thinking of the coming back. I'd come back."

She smiled. "I know. But that's not a life."

He didn't argue with her. He held her for a moment longer, squeezed, and let her go.

"So what do you want to do?"

"I want to go to America. That passport will get me in, won't it?"

"Yeah. I guess so."

"You'll lend me money for the ticket?"

"I'll give you the ticket. You can go to Washington. I have some friends at the *Tribune* who'd help you get settled."

"There's no theater in Washington."

"Sure there is."

"Touring companies from New York, is what I've read."

He smiled. She knew what she wanted and he had to like the way she quietly insisted on getting it.

"So you want to go to New York?"

She nodded.

"But you don't know anyone there."

She shook her head. "There are émigrés. Someone will help me. They live in a place called Brighton Beach, don't they?"

"Yeah. It's in Brooklyn."

"I'll get some kind of job there, and I'll learn English. And then I'll go to the theaters."

He knew he would have to be subtle if he wanted to dissuade her. "I hope it's the right choice for you," he said. "It won't be easy, you know."

She shrugged. "It never has been."

At the airport, he bought both their tickets. Then he got some cash from a teller machine and gave it to her. His flight was boarding. Hers was an hour away.

He put his arm around her and she walked with him to the row of glass booths marked PASSPORT CONTROL. They both got through quickly.

A sign said gates 1–15 were to the left and 15–30 were to the right. He looked at her ticket. "Your flight is at gate 27. I'm at 14."

She hugged him. "Thank you, Colin," she whispered in his ear. "For everything."

He tried to smile, without much success. "No. Thank *you*. For the big story you got me. For everything. You're the best thing that's happened to me in a long time." He hugged her back.

He looked at her. "You never asked me to forget the job and go with you."

She looked back at him. "I thought about it. But it wouldn't have made you happy."

"I guess so," he said.

"We'll be together again," she said. "You'll come to New York."

"Definitely," he said.

"Remember Pasternak," she said. He looked at her, puzzled.

"We had our time at Peredelkino," she explained. "Like him. I'm glad we did. But he did not marry her. The woman in the poem, I mean." Burke nodded. It seemed to make sense.

"When you get to New York, have someone who speaks English call Roger Costello at the *Washington Tribune* and tell him where you are. I'll call him and get your address," he told her.

"All right," she said, and she gave him a tight, strained smile. He hugged her again. "Colin," she said and hesitated.

"Yes?"

"I want you to know something." She hesitated again, dropping her eyes. Then she raised them, and looked at him squarely.

"I love you," she said.

Burke felt a warmth spreading up his body and into his head. It threatened to make his eyes water. He smiled briefly.

"And you never pretend," he said.

"No." She shook her head, solemnly.

"Now go," she said, throwing her arms around him and squeezing.

When she let go, he kissed her quickly. Then he turned and headed for the metal detectors. He looked back, and she was standing there in her new coat and tweed skirt, everything else she had in the world inside a nylon suitcase. She waved, and he waved back. He turned and walked through the metal detectors to the umbilical ramp that led to the plane. As he reached it, and paused, a gust of hot, rough air rumbled from the back of his throat and out through his lips, half laugh, half snort. There was no smile behind it.

"Something funny, Mr. Burke?" the Finnair agent asked him, tearing off his ticket.

"Just an old joke," Burke said.

The agent smiled vaguely. "Staying long in Moscow?"

"I guess so," Burke said.

"It's gotten quite cold there, I hear. Thirty below."

"I'm not surprised," Burke said, and boarded the plane.